ON THE LITTLE CRAZY

Dedication

This book has been a long time in the writing Sometimes, I would dedicate days to the hard work of putting "pen to paper," as they say. Other times, I would put the book aside for several months without writing a word. Always, however, there were those who read my work, provided positive (and needed) feedback, and encouraged me to continue.

This book is dedicated to those encouragers, readers and critical thinkers who were critical in helping to finalize this book. I can think of many. But, my thanks go out to Dave and Deb, who read the first draft and provided needed feedback about character development. Bob, the historian who kept me in the right century. Ann, who used her English major eyes to lead me down the straight and narrow path of punctuation, capitalization and proper grammar. Adam and Mandy, who read, commented, and encouraged. And a special thanks to my wife, Penny, who was always there providing encouragement, suggestions, and a needed push to press ahead to the finish line. Again, thank you all.

Published by:
Powder River Publishing LLC
1014 Black Mountain Road
Thermopolis, Wyoming 82443

Copyright © 2024
ISBN: 978-1-956881-49-3
Printed in the United States of America

www.powderriverpublishing.com

Table of Contents

Prologue

Mining Camp, Big Horn Mountains, Dakota Territory, 1865

A ragged swath of blood red dawn lay across the eastern sky when the first coyote howled—a sharp, chattering bark that rose to a tremulous wail and fell away in a plaintiff whisper. That howl was answered by the staccato yipping of a second wild dog, and a third. Then, there was silence.

"Djavlar!" Lars cursed in his native Swedish, and he eased back into a pool of shadow cast by the early morning light. With eyes the color of glacial melt, he swept the valley floor until a blur of motion drew him to a crescent of darkness at the forest's edge. There, at the edge of the trees, whispered the primeval voice in his brain. Seeking the comforting grip of the Remington Model 1861 cap and ball pistol shoved into his belt, he slid along the log wall to the cabin door, squeezing through the narrow opening and into the dim light inside.

In two strides, he stood over a blanket-covered form lying on the hardpacked dirt floor. "Sven, wake up!" he barked.

Sven snorted and rolled to his side.

Lars reached down and grasped the man's shirt, yanking hard.

"What's wrong with you?" Sven complained as he sat up. "It ain't even daylight yet."

"Listen! Do you hear anything?"

"Hear what?" Sven said, rubbing his eyes.

"I heard howling," Lars said, "Now, there's nothing."

"You woke me to hear nothin'," Sven grumbled. "It's just a wolf, or a coyote."

"No," Lars replied. "It's the Djavlar. The Sioux."

Sven scrambled to his feet and stepped to the open door, peering outside. "What do they want?" he exclaimed. "They've already taken our horses."

"They want us," replied Lars. "Wake the others."

Sven turned and hurried toward a stout, tree-stump of a man named Thompson and shook him hard, and then moved on to the next sleeping form. The sleepy-eyed Thompson sat up, but before he could get to his feet, the cabin door suddenly crashed inward and two Sioux warriors burst into the cabin's dim interior.

His burnished steel knife gleaming in the morning's half-light, one brave howled a battle cry and rushed headlong at the still sleepy-eyed Thompson. The two men fell to the floor, rolling across the hard packed dirt in a tangle of flailing arms and legs until the warrior came up astride the stout miner's chest. Then, in less than a breath, the warrior raised his blade and plunged it deep into Thompson's chest.

Thompson grunted and grasped at the horn handled knife stuck between his ribs. His face darkened, and a ham-sized fist snaked out, grasping the warrior by the throat. Summoning all his strength, the miner rose to his feet and hurled the brave headfirst against the cabin wall. The warrior slumped to the dirt floor, piled in a heap like cast off rags.

While Thompson fought for his life, the second brave feinted at Lars with his blade, drawing blood on the big Swede's forearm. Lars swore and backed away, but the warrior charged like a wild bull, slamming hard into the big Swede and sending him sprawling backward. As Lars fell, he pulled his pistol clear of his belt and flicked its barrel upward, pulling the trigger at point blank range. The Remington spit fire, driving a lead ball through flesh and bone. The brave's body contorted in mid-air, then fell heavily across Lars' belly.

Lars pushed the brave aside and scrambled to his feet. Black smoke curled from the revolver's barrel, rose to the cabin's roof and mushroomed across its surface, carrying with it the tang of burnt powder. Through the haze, Lars caught sight of Thompson standing silently, clutching the blade protruding from his ribs. "Murder," the stricken man whispered as blood pumped from his chest, ran down his belly and pooled in the dirt at his feet. He opened his mouth to speak, but whatever words he wanted to say were lost forever as he pitched forward into the dirt and lay still.

Though the fight had lasted only seconds, three men now lay dead or dying on the cabin floor. Swallowing the fear clogging his throat, Lars focused on his companions. "Benson, blockade the door," he barked out. "The rest of you, gather your rifles. Make sure they're loaded and ready."

The miners turned to their tasks, but Lars caught the arm of one swarthy, darkhaired man as he scurried past. "Olson, see to Thompson," he said quietly. Olson dropped to his knees and laid his head on the man's chest. A moment later, he sat back on his haunches and shook his head. Lars nodded; his face grim.

Olson began to rise, but his eyes fixed on the knife protruding from Thompson's ribs. Reaching out, he grasped the knife by its handle and yanked hard. The steel blade slid free of the dead miner's flesh. Olson wiped the blade on Thompson's shirt, and held the blade up to a shaft of light that beamed through a hole in the cabin's roof. Sunlight danced and shimmered across the shiny steel. Mesmerized, Olson fixed is eyes on the razor-sharp cutting edge, and he turned the glistening blade around and around as if a devilish spell had been cast over his very being.

"Olson," someone called. "We need some help over here."

Olson frowned, but whatever spell had held him in its grip was broken. He slid the dagger into his belt and scuttled after his guns.

With the men busy at their tasks, Lars took stock of his small band. He could count on Sven, his longtime friend, and young Benson, the tall, lanky sailor who had left the sea for adventure in the frontier of America. Behind them stood Williamson, a red-bearded giant who was strong enough to carry a horse, and in the corner squatted Samuelson, a rotund farmer who had left the rocky hillsides of Sweden for the rich farm land of Ohio. Then there was Olson. Stout and ill-tempered, it was rumored he had killed a man in the Old Country and had fled to America just ahead of a hangman's noose.

Each man held a rifle—new Spencers and Henrys—repeating rifles bought before they started their trek. Several carried pistols. Between them, the miners counted three hundred and seventy bullets. They all had knives except Williamson who carried a short-handled, double-bladed axe that hung from a sheath attached to his waist. Razor sharp, it could cut a man in two with one blow.

Six months past, the small group of Swedish prospectors had trekked through the Dakotas and on into Montana in search of gold. They were too late for the placer claims at Grasshopper Creek near Bannock, and they were forced to move on. Turning south, they entered the high country of the Big Horn Mountains, an unexplored wilderness still inhabited by the Sioux. There, they wandered into a high mountain valley, and found placer gold in a small creek that meandered down its length. Working from sunup to sundown, they coaxed yellow dust from the ancient strata of the stream until eight jars of fine gold lay hidden in a cache under the cabin floor—enough gold to make them all rich.

Then three nights ago, a band of Sioux stole their horses. Lars pleaded with the men to pack up what they could carry on their backs and make for Fort Reno down on Powder River before the Indians returned. But the miners wanted more gold and voted to stay. "Just one more shovelful of pay dirt," one said with a smile. The ancients had cast greed as a deadly sin, and true to its form, it could now prove fatal to them all.

The sound of a low whistle penetrated Lars' thoughts. Pressing his eye to a small porthole carved into the wall of the cabin, he scanned the meadow. The Sioux had edged closer to the men's refuge, hiding behind windfalls and clumps of grass. "The sun's up," Lars said. "They're coming. Williamson and Benson, take the north and south walls. Sven and I will guard the east and west. Olson, you take the door. Samuelson, you help wherever you're needed."

As Lars predicted, when the rim of the sun crested the eastern hills, the Sioux broke from their cover. Howling war cries, they charged the cabin. Rifles cocked, the miners waited until the warriors were less than a dozen strides from the log walls, and then they laid down a volley of lead. A half dozen charging warriors went down, forcing the Sioux to retreat to the edge of the woods.

Lars took a deep breath and slid to the cabin floor, drawing a sleeve across his forehead to wipe away the sweat. Silently, the miners waited. Then Benson spoke. "They've built a fire," he said.

Lars returned to the porthole and peered out. A half dozen warriors were holding flaming torches and snaking through the grass toward the cabin. Cursing, he jacked a cartridge into the chamber of his Henry, and turned to face the miners. "Men, it looks like they aim to burn us out. As I see it, our only chance is to make a break down the canyon. If we get past those who are close, we can buy a little time, maybe a minute, before the main band follows."

Olson frowned. "What about the gold?" he asked.

"Too heavy," said Lars. "It'll only slow us down."

"Some of us might want to take our share with us," Olson growled.

"The gold's safe," Lars replied. "If we survive, we can come back and get it later."

"What about the others? What do they think?" retorted Olson, his voice edging towards belligerence.

"Leave it," interjected Sven, and a chorus of "ayes" from the other miners followed. Olson grumbled, but the vote was cast.

Lars eyed the men. "Ready?"

The miners looked at one another and nodded.

Lars threw open the door and stepped outside. Kneeling, he triggered off three blasts in the direction of the advancing warriors as the men took off on a dead run down the creek. Samuelson was the last man out the cabin door and as he passed, Lars fired one more time. Then he sprinted after his companions.

The sight of the six fleeing men caught the warriors by surprise, and the miners made a hundred yards before arrows began whizzing past their heads. Suddenly, in the path ahead, Samuelson stumbled and fell. Lars stopped and grasped the man by the arm. "Get up!" he urged. "We have to keep going."

"Can't. Twisted my ankle," Samuelson panted.

Lars pulled the man to his feet, but before Samuelson could take a step, a Sioux warrior rounded a bend in the trail not more than thirty yards away. Faster than the eye could follow, the brave drew back his bow and fired. An arrow sliced deep into Samuelson's back. He moved his mouth to speak, but eyes rolled back in his head, and with a final gasp, he sagged to the ground.

Rage flooded through Lars' being. Before the brave could nock another feathered shaft in his bow, Lars raised his rifle and fired. With cold satisfaction, he saw the brave crumple. Lowering his gun, Lars took one last look at Samuelson's lifeless body, and then he sprinted down the narrow path.

Less than a half-mile downstream, Lars caught up with his remaining men. Bunched at the confluence of two draws, the miners were hunkered down behind a jumble of boulders. The Sioux warriors, having climbed higher in the rocks, showered their position with arrows. Without slowing down, Lars charged straight up the hill toward the Sioux, firing his pistol as he ran.

The miner's hesitated only a moment before they followed Lars, and the fighting turned into hand-to-hand combat. Williamson swung his axe in wide arcs, scattering warriors before him like windblown leaves. When he slashed one warrior from shoulder to groin, the rest of the Sioux retreated, disappearing into the rocks. Too exhausted to follow, the miners paused for a moment to catch their breath, and then they fled on down the creek.

The rocky terrain slowed the miners' flight, and it wasn't long before the Sioux were again pressing at their heels. Benson took an arrow in the calf, cutting muscle and tendon. He went down, and the Sioux were on him immediately, using their knives on his fallen body. Sven, bleeding from numerous wounds, began to slow, finally stopping in the trail. Lars turned and ran back to where his friend stood.

"Sven, they're coming," Lars shouted as he looked up the trail to see five warriors loping toward them.

"Can't go on. Too weak," Sven wheezed.

The Sioux were closing fast. "I'm sorry," Lars said. "I can't fight them all."

Sven lifted his head. "You must go, but I beg you, old friend. Shoot me before the Sioux get here," the exhausted man pleaded.

Lars shook his head. "I can't," he replied, tears welling up in his eyes.

He turned to leave, but as he started down the trail, he felt the weight of his pistol in his waist band. Turning back, he handed the weapon to his friend. "There's one bullet left. Use it as you will."

Lars had not gone more than thirty steps when the sharp crack of a pistol sounded from behind. Looking over his shoulder, he saw a puff of smoke rising over the top of the grass where he had left his poor friend. An instant later, the first warrior arrived and took a knife to his body. Then, others came. "God have mercy on your soul," Lars whispered. He turned and ran on.

Williamson, the red-bearded giant, had stopped in the trail and had turned to face the Sioux, firing at the approaching warriors. An arrow struck him in the right eye, skinning the flesh off the skull. He turned, pulling the arrow out as he ran, but with blood flowing freely from the wound, the big man was nearly blind. He lagged further and further behind.

Finally, a blood-curdling yell caused Lars to look back over his shoulder. Williamson had stopped running and was standing on a slight rise with his mane of red hair blowing wildly in the wind. Holding his axe high, he turned to face the pursuing Sioux, taunting the braves as they edged closer. Finally surrounded, Williamson screamed, and the last time Lars saw the Norse warrior, he had charged straight into the encircling Sioux, and was slashing wildly at his tormentors with his deadly ax.

Williamson's charge distracted the Sioux long enough for Lars and Olson to put some distance between them and their pursuers. The two men kept a steady pace down the creek until, just before dusk, they came to a stop--physically exhausted and nearly out of ammunition. When he had caught his breath, Lars looked around. They stood at the base of a huge vertical cliff. A rock slide stretched upward into the deepening darkness.

"Olson," Lars said, his hands on his knees, "if we can reach the top of that bluff, we may be able to hold 'em off."

Olson could only nod.

Glancing behind him, Lars spotted two warriors emerging from the woods an arrow's flight away. "They're here." Lars said. Olson took a deep breath, and they began their ascent up the field of stones.

The footing was treacherous, and rocks slid away beneath their feet, clattering down the steep hillside to the canyon below. Twice, a covey of arrows clattered into the rocks around them, but a few well-placed balls kept the Sioux at bay. His lungs crying for oxygen, Lars ached to rest, but he forced every last ounce of strength from his tired legs. Olson kept pace until they finally reached the base of the cliff and threw themselves down on a rocky ledge.

Lars rested for a moment, and then took stock of their situation. A small group of Sioux warriors stood at the bottom of the slide, gesturing to one another. Lars guessed that they had already taken heavy losses, and were reluctant to climb up the open slide where they would be an easy target for Lars' rifle. To the miner's back, the towering overhang stretched for a mile in either direction. With no openings in the sheer wall, the Sioux would be unable to make their way to the top of the ridge.

Parched and hungry, Lars and Olson waited out the night. Once, Lars heard stones clattering down the slope, and he fired a volley through the darkness at the sound. His blasts were rewarded with a yelp, and he knew one of his bullets had drawn blood.

At first light, the two miners crept along the base of the cliff until they found a narrow crevasse that split the overhang from base to rim. Wedging themselves between the two walls of rock, they edged their way up the crack until, an hour later, they pulled themselves over the mesa's rim and rested in the morning sun.

Olson pulled out the knife he had taken from Thompson's chest and turned it over in his hand. One side of the knife's handle was carved the form of an eagle. The other side was smooth and polished. Retrieving a small knife from his boot, the butcher began to carve on the smooth side of the knife's handle.

Lars watched until he could no longer stifle his curiosity. "What are you doing?" he asked.

"See those two peaks in the distance. They make a saddle, and the gold lies in the valley directly beneath the 'V,'" Olson said. "I've carved those peaks into the handle so when we come back to get that gold, we'll be able to find it."

"A map?" Lars asked.

"Yeah," replied Olson holding the knife handle up to examine his work. "Without some landmarks, we may not be able to find the cabin again."

"Probably a good idea," Lars remarked. He reached for the Sioux knife, but Olson pulled away, rising to his feet and shoving the blade back into his waistband.

Lars frowned, but he let the moment pass, and his thoughts turned to their survival. "We should find a spot to hole up for the day," he said, his eyes roaming the surrounding terrain. "Travel at night. There will be less chance the Sioux will spot us."

Olson nodded. The two men trotted toward a thick stand of aspen about a mile away and took shelter under a deadfall. They slept in shifts, always with one eye open and listening intently at every sound. The day passed, and when the moon had risen that evening, they walked south. Seven days later, they trudged into Fort Reno on Powder River and told their incredible story.

The Fort commander listened closely, but he was skeptical about their claims of gold, especially when neither man could, or would, describe exactly where the attack took place. And, despite repeated pleas by the Swedes, the Captain refused to let any of his soldiers accompany them back into the mountains.

Skirmishes between the Sioux and the cavalry increased weekly, confining Lars and Olson to the fort. After two months, the men decided their gold was safe enough beneath the floor of the abandoned cabin, and they traveled to Missouri, planning to mount an expedition to the Big Horns within the year.

It was not to happen. The winter was hard. Lars caught pneumonia and died. Olson tried repeatedly to interest others into going after the gold, but never one willing to provide the financing. What little money he had passed through his hands like water, but it wasn't long before Olson found that he could earn drinks in local saloons by telling his tale of Indians and buried riches.

One night, in a river tavern filled with hardened men, Olson drew the knife from its sheath, and held it out for all to see, explaining in slurred words how he had carved the map in its handle to find his way back to the treasure in Wyoming.

In a dim corner of the barroom, a stranger listened closely. When the miner had finished his story, the man tossed down his drink and left. Later that night, as Olson made his way back to his shack, drunk as usual, he met with death. A robbery, the Sheriff supposed, but the only thing the murderer took was the knife with the eagle carved on one side, and the two peaks in the Big Horn Mountains of Wyoming on the other.

CHAPTER 1. PENNSYLVANIA (CIRCA 1891)

Luke Banister flew through the doorway of the dimly lit saloon, landed on the boardwalk with a bone rattling crunch, and tumbled into the rain-soaked street. A swarthy bear of a man walked after him, stopping before stepping into the mud. "You ain't welcome heah no mo', Banister," he snarled, curling his lip to expose a mouthful of tobacco-stained teeth. "Boss don't want you 'round."

Luke struggled to his feet, mud dripping from his face and clothes. "She can't throw me out. She owes me," he retorted, his words slurred by alcohol.

"She don't owe you nothin'," the bartender spat out. "You've drunk up more than her bill ever was. Now beat it." Squirting a stream of tobacco juice at Luke's feet, the bartender turned and stomped back into the smoky tavern, slamming the door behind him.

Wiping the muck from his face with the sleeve of his ragged jacket, Luke clambered back onto the boardwalk. With trembling hands, he reached out and tested the saloon's door handle. Locked. Rage clouded his gaunt face, and he pounded on the door with his fist, screaming curses until his voice trailed off into a raspy whisper.

It was long past midnight. Luke Banister was cold and sick, and he stunk like bad whiskey. Scanning the darkened streets, his gray eyes lit upon another saloon that lay warm and inviting only a block away. He stumbled toward its closed door, but stopped short when the flickering light of a kerosene lamp drew his eye. For a moment, the dancing flame triggered thoughts of a different time and a different life, and a half smile played at the corner of his mouth.

In the distance, lightening skipped along a tree-covered ridgeline and the night air stirred with a cold, restless energy. Shivering, Luke jammed his fists inside the pockets of his coat and bent into the wind. He had taken but a step when deep within the tattered depths of his pocket, his fingers touched a forgotten bottle. A sly smile spread across his sallow face as he pulled the container from its hiding place. Twisting off the lid, he lifted the flask to his mouth and greedily sucked at its contents.

The whiskey oozed into his blood, and Luke closed his eyes and slumped against the tavern wall, welcoming the numbness that spread through his being. His fingers relaxed, loosening their grip on the rounded flask until it fell from his grasp. When the dull "thud" of glass-on-wood penetrated his sotted brain, his eyes flicked open, coming to rest on the bottle that now lay an arm's length away. Lazily, he reached for it, but a gust of wind thrust it out of his reach and sent it rolling down the walkway.

With a curse, Luke pushed himself upright and lurched after the wayward drink. The wind teased, keeping the bouncing whiskey just a step beyond his reach until the bottle careened off a post and spun into an alley, a dozen steps away.

Luke stumbled to a stop and squinted into the alley's maw. Dark and foreboding, its stale breath reeked of discarded human debris. Seeing nothing in the gloom, he dropped to his knees and crawled forward, his dirty fingers raking through the filth in a frantic search for that which gave him solace. Rats as big as cats scurried across his legs and nipped at his ankles. He struck at them, and they squealed, disappearing into a labyrinth of holes beneath the rotting clapboard buildings. He crawled on until the stench overcame even his deadened senses, and then he emptied his belly into the alley's squalor.

When the spasms had subsided, Luke wearily rose to his feet. Steadying himself against a weathered clapboard wall, he wiped the vomit from his lips with the arm of his jacket, failing to notice the streak of blood that now stained his sleeve. The whiskey forgotten, he shuffled out of the alley into the cold air, his lungs afire with every breath.

Thunder rumbled in the belly of the dark clouds swirling overhead and a squall blew in with sudden fury, slamming against Luke's thin, stooped body and driving him into the boggy street. A primal voice screamed at him to seek shelter. He tried to move, but a heavy, gray mud clutched at his boots and sucked the life from his body.

Suddenly, a bolt of lightning blasted the ground only yards away, searing Luke's eyes with white heat. Blinded, he cried out and fell to his knees, swaying back and forth while wind pummeled his body and whipped his black hair like straw.

For long moments, Luke endured the punishment meted out by the elements, but then his eyes flashed open. With rain running in muddy rivulets down his cheeks, he raised his face skyward and shook his fist at the lightening dancing through the clouds, screaming curses until his voice trailed off into a whimpering plea. Then the spark in his eyes dimmed, and he crumpled into the muck.

#

At first glance, the two men passing by on that cold rainy night mistook the thing they saw in the street for a pile of rags blown there by the squall. But as they drew near, their lantern lit up the wretched figure of a human being.

"Whoa, Lizzie," shouted the driver, pulling hard on the reins. Head down, the old mare halted. Holding onto their hats, the two men clambered down into the street. One reached up to remove a swinging lantern from its holder; the second knelt down and grasped the man's coat, turning his body face up. In this rough part of the city, both men expected to find a corpse, a bullet hole in its head, perhaps, or a knife in its chest. And their instincts were right, or at least, nearly so.

"Hell, Nick," the first man shouted over the storm while he wiped the unconscious man's face with his neckerchief. "It's Luke Banister. I haven't seen him for a year or more, but I'd recognize him anywhere. What's he doing out in this part of town?"

"Looks like he's dead to me, William," Nick replied, shielding his face from the rain.

William lifted Luke's wrist and felt for a pulse. "He's alive, but just barely," he shouted. "And, I don't see any wounds. Give me a hand here. If we don't get him to the hospital soon, we will have a corpse on our hands!" Nick placed the lantern back in its holder, and then helped William drag Luke to the buggy. With much panting, they pushed him onto the seat, wedging the sick man between them. William snapped the whip over the mare's rump and, her tail to the wind, Lizzie took off at a brisk trot.

A half hour later, William wheeled up to the front of a large white structure. A sign painted on the wall boldly proclaimed 'St. Francis Sanitarium'. Before the buggy had stopped moving, William jumped to the ground and hurried inside, reappearing in moments with two men. "Get this man inside at once," he commanded, "and strip these wet clothes off. I'll wash up and be there in a few minutes. And, get Nurse Haddock."

"Certainly, Doctor Bentley," replied one of the men as they lowered Luke down from the buggy seat.

Bentley turned to his traveling companion. "You go on home, Nick," he said quietly. "It's late. The weather's bad. Martha will be worried."

"Are you sure you won't need help?" asked Nick. "I can stay."

"I don't think so. I didn't see any wounds, but from the sounds of his breathing, I think he has other problems. I'll handle this one myself."

"I hate to leave you alone, but I think I'll take you up on it, going

11

home that is. I haven't seen my wife for two days."

Bentley waved his hand. "Nicholas," he said, "I couldn't save the young Johnson boy's life tonight, but maybe I can save this man."

Nick climbed back aboard the buggy and pulled up his collar. He looked Bentley in the eyes. "You might," he said, "if you, and he, are both lucky." With a flick of the whip, he started the mare back out into the night. Bentley watched the buggy disappear. Then he hurried into the hospital.

A middle-aged woman, clad in white, met him in the hallway and led him to the room in which Luke lay. Sturdily built with graying hair pulled back in a bun, she hovered over Luke's form. "He has pneumonia, doesn't he," the nurse said.

"It looks that way," Bentley replied as he placed his hand on Luke's feverish forehead.

"Someone you know?"

"He and I grew up in the same neighborhood."

The nurse gazed at Luke's face. His eyes were sunken; his face drawn and pale. "He looks older than you," she said.

"It's the whiskey," Bentley answered. "His birthday is three days after mine, and I just turned thirty-six. I'll be here tonight. Let me know if he takes a turn."

There was no need for further conversation. Both knew that Luke Banister's chances of making it through the night were less than even, at best.

#

Though a haze clouded his mind, something deep within Luke clung to a tenuous thread of life. A week after his rescue, he opened his eyes to find a stream of warm sunlight flooding into his room. For a long while, he lay still, gazing out a large window at an azure sky and struggling to recall the events of the last few days.

"Looks like you're back from the dead, my old friend," boomed a deep, and oddly familiar, voice. Luke turned to stare at the white coated figure standing in the doorway to his room.

"Who are you?" said Luke sullenly.

"Well, that's a fine how do you do for an old fishing buddy," replied William, feigning hurt feelings. "Though, I guess it has been a long time since we left the neighborhood."

Luke peered at the doctor again, studying him closely. He smiled faintly when he recognized his old friend, William Bentley. Inseparable pals as boys, they had shared many adventures, but the vagaries of life had led the two in much different directions.

"William," he said, "I have to apologize for my memory lapse. It has been a while, you know. Where am I, and what am I doing here?"

"Sure has been," replied the doctor, "a long time, that is." He shook his head. "You're in St. Francis, a Sanitarium. Damn, Luke, I've been worried about you this past week. Thought several times we were going to lose you."

"You needn't have worried."

Bentley raised an eyebrow, but didn't respond as he began to examine Luke's body. Though covered by a short beard, he could tell Luke's face was painfully thin. His shoulders, once strong and broad, were now slumped and tired. "Luke," he said, "it looks like you've taken a turn for the worst along the way."

Luke hung his head. "You never did mince words, William."

William patted Luke on the shoulder. "I have to finish my rounds," he said. "I'll tell the nurse to bring you something to eat. You need some food in your belly." Moving to the window, he pushed it open slightly and a fresh breeze entered the room. "This afternoon, if you feel up to it," he continued, "maybe we can tour the grounds together. We have a lot of catching up to do."

"I don't suppose you ever thought I'd end up this way, did you Will?" asked Luke.

Bentley raised an eyebrow. "I'll be back in an hour. We can talk then."

After Bentley left, Luke gazed out the small window into the hospital garden. Sunlight fell through glass, warming his skin. A fresh breeze swept the cobwebs from his mind, and for the first time in months, he thought clearly. He ran his hand over his square jaw, feeling a week's growth of stubble. I probably look as bad as I feel, he mused.

As promised, Bentley reappeared an hour later. "Luke," he boomed, "let's take a walk."

It was one of those beautiful spring days when the sun was warm and the air was swept fresh by recent rain. Bentley pushed Luke around the gardens in a wheeled chair for a time, chatting about days gone by. When they arrived at a bench bathed in sunshine, Bentley parked Luke's chair and sat down beside him.

"Luke," Bentley began, "the last time I saw you was a year ago, right after Mary died."

Luke gazed off into the distance. "I don't want to talk about it Will.

That part of my life is gone."

Bentley hesitated a moment, and then he looked directly at his friend. "Luke," he said solemnly, "we've been friends a long time, and I'm going to be blunt. You're malnourished. Even if you eat right, it'll be a long while before you regain your strength. And, if you continue to drink, your liver will eat you alive."

Luke reddened at the Doctors words. "You should have just left me where you found me. I was ready to die. It would have been ended there— quick, easy, and done."

"Ended?" Bentley snorted. He leaned forward. "Remember when we were kids, we would spend entire afternoons in the woods out behind your house, fighting bandits and whatever else we could think of. Sometimes we imagined ourselves trapped by a thousand pirates with no way out, but even so, we promised each other we would go out gloriously, with swords drawn and guns blazing."

Bentley paused and took a breath. "We had such great dreams then Luke, and those dreams have not come to an end. I can't make you want to live, but I want you to promise me you won't die curled up in a hole like some rat. Mary is gone. It wasn't your fault. Don't kill yourself for something that doesn't make sense."

For a long while, the two men said nothing. Finally, Luke said sardonically, "You're the man with the answers. What do you think I should do?"

"Throw away the whiskey. You can't take another drink, not one. It's as simple as that," Bentley said. "As for your health, you've contracted pneumonia and the disease has injured your lungs. I suggest you travel to any place with a drier climate. Some people have been able to recover lost lung function by living where the air is dry. Maybe that will work for you."

"I'll never recover what I've lost, William," retorted Luke. "Now, push me back in. I'm cold."

Bentley rose to his feet. "No, you won't recover completely, Luke. Not here, not ever," he said, his voice softening a bit as he wheeled Luke back into the hospital. "But, my friend, you should consider my advice nonetheless. Go someplace new. Learn to live life again. There are no guarantees, but one thing is for sure, brooding around here will get you nothing more than a slow, lonely death."

CHAPTER 2. THE DESTROYING ANGEL (MARCH 1891)

Lord James Atherton leaned back in a highbacked leather chair and let eyes gaze out over the Potomac. On the horizon, a sailing ship cut through the calm sea. Fully rigged, the ship's white sails billowed lazily in the breeze as it moved slowly out into the Atlantic.

Once an officer in the Queen's navy, Atherton smiled as he reflected on voyages and conquests he had made in his younger days, but his reverie was abruptly interrupted by a knock on the office door. Swiveling his chair, he cleared his throat. "Come in," he said, his voice carrying the tone of command one often finds in ranking military officers.

The door swung open, and two men entered the room. One was tall and thin. The other, wearing a long overcoat, was shorter and thicker.

"James," said the tall thin man. "I would like you to meet the Senator. Senator, this is Lord James Atherton."

The squatty politician held out his hand. Atherton stood to clasp it in his own. After exchanging pleasantries, Atherton motioned for the two visitors to sit. The Senator unbuttoned his coat and plopped down in an over-stuffed leather chair; the thinner man stood, pacing nervously.

The Senator spoke first. "Mr. Atherton, I was visiting friends near here and ran into Robert. He tells me you wish to see me."

"Yes, and I thank you so much for coming," replied Atherton, his English accent lending an air of formality to the discussion. "As you know, Senator, Robert and I have certain ranching interests in Northern Wyoming, but I'm here, unofficially, on behalf of the cattlemen of Wyoming. We need your help."

"What would you have me do?" asked the Senator.

Atherton rubbed his chin thoughtfully. "Rustlers are stealing our herds. Homesteaders are staking out the best land. They fence off the creek bottoms and the streams making it difficult to get our cattle to water. If things don't change, we'll be driven into bankruptcy before another year has passed."

"What about the homestead law?" interjected Oglethorpe. "Can you repeal that law? It's drawing the settlers."

"No," the Senator said, shifting uncomfortably in his chair. "Congress passed the homestead laws in 1863 to entice settlers onto free land in the western territories. It has much bigger implications for this country, and it is far too popular with Congress. Even to amend the law would be impossible."

Atherton turned to gaze out over the harbor and fell silent for a moment. At last, he spoke. "We're disappointed of course, Senator, but we have another plan. It's riskier, but it, too, needs, ah...some political help."

Taking a deep breath, Atherton swiveled his chair around to look directly at the politician. "Do you remember what the cattlemen did with the rustlers and outlaws up in Montana during the 1870's?" Atherton asked.

The Senator scowled. "I'm familiar with the Montana raids," he said. "A gang of outlaws were terrorizing the populace—even killed a few folks as I recall. The citizens rose up against the lawless elements. They captured and hung a number of men, and ran many others out of the state. So, what does that have to do with your problem?"

"Senator," Atherton continued, his voice rising in pitch, "some of our friends in Cheyenne were there. They rode in those raids, and they refer to that night as the 'Night of the Destroying Angel'. It is a charming phrase, for those who believe in such things, but they think we can do the same thing in Wyoming."

"Do the same in Wyoming?" said the Senator. "I don't understand."

"We intend to round up these rustlers and mete out the necessary justice, frontier justice, just like they did in Montana," answered Atherton, his eyes glistening.

The Senator raised an eyebrow as Atherton's proposal began to sink in. "These are different times, Mr. Atherton," he said, choosing his words carefully. "The western territories have changed considerably since the lawlessness of twenty years ago. I can guarantee that such an action would not be actively supported by the President. He will not send the military against citizens. As for my state, already the people are taking sides in this war. If the newspapers got wind of such a plan, then all hell would break loose."

"We concede the delicacy of the politics," said Atherton. "But the plan is for the Association to handle the matter itself, privately and quickly. It would be over and done with before the newspapers found out."

"Privately?" asked the Senator. "Then what does this plan have to do with me?"

"All we ask is that the government not interfere," said Atherton, locking eyes with the Senator.

The Senator stroked his beard, deep in thought. Then, with surprising swiftness, he lifted his bulk from the chair. "Your plan carries considerable risk," he said, "though I do see its merits. I'll speak to the necessary people in Washington. I can't assure you that the government will not get involved, but we may buy you some time."

The Senator buttoned his coat. "You're lighting a match to a very dry prairie, Mr. Atherton," he said gravely. "You must be quick about your business lest the fire spread out of control. That would be very bad for you...and me. And one more thing," the Senator said as he placed his derby on his head. "I do not want my name linked with this activity in any way. If the word gets out, there'll be hell to pay from Powder River all the way to Washington D.C."

Atherton smiled as he stood up. Holding out his hand, he said quietly, "We fully understand, Senator. We have already begun preparations and have chosen men for this campaign who will be discreet. There will be no scandal. You have been a good friend of the Association's, and a valuable resource here in Washington. We will ensure that you are not associated with this endeavor in any way."

The Senator turned to leave. As he opened the door, Atherton said pleasantly, "One more thing, Senator. The Queen sends her regards and her thanks for your help."

The Senator grunted. "Good day," he said, stepping through the door and shutting it behind him.

Atherton gazed at the closed door for a few seconds, and then looked at Oglethorpe, his smile fading. "I have just returned from a miserable voyage to England, Cousin Robert," he said disapprovingly, "and the financiers are losing patience with our cattle investments in the west. They are demanding their money. I was forced to make good on my debts. Now, we need to talk about yours."

Startled, Oglethorpe looked up. "It's the rustlers," he said. "They're driving me into financial ruin."

"I sympathize with you, Robert," Atherton countered, "but rustling is not the problem. It's your gambling. Rustlers may cost you a few dollars, but the gaming tables will take the rest."

Robert Oglethorpe hung his head. "I could borrow additional resources given the time."

"Possibly, but you would simply be forestalling the inevitable," replied Atherton. "In any event, borrowing is not the answer, even if you found a lender."

Oglethorpe looked up defiantly. "I just need one big win, just one, and I could pay back everything I owe," he said.

Lord Atherton looked grim. "Whatever you must do, Robert, but should you be unable to meet your obligations, you would have to go into insolvency. That, of course, would disrupt all our family's business lines. We could overcome that, in time, but it would be highly unpleasant. Frankly though, I fear for your health should you not repay your debt, and soon."

Blood drained from Robert Oglethorpe's face, and his eyes shifted nervously like those of a cornered animal. "I understand," he said, his voice suddenly hard and cold. "I'll do whatever I must."

The sharp edge in his cousin's voice caused Atherton to look up. Gazing directly at Oglethorpe's eyes, the older man surmised that his younger relative might have a plan, but he decided to forego the opportunity to talk about it now.

Swiveling his chair, Atherton gazed out the window at the harbor and changed the subject. "Robert," he said, "we are developing a list of men in Wyoming we believe to be rustlers. Our plan is to hunt them down next spring, before the roundup, and hang them where we find them. I will personally be traveling to Wyoming to oversee these operations."

Robert Oglethorpe looked doubtful for a moment. Then he spoke. "This may be fortuitous," he said. "I have been courting a woman who is related to a rancher in Wyoming. His ranch is not far from our own investment, and I understand he is running a herd numbered in the thousands. We could visit there. I would be out of the city, at least for a while, and difficult for the financiers to find."

"Good," said Atherton. "I knew I could count on you to address this situation. Once the rustlers are gone, you might be able to hold out through the fall roundup in September. Your take from the herds should be large enough to pay your debts, and quite possibly, provide a tidy profit as well."

Atherton arose and stepped over to where Oglethorpe stood. Clapping him on the shoulder, he smiled. "Whatever your plan, I suggest you attend to it well. I will help you where I can. If you have need of someone who will, shall I say, take care of problems, then there is a man who has done several unpleasant jobs for me in the past." Atherton withdrew a piece of paper from his vest pocket and wrote a name on its white surface. Handing the paper to Oglethorpe, he continued. "This man will do what you pay him to do, but he doesn't come without a price."

#

Under Bentley's care, Luke recovered steadily, though a hacking cough plagued him unmercifully. Then, three weeks after arriving at the sanitarium, Bentley appeared at Luke's door, a broad smile on his face. "We are releasing you this morning," he said.

Luke waved a thin arm around the bare room. "As you can see, I have my bags packed."

"Listen," William said, his voice turning stern. "I meant what I said about the whiskey. No more or you won't live another five years. And consider my advice about going to a dryer climate. It will help you regain your health."

An aide popped his head in the door. "The carriage is waiting, Doctor Bentley. Joshua said he would drive Mr. Banister home, or wherever he wanted to go."

Together, the men walked down the hall to the sanitarium's entrance. Bentley held out his hand. "I don't know what you'll choose, but if you go off on an adventure, write to me about your travels so I know what I'm missing."

Luke took Bentley's hand. "Thanks, William" he said, "I will when I can, and don't worry about me. I don't mind dying, but it won't be today." With that, Luke walked down the steps to the waiting carriage.

An hour later, Joshua steered the carriage into a long lane leading to a large, pleasant looking house. It clattered up to the front door, and Joshua pulled on the reins, bringing Lizzie to a stop. "This your home?" he asked, admiring the stately structure.

"Yes," Luke said as stepped down from the carriage. "I assume you are available for a trip to go to the city?"

Joshua nodded.

"Wait here, please. I'll be out in a moment."

Luke climbed the steps to his house, opened the door, and stepped inside. It had been weeks since he had last been home, and a musty smell hung in the air. Pulling back a curtain, he threw open a window and let fresh air sweep through the rooms.

Luke went to his office and gathered an armload of files. He stuffed them into a carrying case and returned to the waiting carriage. Clambering aboard, he leaned forward and gave Joshua an address in the city's business district. Joshua slapped the reins, and Lizzie pranced down the lane and out onto the street.

A quarter hour later, Luke found himself in familiar old haunts in the business district of Philadelphia. Tapping on Joshua's shoulder, he pointed at a building on the opposite side of the street. Joshua brought the mare to a stop at the curb.

"Thanks for your help," Luke said, stepping onto the sidewalk. "And, you too," he said, slapping Lizzie on the rump. Dodging oncoming buggies, he hurried across the street toward a glass door that had 'Spencer & Banister, Attorneys at Law' painted in black letters on the glass.

Luke and Ruben Spencer had been friends and successful law partners for more than ten years; nevertheless, Luke paused for a moment, reluctant to enter the office. Finally, he took a deep breath, twisted the knob of the heavy oak door, and shoved it inward. It opened, and as he stepped into the entry, an attractive young girl glanced up from a small desk.

"Hello Miss Aiken," Luke said.

The young woman's eyes widened. "Mr. Bannister?" she asked.

Luke grimaced, realizing it had been months since he had been to the office. "Yes. Is Ruben in," he asked.

"Of course," Kate replied, regaining her composure. "Let me tell him you're here." She rose to her feet. "It is so good to see you," she continued. "Why...why, you're so thin!" With that, she pushed aside her chair and disappeared down the hall. Soon she returned. "Ruben said to come right in," Kate said brightly. "He's been expecting you." Luke thanked the young woman and walked down the hall to Ruben Spencer's office and stepped inside.

Ruben Spencer's office was littered with books and boxes of papers stacked in neat piles on the floor and along the walls. When Luke entered, Ruben stepped out from behind his desk and held out his hand. "It's great to see you again," he said. "I have been keeping tabs on you through our friend, the good doctor. Come. Sit down."

"Thanks," Luke said as he dropped into a highbacked red leather chair. "I'm tired already. I must be getting old."

"Nonsense," said Ruben. "William says you're doing well."

Luke cleared his throat. "On the contrary, he thinks I should move out west where the air is dry."

Ruben leaned back in his chair, assessing the man he had known as a friend and partner. Luke's face was lined and drawn; his body raw-boned, and he breathed hard when he sat. "Go west," Ruben said. "Why on earth would you want to leave Philadelphia?"

"My health, and there are too many memories here, too many places that connect me to the past."

"You're not going, of course."

"Yes, I am. Now let's get down to business."

Ruben grew tense, but Luke continued. "First, you've been carrying this partnership for the past year. There is nothing here that you haven't earned. So, I'm giving my share of everything in this law practice to you. I want nothing, just a few books out of my office. You keep everything else."

Ruben leaned back in his chair and put up a feeble protest, but Luke waved it off. "Only the fact that we are good friends has kept you from throwing me out, Luke continued, "and besides, I'm giving up the practice of law." Luke reached into his satchel. "The second thing is, I'm going to sell all my property, and I'm giving you power of attorney to complete the sale. Here are the necessary documents. They're already signed. After paying my bills with the proceeds, you can deposit whatever funds I have left in my bank. I'll have delivered to you a trunk full of items I want to keep. When I get settled, I'll send you my address, and I trust you will send that trunk to me."

"You know I will," responded Ruben.

The two conversed for about an hour, tying up all the last-minute legal details that accompany business transactions. Finally, Luke sat back in his chair with a sigh. "I'm not used to this," he said. "I hope we're finished."

"I believe so. I don't see anything else that we might need here," Ruben said as he leafed through the stack of papers one more time.

"Good," Luke exclaimed. He stood and held out his hand. "I must be on my way. You've been a good friend and partner. And, I like to think we have done some good along the way. I'll miss our good conversations and debates at the pub. But life sometimes sends you on a different path, and this is the path I have to take."

Ruben grasped Luke's hand. "Then, good luck to you," he said. "I hope you find what you're searching for."

#

At midnight, two weeks after leaving William Bentley's care, Luke sat in his study reading the last legal document finalizing the sale of his business interests. A low flame licked at the split wood in the fireplace, and the faint smell of woodsmoke lent an air of comfort to the room.

Luke tossed a sheaf of papers on his desk and dipped his pen into the nearby ink well. Touching pen to paper, he wrote his name in strong script at the bottom of each page. It was odd, but the finality of his act left him with a sense of relief.

Leaning back in his chair, Luke mused about the past week. He had visited the familiar haunts he had known so well only a year before, but they were different. Even his old friends had moved on with life. As the fire sputtered, Luke concluded what he had known all along—there was nothing left for him in this city. It was time to move on.

Early the next morning, Luke placed the envelope of legal documents in the post. After packing his few remaining belongings, he saddled his horse and rode once more to a nearby graveyard. New grass tinged the ground green and tiny buds covered the boughs of a tall oak that reigned nearby. Dismounting, he tied his horse to a rail and walked to a pile of mounded earth that wore a blanket of colorful flowers. Kneeling, he rested his hand on the soft black soil. "I'm sorry," he whispered. Rising, he strode to his horse, swung into the saddle, and headed west.

CHAPTER 3. THE SKIRMISH

For weeks Luke traveled west. Sometimes, he could trade his labor for food and a place to sleep. Sometimes, he was forced to sleep alongside the road, scavenging for whatever food he could find. He had crossed into West Virginia just two days past, and this particular morning found him riding along a lesser traveled country lane somewhere south of the Ohio River. The two hard biscuits he'd eaten for breakfast left his belly grumbling and tight. To make matters worse, rain drops began to pelt his face.

I don't know why I let William talk me into this, he grumbled to himself, pulling up his collar to ward off the damp.   I'm cold. I'm starving. I'm hundreds of miles from home.

Engrossed in his own thoughts, Luke felt his horse skitter sideways, but it was too late. A second later, he found himself lying on his back in the mud. Cursing, he clambered to his feet, and chased after his mount. "Whoa, calm down," he said, coaxing the animal to a stop.

As he retrieved the reins, a loud guffaw reached his ears. He looked up and cast his eyes on a battered old wagon rolling onto the lane from a side trail about thirty yards ahead. A boy of about seventeen sat on a sack in the wagon box, facing backward, and watching Luke with a grin on his face. A shotgun lay across his knees. An old man clad in brown shirt and pants sat perched atop the wagon seat, handling the team. Beside the old man sat a bearded man dressed in black from head to toe. He too, clutched a shotgun.

The boy turned to say something to his companions. They glanced back and shifted the long guns cradled in their arms. Though the men's looks carried nothing in the way of a welcome, Luke's hunger overrode his caution. *Maybe I can get some directions to the next town, if there is one, he thought, and something to eat.*

Luke calmed his horse and stepped back into the saddle. Spurring ahead, he hurried to catch up with the wagon which, in the meanwhile, had disappeared from view in a creek bottom lined with thick brush. Luke could hear the wagon's iron-rimmed wheels rumbling over exposed river rock. He quickened his pace and caught sight of the wagon just as it emerged from a crossing on the other side of the stream channel.

Suddenly, a rifle boomed from the brush along the side of the road, and a slug slammed into the wagon's box, scattering wooden splinters into the air. The mules reared and bolted, and the two men and the boy leaped from the wagon, diving into the undergrowth alongside the once tranquil road. A second later, the air was filled with thunder as both sides of the road triggered off round after round of fire.

Luke pulled up in the middle of the track. "What the...," he muttered, but before he could react, a volley of lead kicked up fountains of dirt at his horse's feet. The frightened animal reared up on its hind legs, pawing at the air. Luke sawed at the reins, trying to pull the horse back to the ground, but in its panic, the animal threw its head wildly and began to topple over backwards. Kicking his feet out of the stirrups, Luke jumped clear of the half-ton of flesh before it crushed him beneath its weight. His boots had barely hit the ground when another volley of bullets sent him scrambling to the side of the road where he leaped headlong into a stand of brush.

Luke regretted his avenue of escape immediately. Briars ripped at his skin and tore his clothing, but he fought through the thorns until he stepped out into a small open glade a dozen yards off the edge of the track. Spying a downed tree, he sprinted forward, hoping its thick trunk would provide protection from stray bullets. He had almost reached its safety when a bullet zipped through the brush, grazing his left thigh. Luke yelped, but hobbled the last few steps to the stump. Belly first, he slid over the log, falling onto a bed of leaves on its far side.

Rolling to his back, Luke examined the wound. The bullet had passed cleanly through the fleshy part of his upper leg. No bones were broken, at least as near as he could tell. Pulling a neckerchief from his pocket, Luke bound up the wound, knotting the cloth loose enough that his leg kept circulation. Having doctored his limb as best he could, he turned his attention to his face. It was scratched and bloody from the thorns, as were his arms and legs. He wiped away the blood with the sleeve of his shirt and took a deep breath. He didn't know who these people were, or what their argument was about, but whatever it was, he wanted no part of it.

Somewhere out on the trail, a man shouted and, as quickly as it had begun, the shooting stopped. Moments later, the drumming sound of horses' hooves reached Luke's ears, quickly fading into the distance. Minutes passed. The woods were silent. The skirmish, or whatever it was, must be over, Luke concluded, and he raised up and took a quick glance over the log. He was alone.

Luke pulled himself to his feet, but his leg was stiff, and it throbbed in pain. Gingerly, he loosened the bandana tied around his thigh and inspected his leg wound. While the bleeding had stopped, the flesh was already turning a rosy pink. He leaned forward and began to retie the bandana, but the steel on steel click of a hammer locking into firing position slammed against his ears like a clap of thunder.

Startled, Luke snapped his head up and found himself staring direct-ly into the barrel of a revolver. It was held by the man dressed in black who had been riding in the wagon ahead of him only minutes earlier. Luke raised his hands slowly, taking stock of the coarsely dressed stranger that stood a step away. Thin as a fence rail, the man probably weighted a hundred and thirty pounds or less. A thick black beard obscured his face.

"Look, mister, I don't know who you are or what this shooting is all about, but I'm not a part of it," Luke said. "You can see I'm not even armed."

The man sneered and kept the handgun pointed at Luke's chest. "I see'd ya followin' us," he said. "Gun or no. You're a Branscom."

"Branscom," Luke echoed. "I'm not a Branscom. I don't know any Branscom's. I'm just traveling through, that's all."

The man stepped forward and stuck his face so close that Luke could smell his rancid breath. There was no compassion in his eyes, only an emp-ty coldness. "No, yer one of them, for sure," the man snarled. "Ya must've tipped the others off when we came through here. I'm a gonna hav' to kill ya fer that." Before Luke could reply, the bearded stranger pushed his pistol into Luke's chest and squeezed the trigger.

Instinctively, Luke threw himself sideways, expecting the roar of a muzzle blast and a chunk of lead to splinter his ribs and rip into his heart, yet the only sound he heard was a metallic 'click' as the hammer slammed harmlessly onto the cartridge. Grinning stupidly, the man stood still, not quite comprehending that his pistol had failed to fire. For a moment, the two men locked stares, but when the stranger shifted his thumb to pull back the pistol's hammer again, Luke lunged forward, striking out with his right fist. The blow landed squarely on the man's jaw, snapping his head back hard. The stranger's yellowed eyes rolled back in his head, and the pistol fell from his limp fingers as his body slumped to the ground.

Luke stood over his fallen assailant, fist drawn back and ready to punch again. The man lay still for a span of seconds, but then stirred and opened his eyes, focusing on Luke's face. Grinning, he held out his hand, but like a snake, he struck out with his foot, kicking Luke in his wounded leg with the toe of his boot.

A bolt of pain shot through Luke, and he went to the ground as his leg buckled beneath him. The stranger leaped onto his chest and the two men rolled across the grass as brush and briars tore at their skin. Still weak from his bout with pneumonia, Luke was soon gasping for breath, but the bearded man was wiry and strong, and he came up astride Luke's body, pin-ning him to the ground.

His lips parted in a wide, yellow-toothed, grin, the man pulled a short-bladed dagger from his boot. Luke grasped the man's wrist, but the stranger forced the blade toward Luke's throat with his weight. For a split second, Luke wondered what death was going to be like, but something deep inside his soul refused to give up the fight, and with all his remaining strength, he arched himself off the ground. Off balance, the bearded stranger shot forward and landed awkwardly in a stand of grass.

Luke rolled away and scrambled to his feet, panting hard. Spotting a stout tree limb sticking out of a brush pile, he yanked it out and, wielding it like a staff, whirled to face the stranger, ready to fend off another attack. The man lay where he had fallen.

Luke circled his assailant. There was no movement, and the only sound he heard was his own heavy breathing and the soft rustling of the brambles as they swayed in the breeze. Wary of more tricks, Luke prodded the man with his staff. There was no response. He stepped closer, and using the tree limb like a lever, turned the man to his back. The stranger's eyes were open, yet vacant and dull. A trickle of blood ran from a corner of the man's mouth, dribbling to the grass where he lay.

Luke's eyes ran the length of the man's body, and he gasped when they fell on the handle of a knife protruding at an odd angle from the man's throat. In the fight, the stranger had fallen on his own blade, and now it was his blood that stained the ground. Shaking, Luke stepped back and leaned against the old stump, trying to regain his composure.

"I see one of them Branscoms behind that log right here, Pa," a voice shouted. "Careful, son," replied an older, deeper, voice. "See if'n you kin knock 'im down."

Luke jerked his head toward the sound and saw the tops of the brush waving as men made their way toward the meadow. The pain in his leg now pounding, he gritted his teeth limped toward the nearest copse of brush. In quick succession, two blasts boomed from the muzzle of a shotgun and an angry swarm of double ought buckshot whipped past his head.

"Hold up," Luke shouted. "Stop shooting. I'm unarmed."

"Show yourself," the deep voice commanded, "or I'll drill ya full of holes."

Luke rose up out of the brush, his hands high. "I'm shot in the leg," he shouted back. "I can't walk."

"We be a comin' to ya then, mister. If'n you make a move, I'll plug ya, ya hear," growled the unseen voice. Branches crackled as the men made their way forward, and within a few seconds, a long gun barrel poked through the brambles. It was followed by the ruddy face of the old man Luke had seen in the wagon. Trailing a step behind was the boy.

The old man stepped into the small clearing and eyed Luke. "Got a gun?" the old man asked. Luke shook his head. The man scanned the small glade until his eyes lit on the black clad body lying in the grass. "Travis," he shouted excitedly, "see to Willy. I think this man's done hurt 'im."

Stepping over to the still form, the boy knelt and felt the man's pulse. "Willy's daid," exclaimed the boy, backing away.

"Look, I'm sorry about your friend here," said Luke nervously. "I was just trying to defend myself, that's all. I was traveling by myself when the shooting started. I jumped into the brush to get away, but a bullet hit me in the leg. I crawled in here and was laying low when this man just showed up. He called me a Branscom, and then tried to shoot me, but his gun didn't go off. We fought, and during the fight, he fell on his own knife. It was self-defense."

"You talk too much," the old man said. Keeping his eyes glued on Luke, he spoke to the boy. "I reckon we might ought to kill this fella, too, don't ya think Travis?"

The boy hesitated. "I don't know, Pa," he replied. "I'm not sure I cotton to killin' a man for no reason. You can tell by his dress he ain't no Branscom. I suppose he might 'a been traveling like he said."

The old man edged closer and studied Luke's face. Furrowing his brow, he said, "Maybe, maybe not. I guess we can let Jesse decide. Git the wagon, son."

Quickly, the boy disappeared into the brush. The man pulled a long knife from a sheath hanging from his belt and strode over to a nearby tree. With a few deft strokes, he hacked off a forked branch and whittled it into a passable crutch. He handed it to Luke.

"You can walk now," the old man said. Then, prodding Luke with the barrel of his shotgun, he pointed towards the trail leading back through the brambles. "Let's you an' I go down to the road and wait for Travis to git back. Ain't nothing we kin do for Willy here." Relieved that he was not going to be shot where he stood, Luke leaned heavily on the makeshift crutch and hobbled into the brush.

They emerged onto the road just as the boy arrived with the wagon. As the mules slowed to a stop, the old man pushed his shotgun into Luke's belly and waved at the wagon box. "Git in!" he ordered. With little choice, Luke hobbled around to the back and slid into the wagon bed.

The old man looked directly at Luke. "Now, Travis and me are gonna go git Willy. It's only a few steps into the brambles heah, so don't git no idees bout running off. They ain't no place to go, and we'd hunt you down right quickly. Ya hear?"

Luke considered the man's statement. He was right. Luke would not get far even if he could run. He nodded his head, hoping to talk his way out of his predicament later.

The man and the boy disappeared into the brush, reappearing soon half carrying and half dragging Willy's body. "Looks like Willy's the only dead 'un today," grunted the old man as they hoisted the corpse up into the back of the wagon. "I don't see no Branscom's down anywhere."

"I thought I winged one, Pa," said the boy. "But, they all left, so I must of not kilt him."

"Good fer you, Travis," said the old man. "Now, just keep yer gun on this one. If'n he tries anything, shoot him, too. Jesse most likely will anyway." The old man clucked his tongue and the mules leaned into their harnesses.

The wagon headed upwards through the trees. Winding back and forth across the mountainside, they traveled along a rocky road for a mile or more until they crossed a cascading creek. There, the old man turned the mules onto a barely discernable two track path, leaving the main road far behind.

Every rock they crossed sent shooting pains up Luke's leg, but he rode quietly for a while, looking around and wondering where he was being taken. At the first opportunity, he caught the boy's eye. "Where are we going?" Luke asked.

"To our cabin," said the boy. "Up in McGill Holler."

"Who is Jesse?" Luke asked, noting that his fate apparently rested in that person's hands.

"My sister, Jesse McGill," responded the boy proudly. "We're all Mc-Gills."

"Travis, you be talking too much!" cautioned the old man. "Keep yer gun on this fella whilst I tend to the mules."

"Sure, Pa," Travis responded. With that, he pointed the shotgun at Luke's chest and fell silent.

The two track road meandered with the creek channel and at least twice, dipped down into the creek itself, crossing to the other side. The mules labored hard and soon their harnesses were stained black with sweat. Luke's wounded leg throbbed and as they wound their way through the woods, Willy's body bounced around the wagon box like a sack of feed, bumping against Luke's legs. Finally, Luke swallowed his disgust and pushed Willy's stiffening body away, wedging it against the side of the wagon and holding it there with his foot.

After about twenty minutes, the wagon squeezed through a narrow cleft in a rock palisade and passed through a stand of trees, emerging finally into an open meadow.

Curious, Luke swiveled around and scanned the clearing. He guessed it to be about ten acres in size. A roughhewn log cabin stood against a weathered granite cliff at its far end; a stream flowed by within twenty yards of its porch. On the other side of the meadow, opposite the cabin, stood a barn and several outbuildings. The old man guided the wagon up a trail that ran past the moist black earth of a small freshly plowed field. A flock of chickens pecked and scratched for worms and bugs in the overturned sod.

Within a few minutes, the driver pulled into the cabin's yard, and the man the boy called Pa guided the mules up to the cabin, reining them to a stop at the porch. "Halloo," he shouted.

The door of the cabin opened and a slender, darkhaired woman stepped out onto the porch. The woman looked at the wagon's occupants with a puzzled look on her face.

"Pa, I thought you were bringing Willy O'Connell," she said.

The old man gazed at her a moment, gathering his words. Then, in a low voice he replied. "He's in the back of the wagon, Jesse. He's dead. Travis is holding the gun on the man what kilt him."

Gathering her skirt, Jesse climbed up the wheel of the wagon and peered into the box. Luke still had his foot pushed against Willy's body. When the woman gave him a withering look, he sheepishly pulled his foot back.

"I want to know what happened," she said. Curiously, Luke thought he detected a note of relief in her tone.

"Wa'al now, Jesse," replied the old man gently, "we was a coming home and when we reached the bend in the road by the river, we was ambushed there by some of Branscom's men. Things sort of went bad, and we took cover in the woods. Now, in fairness, this fella says he was just passin' by when the shootin' started, but when he hightailed it into the brush, Willy thought he might be a Branscom hidin' out, so's he went in to get 'im but somehow, Willy ended up getting kilt."

Jesse narrowed her eyes and looked at Luke. "What have you to say for yourself?" she asked.

"It's just like this man says," Luke replied, feeling a bit like he was facing a hanging judge. "I don't know any Branscoms. I was just traveling through when the shooting started. Willy, if that's his name, tried to shoot me. I didn't mean to hurt him. I was just trying to keep him from killing me. What happened was an accident."

"You can kill this fella for killing Willy, or if'n you believe him, let him go," the old man interjected solemnly. "It's your desire, Jesse."

"Another killin' won't solve anything," replied Jesse. "Put Willy in the ice house. We'll have a proper burial for him tomorrow. As for this fellow, put him in the smokehouse, and we can decide what to do with him later."

By this time, Luke's patience was exhausted. "Listen, you, whoever you are," he spat out angrily. "I demand that you let me go. You have no right to keep me here."

Jesse stopped abruptly, turned around, and took a couple steps back toward Luke. "Maybe so," she said softly, "but I guess I would have to turn you over to the Sheriff for killing Willy. Usually, when an outsider kills one of our folk, they give them a fair trial and hang them the next day. Would you rather I do that?"

Luke sat speechless. A half-smile played at the corner of Jesse's mouth. "I didn't think so," she said, and turned back toward the cabin, disappearing inside.

The old man crawled down and ambled to the back of the wagon, motioning for Luke to get out. His arguments falling on deaf ears, Luke had little choice. Holding onto his crutch, he scooted to the end of the wagon box and slid out. "Move," the old man commanded, prodding Luke with his shotgun. "To the smokehouse over theah," and he pointed the business end of his gun at a small log structure about a hundred feet away.

Luke hobbled in the direction Pa indicated. When they arrived at the shed, Pa stepped out ahead and removed a stout wooden peg from the hasp that held the door closed. "This heah ole smoke house will hold ya," the old man opined with conviction. "No need of ya even trying to get out." Swinging the door wide, he motioned Luke inside. Luke stooped low and entered the building's dark interior. Pa shut the door behind him and jammed the peg back in the hasp.

"Hey, mister," Luke shouted as Pa walked away. "I'm thirsty. Can someone bring me some water?"

"Patience boy," answered the old man over his shoulder. "I'll send Travis back with a jug."

Luke watched through a hole in the chinking as Pa walked back to the wagon. Then, he turned and surveyed his prison. Though it was made of stout logs, the chinking had fallen out in several places, and shafts of light found their way through the holes to illuminate the dark interior. Sawdust lay deep on the floor, giving each step a soft, springy feel. An old stump sat against one wall, but there was little else.

Luke picked up a small stick poking out of the sawdust on the floor and stuck it behind a piece of chinking. He began prying the mud and twigs loose from between the logs, and soon, he had developed a small opening, about eye-high. He pressed his eyes to the slit, scanning the surrounding meadow.

The sound of a door slamming drew Luke's eyes toward the cabin. He caught sight of Travis climbing into the old wagon. The boy slapped the reins and the wagon groaned as the mules strained forward. *Taking Willy down to the ice house*, he thought. *Hope I don't join him anytime soon.*

The wagon lumbered up to the smokehouse door and stopped. Travis retrieved a fired clay jug from the wagon box and jumped to the ground. "Pa said you needed some water," he said as he unlatched the door and handed the jug to Luke. "This heah's good spring water, best on the mountain." Then, as suddenly as he had come, the boy left, locking the door behind him. Luke lifted the jug to his lips and took a long draught of sweet water. Then wrestling the stump over to one side, he sat down and leaned back against the logs, waiting for whatever came next.

CHAPTER 4. MARRIAGE OR. . .?

By late afternoon, the clouds had dissipated, leaving a hot, yellow sun hanging low in an azure sky. Inside his makeshift prison, Luke paced restlessly until the sound of voices drew him to a crack in the log chinking. Pressing his eye to the slit, he watched silently as Pa and Travis ambled by carrying long handled shovels. They walked to a shaded knoll overlooking the meadow, and Pa sunk his shovel into the sod. With a grunt, he lifted a spade full of black dirt and threw it a short distance away. Travis joined in, and together they worked steadily, shoveling sod and dirt onto a growing pile.

By the time they had finished digging, the afternoon shadows had grown long. Pa pulled out a kerchief, wiped his brow, and then said something to Travis. The boy threw his shovel aside and trudged off toward the barn. Pa strode back to the cabin and disappeared inside. Soon, a pair of chickens arrived and Luke watched idly as the birds scratched for worms in the fresh dirt dug from Willy's grave.

About a half hour later, Jesse and Pa stepped out of the cabin. This time, Pa carried his long-barreled gun. Together, they walked to the smokehouse, arguing in low tones until they stopped at the door. "Bring him out," Jesse said with a sigh.

Cradling his gun in the crook of his arm, Pa pulled the peg from the hasp. The smokehouse door swung open on creaking hinges. "Come on out heah, young fella," the old man commanded. Warily, Luke stepped out into the open air.

After the darkness of the smokehouse, the bright afternoon light stung Luke's eyes. He shaded them with his hand while he eyed Jesse McGill closely. She stood about five and a half feet tall, he estimated, and was clad in a long cotton dress that hugged a trim figure. A full head of jet-black hair fell to the middle of her back, framing a pair of emerald green eyes. Her complexion was smooth and clear save for a few light lines at the corners of her mouth. While a hardscrabble backwoods life aged women early, Luke guessed that she was in her early thirties.

Jesse circled Luke, looking him over like a farmer inspects a mule offered for sale by a scandalous horse trader. "He's pretty scratched up from the briars," Jesse said, addressing Pa. Luke flinched as she stuck out a finger and poked him hard in the stomach. "He's soft, Pa, real soft," she said in a soft drawl. "And pale. Probably hasn't done a lick of work in all his life." Grasping his right hand, she pulled it toward her, turning his palm up. Luke was surprised at how strong her grip was for such a slender woman. He shivered as she ran her fingers lightly over his forearm. "For sure, he hasn't ever plowed a field." She scanned his palms and glanced back at Pa. "No callouses, so he's never chopped much wood either."

Jesse stepped closer and, even in the afternoon sun, Luke could feel the heat emanating from her body. He breathed in the fragrance of the clean dress she wore. She raised her hand and drew it lightly across his cheek, looking intently at his eyes. They locked gazes for a moment, and Luke had the uncomfortable feeling that her piercing eyes could read his character to the depths of his soul. He flushed and looked away.

She stepped back, shaking her head. "He's been sick, too, Pa. I can't say that he would be worth much around here." Turning, she started walking back toward the cabin. Over her shoulder she said, "I don't know, Pa. I suppose he wouldn't be as ugly as some. Maybe he'll do; maybe he won't. I need to think on it a bit more."

Luke turned and looked questioningly at Pa. Pa shrugged his shoulders. "You kilt the man that was arranged fer her," he said. "On this mountain, if'n you kill a woman's man, you're gonna have to replace him."

"Replace him?" asked Luke. "How will I replace him? I don't know anybody around here, let alone any man looking to get married."

Pa grinned and slapped his leg in amusement. "No, you don't understand," he said chuckling. "You're gonna be her husband."

Astonished, Luke blurted out. "Look, old man, I'm not going to be anybody's husband, let alone that woman's."

Pa's smile abruptly faded and he swung the shotgun toward Luke's midsection. "Jesse's gittin' along in years," he said quietly. "Well, she's nigh on to thirty or so, maybe a little more I suppose, though I don't rightly remember. I'm gittin' older, too. Doc says my heart ain't what it used to be. I could go any time. Now, it ain't good for a single woman to be alone in these hills, and I didn't know rightly who would take care of her if I passed on. So, I arranged to bring Willy O'Connell over to see if she might take a shine to him, though she wasn't a bit happy 'bout it. She makes out like she ain't happy with you either, but I think she could cotton to ya, if'n ya treat her right." Pa stopped for a moment to spit on the ground. "But if'n we cain't agree to terms here mister," he continued, his voice now serious, "I'm gonna save the sheriff the trouble of hangin' ya. We'll bury you an' Willy at the same time tomorry."

Then, Pa's grin returned, and he went on, "But to tell ya the truth, she ain't made up her mind yet, and I'd hate to have to shoot ya before I gave ya every chance. Now, I know you don't like bein' held up here, but let me tell ya, she ain't a bad woman. Smarter than a whip, a little high strung maybe, and stubborn once she gits her mind made up 'bout something. Truth is, I've takin' a likin' to ya, mister. Travis has too. Nonetheless, if Jesse decides ye won't do, then so be it, but if'n she says you're good enough, then I've told ya what you're gonna do. Now git back in the smokehouse and take some time to think about what I jist said."

Pa waved his rifle, and Luke retreated into his prison. Pa closed the door, and Luke heard the peg drop in the hasp. With both fists he pounded on the smokehouse door. "You can't keep me here," he shouted. "I've got friends who'll get me out."

"If'n you'd like, I'll send Travis for 'em. Tomorry maybe, or next week," the old man said with a chuckle. Then he ambled back to the cabin and disappeared inside.

Luke turned away from the smokehouse door, stunned at the prospect of having to marry this strange woman to save his life. *I must have been nuts, he berated himself, to let William talk me into leaving Philadelphia. Here I am in the middle of God-knows where, my horse gone, my money stolen. I have no idea how far it is to the next town, or even where it might be. Hell, I'll be lucky if I ever get back to civilization.* He plopped down on the stump in despair.

#

Twilight crept into the meadow, and with it came cooler evening air. When he heard the sound of the cabin door opening Luke peered through a spot in the logs where the chinking had fallen out, and spotted Travis approaching. The boy set a plate of food on a stump next to the smokehouse and removed the wooden peg from the hasp. Stepping back, he said, "Come on out, mister. Jesse fixed you some supper."

Gingerly, Luke stepped through the low door out into the fading light. "Thanks," he said. "I'm about starved." Motioning toward a chopping stump, Luke asked, "Care if I sit down here while I eat? I could use the fresh air." Travis grinned and nodded.

Luke picked up the steaming plate and the smell of ham and beans perked up his appetite. He spooned in one bite, and then another. Though the beans were hot, Luke ate like a starving pilgrim, wolfing down the whole plate with hardly a word of conversation.

After he had wiped the plate clean with a slice of homemade bread,

Luke set it down on the ground and turned his attention to the boy that eyed him with great curiosity. The lad was clad in homespun clothing. His coat hung loosely from a lanky, but strongly built frame. An unruly shock of blonde hair topped a face tanned brown from long hours in the sun.

Travis had waited patiently while Luke was eating, but now he began to pepper Luke with questions, asking about places Luke had been and sights he had seen. The boy listened spellbound while Luke described Philadelphia and life in the city. Travis had come to his defense when Pa wanted to shoot him back down on the road, and for that reason, Luke concluded that he might cultivate him as an ally. Sensing the time was right, Luke slipped in a question of his own. "Who were those people down on the road?" he asked.

"Branscoms," spat out Travis. "We make moonshine. They make moonshine too, but ours is better. Pa is really good at it, minds his mash and temperatures and such. We sell into Wheeling and other places. We an' the rest of the moonshiners on this mountain all got along until this big man named Ben Santelli showed up. He convinced the Branscoms that they ought to control all the moonshinin' round heah. First, they kilt old man Thompson up yonder holler. Then, Bobby Joe Sorrenson disappeared. Now, they're after us, but we ain't quittin'."

Luke listened quietly. Picking up a wood splinter, he stuck it between his teeth and chewed on it for a few seconds. "Travis," Luke said finally, "I want you to know I have nothing to do with the Branscoms."

"I know," Travis replied, hanging his head as if embarrassed. "If it were me, I'd let ya go on yer way. But, the decision is Jesse's. Pa'll do what she says."

Luke wanted to press Travis a little harder, but the door to the cabin suddenly opened. Luke glanced over to see Pa stepping out onto the porch. The old man looked toward where they sat, and cupped his hands around his mouth. "Travis, you done out there?" he shouted. Travis stood up and in a loud voice replied, "Yeah, Pa. I'll be there in a minute." Turning to Luke, he said, "Now, mister, it's time to go back into the smokehouse."

Luke handed the plate back to Travis, and obediently limped back into the dark interior of the building. "Thanks," he said. Travis placed the peg back into the hasp. As he turned to leave, Luke called out through the small peephole, "Tell Jesse the ham and beans were good. Best I've ever had."

"I'll tell 'er," Travis said with a grin, and he trotted back to the cabin.

#

About an hour later, Jesse appeared at the cabin door carrying a bundle and a large tin mug. Stepping off the porch, she walked purposefully toward the smokehouse and stopped in front of the door. Lifting the peg from the hasp, she pushed the door open and stepped inside. Brushing the hair back from her face, she handed the bundle to Luke. "There's a woolen blanket to ward off the night air," she said in a soft drawl. "There's no sense in catching your death of pneumonia out here. This cup contains hot tea and a mix of medicinal herbs. Drink the tea, it'll help your stomach and your cough. Here's a bag of clean cotton strips to wrap the herbs against your wounds. It's a poultice. The herbs will keep the infection away."

Luke stepped to the doorway and took the cloth from Jesse's outstretched hand. "What are you," he asked skeptically, "some kind of a backwoods medicine man?"

Jesse's green eyes flashed like lightning on a summers evening, but a smile played at the corner of her mouth. "Just do as I say," she replied evenly. "You don't want that leg to get gangrene. Pa's not all that good with a saw."

Luke opened his mouth to protest, but before he could speak, she stepped out of the smokehouse and back into the night air. Shutting the door, she replaced the peg in the hasp. Luke pressed his cheek to the gap between the logs and watched her walk away. *She is, he admitted reluctantly, a rather handsome looking woman.*

Left alone, Luke turned his attention to the mug Jesse had left. Sniffing its contents, he was pleasantly surprised by its minty aroma. *At least it smells better than some of William's medicines, so I guess it can't hurt.* He sipped the tea until it was gone. It soothed his throat. Then, he lowered his trousers and rubbed the herbs on the reddening wound, binding them to his leg with the cloth strips. Spreading the blanket on the sawdust, he lay down to rest.

There was little activity throughout the rest of the evening. Jesse stayed in the cabin, but Pa brought some additional tea and herbs for his wound. The redness that had been slowly creeping up his leg began to fade, and he wondered if the home styled medicines could actually be helping. *I can only imagine what William would say about this poultice, he thought, and he smiled inwardly knowing his friend was quite finicky about using only scientific remedies for his patients.*

Later that evening, Luke heard the cabin door open once again. He pressed an eye to the hole in the chinking and saw Jesse's trim figure silhouetted by lantern light that spilled through the open doorway. She walked to the end of the porch and sat down in an old rocking chair, swinging rhythmically back and forth and gazing out over the valley.

A full moon had risen over the hills, washing the valley in a luminous yellow haze and leaving the cabin glimmering as if made of burnished gold. Luke couldn't remember the last time he had seen anything so beautiful, and as he beheld this world of dreamlike splendor, long-stifled feelings stirred within him. He lingered at the gap in the chinking and watched until the moon slipped behind a cloud and shadows enfolded the meadow. The ephemeral scene passed and a chill filled the air. Jesse rose from her rocker and went into the cabin, shutting the door behind her.

#

A coughing fit brought on by the damp mountain air awoke Luke an hour before sunrise. Sitting up, he groped in the darkness for the water jug Travis had left, finally locating the vessel in a dark corner of the smokehouse. Luke wrestled the wooden peg from the spout and raised the jug to his lips, taking a long drink of cool water. The water soothed his throat and, after sitting for a few moments staring into the darkness, he replaced the wooden peg and set the jug back where he found it. Yawning, he lay back on the sawdust, pulling the woolen blanket up around his neck to ward off the chill. Near silence reigned outside his small prison; only the slight murmur of leaves rustling in the early morning breeze penetrated the logs forming his cell.

Luke tossed and turned, a thousand questions flooding through his mind. *What if I am forced to marry Jesse? I know what will happen if I refuse, but what if I go through with it, but up and disappear one day? I could get out of here that way, maybe.* None of the questions came with an answer. To quiet his mind, he focused on a dim shaft of light that fell through a gap in the smokehouse wall, but the more he strained to see it, the fainter it became. He stood up and widened the gap between the logs by loosening a bit more chinking with his fingers. A soft radiance spilled into his dark chamber. He pressed his cheek to the wood and peered outside.

The smokehouse afforded a panoramic view of the entire meadow, and Luke's eyes strained to see as much of the exterior world as he could. His eyes were about to give out when a faint noise floated through the night air. It emanated from the impenetrable blackness that lay just beyond the forest's edge, and in the silence of the valley it seemed discordant and out of place.

His curiosity piqued, Luke pressed his brow hard against the rough log walls to see if he could locate the source of the sound. *A deer, he thought, or maybe a bear.* He held his breath and listened intently, but he heard only stillness. *The wind, he assured himself as he stepped away from the wall, but a few seconds later, the distinct sound of muffled voices came to his ears.*

"The McGills?" he wondered aloud, but, when he placed his eye to the view slit, the moonlight revealed no discernible movement around the cabin, and no lantern shone from within.

Shifting his gaze, Luke strained his eyes, trying to see through the dim light. As his eyes focused, he detected a slight movement alongside the trail leading up to the meadow from the main road. Whatever was out there moved quietly, and intentionally kept to the shadows at the forest's edge.

Luke glanced at the horizon and noted that in less than a quarter hour, the first light of day would be breaking over the tops of the hills. He stayed glued to his vantage point and, as the shadows retreated, began to make out shapes. His eyes widened with surprise when he counted two, three, and then five figures slinking through the trees at the clearing's edge.

The men approached to within fifty yards of the cabin, stopping in a huddle as one man held up his hand. Luke could discern muffled voices as they conferred together. By this time, the sun had risen to the point where Luke could see the features of the man who appeared to be doing most of the talking. He was a big man, narrow-shouldered, but large waisted. He wore a black, flat-brimmed hat and long, dark coat. While his voice was inaudible, his hands and arms were very animated as he spoke, and he punctuated his statements with explosive jabs in the air. After a few moments of discussion, one of the men scurried off toward the log barn; two others made their way into the woods.

When the intruders had taken their places, the big man and one other minion began to move quietly toward where the McGill's slept. They reached a wooden horse trough about fifty yards from the cabin, and hunkered down, concealing themselves from the view of anyone who might look out a cabin window.

Luke watched, perplexed. Who were these men, and what were they up to? he wondered, stepping from one side of the tiny smokehouse to another. He dug at the chinking with a stick, trying to enlarge the hole, but when he heard the cabin door opening, he pressed his face hard against the logs. Emerging from the cabin, yawning and stretching, and entirely unaware of the danger that charged the early morning air, he saw Travis.

CHAPTER 5. BRANSCOMS

Travis stepped out onto the porch and shambled across the wooden deck, loitering at its edge for a moment while rubbing the sleep from his eyes. Jesse appeared at the still-open door and gently scolded the young man for leaving it ajar. Handing him an oak water bucket, she pointed toward the water well that lay about thirty yards away, and then disappeared back into the cabin, closing the door behind her.

Travis stifled a yawn and casually glanced around the valley. The spring grass bent gracefully under the weight of the morning dew. A wisp of fog drifted across the meadow. The air was still and quiet. He threw the wooden bucket over his shoulder, stepped off the porch, and trudged down a worn path toward the well.

#

Luke changed his position, trying to get a better look at the men who had invaded the McGill meadow. "Branscoms, I'll bet," he muttered to himself. "They're back for another try."

Luke stepped from side to side in the tiny building, trying to keep track of both Travis and the men at the water trough. Conflicting thoughts ran through his mind, but of two things he was sure. These men, whoever they were, were not there to rescue him and while he was angry at being imprisoned by the McGills, he had no desire to see them come to any harm.

Seconds passed and Luke agonized about what to do, but when the click of a hammer being locked into firing position knifed through the early morning air, he was galvanized into action. Throwing caution to the wind, he shouted a warning to Travis just a heartbeat before the deadly rifle roared a malevolent greeting of its own.

#

At Luke's yell, Travis ducked and jerked his head toward the smokehouse. The slug from the long rifle smashed into the large oaken bucket slung over his shoulder, spinning him around and knocking him to the ground. He scrambled to the granite lip of the hand-dug well, hugging the rock for cover. A lead smashed into the stone, ricocheting and whining away into the misty light of morning.

Suddenly, from the McGill cabin, Luke heard one blast and then another. Jesse and Pa were returning fire, he concluded, and he cheered inwardly. He pressed his eye to a crack in the smokehouse chinking and focused on the strangers. They hugged the ground as bullets fired from the cabin thumped into the side of the horse trough. The McGill's answering fire diverted the ambusher's attention away from Travis for a moment, but soon, the rest of the intruders began peppering the cabin with volleys of their own. Dozens of rounds plunked into the structure's thick log walls and bullets shattered the cabin's windows, showering razor-like shards of glass into the interior.

#

With the fire now concentrated on the cabin, Travis braved a glance over the lip of the well. He counted at least four men firing at the cabin with rifles. A flash of movement in the woods caught his attention, and he spotted a fifth man stealthily working his way through the trees.

Travis ducked his head back behind the rocks. In a few seconds, the man at the edge of the woods would have a clear shot at where he now lay. He could make a run for the cabin but with the lead slashing through the air, he knew that such a move would be suicidal, and running for the cover of the forest would be like running into the arms of death itself.

Where? How? Travis shouted inwardly, and he clenched his fist, slamming it against the rocks, trying to slow the rising panic that threatened to turn his thoughts into whirling chaos. The rough granite tore the flesh of his knuckles and blood dripped onto the ground, but the pain made him focus. "Of course, the well," he muttered as he remembered the slab that had fallen out of one side of the well when he and Pa had dug it three years ago. It had taken them days of hammering to break up the stone and haul it to the surface in buckets. Travis had cursed the rock at the time, but it had left a niche in the wall about four feet high by two feet deep and two feet wide. He had used it as a perch when cleaning the well. Now, it was a hiding place, and if he were lucky, it might save his life.

He glanced once again at the shooters. The four men in the main band and still preoccupied with the cabin, but the man in the woods had disappeared from sight. Like a snake, he slithered up and over the lip of the well, and grasping the bucket rope, lowered himself into the dark, stone cylinder. He slipped down the rope until he reached the cavity from which the rock had fallen. He swung over and set his feet on the solid rock. Though icy water came to his waist, he crouched low and flattened his body against the cold, mossy stone, out of sight of anybody looking down from above.

#

For a quarter of an hour, gunfire rattled the valley. The cabin windows were shattered. The heavy oak door was split and shredded. Through it all, Pa and Jesse returned a steady stream of buckshot and lead that kept the attackers at bay.

Maybe they'll be able to fight off these ambushers, Luke thought as he shifted his vantage point to see the rest of the meadow, but seconds later his heart fell. Unseen by either Pa or Jesse, a man with a lighted torch was edging along the perimeter of the woods, heading directly toward the McGill cabin. When he had worked his way to within thirty feet of the cabin's porch, he left the cover of the trees and ran forward. With one final lunge, he tossed the torch onto the roof of the wooden building and turned to retreat, but before he had taken a half-dozen steps, a double-barreled shotgun appeared at one of the shattered windows and a lone blast boomed across the meadow. The man screamed and crumpled into the grass.

Luke's eyes flicked to the cabin and he caught a flash of Jesse's face as she withdrew the weapon. His eyes narrowed. *Good girl he thought. At least one man isn't going to walk away from here.*

Though mortally wounded, the man had done his job. The cabin roof began to smolder and tongues of flame started to work their way down the cabin's log walls. Within minutes, white smoke billowed out of the broken windows, rising high above the meadow floor.

Aghast, Luke observed the horrific scene through the hole in the chinking. *The interior of that cabin must be a hell, he thought. They have to come out soon.*

As if reading his mind, the cabin door opened and Pa emerged, coughing and wheezing and waving a white bandana. Jesse followed close behind, a strip of cloth over her mouth and nose, but still carrying a long-barreled shotgun.

"We want to palaver," Pa choked out.

"Come on out to the yard," ordered the big man from behind the horse trough. "And have that she-devil with you put that shotgun down."

Pa laid his hand on Jesse's arm. She shook her head but let the shotgun drop from her hands to the wooden porch. Holding on to one another, they stumbled out into the yard just as part of the cabin roof fell inward, sending a shower of sparks and smoke into the morning sky.

Jesse and Pa held on to one another as they made their way toward the horse trough but, inexplicably, stopped where Luke could see both McGill's clearly. Soot blackened Pa's face and blood oozed from a wound in his cheek. Jesse's black hair was peppered with gray ash; the whites of her green eyes reddened by smoke. Both grimaced in pain, but still they stood together, defiant and proud.

The two men at the horse tank stood up. The big one strutted forward, stopping directly in front of the two McGills. Powerfully built, the man stood more than six feet tall and weighed a good 220 pounds. A hooked nose hung from a face that was sallow and fleshy. Black boots, decorated by a silver buckle at the ankle, shod his feet.

This must be Ben Santelli, Luke thought, the man Travis was talking about.

"Wa'al, Bakky," the man said arrogantly, turning back toward his companion. "Now look who's here asking to palaver."

"Looks like they ain't so high and mighty now, Ben," Bakky replied with a nervous giggle.

"Santelli," spoke up Pa, his voice raspy. "You done burnt us out. We ain't got nothin' left. Now, you and the Branscoms go away and leave us be."

Santelli only grunted. By this time, the two other men in the band had joined their comrades.

"We saw Travis go down," reported the first man to arrive. "We looked for 'im and found a little blood, but he jist disappeared. He must've crawled into the woods cause we cain't find him nowhere round heah."

The big man erupted with anger. "Weed and Seth, surely you're two of the biggest fools in these hills. Spread out and comb the woods around heah. He can't be far with a bullet in 'im. If that whelp gits away, there'll be hell to pay." Like whipped dogs, the two men turned and scurried off.

Santelli watched the two men retreat, and then he whirled and slammed a ham sized fist into Pa's midsection. The old man fell to the ground and rolled into a fetal position, gasping for air. Screaming, Jesse fell on top of her father, covering his body with her own. "You're a pig, Santelli," she shouted.

Santelli squatted and grabbed her by the hair, twisting her neck until she squirmed in pain. Then, he backhanded her across the cheek, drawing blood from the corner of her mouth.

"That's for killing Zeke," he snarled. "Now, where's Willy? I know he's supposed to be around here somewhere."

"Willy's gone," Jesse lied through bruised lips. "He's gone to git the Sheriff. He'll be back here anytime."

Santelli let go of Jesse's hair and stood up. "The Sheriff?" he mocked, looking over at the man who had been with him behind the horse tank. "Why, the Sheriff is Bakky's cousin, ain't that right Bakky? And, it ain't likely he'll come to help the likes of you, Jesse McGill."

Scanning the woods and the buildings, Santelli continued. "As for Willy, I don't believe ya. He's around here somewhere. Bakky, check the barn and the other buildings for Willy and the boy."

Bakky nodded and trotted down toward the barn. Pushing the barn door inward, he disappeared into its interior, reappearing a few minutes later. Shaking his head, he turned his attention to the ice house, gingerly pushing that door open with the barrel of his rifle. He stepped inside, emerging a second later with a triumphant whoop.

"Ben," Bakky chortled loudly. "Willy's down heah in the ice house, and he's stone cold daid." With that, he hurried back to where Pa and Jesse stood. "We musta kilt him yestidy," he snickered as he arrived.

"So, Willy's dead," Santelli said, leering at the McGills, "and Travis has a bullet in him. He won't make it far with Seth and Weed on his track. So now it's just the two of you."

At that time, Seth and Weed returned. "We didn't see Travis anywhere, Ben," one offered deferentially. "We saw some blood, but he's just disappeared. We even looked in the well, but we couldn't spot anything."

Santelli quieted for a moment. "No matter," he said rubbing his jaw. "We can hunt him down and kill him when we find him. Right now, we need to finish this job. Folks may git to wondering what this smoke is all about and start showing up heah." He turned to the two men. "Seth, you go git the horses. Weed, go see to Zeke and help Seth load him up when he returns."

Then, Santelli turned back to the McGills, an evil grin playing at the corners of his mouth. "Bakky and me will take care of these two." The big man prodded the two McGills with his boot. "Get up," he commanded. "We got some unfinished business."

Jesse helped Pa to his feet, and Santelli shoved them roughly toward the barn. Bakky trailed behind, his gun at ready. Luke stood transfixed by the scene unfolding before him, watching helplessly as the two men prodded Pa and Jesse forward with the barrel of their guns.

As they arrived at the barn, Jesse stumbled. Pa reached out to catch her, but Santelli slammed him with the butt of his rifle. Pa cried out. "Move on," Santelli growled, clearly enjoying the pain he had inflicted. "We ain't got all day."

Jesse rushed to Pa's side, screaming at Santelli, "You don't have to hurt him anymore. He's an old man. He can't do anything to you." Santelli pushed her hard against the barn. "Get in there," he smirked. "I've got somethin' for ya." Turning toward Bakky, he said, "Bring in the old man, too." Bakky shoved Pa into the barn's interior and shut the door behind them.

Though it was early morning, the inside of the barn lay shadowed. Santelli spotted a kerosene lantern hanging from a peg drilled into the center beam of the barn. He strode over, lifted the lantern from its holder, and lit the wick. When the lantern was hung back on its peg, it swung back and forth, casting eerie dancing shadows against the wooden slats of the barn wall.

Santelli turned and leered at Jesse. "Watch Pa," he ordered Bakky. "I need some light to finish my business with Jesse here." The big man moved toward Jesse, stalking her like an animal stalks its prey. Desperately, she tried to evade his bruising grasp, but he herded her into a corner of the barn, and when she tried to run past him, his hand shot out like a coiled spring, grasping her wrist in a steel vise. She scratched and kicked, but he dragged her toward a horse stall with one hand, while he unbuckled his belt with the other. Jesse battled with all she had, but Santelli's strength was too much. He threw her down, and then fell on her body, crushing her beneath his weight.

Bakky watched the ongoing struggle. He feared Santelli, but soon his eyes took on a vile gleam. "Why cain't I do my business, too?" he demanded sullenly, his lust overcoming the fear he felt for this huge man.

Seeing Bakky's distraction, Pa sprang forward with speed and agility that belied his age, flailing at Bakky with all the strength he could muster. Taken by surprise, Bakky stumbled backward and fell, dropping his rifle as he hit the barn floor. The momentum of Pa's attack propelled him forward, and he fell on top of Bakky, pinning him momentarily to the ground. They wrestled across the dirt and straw, but Bakky's strength was too great, and he shoved Pa aside.

Gasping for air, Pa rolled away from the foul-smelling man, but his hand fell on Bakky's rifle. Pulling it to his side, he leveled the barrel at Bakky's belly. "Git back," Pa commanded as he rose to his feet. Bakky, only a trigger pull away from death, obligingly stepped back against the barn wall.

Pa raised the barrel of the rifle and triggered off a lone blast. "Stop, Santelli," Pa cried, "or I'll kill 'ya!" And, he swung the gun around to Santelli.

Santelli stopped his attack and slowly rose from the barn floor. Bruised, Jesse rose to her feet, holding her torn dress together with one hand. Edging past her attacker, she spit at his face defiantly. Santelli's eyes bore a look of near insanity, but his voice was honey-smooth as he wiped away the spittle.

"Look, old man, we didn't mean no harm," Santelli purred. "We were just having a little fun with Jesse here, that's all."

"Yeah," chimed in Bakky. "Jist a little fun." He took a step toward Pa.

Pa swung the barrel of the gun away from Santelli and pointed it toward Bakky. It was a fatal mistake. In the second that Pa glanced away, Santelli whipped out a bone handled knife from his waistband, and with one huge hand spun Jesse in front of him, holding her in a steel grip as he brought the knife blade to her neck.

"Now old man, give me the gun, or I'll slit Jesse's throat from ear to ear," he hissed, pressing the knife blade tightly against Jesse's skin. Jesse cried out in pain as a thin, red line of blood oozed from the white flesh of her neck.

Pa stepped back. Suddenly, he clutched at his chest, and the blood drained from his face, leaving his cheeks a grayish pale. Dropping to his knees, he focused glassy eyes on Jesse, reaching out and whispering, "I'm sorry, Jesse. My heart. It's my heart. I cain't...." A bolt of pain shot through him, cutting off his words. He leaned back on his haunches, hugging his chest in a futile effort to keep his heart from exploding. The rifle slipped from his grasp and fell to the barn floor.

Bakky snatched up the weapon and danced away, chortling in glee, but in the span of a breath, his expression changed to pitiless malevolence. Leveling the rifle at the old man's chest, Bakky pulled the trigger. A tongue of flame erupted from the rifle's muzzle, and like a puppet on a string, Pa's body jerked backward, his life blood spilling onto the straw.

For a moment, Jesse stood with mouth open, stunned. Then she struck, clawing at Santelli's eyes with her free hand and raking deep furrows in his flesh. Howling in pain, Santelli dropped the knife and reached for his face. Freed from his iron grip, Jesse scooped up the knife and slashed at the big man, cutting him from thumb to mid-forearm.

Roaring like an enraged bear, Santelli struck out blindly, catching Jesse on the cheek with his fist. The force of his blow sent her sprawling backward onto the straw floor. The knife whirled away into the darkness. Jesse shook her head to clear her mind, and then crawled to where Pa's body lay. Sobbing, she lifted the old man's white-haired head and cradled it in her lap for a moment. Then, she laid Pa's head back in the straw and, slowly, stood upright, looking her two assailants square in the eyes. "You're cowards and pigs," she spit out, hate dripping from her voice.

Santelli raged as he held onto his bleeding arm. "Shoot her!" he screeched at Bakky. "Kill her!"

Inexplicably, Bakky hesitated, but Santelli lunged forward and ripped the rifle from the smaller man's grasp. Whirling, he swung the long barrel toward Jesse and pulled the trigger. Again, the rifle boomed and the slug slammed high into the right side of Jesse's chest, spinning her around. When she finally steadied herself and looked down, blood trickled from a small round hole in her dress.

Shock flooded through Jesse's body, and she stumbled toward Pa's body. She reached out to steady herself and her hand brushed against the lantern hanging from the center beam of the barn. In one swift motion, she pulled it from its peg. Swaying back and forth, her eyes bleary and dim, she gathered her last bit of strength. "I'll see you both in hell," she whispered through clenched teeth. Swiftly, she swung the lantern above her head, and smashed it hard against the center post of the barn. The lantern shattered, scattering burning kerosene across the barn floor and igniting piles of straw like dry tinder. Swiftly, a wall of flame roared to life, separating Jesse and her two assailants. Driven back by the heat, she stumbled to the far barn wall and slumped to the ground, closing her eyes. Blood drained from her face, while a bright red stain spread across her breast.

"She has my knife," Santelli bellowed, and as if demon possessed, he rushed forward, trying to fight his way through the sparks and cinders, but the flames were too hot, and he was driven back. He tried to skirt the wall of fire, but again the heat turned him away. Smoke billowed up so thick that it obscured Jesse's body.

"Come on Ben. We need to git out of here," Bakky shouted as he fled out the barn door. Choking and gasping, his flesh seared and his lungs full of smoke, Santelli was forced to retreat, too. On hands and knees, he crawled from the building into the open air.

Bakky feared Santelli's madness, but gathering his courage, he spoke urgently. "Ben, this smoke is bound to bring someone some of the neighbors soon."

Santelli rose to his feet and his rage abated long enough for a sense of sanity to return. Wiping the ashes from his face, he said, "I want you to fire everything—all the buildings. Kill everything that moves."

"What about Travis?" Bakky asked.

"When everything is burning, go help Seth and Weed look for him. Don't come back until he's dead. If you kill him, there won't be no one left to tell any tales."

Though Santelli's manner had turned lucid, his eyes burned red and Bakky knew better than to argue. He turned from the big man and trotted over to the ruins of the cabin. Pulling a burning log from the smoking embers, he dragged it to the icehouse. With one heave, he threw the log up onto the roof. Returning to the cabin, he dragged another log from the embers, and turned toward the smokehouse.

#

Luke witnessed everything that had occurred, and as Bakky approached with the burning log, Luke stepped away from the smokehouse wall, saying nothing. Bakky tossed the log up onto the roof, and with a few minutes, the roof of his prison started smoldering. Smoke began to curl from the roof into the interior of the shed. Horror-stricken, Luke realized he was about to burn to death.

CHAPTER 6. ESCAPE

Jesse's eyes flickered open, and she found herself lying face down on the barn floor, struggling for breath. Flames danced at her feet and smoke roiled in a haze that hung from the barn's roof. Through burning eyes, Jesse spotted Pa lying on his back a dozen feet away. She crawled to where he lay and shook him, calling his name, but his eyes were unblinking and dull. Reaching out, she touched the splotch of blood on his shirt. It was wet and sticky.

The horror of the past minutes came flooding back to Jesse, and a scream caught in her throat, but there was no time to mourn. Already, her dress was beginning to smolder, and she knew if she did not find a way out of the barn in the next few seconds, she would be consumed by the flames.

Hugging the ground, she took deep breaths of air as she crawled away from the heat, but her escape came to a sudden end when she banged against the barn's wall. Hugging the ground, she pressed her mouth against a crack in the wood, sucking in fresh air from the outside like a parched man drinks in cold water. A few deep breaths cleared her mind, but the inferno's roar grew louder, and a moment later, part of the barn's roof crashed inward, showering her with ash and sparks. When the dust had cleared, her heart fell when she saw that the fallen roof now blocked all avenues of escape.

Jesse shrank back and dug her heels into the dirt, pushing her body hard against the barn wall, but it was strong and solid. She turned and kicked at the planks, and felt one plank move ever so slightly. Frantically, she searched for something with which to pry the board loose, and a glimmering piece of metal caught her eye. It was Santelli's knife. She scooped it up, and thrusting its sturdy blade between the planks, pried with all her strength. The plank swung aside, opening a narrow gap. Sticking her head through the opening, Jesse dug her fingers into the barnyard debris and wriggled her lithe body through the hole, tumbling at last into the cool, fresh air of the world outside.

For a moment, she lay still, drinking in sweet breaths of air. Her body ached and she wanted to lay in the dirt forever, but she knew she had to move, and quickly. Grimacing, she rose to her feet and forced her legs to move, one ahead of the other, until she stumbled into the shadows of the woods at the edge of the meadow. Under cover of the leaves, she staggered down a barely discernible path until pain overcame her will to go on.

As the din of rifle fire from above reverberated in the well, Travis shrank back against the cold, mossy wall and prayed that no one had seem him climb into the well. Though his bones ached from the cold water, he waited. Once he leaned out to glance up, and he thought he saw a wisp of gray smoke floating by, but when someone fired into the water from above, he again flattened his body against the rock.

Abruptly, the shooting stopped, and an alarming quiet settled over the dark cylinder of stone. Travis held his breath and listened for any sound that might filter down the well bore. Finally, he heard voices. Maybe it's Pa, or Jesse, he tried to convince himself, but he resisted an urge to shout out. Leaning out of the cavity, he peeked up the well shaft, but could see only blue sky. A moment later, the sound of voices grew more distant, and then faded away.

Travis really wasn't sure how long he had been crouched in the dark cornice, but the icy water lapping at his chest was steadily drawing the heat from his body, leaving it numb and lethargic. He knew he would have to get out of the well soon, or he would die of the cold.

Reaching out, Travis took hold of the rope attached to the windlass. He pulled hard. It held securely. Gripping the cord with both hands, he began to climb, hand over hand. The rope was slick with moss, and once he slipped all the way back to where his boots dangled in the water, but he redoubled his effort and finally pulled himself to the top of the well.

Clinging precariously to the rope, Travis scanned McGill Holler until his eyes came to rest on the mass of billowing smoke and flames that had once been the McGill cabin. Stunned, the young man clambered over the lip of the well and, abandoning all thoughts of his own safety, raced toward the burning rubble that was once his home. Leaping onto the porch, he tried to force his way inside. Tongues of flame drove him back. Shielding his face, he retreated from the broiling heat to stand alone in the meadow, staring at the ruins. He would not let himself think about what might have happened to Jesse and Pa, but a sense of dread and hopelessness ripped at his gut.

Jesse came to once again and found herself lying on an animal trail just off the edge of the woods, still clutching Santelli's knife. She was exhausted and confused, and when she moved, a spot above her breast burned like fire. Instinctively, she reached up and touched her shoulder. It was wet. And when she brought her hand away, the tips of her fingers were red with blood. Stared into space for a moment, then images of the last few minutes flooded her mind—Pa lying dead, and Santelli's evil laughter.

Fear and rage welled up within her, but the emotions gave her strength to focus her mind—strength to move on. Think, she thought to herself. Stay alert. If she stayed where she was, Santelli would find her, that she knew. Moaning quietly, she forced herself to her feet and pushed on through the brush, following the game trail as it wound through the dense forest. Ancient, lichen-covered logs blocked her way, forcing her off the path and into undergrowth that grabbed and tripped her at every turn. Stumbling and crawling, she pressed on, using all the woods knowledge Pa had taught her.

She had gone a little more than a quarter mile when she heard a low whistle behind her. Another whistle answered, further away and lower in pitch. The whistles were not made by any forest bird she knew. Faster! I have to move faster! she told herself. They'll catch me if I stop. She quickened her pace.

Stumbling around a corner in the trail, she came upon a massive, downed tree that lay across the path, blocking her way. Too weak to climb over the stump, she turned off the trail and struggled through the brush, but this time, luck was with her. When the tree had crashed to the ground, it had fallen onto a stand of saplings, crushing them with the weight of its trunk. Still alive, the leafy young trees had bent over, forming a small, hollow cavity beneath the log. It was a perfect hiding place.

With feverish intensity, Jesse crawled into the hollow made by the saplings, pressing so hard against the rough bark of the downed tree that it ripped her dress and drew blood on the skin of her back. She ignored the pain and lay still, holding Santelli's knife at ready.

#

Bakky was born to the woods and could track a coon across solid granite, but he could find no trace of Travis. He made his way along the edge of the forest until he reached the back of the barn. It was there he noticed something dark on the grass. Squatting down, he stretched out one finger and touched the spot. It left a streak of red on his finger tip

He stood and whistled. Weed answered with a whistle of his own, and the two men began to move slowly forward, meeting where two trails converged.

"There's blood heah. It might be Travis. You stay next to the edge of the trees," Bakky whispered. "I"ll look on further to see if I kin flush 'em out."

Weed nodded.

With backwoods cunning and skill, Bakky followed the trail. He stopped occasionally to listen, but whoever or whatever, had left the blood sign wasn't moving. The forest lay quiet except for the occasional call of a quarrelsome magpie. Even so, his instincts told him that his quarry was nearby. He continued on until he came upon the large log lying across the narrow path. Clambering onto the fallen tree, he slowly walked its length, listening for the slightest rustle, the faintest sound out of place.

#

Jesse listened as heavy boots clumped along the downed log, stopping just above Jesse's shelter. A wood tick lazily worked its way up Jesse's arm. She yearned to flick it away, but she forced herself to lay motionless. She held her breath as bits of bark rolled off the log and fell onto the hem of her dress. Slowly, she pulled the cloth closer to her, tucking its folds beneath her legs.

Just when she thought her lungs would burst, the sound of a shrill whistle floated to her ears from the direction of McGill Holler. Whoever was on top of the log hesitated a moment, and then jumped back onto the trail, retreating the way they had come. Jesse listened to the boots clumping rhythmically on the ground until the sound faded away. Then, she exhaled slowly, rose to her feet, and moved quietly on down the path, putting distance between her and McGill Holler.

#

Luke threw his shoulder into the smokehouse door again and again, but the oak held. Through cracks in the logs, he could see flames licking at the edge of the smokehouse roof. Smoke trickled in from beneath the shingles, fouling the air and causing him to cough. This is it, he thought. With his breaths coming fast and shallow, he knelt and crawled to a side wall, trying to inhale fresh air from openings between the logs. He had almost given up hope when his burning eyes caught a flash of movement. It was Travis. Luke shouted as loud as he could. "Travis, I'm in the smokehouse still. Get me out of here!"

The boy came to a halt and stared for a moment, trying to locate where the sound had come from.

Luke shouted again. "Over here. Help!" He crawled on hands and knees to the door, pounding on the oak slab with his fists.

For a moment, Travis looked uncertain, but then he sprinted over to the shed. Yanking on the wooden peg holding the door closed, he flung the door open. Luke tumbled out onto the ground, gasping for breath. "Thanks, Travis, I don't mind dying, but I didn't really want to die today. Those people are animals."

"I know, they're Branscoms," replied Travis as he cast his eyes excitedly around the meadow. "Where's Jesse and Pa?"

Luke didn't answer, but he couldn't stop himself from looking at the barn. Travis' eyes grew wide as the implication sunk in, and without waiting for a reply, he turned and ran toward the fired building.

Luke gathered himself and stumbled after the boy. He caught up with him as Travis frantically probed the burning structure, trying to find some way in. Luke threw has arms around the young man's chest and wrestled him to the ground.

"Let me go!" Travis shouted as he struggled to throw Luke aside. "I have to get Pa and Jesse out!"

"No one could have survived in there," Luke said through clenched teeth. "After those men ambushed you, they set fire to the cabin. When Jesse and Pa came out, they dragged them both down to the barn. I heard two shots, and then the fire started."

Travis' eyes took on a look of disbelief. "I don't believe you," he said, his voice choking with emotion. "Pa has always fought the Branscoms, and he's always won. And, Jesse, she was so smart nobody could get the best of her. They can't be dead."

"I'm sorry, Travis, but there was nothing either of us could do."

Slowly, Travis stopped struggling. He lay face down in the dirt, his head cradled in his arms. Luke relaxed and let the boy go. "The men who did this thought you escaped," Luke said as he stood. "Two men were sent into the woods to track you down. They'll be back. We have no guns, nothing to protect ourselves. We need to get out of here as fast as we can and contact a lawman in the nearest town to report what happened here today. Let the law take care of this."

"Can't," replied Travis, wiping away tears as he rose to his feet. "The Sheriff's a Branscom. He runs the county, and if'n we showed up, we'd be dead before nightfall."

#

Weed stopped at the edge of the woods, holding up his hand to halt Bakky. "I see Travis, there by the barn," he whispered, pointing at the burning structure. "Somebody's with him. Ain't nobody I've ever seen befo."

Bakky peered through the brush. "Anybody else theah?" he asked. "Don't see nobody," said Weed.

"Then, let's kill 'em both," Bakky replied. He brought up his rifle and leveled it at Travis' chest.

#

Luke nervously scanned the line of trees that edged the meadow, and out of the corner of his eye he caught the glint of sunlight off polished metal. Instinctively, he shoved Travis to the ground as he dove for cover himself. A rifle thundered, and a slug whistled overhead. While the first muzzle blast was still echoing from ridge to ridge, a second sent a bullet that kicked up turf just in front of where they lay. Both Luke and Travis scrambled toward a pile of straw.

"Bakky Branscom," spit out Travis, as he peeked around the straw. He jerked on Luke's shirt and pointed toward the smoldering cabin. "Come with me," he whispered. "If we can get to the back of the cabin, we can get out of here."

With that, Travis leaped to his feet and broke toward the smoking ruins of the cabin, disappearing into a small opening in the dense underbrush behind the blackened shell of his home. With no option but to follow, Luke scrambled to his feet and, throwing aside the pain in his leg, took off after Travis. He set a course for the same brush into which Travis had disappeared and plunged into the opening just about the time a slug zipped by his ear.

Luke forced his way deep through the brambles until he stumbled onto a narrow path concealed by thick shrubs on one side and guarded by the sheer rock cliff on the other. He stopped for a moment and cast his eyes up and down the trail. To his left, the trail wound along the base of the rock formation; to his right, it climbed precipitously up the cliff. Travis was nowhere to be seen.

The sound of a branch breaking caused Luke to glance back the way he had come. Santelli's men were closing in. His time running out, Luke turned right and began to climb upward.

The trail followed a narrow ledge that ran close to the face of the cliff. It ended at a huge slab or rock that looked as though it had broken off the cliff eons ago. Travis popped out from behind the slab and pointed to a small crevice in the cliff's face.

"There's a cave here that winds through the mountain and opens up on the other side of the ridge, down toward the river," Travis whispered. "It's got a lot of forks and turns, but jist follow me, and keep yer right hand on the wall. If'n you take it off, you'll get lost for sure. You might never make it back out."

Luke hesitated. He hated dark, closed places, but he followed Travis into the foreboding opening in the mountain.

For the first twenty yards, the cave was light and airy, but as they moved away from the entrance, the light dimmed, and the cave grew black as coal. Luke breathed hard, taking in air that was cool and smooth and velvety soft with moisture. Remembering Travis' warning, he hugged the cave wall, keeping his right hand always pressed against the damp limestone rock, and he concentrated on the sounds of Travis' boots scraping on the stone ahead.

The roof of the cave got lower, and the walls closer. At times, Luke crawled through mud. Once, he waded through waist deep water. Always, he fought with the fear that rose in his throat—a primeval fear of being buried alive in the dark. In the darkness, he lost all concept of time. What seemed like hours, may have been mere minutes. Just when he was sure that they would be in the bowels of the mountain for eternity, he noticed that he could see his own hand. Light, he thought joyously, and with renewed vigor, he pressed on. The cave grew brighter, and shortly, they crawled out of the dark dank hole and back under blue sky.

Luke brushed the dirt and mud from his clothes, and sat down on a rock to let his eyes adjust to the light. They had emerged from the cave onto a bluff high above the Ohio River. Wide and rugged, the river stretched for miles in either direction. Under different circumstances, he would have enjoyed the magnificent view of the river valley below. But today, he had no time for reflection. He turned to Travis. "Where are we?" he asked.

Travis pointed to a trail barely discernible through the trees. "Down there's the river road," he said. "Pa's cabin sat in a holler surrounded by a horseshoe shaped ridge. The cave we just came through goes from one side of the ridge to the other. Pa and Jesse and I always figured we could escape through the cave if the Branscoms ever came for us, but when they fired the cabin, Jesse and Pa couldn't git out."

"You know this country, where do we go from here?"

"We should go down river. Pa always talked about relatives in Wheeling." Tears welled up in Travis' eyes as he spoke. "I guess those are the only kin I've got now."

Luke stood silent for a moment. "I'm sorry about Jesse and Pa," he said.

Travis turned away and stood up. "We best be goin' now," he said. "The Branscoms always suspected we had some kind of route out of the holler. They ain't never found it, but before long they'll be a watchin' the road and combin' this ridge, trying to flush us out."

Luke looked askance at Travis. "Exactly how are we going to get down river if the road is guarded?" he asked.

"There's a log raft in the slough, yonder," replied Travis, pointing toward a marsh along the river's edge. "I saw it a week ago when I was fishin'. If we kin push that raft out on the river, we kin float to Wheeling. They'll never catch us."

Luke gazed down at the winding river. "I hope it's a good raft," he replied, wrinkling his forehead into a frown. "I can't swim."

CHAPTER 7. CROSSING THE RIVER

"This is how we get to the river," Travis said, pointing to a well-used animal trail that wound its way down the mountain.

Luke followed the track with his eyes until it disappeared into the underbrush. "Lead the way," he said.

Steadily, but quickly, they wound their way down the hillside, stopping now and then to survey the road down below. A half hour later, they found themselves crouching behind a thick bush not more than a dozen yards from the main road.

Travis pointed toward a marshy inlet about fifty yards away. "I think the raft is in that slough, in among the reeds," he said.

"Aren't you sure?" Luke asked with mild surprise. "I thought you said this was the one when we were up on the ridge."

"Well, to tell ya the truth," replied Travis with an apologetic grin. "There's that slough, and there's one downriver a ways from here. Now that I think about it, I'm just not sure which one it's in."

Luke surveyed the area, gritting his teeth as a bolt of pain shot up his leg. There was little protection between where they were crouched and the cover of the reeds. "Let's get across the road and make our way down to the slough," he said. "The raft shouldn't be too hard to find,"

Travis agreed. He stepped through the brush and started across the open space.

"Wait, someone's coming," Luke warned as the pounding beat of hoof beats reached their ears. "Listen, Travis, we don't have much time. With this leg, I'd just slow you down. I'll stay here. You go find the raft, and when you find it, give me a signal. I'll catch up."

Travis nodded and sprinted across the road toward the cat tail marsh. He was yet thirty yards from the reeds when two riders galloped headlong around the bend of the road. The boy dove over a log and disappeared from sight.

The riders pulled up about twenty yards from where Luke lay hidden. He shrank back into the brush, and peering intently through the leaves, studied the men who had just arrived.

The lead rider sat astride a big gray horse, his back toward Luke. He spurred the gray and circled the area, scanning the river for any signs of life. Then, jerking on the reins, he spun his horse around so he could survey the ridge. It was then that Luke got a good look at the man's heavy jowled face. His blood ran cold when he recognized the sallow features of Ben Santelli.

"Seth, search along the river," Santelli commanded, his voice gruff and harsh. Seth dismounted and pulled a rifle from his saddle scabbard. Tying his horse to a log, he headed toward the water's edge, poking his rifle barrel into each thicket and stand of grass as he passed. Luke watched in growing alarm as Seth headed directly toward the log where Travis lay hidden.

With little time for thought, Luke acted. Standing, he coughed and stepped nonchalantly out of the brush. Whistling a tune, he made his way out onto the road, all the while fumbling with the buttons on his pants.

Startled, Santelli swung his horse around to face the stranger hobbling toward him. He cantered to within a few steps of Luke and stopped, blocking Luke's way. Leaning forward in the saddle, Santelli growled. "Who are you?"

Luke was stunned at Santelli's appearance. Deep red scratches ran from the man's forehead to his chin, and his left arm was bound up in a blood-soaked rag. Jesse and Pa had given a good account of themselves before they were killed, he thought with some satisfaction.

"Name's Banister, Luke Banister," Luke said, immediately regretting the use of his real name.

Santelli narrowed his eyes. "You seen anybody on this road, maybe a boy about seventeen or so?"

Luke thought fast. Hoping the quiver in his voice wouldn't give away his lie, he pointed down the road. "Well, now that you mention it, I did see someone come out of the brush just down the road there about a half-mile or so. He saw me and high tailed it back up on the ridge. Wasn't more than twenty minutes ago. I couldn't see the person all that well. Might've been a boy for all I know."

Santelli eyed Luke for a moment, and then he whistled for Seth, motioning him in the direction Luke indicated. Seth abandoned his search and trotted down the road. Over the big man's shoulder, Luke caught a flash of movement and a brief glimpse of Travis quietly making his way toward the slough. Moments later, the boy vanished into the mass of reeds and cat tails.

"What are you doing here?" asked Santelli, taking in Luke's mud-covered clothes.

"You the law around here?" asked Luke insolently.

"As much law as I need to be," the big man answered, malice creeping into his voice.

Luke spit on the ground. "If you aren't the law," he replied, "then what business is it of yours?"

Luke's impertinence irritated Santelli. With surprising swiftness, the big man swung out of the saddle and, in two quick steps, stuck his fleshy jowls close to Luke's face. "Mister, I asked you a question," he hissed.

Santelli's rank breath assaulted Luke's nostrils, but Luke held his ground. Pulling at his belt buckle, he forced a grin. "Look, I meant no harm. I was down at the river an hour ago trying to catch something to eat when I fell over a log into the mud. I'm just traveling through and was doing my business up behind a tree when you folks stopped, that's all," he said.

Santelli's black eyes burned like hot coals. Over the years, Luke had defended a number of criminal clients in his legal practice. Some were men who simply made bad decisions and paid for it. But there were others, the worst, who in unguarded moments, had a cold look of insanity in their eyes. Santelli had that look.

"I've killed men for talking to me the way you just did," Santelli snarled, and like a timber rattler, his right arm struck like a snake, catching Luke by the throat.

Surprised by the sudden attack, Luke struggled, gasping for air, but the big man's grip was like iron. The grey edges of consciousness began to close in on Luke's brain, and he knew he had only little time left. With as much force as he could muster, he brought his fist up hard, smashing against Santelli's chin. The big man flinched and loosened his grip. Luke struck out again, and this time his knuckles landed hard against the big man's nose.

Santelli howled and released his grip on Luke's throat. His hands flew to his face, wiping at the blood that dripped from his chin. Luke caught a breath, and then struck out toward the slough, hobbling as fast as his bad leg would allow.

Cursing, Santelli rushed back toward his horse, grabbing at the carbine resting in the saddle scabbard. Spooked by the sudden noise, the gray skittered sideways. Santelli lunged at the reins, gathering them up in his huge hand, but the frightened horse reared, pulling the man off his feet and dragging him cursing and yelling down the road.

Santelli's shouts brought Seth scrambling back down the slope. He caught Santelli's horse and held the animal by the bridle while the enraged man struggled to his feet. With the veins in his forehead sticking out like angry red pipes, Santelli raged, "He ran toward the river. I want that man dead. Do you hear me? I want him dead!"

By this time, Luke had reached the edge of the slough. He paused, looking back, but when Seth sent a slug winging in his direction, Luke spun around and stepped off into the marsh.

The slough's water was ice cold, but the cattails hid Luke from his pursuers. He pushed deeper into its reaches, bending low to avoid being seen.

Santelli and Seth ran to the edge of the slough and, at the slightest sound, fired blindly into the reeds. Bullets clipped the cattails as they zipped by, but Luke pressed on. Then, as quickly as it had begun, the shooting stopped. The swamp was silent for a moment, but the rifle blasts were soon replaced by the sounds of Luke's pursuers splashing noisily along Luke's back trail. They were closing on him fast.

"Where is that raft?" Luke muttered to himself as he floundered through the mud. "Where's Travis?"

Luke's heart leaped into his throat when he felt a tap on his shoulder. Whirling, he found Travis standing only an arm's length away. "You scared me half to death," Luke whispered.

Travis shrugged and pointed at a small log raft barely visible through the reeds. "It's bogged down in the mud," he whispered excitedly. "I can't get it out."

Luke motioned for Travis to follow, and they sloshed to the back of the raft. A quick survey of the craft made Luke's heart sink. It was small, hardly big enough to navigate the river. It must have been there for several years because the end of one of the logs was soft and rotten. Unsure of whether the raft would even float, Luke looked for another avenue of escape, but they were hemmed in by the river on one side, and their pursuers on the other. A shout from the reeds, somewhere behind them, caused panic to rise in Luke's throat. It was only a matter of seconds before Santelli found where they were hidden.

Luke leaned into the craft on one side and motioned for Travis to do the same on the other. With strength enhanced by fear, they pushed, but the raft moved forward only slightly. Luke splashed around to the front of the craft, frantically pulling at the reeds in a desperate effort to clear a path. Travis did the same on the other side of the small vessel. Returning to the back of the raft, they anchored their boots in the mud and pushed with all their strength. Slowly, the raft moved ahead, its bottom sliding along the river mud until it finally breached the slough and nosed out into open water.

With the agility of youth, Travis scrambled aboard the small vessel, but the river bottom muck had taken hold of Luke's boot, and try as he might, he could not pull it free. The raft began to drift. Desperately, Luke lunged forward, grabbing hold of one of the logs before the craft floated out of his reach.

A shout arose from the marsh. Luke looked back and caught sight of Santelli and Seth standing in the cattails just a stone's throw up river. He redoubled his struggles, and slowly, the mud let go its grip.

As the river current pulled the raft downstream, a shotgun roared, and buckshot splattered like raindrops against the back of the craft. Most of the pellets bounced off the heavy logs, but one ricocheted and stung Luke in the cheek, drawing a trickle of blood. Moments later, a rifle slug splintered the wood of a log beside Luke's head. Travis dropped to the deck of the craft and flattened out. Luke submerged his body deeper into the cold water, leaving only his eyes and nose exposed.

Pulled by the current, the raft picked up speed, and soon it was more than a hundred yards downriver. Santelli's short barreled carbine lacked range and his slugs fell short of their intended target. With the river roaring in his ears, Luke raised his head to take one last look back and caught sight of Ben Santelli standing in waist deep water watching their progress. Then, the gargantuan hand of the river spun the raft like a top and pulled it further out into the swift current.

Rough and unruly from the spring rains, the Ohio's relentless current carried them downstream at ever increasing speed. Luke struggled to pull himself aboard the raft, but the river assaulted him mercilessly, dragging him over hidden rocks and battering his body against piles of debris. In one angry rapid, Travis was swept overboard, but he surfaced downstream, and just before the raft passed him by, he reached out and latched onto the side. Unable to crawl back aboard the raft in the maelstrom of the river, the two refugees kicked and swam, always trying to push through the fast-moving torrent to the far bank, but after about twenty minutes, Luke began to struggle with the numbing cold that spread throughout his entire body.

Shivering, he raised his head to look at the far shore. They were still more than fifty yards from hard ground. Luke glanced at Travis. The boy was almost spent. His head hung low in the water, and his movements were slow and mechanical. Luke tried to speak, to urge Travis on, but he was unable form any words.

Turning his attention once more to the river bank, Luke picked out a small cove that might give them refuge. Though his body cried out for rest, he bowed his head and kicked with all his remaining strength in an effort to propel the raft toward calmer waters. It was only a few minutes, but it seemed an eternity before Luke's feet touched the hard bottom of the river. A few more feet, and he walked on hard sand. His body numb to the core, he pulled the raft behind him, finally beaching it on the sand bar.

Luke turned to look at Travis. The boy had let go of the raft and was drifting away, his head and body slowly submerging beneath the muddy water. Luke splashed through the shallows and reached out for the drifting body. He pulled the boy's head above the water, and then, through sheer force of will, waded the last few yards to dry ground, towing Travis behind him. Luke dragged the young man onto a sandbar, and then collapsed into the sand beside him.

CHAPTER 8. RESCUE

Fear gave Jesse strength, and a burning hatred for Ben Santelli drove her on. She stumbled through the forest for more than an hour, weak and losing blood, and longing to lie down and rest in the soft, green grass. When she finally came upon a wagon road, even fear and hatred could drive her no further. She fell to the ground, and lay still.

Jessee drifted in and out of consciousness, but through the veil of gray, she heard a voice saying, "Oh my, Abe, it's Jesse McGill." Another voice, this one deeper and louder, exclaimed, "She's been shot, Sarah. She needs a doctor, quick. Let's take her to our place and figure out what to do from there."

Jesse felt strong hands lift her from the ground and place her gently in a wagon box. She writhed in pain and cried out, but the woman held her hand and spoke soothingly. "Hang on there, missy, we'll git you on up to the cabin and take a look at this heah wound." Jesse felt the wagon begin to move, but mercifully, she passed again into unconsciousness.

#

The mid-afternoon sun was bright and hot, and Luke and Travis absorbed its heat like a starving man gobbles down bread. Their ordeal on the river had left both battered, bruised and hungry.

"Looks like we made it across," Luke said as he stretched out his leg.

"Yeah, thanks," replied Travis. "I wasn't sure..." and his voice trailed off as he examined a long scrape on the back of his hand.

Luke nodded. "I guess we're even now."

They sat quietly for a few minutes, recovering their strength. Finally, Luke spoke again. "We need to dry out our clothes. We better find some shelter where we can make a fire and not be seen. Do you know anyone on this side of the river?"

"Nobody," said Travis. "Ain't never bin on this side of the Ohio."

Luke began to consider other options, when Travis lifted his nose to the river breeze. "I smell wood smoke," he said, as he turned his head back and forth, sampling the air.

Luke stood up and sniffed the wind. Someone has a camp close by, in that direction." He said, pointing toward the woods. "Maybe it's someplace we could dry out."

"I'll go with ya," Travis said. "Two might have better luck than one."

The two bedraggled men followed the smell of burning wood until they came to the edge of a small clearing. Voices floated through the brush, and Luke held his hand up and motioned for Travis to stop. Creeping forward, Luke parted a bramble to reveal, not more than thirty yards away, a caravan of wagons arranged in a circle. A group of women busied themselves with pots hung over a blazing fire. Several men sat on logs, laughing and talking to one another.

"Gypsies," Luke said.

Travis' slender frame shook with cold. ""We can't go back across the river. We might was well take our chances with these folks," he said.

Luke ran his hand through his matted beard. "You stay here," he said. "I'll go in first. If things go well, then you can follow me in."

Luke parted the brush and took a step forward, but Travis laid a hand on his arm as three riders suddenly thundered into the clearing. Luke faded back into the brush and watched as one of the men drew his rifle and stopped at the edge of the meadow, sealing off the road. Another continued on, but hung back just outside the circled wagons. The third man galloped straight to the fire, scattering women and children as he reined his horse to a stop.

The rider was close to where Luke and Travis sat concealed in the brush, and Luke could see the man clearly. He was a thick bodied sort with a bullet head. His bearded face wore a permanent frown of disapproval. A sheriff's badge hung on the lapel of his leather vest, glinting in the sunlight.

The beefy lawman scanned the clearing, his eyes boring into the very brush in which Luke and Travis were hiding. They shrank back and watched as a Gypsy stepped forward.

"Who are you folks, and what are you doing here?" the Sheriff inquired gruffly.

"We are simply travelers," replied the Gypsy, bowing deeply, "who have stopped to rest along our way."

"I'm going to ask again. Where did you come from, and where are you headed?" snarled the sheriff. "And I want straight talk, no riddles or lies."

"Certainly," the man replied calmly. Luke admired his aplomb. Obviously, the Gypsy had answered lawmen's questions many times before. "We are poor Gypsies who are traveling from the Virginias to Ohio. We left no home, and are going to none. Our home is always where our wagons and our families are."

The Sheriff was not satisfied with the answer though he had no reason to doubt it. He scanned the campground, peering closely at the Gypsies standing near the fire. "Is this all the people you have with you?" he growled.

"All but a few children who are asleep in the wagons," replied the Gypsy.

The Sheriff continued. "We got word from across the river that a man and a boy might have landed a raft near here. We've reports they murdered a man and a woman up in McGill Holler. If you see them, there's a reward of a five hundred dollars for each man."

The Gypsy raised his bushy eyebrows, and a murmur went up around the fire.

The Sheriff edged his horse closer. "Is that your daughter?" he asked, leering at the young girl. "I can see some resemblance."

The Gypsy fingered the hilt of his knife. "Yes," he replied cautiously as he placed a protective arm around her shoulders. "She is my flesh and blood."

"She's a purdy thing," the Sheriff replied, leering at the young girl.

The Gypsy's eyes narrowed, and though he didn't blink under the Sheriff's menacing stare, his hand never left the handle of his knife.

The Sheriff broke off his gaze, and slowly walked his horse around the campfire, looking at each person closely. "I want these two men," he said, the softness of his voice belying the sinister message he spoke from cruel lips. "If you are hiding them around here," he continued, coming full circle to the Gypsy leader, "I will find out." Then, leaning forward, he stared directly into the man's dark eyes. "In such case, things will go badly for you and your people."

The Gypsy said nothing.

The Sheriff spurred his horse and galloped out of the clearing. As he passed, the deputies fell in line behind him.

#

Luke watched until the sheriff vanished in the trees. "Travis," said Luke, his gaunt body shivering with cold. "I don't like the looks of this." Travis replied, anger reflected in his voice. "That Sheriff is kin to the Branscoms. I've seen him before on our side of the river. I told ya we couldn't trust the law."

Luke sat down and took off a boot, squeezing water out of his socks. "The man said there's a reward out for us. If they're paying money, we can't trust anybody."

Travis nodded in agreement.

"It's best we find another place for the night," Luke said. "Let's continue on down river till dark." Luke pulled his boot back on, and stealthily, they made their way back toward where they had landed the raft.

Luke searched the water's edge until he found two long driftwood poles. Handing one to Travis, they boarded the raft and plunged the poles into the water. Straining hard, they edged back out onto the river.

The current pulled the raft along at a good pace. When the water turned rough, they maneuvered closer to shore. Sometimes, they struggled to avoid rocks or debris that lay at the surface. At least once, they hit a sandbar, but were able to work themselves free and continue on downstream. When the water was smooth and too deep for the poles to reach bottom, they rested, and let themselves be carried along by the water.

On one calm stretch of the river, Luke took better stock of the raft's condition. It was about fifteen feet long and not more than ten feet across at its widest point. It rode low in the water, but the vessel was in better condition than he first thought. On the raft's deck stood a small enclosed shelter, five feet wide and six feet long. It was just big enough to provide refuge from the weather for two men. The remnants of a ragged blanket covered its doorway, fluttering in the breeze.

Luke pulled aside the tattered cloth and peered inside. The interior was dark, and at first, he saw nothing, but as his eyes adjusted he was elated to find its previous owner had left behind several tins of food. They were rusty on the outside, but seemed to be sound. And, in a dark corner, he found a leather pouch containing flint and steel. He picked up the pouch and backed out of the small shelter.

Several hours later, when the sun began to wane, they came upon a river village. A small mercantile district consisting of three stores sat at the river's edge. Moored at one pier floated a riverboat with the name "Golden Girl" painted in large letters on its stern.

Though they were both hungry, Luke was loath to land the raft at the village itself. They floated a half-mile on downstream until they came upon a stand of cattails where a small creek flowed into the Ohio. They glided into the reeds until the raft came to a stop. Slipping into the water, they pulled the raft towards shore, and hid it as best they could.

"I'm gonna go hunt squirrels," Travis said, placing a number of smooth river rocks in his pocket. With that, he disappeared into the woods.

From the raft's shelter, Luke retrieved two tins of food and the pouch of flint and steel. Gathering a few sticks of driftwood and some dry moss for kindling, he arranged them on the sand so that they would burn well. His stiff fingers fumbled with the flint and steel, but soon he was raining sparks onto the kindling. The wood began to smolder, and with a few breaths, Luke coaxed it to life. By the time he had nursed the fire into a roaring blaze, Travis had returned—carrying a chicken.

Luke arched his eyebrows. "Oddest looking squirrel I've ever seen," he said.

"Tastes the same," chuckled Travis, "but not as stringy."

A short time later, the chicken was cooking over a hastily built spit, and with the abandoned tins of food left by the raft's previous owner, they dined like kings.

#

At dusk, Santelli, Bakky and Weed slipped out of the woods into the twilight of McGill Holler. McGill's cabin lay in ruins; the logs of the barn were still smoldering, and the smell of smoke hung heavy in the air.

"Keep a watch," Santelli growled at Weed. "Bakky, you come with me." With Bakky in tow, the big man strode to the barn and, without hesitation, stepped into the smoking rubble. He spit on a hot ember, and his saliva sizzled and popped. Hot coals flared under the soles of his boots, and a slight breeze lifted sparks from the ashes, swirling them around his head. Santelli ignored the stinging heat and purposefully made his way toward where he saw Jesse fall. Kicking aside blackened timbers, he squatted down and swept away the ashes with his hand, looking for Jesse's body. Finding nothing, he moved to another spot and repeated the process, but with no success. Within minutes, he had covered the entire floor area of the small structure.

Santelli cursed and stood upright, scanning the ruins in puzzlement. Angrily kicking aside charred logs, he bulled his way out of the blackened structure and into the grassy meadow at the back of the barn. Bakky trotted along behind.

Slowly, Santelli walked toward the woods, scanning the ground intensely. His keen eyes spotted a dark stain on a tuft of grass. Squatting on his haunches, he picked a single grass blade, and holding it close in the dimming light, rolled the blade between his fingers. Dried blood crumbled into his hand.

A frown spread across Santelli's face, and he scanned the dark edges of the forest. "She got out, Bakky. She's in there somewhere," he said, pointing toward the woods. "Get Weed. Have him search for her trail. And Bakky, tell him to stay around here close. It might be two or three weeks, but sooner or later, she'll show up. When she does, I want her brought to me. She's got something of mine. I want it back."

Santelli walked to his horse. "I've got an appointment downriver," he said as he mounted the big gray. "Hunt Travis down." Santelli looked at the two men with thinly concealed loathing. "If he ain't dead when I get back, I'll kill you both." Spinning his mount, he cantered away.

#

A dull, pounding pain brought Jesse awake. Moaning softly, she opened her eyes to find herself in a house that looked strangely familiar. Immediately, a soft wrinkled hand touched her on the shoulder. "Gracious, child," a soothing voice intoned. "I declare, you have been asleep for two days."

Jesse turned her head in the direction of the voice, and as the haze slowly left her eyes, she recognized the McGills closest neighbor, Sarah Benson. Sarah had been in the hills for as long as Jesse could remember. She was a tall, big boned woman of about 65, give or take a year. At one time, she might have had blonde hair, but now it was a silvery gray, and it framed her wrinkled head like a knitted cap.

"Sarah, how did I get here?" Jesse asked weakly.

"Child," answered Sarah, "we can talk later. Right now, you need some nourishment. I've got some broth simmerin' on the stove. Let me get you a cup. You need some food in your stomach." Sarah laid her knitting on the floor, rose from her rocking chair, and walked over to a black iron stove standing against one wall. Taking a heavy mug from a pantry shelf, she ladled out a spoonful of golden broth and brought it back to where Jesse lay.

Sarah set the broth down, and helped Jesse to a sitting position. "Drink this child," Sarah said as she handed her the broth, "it will help. In a week or two, I declare, you'll be good as new."

Jesse gave Sarah a weak smile and sipped the broth slowly. She had just opened her mouth to ask more questions when a set of heavy boots stomped up the steps of the cabin and onto the porch. A second later the door opened, and Abe Benson walked into the room.

Abe was the perfect antithesis of his wife, Sarah. He was about five years older than she, and only a little over five foot tall, but tough as leather. Ruddy faced, he was bald as a baby, and sported a bushy gray beard that hung to his chest. His mannerisms were generally gruff, but Jesse liked to tease him when he was around, because it made him blush like a small boy.

"Abe," said Sarah as he shut the door behind him. "Look who's awake."

65

CHAPTER 9. WHEELING

Overnight, a cool mist settled into the river bottom. Its chill dampness seeped through the thin walls of the raft's tiny shelter, and by dawn, Luke was shivering with cold. When the day's first light fell dimly through the knotholes in the shelter's roof, he happily left a snoring Travis behind and crawled from the hut into the early morning air.

Standing, Luke stretched, grimacing as his injured leg protested with a dull pain. He inspected the wound, but found it to be healing well. "Maybe Jesse's poultice worked after all," he muttered to himself. "I should write that horse doctor William and tell him he has some competition."

Pulling the collar of his coat tight around his neck, Luke stepped from the raft onto the sandy beach and walked briskly along the river's edge, flapping his lean arms in an effort to generate some internal warmth. Another shiver raced through his lean body, and the thought of a warm fire drove him to retrieve the flint and steel from the raft. Soon, he was huddled next to a small blaze, pondering the events of the last few days. Only three weeks away from home, he thought, and I'm on the run from the law and wanted for a murder I didn't commit. His legal training told him that he should turn himself in and fight the charges, but Travis' warning that he would most likely be murdered before a trial ever took place rang strong in his head. In the end, Luke's confidence in the rule of law won out, and he concluded that his only viable option was to face the charges in court.

As Luke wrestled with his future, a faint rumble from somewhere up river penetrated his thoughts. The rumble grew louder and more powerful until the ground throbbed with its resonance. Startled, Luke jumped to his feet and retreated from the edge of the cove, turning back to the river just in time to see the prow of a huge river boat emerge like a ghost from a break in the mist.

Seemingly close enough to touch, the boat glided into full view, splendid and dazzling in the diffuse morning light. The decks of the massive craft were painted a gleaming white; the trim a glistening ebony. Twin stacks belched black smoke as the engines below decks labored at their work, driving paddle wheels that churned the river to a bubbly froth. The ship's bow bore the vessel's name: The Golden Girl.

The boat passed by quickly, and in moments the haze had enveloped the forward part of the ship, leaving only the stern visible. Luke's keen eyes took in every part of the vessel as it passed, but they came to rest on a man dressed in a long black coat leaning against the aft deck rail.

An officer, thought Luke, and he watched with curiosity as the man hoisted the stub of a black cigar to his lips, took a puff, and then flicked it into the river. As the black coated man turned to leave, he caught sight of Luke standing at the river's edge. He leaned forward and locked eyes with Luke just before the ship disappeared into the swirling mist, leaving only the boat's whistle sounding through the fog.

The passing river boat had shaken Travis awake. They ate a slim breakfast, and then pushed back out onto the river. By mid-day, they were far downstream, floating past small settlements that appeared with regularity along the river's banks. River traffic picked up as well, and as the raft passed one slow moving barge, Luke spied a man lounging on the barge's deck.

"Halloo! How far to Wheeling?" Luke shouted.

"About two miles down river," the man replied as he looked up from his task. Then, spitting tobacco juice into the water, he continued. "It'll take ye about an hour to git theah. It's busy. A small raft liken yours might git run over by a barge. Ye might wanna tie up early and ketch a ride in ta town."

"Thanks," Luke shouted back.

A half hour later, they rounded a river bend and spotted a quiet cove ahead. Poling hard, they glided across the cove's calmer waters and beached the raft on a sand bar. Travis jumped off and waded the remaining few yards to dry land. He tethered the raft to a small log and scrambled up the river bank to see what lay ahead.

Luke retrieved the pouch of flint and steel. The last few days seemed like a dream, no, a nightmare, but now, he felt more convinced than ever that he should contact the local authorities. Wheeling is a city, he thought. Here, there should be no corrupt backwoods sheriff wielding the power of life and death, and no Ben Santelli, who seems to be able to kill with impunity. His thoughts were interrupted when Travis piled back over the river bank surrounding the cove. "There's a wagon road not more than a hundred yards away," he said excitedly. "We can catch a ride into town there."

Luke smiled at the young man's enthusiasm. "I guess we won't need this anymore," he said, pushing the raft back into the river. "It's best that we leave no clues about where we came ashore." They climbed the river bank and watched the raft until it disappeared from sight. Then, they trudged to the road, hoping for a ride into the city.

It wasn't long before a farm wagon, pulled by a matched pair of well-kept mules, drew abreast of the two men. Luke glanced over at the farmer and his cargo; a load of chickens bound for market. The farmer eyed the pair's wet boots and trousers, and dirty disheveled appearance, but said nothing for a moment. Then, pursing his lips, he struck up a conversation.

"You jist git off the river?

"What makes you think that?" Luke responded looking over at the wagon driver from beneath his shaggy untrimmed hair.

"A guess," answered back the farmer in a gruff but pleasant voice as he eyed Luke's thin body. "When I git to town, I could sure use some help unloadin' these here chickens," he continued. "I could pay fifty cents each if'n yer lookin' for some work. You two hungry?"

Luke's belly rumbled. The thought of real food was tempting. "Yeah, we're hungry."

"Well, heah," said the farmer as he rummaged around in a sack on the floor of the wagon, "My missus made up some grub for me today. I'll give you one o' her specialties if you hire on for an hour or two." From the sack he produced a thick piece of ham, topped by a chunk of yellow cheese and sandwiched between two large slices of home baked bread.

It was more temptation than either Luke or Travis could stand. "You have a deal," they exclaimed, almost in unison. Luke grabbed hold of the wagon box, and using the wagon's momentum, swung himself up into the seat alongside the farmer. Travis clambered into the back.

For Luke, the ride to Wheeling was pleasant. The farmer chatted amiably about the weather and farm prices, but refrained from asking any further direct questions about who they were. Luke found the man to be surprisingly well versed on the issues of the day. Time passed quickly, and soon, they reached the outskirts of town.

It was market day and the town was bustling with people and wagons. Guided skillfully by the farmer, the mules plodded along until they reached the market square. As he rolled up to the appropriate stall, the farmer pulled on reins and shouted, "Whoa." The mules came to halt.

Luke and Travis jumped down from the wagon and went to work immediately. An hour later, the crates of chickens and other farm produce were unloaded, and the stall was neatly arranged. Thanking the farmer for the ride, they turned to leave. "Hold on there," the farmer said as he fished deep in his pocket. "I still owe ya something." The man pulled two half dollars from his pocket, flipping one to Travis and one to Luke.

"Thanks for the help, and the conversation." the farmer said gratefully. "You certainly talk better than you look. By the way, there's a woman who runs a hotel down by the riverfront. For two bits you can get yourself a good meal. Oh, and across the street be a barber shop and laundry. Another two bits will get you a bath, a shave and a haircut, if you're interested. Tell 'em Henry sent ya."

"Thanks," Luke grunted, embarrassed at the pointed reference to his disheveled looks.

As the two turned to walk away, the farmer yelled after him. "Hey fellas, good luck. If you need some more work, I could use a couple of good hands back on the farm. I'll be here all day."

Luke nodded and waved as he and Travis headed off in the direction of town. The farmer grinned and turned back to his chickens.

Luke and Travis walked along in silence for a while. Finally, Travis spoke up, a twinge of sadness in his voice, "My kin live north of town, maybe a mile or two. I guess I should find them."

"Then, this is where we part ways," responded Luke, clasping the young man on the shoulder and holding out his hand. "I'm going to get cleaned up a bit, and then I'll go see the sheriff. I'm sure he'll want to talk with you soon. They'll need your testimony."

Travis shook his head, and then grasped Luke's hand in his strong grip. "I'll do whatever I have to for Jesse and Pa," he said, a tear welling up in his eye.

Wishing each other luck, Travis headed north, and Luke headed into the city.

#

Luke made his way to the riverfront and found the hotel Henry had recommended. For a moment, he paused at the hotel's window, watching the activity inside, and slowly he became aware of his reflection in the glass. He leaned closer and touched his scruffy black beard and, with some dismay, ran his hand through his hair. It was thick and matted. When he looked at his hands, they were brown with dirt. His eyes wandered to his pants, and he realized they were wrinkled and dirty.

"I can't go in like this," Luke muttered disgustedly. Turning away from the hotel window, he searched the storefronts for the barbershop Henry had mentioned. Spotting a red and white striped pole on the far side of the road, Luke strolled across the street to the barber's door and ducked inside.

The interior of the shop was small but clean. Shaving lotions and hair tonics in bottles colored red and blue and green stood on crowded shelves, their aroma permeating the air. A thin, balding barber stood at a counter reading the morning paper. He looked up and greeted Luke good naturedly, motioning him toward an empty chair. Luke sat down. "Henry sent me," he said.

"He did, did he?"inquired the barber. "I suppose he thought you might need a shave or a haircut?"

"Both," Luke answered emphatically. "And, I want a bath and my clothes washed. How much?"

"Two bits," the barber replied.

Luke nodded, and the barber went to work. Thirty minutes later, Luke's black hair was neatly trimmed, and his face clean shaven.

"Bath next," said the barber, motioning for Luke to follow.

Luke rose from the chair, and stepped through a curtain into the back of the barbershop. A large galvanized tub, full of hot steaming water, sat in the middle of the floor. The barber left, and Luke stripped off his clothes. He stepped into the tub and luxuriated in the first hot bath he had taken in weeks.

A polite knock announced the arrival of an older woman who stepped into the room. She hung up a robe and gathered his clothing, holding them at arms-length. "I'll bring these back soon," she said, exiting through the curtain.

Luke enjoyed his bath until, sometime later, the older woman returned, bringing a shirt and trousers not his own. "Sorry, mister, but your clothes were plumb worn out," she said. "Even looked like there might be a bullet hole in one leg of your trousers." She grinned, but didn't wait for Luke to respond. "No matter," she continued. "I tossed them into the rag pile, and brought you a pair of trousers and a shirt that look to be your size. They were left here about a year ago by another gentleman. Don't know what happened to him, but he never came back. I'll just give them to you."

Luke accepted the clothes graciously. He dressed and returned to the front of the barber shop. "Thanks," he said, handing the barber a quarter. "By the way, Henry said the hotel across the street is a good place to eat. That true?"

"Yep," replied the barber. "Good food and cheap price."

Luke left the barbershop and walked to the hotel. This time, he stepped inside without hesitation, stopping at the entrance just long enough to spot a plump, middle-aged woman who seemed to preside over the eatery. "Afternoon, ma'am," he said politely, tipping his hat. "Henry said this is a good place to have dinner."

"So, he says, does he," replied the woman jovially. "Well, mister, if you want good food, then you've came to the right place. What did you have in mind, handsome?"

"Meat would be good," replied Luke with a smile, looking longingly at the thick cut of beef sizzling in the skillet.

"Mister, we've got the best steaks in West Virginia," boasted the woman.

"I'm sure you have at that," Luke answered, "but I'm more interested in the price at this moment."

"How much you got?" she inquired, scanning him from head to toe.

Luke scrounged through his pockets, coming up with the remaining two bits earned from the farmer. "I've got a quarter-dollar," he said as he eyed the homemade rolls setting in a pan in the warming cabinet. "That's all."

"Then a quarter-dollar it is, mister," she replied laughingly. "Find yourself a table, and I'll bring you the best steak cooked on the Ohio River."

Luke grinned and turned to look at the available tables. He chose one that stood in a secluded corner, and sat down with his back to the wall.

The buxomly woman grabbed a heavy plate and slapped on a huge chunk of beef. Mounding up fried potatoes on the side, she brought the plate to Luke and plunked it down on the table.

"Hope that suits ya," she said, looking him over. "Bon appetite."

"Mercie," Luke responded and dove in.

Minutes later, the waitress came by with a steaming mug of black coffee. He lifted the brew to his lips and took a sip, reveling in its taste and aroma.

Luke had been so engrossed in his meal that he had paid little attention to the other diners in the hotel. Now, as he took time to assess his surroundings, he realized that he had drawn the attention of a trim and proper man at a table nearby. The man wore a stiff black, captain's uniform, and watched him intently.

"Pretty good cook, wouldn't you say," the man said good naturedly through a strong New England accent.

"Good enough," Luke replied, not eager to enter into conversation with a stranger.

"But of course," the stranger said, sensing Luke's reluctance to talk. "Let me introduce myself. I'm the captain of the Golden Girl. John Smith is my name. Just call me Captain. We're tied up at Dock 3. I must apologize, but I overheard your conversation with the waitress. Are you French?"

"No. I learned the language in school."

"School? You can you write and cipher then?"

"Well enough."

Captain Smith eyed Luke's worn clothing. "Are you looking for work?" the man asked.

"I might be," replied Luke, his interest picking up.

"Good. I have a job for a purser. My last one disappeared. Rumor is he was in a poker game that went bad. We leave for St. Louis in two hours. Stop by before then if you're interested. It pays well. Job includes a warm bed and food."

Luke nodded. Captain Smith rose from his chair, spun smartly on his heel, and marched across the room. Luke watched until he opened the door to the restaurant and vanished from sight.

Luke nursed his coffee and mulled over his options. Work would result in money, something that was now in short supply, but his training and experience drove him to the conclusion that he must contact law enforcement in Wheeling and tell them about Pa and Jesse. His mind made up, he tossed down the last swallow of coffee and set his cup on the table. At that moment, two men entered the restaurant.

Luke eyed the newcomers. The first man wore a badge pinned to his jacket and seemed familiar with the place. Probably a local constable, Luke thought to himself. The second man stood with his back to Luke, staring out the window, but when the newcomer turned and walked toward a nearby table, Luke lowered his eyes in dismay. The second man was Ben Santelli.

CHAPTER 10. RUNNING

The constable greeted the cook. Then both men sat at a table not far from Luke, giving him but a cursory glance.

Santelli spoke first. "Sheriff, the killer is here, in this town," he insisted, his voice loud enough for Luke to hear.

"Maybe." responded the lawman. "But Wheeling's not that big of a city. As far as I know, he's a stranger here and has no place to hide. If he's around, we'll find 'im. "

"When you catch up with him, you know I'm authorized to take him back for the McGill murders, don't you?" growled Santelli. "Sheriff Branscom signed the warrant."

"I've got it right here," the constable replied, tapping his vest pocket. "It's properly executed. We're looking for a man named Luke Banister."

"Good," Santelli grunted. "Now, I'll be gone for a few days, but when I get back, I expect him to be in your custody."

Luke was struck speechless. A million thoughts raced through his head, but one thought stuck. Santelli was trying to frame him for the murder of Pa and Jessee McGill. Nursing his empty coffee cup, Luke slumped in his chair while straining to overhear the rest of Santelli's conversation, but the big man lowered his voice and spoke in quieter tones. Luke could hear little.

When Santelli and the constable had finished eating, they paid their bill and left. Luke watched through the window as they crossed the street. Luke waited several minutes before settling up with the cook. Then, he exited the hotel. Trying to appear nonchalant, he loitered for a moment on the sidewalk while he glanced up and down the street. He saw neither Santelli nor the Sheriff.

Luke's resolve to go to the local sheriff melted away, and he walked aimlessly up the street until he found himself passing in front of the barber shop that he had visited earlier. He could not have chosen a worse route. As Luke peered through the glass, he could see the barber engaged in conversation with the constable and Ben Santelli. Luke's shadow in the window drew the barber's eyes and the man recognized his recent customer. He immediately said something to Santelli and the big man whirled to stare at Luke.

For a moment the two men locked eyes, then Luke cursed and ran. Ducking into an alley way, he sprinted down its narrow passage, wincing as his injured leg protested every step. Santelli, trailed by the constable, rushed out of the barber shop to give chase.

Luke ran blindly through a maze of alleys and streets, startling people as he flew past. Dogs yapped at his heels and his breath came in gasps, but every time he slowed, the clumping boots behind him gained ground. The local constable knew his territory, and before long, Luke realized that he was methodically being driven toward the river. Finally, Luke careened around the corner of a wood frame building and skidded to a stop. He was trapped. Not more than twenty yards ahead stood Ben Santelli, his pistol drawn and cocked.

Luke frantically looked back the way he had come, but he could hear the constable's boots as he closed from behind. He stepped back, keeping his eyes fixed on Santelli. Be calm, he thought.

"You're done for, mister," panted the big man as he advanced. "Where's the boy?"

"What boy?" returned Luke, stalling for time.

"I don't need you, mister. I'll find the whelp sooner or later, but it would be easier if you told me where he was. I might even be inclined to let you go if'n you did that," Santelli responded.

Luke's mind raced. If he were taken into custody now, he would most likely be turned over to Santelli, and he would never make it back to McGill Holler alive. Luke took another step back. "Look," he said, "I don't know who you're talking about."

Santelli thumbed back the hammer on his pistol. "No matter," the big man sneered. "I'll find Travis sooner or later."

Luke looked for an escape and his eye caught sight of a narrow passageway directly to his right. Through its length, Luke could see the docks and beyond that, lay the river. He dove for the opening and a split second later was sprinting down the passageway's narrow confines. Behind him, a pistol roared and a slug splintered a wooden post just ahead.

Seconds later, Luke emerged onto the riverfront. The docks were bustling with people, and he ducked into the crowd, trying to lose himself in the scurrying throng. A tram of luggage passed by. He slipped to its far side, out of sight of either Santelli or the constable. As it moved, he walked with it, keeping pace until it came to a stop at a huge paddle-wheel steamer tethered to the dock with ropes as thick as a man's forearm. It bore the name "Golden Girl."

The riverboat's decks teemed with activity as passengers boarded. Concealed by the crowd, Luke crouched behind the tram, uncertain about what to do next. But when he caught sight of the Sheriff and Ben Santelli pushing toward him through the throng, guns drawn, he knew there would be no justice on this dock. He would be lucky to escape with his life. Melding into a group of passengers, he climbed the gangplank and stepped out onto the main deck of the vessel.

A ship's officer checked the passenger's tickets and then turned to him. "May I see your ticket, please?" the officer asked.

"I'm not a passenger," Luke said, looking over his shoulder at the docks below. "Captain Smith offered me a job as the purser."

The officer looked Luke up and down, noting the patched and shabby trousers he wore. "You, a purser?" the officer said with derision. He stepped menacingly toward Luke. "If you don't have a ticket, then get off this ship before I have you thrown off."

"Hold on there, Mister Stafford," boomed a voice from an upper deck.

Luke looked up to see Captain Smith descending a set of stairs. When he reached the lower deck, Smith strode over to Luke. "I'm glad to see you could make it," he exclaimed. "You're here for the purser's job, I assume?"

"Yes, I am," said Luke, again glancing over the rail at the crowd milling around below. He spotted the constable stopping and questioning people though Santelli was nowhere to be seen.

"And you can read and write?"

"Very well, Captain," answered Luke, giving the ensign a cold stare.

"Good!" the captain exclaimed. "I don't have time to find an experienced purser at this late moment, but we need someone to check in the passenger's valuables. Have you ever worked on the river before?"

"No, Captain, I haven't," replied Luke truthfully. "But I have been schooled in accounting, among other things. If you give me a day to learn the position, I'm sure I'll do the job to your satisfaction."

"Very well, then," stated the captain with finality. "You're hired. I'm Captain Smith, captain of the Golden Girl. And, you...?"

"Banister, Luke Banister," Luke replied.

"Excellent! Follow me and I'll show you your duty station."

Captain Smith spun on his heel and marched across the deck. Luke fell in behind, feeling a bit like a military recruit headed for boot camp. Ensign Stafford could only glare.

CHAPTER 11. THE GAME

The captain led Luke across the deck to a small cabin and unlocked the door. "This is the purser's office," he said, motioning Luke inside. "You start now." He reached into a vest pocket, and producing a small folded paper, handed it to Luke. "Here's the combination to the safe. It remains open while you're in the office. Any time you leave here, it must be closed and locked. Is that clear?"

"Of course," replied Luke as he unfolded the paper and looked at the numbers written neatly thereon.

"I want you to memorize the combination. Do so quickly, sir, and bring the combination back to me at mess," commanded the captain. "Don't lose it. Don't show it to anyone else. There are receipts for the passenger's valuables in the drawer along with pen and ink and other necessary items. After we get under way, I'll send the cabin boy down to show you your room."

"Thank you, sir," replied Luke.

"Oh, and one more thing," the captain continued. "Can you play poker?"

Curious at the question, Luke looked up. "I've played some in the past," he answered. "Why do you ask?"

"One of your jobs is to represent the house in the evening poker game," Captain Smith said. "It's no matter how skilled you are here. The house always has the odds on its side."

Luke took in the captain's stern face, and before he could form a question, Smith continued. "The first game starts at seven p.m. sharp, right after mess. You play until midnight. Someone will relieve you at that time. Do you have any questions, Mr. Banister?"

"Not right now."

"Good. Welcome aboard."

The captain stepped through the doorway, but turned back for a moment to look at Luke. "One more thing, Mr. Banister," he said quietly. "If anything comes up missing, I'll hang you from the yardarm at the next sunrise." With that, the captain closed the door and strode away.

Luke watched the retreating captain until a salesman clad in a pinstriped suit interrupted his thoughts. "Mister, are you the purser, here?" he asked. "I have some valuables that I need to put in the ship's safe." Luke pulled a pencil and a receipt book from the desk and went to work.

The number of passengers wanting to check valuables seemed never ending. Luke worked steadily, documenting each person's goods and placing them in the heavy steel safe. At a quarter to five, he was readying to close the office when he looked up from the desk to see a stunning pair of blue eyes looking directly at him. The eyes were framed by blond hair that started high atop the woman's head and fell in a cascade to the middle of her back. In one hand, the woman held a diamond necklace, and the other a large emerald brooch. She waited impatiently.

Luke stuttered, "May I...uh, help you, ma'am?"

"Sir," the woman said with a southern drawl, "I have several pieces of jewelry I need you to safeguard. Would you be so kind as to place these in the safe for me?" and she held out the necklace and the brooch.

Luke took the jewelry, noticing that the woman's hands were soft, white, and delicate. She turned to walk away.

"Wait, Miss," he said, "I need your name, and you need a receipt."

"Grace West," replied the woman as she turned back to face Luke. Luke wrote the name. "Miss West," he said as he recovered from the onslaught of emotions. "Your receipt."

"Why, thank you Mister...," and she leaned forward, awaiting an answer.

"Banister, Luke Banister," replied Luke.

"Then, thank you Luke Banister. Silly me, I had plumb forgot the receipt." With that, the woman plucked the paper from Luke's hand, and swept out the door.

#

At precisely five o'clock, the ship's boy, a lad of about twelve, showed up at the purser's office. Poking his head in the door, he said, "You must be Mister Banister?"

"Yes, I am," replied Luke, amused by the boy's impertinence.

"I'm Sam. Captain told me to show you your quarters. Lock the door and follow me," he commanded.

Luke smiled, grabbed his coat and stepped out the door. Remembering the captain's warning, he ensured that it was locked.

Luke followed the boy down several flights of stairs and through a narrow passageway to the crew quarters in the lower deck. When they reached a door at the far end of the passage, the boy knocked. A voice from within shouted, "Come in."

Sam quickly opened the door. "Ensign Stafford, this is Luke Banister, our new purser," said the boy. "Captain said he's your new bunkmate till we get to St. Louis." The boy grinned mischievously and left as quickly as he had appeared.

Ensign Stafford stood up and a look of recognition came over his face. "You're the man who needed a job, aren't you?" he said mockingly. "Well, you got one. I hope it's to your liking." He motioned toward an empty bunk fastened to the wall. "That's yours. You can stow your clothes, if you have any, in the locker there," and he pointed to a chest at the foot of the bed. "You can wash up down the hall. As an officer, you're expected to be well-groomed every day," he said, barely concealing his disdain for Luke's clothing.

"Look," replied Luke, "I'm just working my way down river. I'm not looking for trouble, with you or anybody else."

"Have you had any river-time before, Mr. Banister," asked the Ensign, his tone softening a little.

"None."

"I'll give you fair warning then. Be on the watch. There are many people who work this river for their own purposes, many of them illegal. And, if you run afoul of any one of them, your fate can be cruel."

The Ensign's response resulted in more questions than answers, but before Luke could follow up, he felt the ship move slightly. Looking out the cabin window, he saw the dock receding as the ship got underway. The ensign rose. "Duty calls," he said. Grabbing his cap, he left.

About a minute later, Sam reappeared clutching a clean uniform under one arm and shoes under the other. He also carried a bucket of hot water.

"Cap'n said to try these on. He had 'em hanging in the closet. " Thy don't fit him anymore," Sam said with a smirk. "He's getting a little big 'round the middle, ifn' you know what I mean. The water's for washing. This was the purser's room before, and he left shaving gear in the drawer over there. Captain says you can use that. Officer's mess is served promptly at six." Without waiting for a reply, the boy scampered off on another errand.

Luke took off his old clothes and donned the uniform. It fit, though it hung a little on his gaunt frame. At 5:45 sharp, he left the room and went out for a stroll on deck.

The afternoon proved to be warm and inviting, and many passengers leaned against the deck rails, basking in the last rays of sunshine. Luke strode along the deck, stopping occasionally to gaze at a barge headed up-river or to a village on the river bank. He wandered aimlessly until he found himself at the aft end of the boat. On rounding a corner, his eyes caught a brief glimpse of a hulking figure disappearing down a set of stairs to a lower deck. Startled, Luke hurried forward, stopping at the top of the stairs. There was no one on the deck below.

Luke descended the stairs and scanned the lower deck in both directions. The man, whoever he might have been, had disappeared. Luke frowned. "I must be jumpy," he muttered. "It's impossible for Santelli to be on this boat." Just then, the ship's whistle sounded. Not wishing to be late for mess on the first day of work, Luke abandoned his search and hurried back the way he had come.

The evening meal was enjoyable. The other crew members were pleasant, but Luke ate quickly and hurried to the game room on the second level of the riverboat. He arrived fifteen minutes before the gaming table opened up. Captain Smith was already seated, shuffling a deck of cards.

"Good evening," boomed the Captain as Luke strode into the game room. "I trust your first day went well?"

"It was fine," replied Luke as he adjusted his shirt collar.

"Good, good," replied Smith, rubbing hands together in pleasure. "Now, you know how to play poker?" he said, implying more of a question than a statement.

"Well, Captain, I can hold my own, but I'm not a professional, if that's what you mean."

"No need, no need," Smith replied. "We always take our share. It's our pay for operating this establishment. Unless someone is cheating, that is, and if we catch them cheating, then well..." and he let his sentence trail off.

Luke assumed the unspoken consequences were as much a warning for him as it was for other players.

The captain motioned toward a chair. "Sit. Let me show you the games we play on this vessel." And with that, he gave Luke a few minutes of instruction on five card stud and draw poker. Precisely at seven o'clock, sharp, the lessons were interrupted by a polite drawl "Is this heah table open?"

Luke glanced up to see an aristocratic-looking older gentleman, dressed in white. The man sported mutton-chops down to his jaw-bone, and long gray hair curled at his collar. When he pulled out a chair, Luke observed that the man's hands were large; his fingers long and agile.

Captain Smith frowned. The newcomer was obviously someone with whom he was acquainted. "This is our new purser, Harry," Captain Smith growled. "No tricks tonight."

The older gentleman feigned a pained expression and replied, "Captain, I'm astonished that you would have any concerns about a gentleman such as myself."

Clearly unimpressed by the man's mannerisms, Smith continued. "You know the penalty for palming cards, Harry. Off the boat you go, wherever we are. Is that clear?"

The man nodded and smiled. "Never liked a cheater myself, Captain. Can't afford to lose to one either. I'll look out for your new protégé here tonight and keep everybody honest," he replied with a chuckle.

Captain Smith permitted himself a smile. Pushing his chair back, he stood and tapped Luke on the shoulder. "You're on your own, Mr. Banister. Good luck."

Luke turned to the southern gentleman. "Table's open, mister. Pull up a chair." The man sat down. Luke shuffled the deck, and dealt the first hand.

The captain watched the play from across the room for a while, then he left to tend to other tasks. Luke played well, holding his own and even winning a few dollars here and there. Other passengers sat in on the card game, trying to try their luck, stayed for several hours; some lost their stakes quickly and retired.

About a quarter to ten in the evening, Luke threw in a hand and pushed away from the table. As he stretched his legs, he caught sight of a tall, thin man making his way across the floor. On one arm, clung Grace West.

When the couple arrived at the table, a dry goods salesman was cashing in his chips. The thin man stood when they arrived. Impatient, he waited for the salesman's chair to open.

"Are you going to play that nasty ole game again tonight?" pouted Grace.

The thin man replied smoothly, "Yes, I am, dear, for a few hours."

Pursing her lips, Grace said, "Why Robert, last night you didn't get in until after daylight. You know I get lonely when I'm by myself."

The man grasped her by the hand. "As soon as I get even with what I lost last night, I'll be along. Now, do be a good girl and go on down to the cabin," he said. I'll be there soon."

The woman's eyes flashed, and she stepped back. She glanced at the players gathered around the table, catching Luke's eye. Smiling, she strutted around to where he sat and placed her hand on his shoulder, drawing it slowly across his back from one side to the other. "Maybe this handsome man would escort me to my cabin," she said coyly.

The thin man flushed red and took a step toward his blond companion, but Luke rose from his chair and blocked his way. The man stopped short, unsure of himself and unwilling to start an altercation in front of so many people.

Turning to the woman, Luke said politely. "Miss, it would be a pleasure. Unfortunately, I'm on duty right now, and while the captain would certainly understand me escorting such a beautiful woman to her room, I doubt that he would he would forgive me for abandoning my post."

As he spoke, Luke spied Sam scurrying through the crowd. He reached out and grasped the young boy by the collar, jerking him to a quick stop. Luke continued, "And though I have to forego the pleasure of your company, I've the best-looking young man on the ship right here." He pulled Sam around in front of him. "He would be happy to escort you to your cabin, wouldn't you Sam?"

Sam's eyes opened wide, and he gulped as he looked at the blonde. "Why, why...sure, Mr. Banister," he stammered.

The woman looked contemptuously at the boy, and with a glare at both men, tossed her head and stalked out of the room.

The incident had drawn the room's attention, but when Grace West left, all returned to their former pursuits. The dry goods salesman pocketed his money and vacated his chair opposite Luke. The thin man placed his hand on its back and moved in immediately." I assume this chair is open," he said in a cultured British accent. Without waiting for Luke's reply, he sat down in the vacant seat.

"Apparently," replied Luke.

"Oglethorpe. Robert Oglethorpe of London, and more recently, Boston." The Englishman leaned forward in his chair and in a low measured tone, he continued. "I dare say, mister, that if you ever come between me and my woman again, I will thrash you within an inch of your life."

Startled, Luke looked up. It wasn't the threat of being whipped by a British dandy that gave Luke pause. He had often been threatened in his legal practice by more than one unhappy adversary. But the English British accent was so out-of-place on a riverboat plying the Ohio that he almost laughed aloud.

The threat was real, however, and Luke focused his attention on the Englishman for a moment, looking him over closely. The man was narrow faced, and sported a pencil thin moustache beneath his rather patrician nose. His tailored suit covered a tall and slender, but wiry, build, and a derby hat perched at a rakish angle on his head. Luke shrugged off the Englishman's threats, but there was something about Robert Oglethorpe that Luke disliked immediately.

Luke shuffled the deck and slid the first card across the table. "Boston and London," Luke said. "You're a long way from home. What brings you out on the Ohio River, if you don't mind my asking?"

"I'm traveling to Wyoming on business, though it is no concern of yours," Oglethorpe replied, arrogance dripping from his voice.

"Wyoming," Luke responded, lifting his eyebrows as he dealt the cards. "Wyoming out in the Dakota territory? Why, it just became a state last year. I hear tell it's filled with outlaws and cattle thieves."

Oglethorpe laughed, but there was little humor in his response. "You read too many dime novels," he said, assuming, as intended, that Luke was an itinerant gambler, "though I do have some interest in the cattle business there and we have our share of highwaymen."

While he sensed Oglethorpe's growing irritation with the conversation, Luke pressed on with another question. "Why Wyoming?"

"Land and grass," replied Oglethorpe. "The grass is free, and the land stretches unfenced for a hundred miles. A man can run thousands of head of cattle on that range. Now, are we going to play cards, or talk?"

Luke grinned inwardly. Though the conversation was short, Oglethorpe's statements about opportunities in Wyoming wandered enticingly through his mind. He silently vowed to investigate further the first chance he got.

CHAPTER 12. JUMPING

The night wore on. Players changed, but Robert Oglethorpe stayed. Luke raked in his share of winnings, but luck abandoned Oglethorpe, and he became more irritable with each hand lost. The Englishman began raising the stakes with each bet, and by midnight, his purse was empty. Slamming his cards on the table, he kicked back his chair and stood up. "I'm not convinced this is a fair and honorable game," he complained. "I've lost over three thousand dollars tonight!"

"Are you saying you were cheated?" Luke asked, rising to face the red-faced Englishman.

At that moment, Captain Smith crossed the gaming room to where the two men stood eyeing one another.

"Mr. Oglethorpe," the captain interjected. "I'm sorry to see that your luck was worse than you might have hoped. Possibly, tomorrow you will do better."

The Englishman glared at Smith. "Gentlemen, I'll be here," he retorted, "and I expect an honest game. Obviously, I have my suspicions about this evening." He stalked out.

"Game's over for the night, Mr. Banister," Captain Smith said as he watched Oglethorpe leave the room. Removing a leather bag from his waistband, he threw it on the table. "Take five percent for yourself. Stow the rest in the purser's safe. Oh, and one other thing," Smith said. "Mr. Oglethorpe will still be aboard tomorrow night. He's lost heavy over the last two nights. Perhaps it's time to bar him from the table."

"Perhaps," Luke replied.

"If he comes in to play, let me know," Smith said and headed off toward another gaming table.

Luke counted the cash, separating out five percent of the earnings. After shoving his share into his pocket, he stuffed the rest of the winnings into the bag. Happy to escape the smoky haze that lay heavy in the gaming room, he stepped out onto the deck and stood at the rail, inhaling the fresh, cool river air and gazing at the lights of riverside villages as they passed slowly by.

Purser's hours start early, he thought. Reluctantly, he pushed away from the deck rail and headed toward the purser's office on the lower deck. As Luke made his way aft, the lights from the gaming room faded while the cacophony of voices and sounds died away. By the time he reached the stairs connecting the upper and lower decks, he found himself alone with only his footsteps and the sounds of the river breaking the night air. Suddenly, he was startled by a plaintiff voice that called to him out of the darkness.

"Hey, mister, can you get me something to eat? I haven't eaten all day."

Luke spun around in surprise. There was something oddly familiar about the voice. "Who's there?" he demanded, searching the shadows.

"It's me mister," responded the faceless voice, and a slender figure stepped out of the darkness of a corner into a thin beam of light.

Luke gasped in surprise. "Travis!" he exclaimed.

The young man grinned weakly when he recognized his former traveling companion. "Luke. My kin ain't in Wheeling anymore. They moved on to Kansas City. I ain't got no way of getting there, so I stowed away on this heah boat."

Luke scanned the deck. It was empty save the two of them. "Travis, do you know what they do to stowaways?" he asked. "I heard the captain talk about it today. They use the lash on them and toss them overboard. They'll do that to you, and the same to me, if they catch us here together."

Travis' eyes grew large, but then he sighed. "Wa'll, I cain't get off until the next stop, and I'll worry about the whippin' if'n they catch me. Right now, I'm so hungry I could eat a whole chicken."

Luke glanced over his shoulder. "Where are you hiding?"

Travis pointed. "In that lifeboat there. It isn't much for comfort, but it had a blanket in the storage area and a tarp over the top. At least I can stay warm and dry."

Luke thought for a moment. "Stay here, and stay out of sight," he said finally. "I'll go down to the galley and get you something to eat. We'll talk further when I get back." Travis nodded and crawled back into his hiding place. Luke pulled the canvas tarp over the boat; then, moving stealthily, he descended the stairs to the galley, below.

Moonlight cast shadows on this side of the riverboat, but other than the distant throbbing of the engines, there was little sound. Luke made his way to the galley door, twisted the door's handle, and shoved the heavy wooden door inward. Stepping inside, he closed the door behind him.

The interior of the galley was blacker than coal. Luke struck a match and lit a lantern. After setting it on a table, he retrieved a bag from the wall, opened the food storage locker and grabbed a loaf of bread, stuffing it into the bag. Next, he scavenged two apples from a barrel along with a pack of dried meat. Satisfied that the food would hold Travis for at least a day, he grabbed a jug of fresh water and slipped out the galley door, felt his way through the shadows, and climbed the stairs. When he stepped onto the riverboat's upper deck, he breathed a sigh of relief. He had taken only a step back toward Travis' refuge when out of the darkness stepped a dark-coated man, the barrel of a nickel-plated revolver glimmering in his hand.

"Ah, Mr. Banister, we meet again," the man said, waving the revolver. "I trust you still have my money."

Luke instantly recognized the clipped English accent of Robert Oglethorpe. Instinctively, he stepped back. "Mr. Oglethorpe," he said, a thousand thoughts racing through his head. "Are you referring to the money you lost tonight?"

"Yes. Of course," responded the Englishman. "The game was crooked."

"Hardly," Luke retorted. "You played poorly."

"However I played," Oglethorpe said, his voice growing impatient, "I want it back. Now hand it over."

Luke edged back until the ship's rail pressed into his back. The Brit did not intend to let him go free, that he knew. Buying time, Luke dropped the food and slowly withdrew the leather bag of poker winnings from his jacket. "You win, mister." he said. "It's all here in this bag. Every cent."

Eyes gleaming, Oglethorpe stepped forward, but as he reached out, Luke swung it out over the rail, holding it high above the dark water slipping by below. "On the other hand," Luke said, "we may be at an impasse here, Mr. Oglethorpe. If you shoot me, then this bag goes into the river. Your money will be lost. You'll never get it back."

Oglethorpe pulled up short, now hesitant. He held out his hand. "Hand me the bag, Banister," he said, "and I'll let you live."

The words had scarcely left Oglethorpe's mouth when something flashed through the moonlight, smacking the Englishman in the face. With a stunned grunt, the man reeled backward and sprawled on the deck. Like a ghost, Travis appeared out of the darkness, an oar from the life boat still in his hand.

Before Luke could act the Brit scrambled to his feet, still holding the pistol. He leveled it at Travis and thumbed the hammer, backing the young man away. "I don't know who you are, boy," Oglethorpe spit out through bloody lips, "but you're going to meet the same fate as this commoner."

Desperately, Luke hurled the leather money bag at the Englishman, hitting Oglethorpe on the arm. The blow deflected the man's aim, but the Brit triggered off a blast that slammed into the rail beside Luke. The bag skittered across the deck, coins and paper bills spilling from its open mouth.

"Jump! Now!" Luke shouted to Travis, and he leaped over the rail as far out into the inky blackness as he could. Without hesitation, Travis sprinted forward and dove over the rail after him.

Screaming in rage, Oglethorpe lunged forward and emptied his revolver into the roiling black water below. His knuckles white, the Englishman gripped the railing and scanned the darkness, but he saw nothing. It was as if the river had swallowed the two men whole.

#

Luke splashed into the icy Ohio and went under, popping up moments later spitting muddy water from his mouth.

Travis bobbed to the surface a few yards away. "Swim away from the riverboat," he yelled.

Luke kicked and thrashed through the river's current, but the riverboat's wake buffeted him hard. He went under again, surfacing some yards downstream, choking and gagging from swallowing too much water.

"Luke," Travis shouted as he swam toward the sound. "Say something so I can find you!"

Luke managed a strangled "I'm over here."

"Keep talking," shouted Travis as he swam toward the sound. In a moment, his hands touched Luke's shoulder. "Hold on," Travis pulled Luke toward the river's edge. Before long, they encountered shallow water, and then a sand bar that allowed them to wade ashore.

"Damn," Luke said as he crawled from the water exhausted. "You're going to have to teach me to swim."

"I can do that," replied Travis, shivering in the night air. "I'll make a trade right here. I'll teach you to swim if'n you teach me to read and write."

"You can't read?" Luke asked, a little surprised.

"Never learned," replied Travis. "Jesse can. Real good, but Pa said all I needed to know was how to make moonshine. And I've memorized the fixin's for his moonshine recipe so I didn't have to read nothin'. Weren't no schools back in the hollers anyway."

"It's a deal," exclaimed Luke as they climbed the river bank.

#

The galley door of the Golden Girl creaked open. A man, silhouetted by moonlight, entered the room. He was followed by a second figure. In a voice dripping with exasperation, the first man spoke. "Where have you been? I expected to meet you earlier, up on deck, or in the gaming room."

"I don't like crowds, and I'm not a gambler. You can't trust luck to be on your side when you need it," the second man responded, his raspy voice exaggerated in the darkness.

"Then, let's get down to business," said the first man. "You come highly recommended by my cousin, James Atherton. He said that you might be willing to do a certain job, that I, shall I say, find distasteful, and that you would be discreet about the job afterward."

"For the right price, I can do just about anything. What did you have in mind?"

The first man cleared his throat. "I need a certain man to meet with an accident, a fatal accident. I need you to make happen."

"Who is the man?" Is he here? Can it be done tonight?"

"No," he is not here. He lives far from here--in Wyoming. But the job can be done any time in the next six months."

"Wyoming? That is a far piece from here." The room was quiet for a moment, and then the man with the raspy voice continued. "I might have reason to go there, but it cost you a lot."

"I'm prepared to pay a reasonable price, of course."

"I'll need ten thousand—half now and half when the job is done."

"Ten thousand! That's a steep price."

"It's a long way to travel, and for these things to occur discreetly, the price is always high," the raspy voiced man said, his voice taking on a stubborn tone. "If it's too high, I'll get off at the next stop and the deal is off."

"I guess I have little choice," the first man replied after a moment of silence. He reached into a leather bag and pulled out a sheaf of paper bills. "This should be half of your price. As agreed, I'll pay the rest when you've finished your task."

The first man took the bills and stuffed them into his vest pocket. "I'll send you a message when I'm ready to head west," he said. "Until then, don't try to contact me again." The door opened and both men left the room.

#

Robert Oglethorpe stomped into the gaming room and thrust out his chin. "I caught your poker player stealing food from the galley," he said haughtily, dropping the bag of food at Captain Smith's feet. "He had some-one with him, a boy I think, a stow-a-way, and they tried to rob me. No, Captain, they tried to murder me. Look at my face."

Captain Smith surveyed Oglethorpe's puffy lips and cut chin. "Where

87

is Banister?" he asked.

"They jumped over the side of the ship," Oglethorpe said. "Banister had a bag with him, a bag of money from the poker game I dare say, and he took it with him. It was your money, so he robbed you as well, Captain."

Smith shook his head. He considered himself a good judge of character, and he was reluctant to admit that he had made a mistake by hiring this stranger named Luke Banister. "I'll ensure that the authorities are alerted at the next stop," he responded.

#

Sunrise found Luke and Travis trudging along the river road. Cold and wet, they had been walking in silence for over an hour when Luke spoke. "Travis, I never got a chance to say this before, but I'm sorry about Willy."

Travis shrugged his shoulders. "It was all Pa's doin', ya know. Pa was getting along in years, and he was afraid Jesse would be left all alone if he passed on, so he set up this marriage with Willy. There aren't many men folk around that part of West Virginia that are willing to take on a woman her age, you know, being nigh on to thirty or so. He arranged what he could, I guess. Trouble is, Willy drank about as much moonshine as he made. That didn't set well with Jesse. She said something about it once, and he drew back like he was gonna hit her. Would've too if Pa hadn't been standin' there. To tell ya the truth, if'n you hadn't kilt him, Pa woulda if he'd hit Jesse. That's why Pa didn't shoot ya right off. He sorta knew that Jesse needed a different kind of husband. Jesse has something special. She's smart. Too smart, I think. She scared off most men, but Pa was hopin' you might take a fancy to Jesse once you got to know her. And, she, you, for that matter."

Before he could think too much about what Travis had just said, a deep rumble interrupted his thoughts. Glancing back down the road, he spotted a lumber wagon approaching. "Travis," he said. "I think we've got us a ride."

#

Captain Smith docked the Golden Girl at the nearest town, and met with the town Sheriff. Soon, the town was abuzz with rumor of two men who had jumped into the river after trying to rob and murder a man on the Golden Girl. The sheriff organized a search of the river banks, but returned home empty-handed. Most folks familiar with the dangers of the river argued that the current probably claimed the two men, and speculated that their bodies would turn up along the river bank somewhere.

But Luke and Travis had escaped the river's grasp, and a half a day later, they were eating at a riverside tavern. At the next table, two men began talking about the fracas aboard The Golden Girl. When one man mentioned a reward, Luke gave Travis a knowing look. Stuffing the rest of their food into their pockets, they quietly exited through the back door of the tavern. Now marked men on the river, they had no choice but to travel overland. Using some of the money Luke had won in the poker game, they purchased supplies and struck out cross-country, heading west toward Kansas City. Days later, dusty and tired, they arrived in the bustling town on the back of a freight wagon.

Kansas City hummed with activity. Settlers and sod-busters were buying equipment for their lands; hustlers were plying their trade and trying to separate people from their money. When the wagon stopped at a local warehouse, Luke and Travis hopped out, thanking the wagon driver for the ride.

Luke turned and clasped his young companion on the shoulder. "Travis," he said, "I guess it's time for you to find your kin. Do you have any idea where they might be?"

Travis nodded. "A neighbor of theirs in Wheeling gave me a street and number, and I memorized it. I'll just ask around until I find somebody who knows where it's at. I guess it can't be that hard to find."

"Why don't I go with you," Luke spoke up, sensing Travis' hesitancy. "This time, we'll make sure you have a place to stay."

Luke fished in his pocket and withdrew a thin bundle of paper money. "Let's take a cab," he said. "I'm tired of bouncing around in the back of an old wagon." Travis grinned and agreed. Luke hailed the next cab and gave the driver the address. The driver nodded and slapping the reins, set his team in motion. The team pranced ahead, and in about ten minutes, they entered a pleasant residential neighborhood. The driver turned and headed down a tree-lined street, stopping in the front of a frame house.

"This is the address," the cabby said.

The two riders clambered out. Luke paid the driver while Travis strode to the front door and knocked. From within, a voice could be heard. "Hold on, I'll be there in a minute." Soon, the door opened, and a portly woman appeared, almost filling the door frame.

"May Belle Lee?" Travis inquired.

"Yes," replied the woman.

"I'm Travis, Travis McGill, your cousin."

The woman stared at Travis for a moment, and then she let out a whoop. "Burley, come see what jist knocked on our door!" she shouted. Waddling forward, she threw her arms around Travis and hugged him to her bosom. Moments later, a man at least as large as May Belle appeared at the door. May Belle turned Travis loose and introduced her husband, Burley. By this time, Luke had arrived at the front door. "Pleased to meet you. I'm Luke Banister," he said.

"Land o' Goshen!" May Belle exclaimed. "Are you some kind of relation, too?"

Luke smiled. "No, ma'am. None at all. I've just accompanied Travis here to find you. We have a story you might want to hear."

"Come on in, then," May Belle insisted.

Luke and Travis stepped inside. Travis told the whole story, from beginning to end, of what had befallen them since they had left West Virginia. He hung his head and fought through tears when he spoke of Pa and Jesse being shot.

When he was finished, May Belle cried and patted Travis on the shoulder. "We must do something," she insisted. "Can't we go back and get the Sheriff to arrest this...this madman, Santelli?"

"May Belle," interjected Luke. "We'd be arrested the minute we got anywhere close to the Ohio River. And, what Travis didn't say is that we can't go back to West Virginia right now. The Sheriff is in league with Santelli and would clap us in jail if we showed our faces. We'd most likely be dead before first light the next day."

Luke stood up. "I have to go," he said politely, shaking Burley's hand. "I thank you kindly for all your hospitality."

Travis looked at him quizzically. "Where are you going from here?" he asked.

"I saw a hotel not far up the road. I'll spend the night there. Tomorrow, I think I'll take the Union Pacific on west," Luke replied thoughtfully. I have a friend, a doctor, who said I have to live in a drier climate for my health. I don't know where that will be, in the end, but I've decided to try Wyoming, first. I met a man who said there's endless grass and prairie there, and lots of new opportunity. Don't know what I'll find for sure, but I'm hoping there's room for me."

May Belle gave Luke a hug, and then she and Burley followed him out of the house. They stood on the porch while Travis accompanied him down the walkway to the street. At the front gate, Luke stuck out his hand. "You take care, Travis. We'll meet up again sometime."

Travis hung his head, but then looked up, a grin spreading across his face. "Wait," he said. "I'm going with you."

"But, Travis," Luke replied, "don't you want to stay with your cousin?"

Travis looked back at the house. "She and Burley are good people, I'm sure," he said. "But they have their own lives. I'm nearly grown, and its time I make a new life for myself, even if it's out west. I want to go with you, if you'll let me."

Luke thought for a moment. "Well, I guess I could use a partner," he said. "And you haven't taught me how to swim yet, so our bargain is still good."

Travis grinned. Turning, he ran back to May Belle and gave her a big hug. "I'm going west," he said.

Tears welled up in May Belle's eyes. "Then, you take care, young man," she said. "And be sure and write when you find a place to settle down for more than a few days."

Travis nodded. Stepping back, he shook Burley's hand, turned, and ran to join Luke.

#

Miles to the east, Sarah Benson and Jesse McGill sat on the porch of the Benson cabin enjoying the early morning coolness. It had been nearly three weeks since Jesse had been shot in the Branscom raid, and her wounds were healing well under Sarah's watchful eye and herbal medicine care. Deep in thought, Jesse rocked back and forth. Finally, she spoke. "Sarah, I know Travis is out there somewhere."

Sarah looked up. She chose her words carefully. "Jesse, my child, no one around here has seen Travis since...since the Branscoms burned you out. We don't have any idea where he's gone, or even if he's..." and Sarah's voice trailed off.

Jesse gazed out over a meadow filled with wild flowers. "Alive, you mean," she said, finishing Sarah's unspoken thoughts. Turning to look at the gray-haired woman, Jesse continued. "Sarah, I know Travis is alive. I'm going to find him."

"But, Jesse," replied Sarah softly, "word on the mountain is that Ben Santelli is still looking for you. Why, just last week Abe said Billy Thompson over on Carlton Creek was asked by Bakky Branscom if he had heard any rumors about where you might be."

"Sarah, I value your words, and I'm grateful for the way you've cared for me, but I'm not going to hide in these hills forever," Jesse replied. Then, a tone of defiance crept into her voice. "And, I swear to you that I'm going to

91

see Ben Santelli pay for his crimes, even if it's the last thing I ever do."

Sarah knew that Jesse's mind was made up. She bit her tongue and kept silent.

Several days later, Abe Benson left the cabin early to go hunting. At mid-morning, Sarah pulled on a bonnet and walked to the neighbors to visit. Left alone, Jesse sat on the Benson's porch, rocking and staring across the meadow. Something beyond seemed to be calling to her. Rising from the rocker, she stepped off the porch and walked to the edge of the woods. She paused for a moment, and then, with a determined stride, pushed deeper into the forest.

Jesse followed the road through the West Virginia countryside until she arrived at the last place she remembered being before the Benson's had found her. She kept her eyes focused and moved straight ahead, following the faint trail that she had walked that day. Determined that fear would not turn her back from her mission, she pressed on, deeper into the forest, until her eyes spotted something shiny that lay partially hidden in the grass and leaves. Kneeling, she brushed away the leaves, and there, resting in the black soil, lay the knife she had taken from Ben Santelli.

Jesse picked the knife up, and held it in the palm of her hand, inspecting the weapon more closely. It was almost primitive in construction, but strong and well-made. A carving of a soaring eagle graced one side of the handle while two mountain peaks adorned the other. It had a story to tell, but whose? Who owned it before Santelli? What secrets did it hold? But then, a chill raked her body when her eyes fell on the dark red stain on the blade. Blood! And, it was hers! She rose to her feet, wanting to throw the knife deep into the woods, but instead, she wrapped her fingers around the handle. Strangely, it felt comfortable in her hand. Slowly, she drew the blade through the grass, wiping the steel clean. Sticking the knife in her apron, she rose, and continued down the path, a sense of urgency driving her on.

A half hour later, Jesse stood at the edge of the woods surrounding McGill Holler. Sadness gripped her as her eyes played over the ruined buildings. In her mind, she could visualize Pa or Travis to coming to greet her, but there were no signs of life. Taking a deep breath, she left the woods and hurried across the meadow to the charred cabin. Pulling the bone-handled knife from her pocket, she sank its blade into the soft dirt beneath one corner of the burned-out structure, digging until she uncovered a flat, round rock. Working swiftly, she levered the rock from its resting place, revealing an oil skin bag stuffed with paper money and gold coins. Glancing furtively around the meadow, she removed the bag and placed it in her apron.

Jesse turned and started back the way she had come. She was almost in the safety of the woods when Weed Branscom stepped from behind a tree, blocking her path. Weed grinned through teeth blackened with rot. "Wa'al now, if it ain't Jesse McGill. We all figured you made it out of that barn. Ben Santelli said you was alive out there somewhere and would come back heah jist like a mother hen comes back to the roost."

"You pig," Jesse spit out, fear rising in her throat. She pulled the bone-handled knife from her apron, waving its sharp point at Weed. "Get out of my way."

"Well, sure you know I will," Weed replied, his eyes narrowing to slits as he stared at the knife, "Santelli says you have something of his'n, that knife you got right there. Ben tole me one time that knife is a treasure map. A map to gold somewhere out west. Wyoming, I think." He moved closer, "He also has some unfinished bidness wit ya, but so's I."

Jesse retreated, holding Weed at bay with the knife. "What have you done with Travis?"

"Travis, that good fer nothin' brother o' yourn," said Weed, leering at the frightened woman. "Last I heerd, he and some other fella were heading down river. He thought you was daid, Jesse. "Wa'al, you ain't now, are ya. You're jist as alive as me, but being alive heah now ain't gonna do you no good no how."

Frantically, Jesse scanned the meadow for an escape, but she was hemmed in. Weed moved forward, but before he could launch an assault, a rifle boomed from the darkness of the forest. Weed's face took on a surprised look, and blood appeared at the corner of his mouth. He took one step toward Jesse. The long gun fell from his fingers, and with a gargling cry, he pitched forward into the grass.

Jesse danced backward, her frantic eyes scanning the tree line from where the rifle blast came. When she saw Abe Benson appear from the woods, she let out a long slow breath. He came toward her cautiously, holding his rifle at ready, its barrel still smoking.

Abe strode over to Jesse. Without emotion, he said quietly, "He killed my brother last year, but I take no pleasure in killing this man. 'Revenge is mine, saith the Lord,' though sometimes we are but tools for his work." Tearing his gaze from Weed's lifeless form, he searched the meadow closely. "Bakky's most likely out there somewhere. If he heard the shot, he'll be here soon. Quickly, we must go."

Jesse gathered her skirt, and they hurried back into the darkness of the forest.

CHAPTER 13. THE TRANSCONTINENTAL

The transcontinental passenger train steamed westward, its iron wheels clicking rhythmically on the long ribbon of steel track. The monotonous rhythm was broken only by stops at dusty outposts that hugged the rails. There, travelers would disembark. Others would board. Then, billowing a cloud of steam, smoke and cinders, the engine would strain forward, pressing on to the next stop on its journey, and the rhythm would continue.

For Luke and Travis, each settlement became a welcome distraction from the relentless clickity-clack of iron on iron. Hours became days, and days wore into nights until, on the morning of the third day, Luke awoke bleary-eyed from a restless sleep. Leaning against the side wall of the Union Pacific passenger car, he let the April sun stream through the window to warm his body. He would have been perfectly content there, but it had taken the better part of three days to travel from Kansas City to Cheyenne, Wyoming, and his muscles ached from inactivity. He pushed back his black hair and rocked forward, letting his legs drop down to the floor of the passenger car.

Luke pulled out his pocket watch and glanced at the face. It read seven-o-five. Shading his eyes, he squinted out the train window to see a familiar sun staring back from a blue, cloudless, sky, but the landscape that lay beyond the glass was alien to his eyes. During the night's run, the land had turned from forested hills to a greening prairie. Sagebrush peppered the land, bent to the southeast by the relentless wind. Otherwise, only distant bluffs and stands of tall cottonwood trees broke the panorama that stretched on to a distant horizon.

At the sound of the train's whistle, Luke tore his eyes from the passing countryside. He retrieved his hat from the seat beside him and pulled it down on his head. Next stop, Cheyenne, he thought, stretching his aching limbs.

Travis, his hat cocked at an odd angle over his eyes, stirred several seats away. A drummer with a suitcase full of goods sat three rows ahead staring out the window. A sheriff's deputy sat across the aisle, looking out the train window, and a woman with two young boys, seemingly bent on mischief, occupied the seats near the end of the car.

The train began to slow, and a few minutes later, it hissed into the station. As it rolled to a stop, Travis sat up and peered out the window. "Is this Cheyenne?" he asked, yawning broadly.

"Sho 'nuff, pardner," Luke replied, emulating the best dime novel prose he could muster.

The passenger car doors opened, and Travis wasted little time in jumping to the platform, eager to experience the amenities of this legendary western city. Luke followed, stepping off the train into a gusty wind that pulled his hat from his head and sent it whirling toward the depot. Cursing, Luke sprinted after the hat, but the wind rolled it like a hoop, and kept it just out of his reach.

The hat had rolled to the end of the train station, when suddenly a tall, long-legged cowboy wearing a black Stetson appeared round the corner of the depot. Spotting the hat rolling by, the cowboy lifted his foot and stomped down hard, effectively stopping the wayward hat.

Luke skidded to a stop in front of the cowboy, a look of dismay on his face. The cowboy leaned down and retrieved the hat, dusting it off. "This yours, mister?" the cowboy asked, trying to pop the fedora back into shape before handing it back to Luke.

Luke examined his smashed head gear. "It was," he said forlornly. "I don't know if it'll be much good to me now."

"Sorry," the cowboy replied pushing back a broad-brimmed hat graced with the feather of a wild hawk. "I couldn't catch it, but thought I could stop it. Guess my foot got a little heavy."

About that time, Travis arrived. He took one look at the bedraggled hat and snickered. The lanky cowboy began to walk away, but then turned to face the two newcomers. "Would you two gents be looking for work?" he asked. "I've got a thousand head of cows I need to trail three hundred miles north. I'm short a couple of hands. Looks like they had a little trouble with the law here in Cheyenne last night. Can't wait for 'em, though," growled the cowboy as he shook his head. "Pay's thirty dollars a month. I'll furnish the horses and bedrolls. Hell, you can have the fella's bedrolls that didn't show up this morning. You get three squares a day, beans with Howard's biscuits, and as much coffee as you can drink. What do ya say?"

Luke looked askance at the talkative fellow in front of him, "Do I look like a cowboy, mister?" he replied, comparing his shoes and bare head to the boots and Stetson the rangy cowboy wore.

"Well, no, no ya don't," replied the man as he removed his Stetson to scratch his head, revealing a shock of thick, red hair. He pushed his hat back on his head and looked at Luke and Travis closely. "But you all do look like you could use some work. I'd be willin' to cut you some slack on the experience side if you'd hire on. I can make a cowhand out of ya in a week."

Luke shook his head, amused at the man's persistence. "Can't say as we're interested," he replied.

"Hell," the man grinned. "I know I didn't offer you enough. I'll make it forty dollars a month plus a bonus if we get the herd there in thirty days. I'll admit, it's work, hard work, but you get fed three times a day, and you have a place to sleep at night."

Travis tugged at Luke's sleeve. "Listen, Luke," he whispered, wide-eyed. "That's a whole lot o' money, more money than I've made my entire life. We ain't got no place else to go, and it'll give us a grubstake."

Luke hesitated, considering Travis' words. Turning to the red-headed cowboy, he said. "My partner wants us to hire on. I'll go with that, but you have two fairly green hands here."

A broad grin spread across the cowboy's face, and he held out his hand. "Welcome aboard. My name is John Walker, and most of the time, I answer to one name or the other. I'm the trail boss. Wagon is over there. Throw your bags in the back, and we'll be ready to roll."

Luke and Travis carried their bags over to the wagon and tossed them in the back, clambering in after them. Walker settled into the wagon seat like he had been born there, and with a slap of the reins, set the team in motion. They headed down the street and out of Cheyenne to the west.

A few miles from the city, they came to a makeshift corral. A herd of horses milled around inside. Two cowhands, one young and one near middle-age, were seated around a campfire cradling a tin cup between their hands. John pulled in to the camp, and brought the wagon to a stop. "Step down fellas," he said to Luke and Travis. "I'll introduce you to the hands."

Trailed by his two new hires, the big red-headed cowboy strode over to the campfire. "Sam, Billy," he called out to the hands sitting around the fire. "This is ah..., I guess I didn't catch your names," he said apologetically.

"I'm Luke Banister," Luke filled in, "and this is Travis McGill."

"Luke and Travis. Good! Gentlemen, they'll be riding with us on this trip."

"Howdy," Billy said, jumping up to greet the newcomers. "Sam Rivers," the older man said quietly, holding out a gnarled hand. Travis and Luke greeted each man, shaking their hand in turn.

Luke surveyed the two cowboys and was struck at their differences. Billy was as young as Travis, thin, and angular. Sam was older, late forties maybe, weathered by the sun and a hard life. Lean and wiry, he wore a six gun on one hip, tied low to his leg.

At that moment, a bald-headed, whiskered gentleman of about seventy appeared around the corner of the chuckwagon, carrying on an animated conversation with himself. "And that," John Walker said with a chuckle, "is Howard. He's our cook. Howard, meet our new hands."

Howard glared at the newcomers. "Two more mouths to feed," he growled. "Hope yer not expecting any coddling. No sirree, cause there won't be any on this drive. You'll eat what I cook or ye won't be eating at all." Without waiting for a reply, the old codger continued on with his tasks, still muttering to no one in particular.

Walker watched the man disappear around the corner of the chuckwagon. Then, he turned to the two newcomers. "Don't mind Howard," he said. "He's all gruff and growl, no bite." Walker turned serious. "Travis, can ya handle a rope, son?" he asked.

Travis nodded.

"Good. Grab a riata over there and take your pick of those hammerheads," Walker commanded, pointing at the corral. "When you get a loop on one of them, saddles are over by the wagon. Be ready to ride in an hour."

Travis strode over to the corral post and removed one of the lariats. Climbing to the top rail of the corral, he surveyed the horseflesh milling nervously about. A big buckskin caught his eye, and he jumped into the pen, swinging his loop. Wild-eyed, the buckskin tried to break by the boy, but he tossed his lasso and held on as the loop settled neatly over the buckskin's neck. Travis snubbed the rope to a corral post, and slowly pulled the horse in, talking low and easy to the skittish animal.

Walker watched, nodding his approval. "Looks like he's gonna be fine," he remarked. Then, he turned to Luke. "Riding broncs is a young man's game. Now, I ain't saying that you're old, but you're certainly not twenty either. Those old cayuses will bust you up quick if you're not used to 'im. I think I'll start you on the hoodlum wagon, carrying bedrolls and tents, supplies and such. You do know how to drive a wagon don't ya?"
Luke, slightly insulted by John Walker's observation, replied. "I'm not that green."

John grinned. "Good," he said. Then he pointed toward a heavy, canvas-covered wagon standing by the corral. "That one's yours. The team's already hitched and ready to go. Check 'em out. Be ready to roll in an hour." Luke retrieved his bag, along with Travis', and lugged both to the hoodlum wagon. He went about his assigned tasks, inspecting the team and checking the traces and harness.

True to his word, within an hour Walker gave the command to roll. They started north, traveling about three miles before they came upon the main herd. Luke gazed out over the grazing cattle, impressed by the sight of a thousand head bunched together, but he had little time to take it all in. Walker rode around the herd, issuing commands to each cowboy along the way, and soon, all were plodding north at a slow, steady pace.

The day wore on without incident. That night, during the evening meal, Luke met the other hands. There was Nick, a happy go lucky sort who always had a smile on his face, and Zack, an experienced hand who was full of advice. Then, there was a dour man who went by the name of Frank Kelly, who seemed to take an immediate dislike of Luke, disagreeing with everything he said. Luke found Kelly's attitude to be the lone thorn in an otherwise pleasant day, and he resolved to keep his interaction with the sour man at a minimum.

Several days had passed when one morning Walker galloped up to the hoodlum wagon, reining his mount in beside Luke. "Billy's horse shied away from a rattler and pitched him off," he said. "His leg is banged up. Don't think it's broke, but he can't ride. I'll need you to ride point for the next few days. Billy can drive the wagon."

"Be happy to," Luke replied, anxious to try his hand at something else. "I'll take the wagon up and trade out with him."

Walker wheeled his horse and headed back to the front of the herd. Luke slapped his reins against the rump of his team, pushing them into a faster pace and within a quarter hour, the wagon pulled abreast of where Billy sat on a rock, leg out-stretched. Pulling in close, Luke called out, "John said you took a bad spill there, Billy. Wants us to change out for a couple of days. You ride the wagon, and I'll ride point."

Billy spit a brown stream of chew into the dust. "Damned old hammerhead! Snake skeered him and he blew up on me without any warning."

Luke clambered down from the wagon and helped the boy climb into the driver's seat. "You should get Howard to take a look at your leg when you get a chance," Luke said, "just to make sure it isn't broke."

"Takes more than an ole rattler to stop me," Billy retorted, settling into the driver's seat. Luke smiled at the young man's bravado. Then, after adjusting the stirrups on Billy's saddle, he mounted and bid the young man goodbye. Spurring his new mount, he galloped to the front of the herd and joined Sam at the point, happy to be out of the dust cloud kicked up by the cattle.

By evening, they were nearing Chugwater Creek, some forty miles north of Cheyenne. Walker chose a wide, open meadow in which to bed the herd. The small village of Chugwater lay several miles distant, and Walker took the wagon, along with Howard and Travis, into the town to buy supplies. After Howard's usual supper fare of wild game and beans, Luke sat by the campfire telling Billy about Pennsylvania while the other cowboys listened—all of them, that is, except Frank Kelly.

As soon as Walker left camp, Kelly produced a bottle of whiskey from his bedroll. He sat alone outside the flickering shadows cast by the fire, cursing the foreman and complaining. With each draught on the bottle, he became louder and more abusive. The men ignored his rants until Kelly stood up and, draining the last swig of whisky from the bottom of the bottle, threw it into the fire. Then, he stumbled over and stood in front of Luke.

"We don't need to hear any more dude stories, especially from you, you yellow-bellied snake," Kelly spit out.

Luke looked up. Kelly was drunk and spoiling for a fight. Luke glanced at the other hands, but all sat watching him, waiting for his response. With a sinking feeling, Luke realized that he couldn't ignore Kelly's challenge. If he backed down, he would be branded a coward by the crew, and he would be the target of Kelly's bullying for the rest of the drive. He had no choice but to take on the drunken Irishman.

Luke stood and looked Kelly in the eye. The man was about Luke's height, but stocky as a bear, and he outweighed Luke by a good forty pounds. Square-jawed and beetle-browed, his knuckles were calloused and scarred. This is going to hurt, Luke thought, but with Kelly looming in front of him, there was no way of backing out. Steeling himself for the unavoidable onslaught, he said quietly, "Kelly, you're being a jackass."

Luke's refusal to back down surprised Kelly, and he stared through blood-shot eyes while his sotted brain tried to process the challenge. He stepped back, clenching and unclenching his fists nervously. Then, the whiskey took over again, and bellowing like an angry bull, he rushed forward.

Kelly aimed to hit Luke straight on, trying to flatten him with the brute force of his charge, but Luke stepped aside, and struck the onrushing man hard with his right hand. The blow landed square on Kelly's jaw. The Irishman stumbled and sprawled into the dirt. Lumbering to his feet, he backed away, rubbing his chin.

For a second, Kelly stared at Luke with hatred burning in his eyes. Then, he lowered his shoulders and charged again. This time, he head-butted Luke square in the gut, knocking the air from his lungs. Gasping for breath, Luke was driven backward until he tripped and fell into a stand of sage. Kelly piled on, holding Luke to the ground while his fists rained blows on Luke's head.

As best he could, Luke fended off Kelly's punches, but soon, blood was flowing from his face. Remembering the school yard wrestling trick he had used against Willy, Luke arched hard, thrusting the man forward over his head into the dirt. Kelly scrambled to his feet, but Luke rolled away and came up slowly, wiping blood from his nose.

Luke had been able to land a few blows, and blood dripped from the corner of Kelly's mouth, but any pain the big man felt was dulled by the whiskey. The two men circled one another warily until Kelly waded into Luke, landing a right to his belly, and a left to his cheek. Luke counter-punched, but Kelly swung wildly. A roundhouse caught Luke on the side of his head and sent him reeling to the ground. Kelly stood over his prostrate form.

"I didn't like you from the moment we first met," the Irishman snarled through bloody lips, and he drew back his fist to smash it against Luke's face. Luke raised his arm to ward off the blow, but before Kelly could strike, a pistol roared from the darkness. Kelly screamed and clutched at his right ear. He stumbled away, blood trickling from between his fingers. Luke raised his head, and through bleary eyes caught sight of John Walker standing by the campfire, a grim look on his face. In one hand, he held a smoking six gun.

"Do you want any more of this?" the trail boss asked Kelly angrily.

Kelly shook his head and backed away, but hatred still fired his eyes. Walker stepped over and bent down to check Luke. "Sam, Travis," Walker ordered. "Get this man over to the wagon."

The two men stepped forward. Pulling Luke from the sod, they carried him to the hoodlum wagon where they set him down. Howard poured a pan of cold water, grabbed a rag, and cleansed Luke's wounds. Then, he rummaged around in his medicine bag, producing a can of salve. After swabbing it liberally on Luke's face, he carried the medicine bag over to Kelly and proceeded to bandage his ear.

"Are you going to make it?" Walker asked Luke.

"I'm alright, but I'm not going to be too pretty for the next few days," Luke responded through puffy lips. While battered, Luke considered himself lucky. He could have been beaten into a pulp by Kelly if John had not returned when he did.

Walker nodded, and then strode over to Kelly. "You know the rule," he said angrily. "No whiskey in camp. Where is it?"

Kelly glanced involuntarily at his bedroll. Walker strode over to the blankets and fished out two more bottles of whiskey. Walking to a nearby boulder, he smashed the bottles against its granite face. Kelly looked on with dismay as the whiskey washed down the face of the rock and dripped to the ground.

Walker turned back to the crew. "Sun rises early these days, gentlemen," he growled, "and it'll be a long day tomorrow. Kelly, you're on night duty. Get your stuff and head out. I'll be checking on you every hour. Everybody else, put out the fire and turn in."

Bruised and stiff, Luke rose early the next morning and made his way to the campfire. Walker was already up and taking breakfast. The big red-head looked at him quizzically, but Luke said nothing. Kelly, his eyes red rimmed from the whiskey, leered at him from across the campfire, and except for Travis, the other hands avoided eye contact. Luke downed a mug of hot coffee, straddled his horse, and rode out to check the cattle.

On the trail, Luke rode for several hours, deep in his own thoughts. Around mid-morning, Walker rode up and fell in beside him. "From the looks of Kelly this morning, I'd say you gave a good account of yourself last night, better than I expected from a dude," Walker said, a hint of admiration in his voice.

"Thanks," Luke said through bruised lips, "but he doesn't look nearly as bad as I feel."

They rode along silently for a few minutes, and then Walker spoke again. "Kelly's a good cowhand, but when he gets whiskey in him, he goes bad, all crazy-like. That's why none of the boys stepped in. He's whipped them all before, and they didn't want to face him again. Watch him. He carries a grudge, but next time, you'll give him a better go."

"John," Luke said, narrowing his gray eyes. "There won't be a next time. I'm not going to let him, or anyone, do that to me ever again."

John looked at Luke sideways and started to say something, but thought better of it. "We'll talk again later," he said. With that, he spurred his horse and headed back down the long line of cattle strung out along the trail.

Later that afternoon, the trail boss rode up and fell in beside Luke. "We're headed into some rough country over the next several weeks," he said. "You'll need to be prepared."

"Rough country?" Luke echoed, wincing as he arched his brow above a blackened eye. "What do you mean?"

"I mean it's nearly lawless," the trail boss continued. "A dozen killings over the last year or so, mostly over cattle rustling, but several men were ambushed or killed out of sheer meanness."

"What does that have to do with me?"

"You need a gun. And, you need to know how to use it," responded Walker. "We may end up with a pack of rustlers trying to cull a few cows from the herd, or a wolf or two might want to take down a steer. Who knows what else might happen."

"I don't have a gun," replied Luke, his face reddening. "Lost it back in West Virginia."

Walker grinned. "I've got one I'll give to you. It belonged to another man, but he doesn't need it anymore," he said. "I'll teach you how to use it."

That evening after Howard had served his usual fare of beans and biscuits, Walker pawed through his trunk, digging out a black, pearl-handled revolver from the very bottom. It nestled snugly in a leather holster. Grabbing a box of cartridges from the supply wagon, he motioned for Luke to follow him out in the brush.

Walker stopped about a quarter mile from the camp and handed Luke the pistol and six cartridges. Luke balanced the weapon in his hands. It felt light, almost as if it had a life of its own. Luke opened the cylinder, placing a cartridge in five of its chambers. When he snapped the cylinder shut, Walker said, "Always load just five. Keep one cylinder open, and keep the hammer there. It's so you don't shoot yourself in the foot." Then, he pointed at a rock about twenty yards away. "Hit that," he said.

Luke lifted the pistol to eye level and, sighting down the barrel at the rock, thumbed back the hammer. The cylinder rotated, and, slowly, he squeezed the trigger. The hammer slammed forward, and the pistol jerked upward in his hand as a loud blast echoed across the prairie. The rock flew into two pieces.

"Lucky shot," drawled Walker. He retrieved an empty bean can from camp, walked out about thirty yards and set it on a stump. When he returned, he said, "I'll bet you a whiskey you can't do that again."

"I'll pass on the whiskey," Luke said, but once more he raised the pistol. Sighting down the barrel, he squeezed the trigger. Again, the pistol roared. The can flew away into the sage as if jerked by a rope. Walker ambled out to retrieve it, bringing it back to where Luke was standing. Holding it up, he stuck his finger in a large hole punched in the can's center.

"Well, I'll be," he remarked with some amusement. "Looks like you're a natural pistolero, Luke. Sure you haven't done this before?"

Luke smiled and shook his head. They continued to practice, and after Luke had shot up the box of shells, they returned to camp.

Luke had never felt the need of a pistol before, but in this territory, it seemed a gun was almost a necessity. Like the other drovers, he began to belt it on each morning and soon, it came to feel like it had always been a part of him. Every day, somewhere along the trail, he practiced with the weapon and got very good at placing his shots, whether from a horse or afoot. Walker began showing him how to position the holster so that the pistol could be drawn quickly. That too, he practiced, and in a short time he was clearing leather faster than the eye could follow.

As the drive wore on, the other drovers began to take notice of his improving skills, and around the campfire at night they talked about it with admiration. When Luke had the pistol strapped to his leg, even Frank Kelly held his acrid tongue, though his black eyes still burned.

CHAPTER 14. CHOLERA

It was a warm afternoon in mid-May when the herd arrived at the Platte River in central Wyoming. Astride a dun mare, Luke watched as the river, running high with snow melt, rolled past. They had been on the trail for over two weeks, and Luke guessed they had come nearly 140 miles. To reach the Powder River Country, he reckoned they would have to travel another 100 miles—ten days at least. He didn't mind. Over the last few weeks, he had come to feel at home in this land.

Luke's musing were interrupted when Walker reined up beside him. "Ride with me down to the river. We'll look over the crossing," Walker said. Luke nodded and followed the trail boss down the narrow trail to the river's edge. Luke halted on the bank, but Walker let his mount splash into the current. "Bottom's good, but the river is fast," he shouted from half-way out in the stream.

"Some of the smaller ones might turn with the current, "Luke responded. "We might have to station a couple of hands downstream to pick up those that get washed away."

Wheeling his horse, Walker splashed back to shore. "Let's pitch camp on this side tonight, and we'll cross first thing in the morning," he said. "River is lower then. Run-off drops during the night. Besides, it's too late in the day to be fishing cows out of the river." Luke nodded in agreement.

On returning to the herd, Walker ordered the drovers to bed down the cattle and set up camp. Howard cooked an early supper, and drovers joked around the campfire for a bit before they turned in early. Billy and Travis had drawn the midnight watch, and they threw out their bedrolls, trying to catch some shuteye before their turn on guard. Luke and Sam had drawn the ten o'clock watch. Sam made use of his time by dozing beneath the hoodlum wagon, while Luke leaned against his saddle at the campfire, gazing into its dying embers.

Walker walked down to check the remuda, and then wandered back to camp. Picking a piece of dry wood from the wood pile, he carried it to the campfire and threw it into the embers. He watched as sparks rose into the night sky, and then sat down on a log not far from Luke. "What brings you out here, Luke?" he asked, abruptly. "You're not a boy of sixteen, run away from home. You're a book-educated man, as near as I can make out. You must have a family somewhere."

Luke glanced at Walker and smiled. "Nope," he said. "I'm certainly not sixteen anymore. I can feel that every morning I get off this hard ground."

"Well, you seem out of place here." Walker said. "These young boys are either running from a Pa who beat 'em, or looking for adventure. The old men, well, most of them are running too—some from the law, some from women, some from themselves. But the only schooling these ole boys have is the education that comes of a hard life. You're not wanted anywhere, are you, for robbing a bank, or a killin'?"

"Nope," Luke said. "At least not for robbing a bank."

Luke looked up at the canopy of stars and a sense of peace entered his soul. He had not talked about his wife to anyone since her death, even to his friend William, but here under the night sky, the words began to flow. "I was married once, John, though it seems like a hundred years ago now. My wife's name was Mary. She was a beautiful woman, and I loved her more than life itself. I was an attorney in Pennsylvania, and a successful one at that, I suppose, by some men's standards. But some cases took me away from home on extended business trips. About a year ago, I had a case up state, but Mary took ill the day before I was to leave. Doc came in, looked her over, and told me she would be fine. She told me to go on with the trip, and though I knew she really didn't want me to go, I went anyway. Three days later, I received a telegram saying that she had died during the night."

Luke paused, and stared into the fire. "I blamed myself for her death, I guess, and afterward, I lived a melancholy existence. I rarely left the house, but one afternoon, a neighbor brought over a jug of moonshine whiskey. We had a few shots, and when he left, I kept the jug."

"The whiskey made me numb, but when I sobered up the melancholy returned. After a few days, I rode over to the neighbors and bought another jug. When it was gone, I bought still more. Three months ago, a friend found me in a muddy gutter in some unnamed town, half-frozen and nearly dead with pneumonia. I spent weeks in a hospital, but it gave me plenty of time to think. I knew there was nothing left for me in Pennsylvania, so, after I left the hospital, I put my affairs in order. Then, one day, I saddled my horse and left."

By the time Luke had finished, the moon was high. "Sorry about your loss," Walker said. "It must have been hard."

"It was," Luke responded, "but the hardest part is trying to forgive yourself." He pulled out his pocket watch and flipped open the cover. "It's nearly ten o'clock. I should be relieving one of the boys," he said. Standing, he pulled his hat down tight and headed to the picket line. Picking a raw-boned black out of the remuda, he threw the saddle on its back, and pulled the leather cinch tight. Speaking softly, he stepped into the stirrup and swung a leg over the horse's back, and was relieved when his mount trotted forward docilely.

Must be as tired as I am, Luke thought.

Luke circled the herd, gathering a few wandering strays and pushing them back to the main bunch. As the evening wore on, the herd quieted. Luke relaxed, listening to the plaintive bawl of a lost calf, and the howl of a lonely coyote drifting in on the night air. Midnight came and went, and Luke waited patiently for Billy to show up in relief. He never came.

Around 1:00 a.m., Luke concluded that the young man was still asleep by the fire. Riding back to camp, he reined in his horse near Billy's bedroll and dismounted. He leaned down to shake the young man awake, but Billy didn't move. He shook him again. This time, the boy only moaned. Luke laid his hand on Billy's forehead. His skin was hot to the touch.

Luke hurried over to the chuckwagon and tapped Howard on the shoulder. "Howard," whispered Luke. "Get up. Something's wrong with Billy."

Howard grumped and snorted, but he threw aside his blankets and rolled to his feet. "Grab a lantern," he said as he limped over to Billy's bedroll.

Luke picked up the lantern and lit the wick. Then he followed stepped toward where Billy lay.

Howard knelt beside the young man and examined him closely. "Wake up the boss," he whispered. "We might have a case of cholera."

Luke hurried over to Walker's bedroll and shook the trail boss awake. "Billy's sick," Luke said.

Walker pulled on his boots and strode over to where Howard sat. "What's the matter?" he asked.

Howard scratched his head. "I can't be sure, but it looks like cholera."

"He was down at the river. Do ya suppose he drank some of that water?" asked Walker.

"Don't know," Howard said over his shoulder as he scurried off to retrieve medicines from his stores.

His face grim, Walker turned to Luke. "I'll get Kelly to take his shift. Do what you can to help Howard."

Howard hurried back with can of foul-smelling liquid. He poured some down Billy's throat, but there was little either one of them could do. As the morning drew closer, Luke laid down and tried to catch a few hours of sleep.

At dawn, the crew awoke and began to ready themselves for the day's work. Walker called them all together. He had been up most of the night; his face looked lined and haggard. "Billy's sick," he announced, "too sick to travel, but we have to move on. The cattle will deplete the available grass in a day, and then they'll begin to scatter. We won't be able to hold the herd together."

Walker paused. "We need a volunteer to stay with him," he said. "He needs water and care. If it's what I think it is, the next day will tell whether he lives or...," and his voice trailed off.

The hands looked down, fiddling with their hats, but Luke stepped forward. "I'll stay."

Walker peered at him closely. "Get a tent and food and water for three or four days. When Billy gets well, you two can catch up." Luke nodded and followed Howard to the supply wagon.

Walker gave out the day's orders, and soon the herd was headed north. Howard lingered until the last cowboy had left. Then he stepped over to the back of the wagon and reappeared with a shovel and a black book. He handed both to Luke.

"A Bible and a shovel? What are these for?" Luke asked with a frown.

Howard's face took on a grim look. "You'll know when the time comes," he said, clambering into the wagon. Whistling to the team, he drove the wagon forward, leaving Luke standing alone with Billy in the abandoned campsite.

Luke watched until the wagon disappeared beyond the rolling hills, leaving only a billowing cloud of dust as evidence of its existence. Then he turned to his task.

Throughout the day, Luke tended Billy, bringing him water, and forcing it past his lips. The fever raged fiercely. The boy drifted in and out of consciousness. Morning wore into afternoon, and afternoon into night. On the horizon, cumulus clouds rose thousands of feet into the evening sky, their bellies lit by flashes of lightening. Distant thunder rumbled across dozens of miles of unbroken prairie, and occasionally, a lone coyote howled to his pack.

About midnight, Billy woke suddenly. He raised his head and focused his glazed eyes on Luke. "I want you to tell my mama, Mr. Banister, that I was a good cowhand," Billy said, his voice low and raspy.

"You can tell her yourself, Billy, when you get back to Texas," Luke answered, relieved that the boy was conscious. "Do you want some water?"

Billy nodded. Luke put his arm under the boy's shoulders and raised him to a sitting position. Billy drank lightly through parched lips. Then, Luke laid him back down.

"I ain't gonna live to get back to Texas, Mr. Banister."

"Don't talk like that Billy! You'll be fine by morning."

"And, I'm gonna miss all this. The stars at night. The coyotes howling somewhere far off." Billy paused. "Did you know, Mr. Banister, that I wanted to be like you?" he continued.

"Me?" asked Luke. "Billy, you could be better than I am."

"Did you know that I can't read. I been watching you teach Travis, and I wanted to learn to read, too."

"I'll teach you. We'll start tomorrow," Luke said, "but now you have to rest."

Billy laid back and closed his eyes. "I wanted to read about far-away places," he said, his voice low and quiet. "I wanted...," and he passed again into a restless unconsciousness.

Luke sat next to Billy's side, maintaining his vigil. Every fifteen minutes, he would try to get some water down the young man's throat, even if only to wet his lips. About two o'clock in the morning, Luke reached out to touch Billy's forehead. The boy's skin felt cool, and for a moment Luke's heart lifted with the thought that his fever had broke. But, Billy didn't move when touched, and when Luke leaned down, he could hear no breathing. With a sinking heart, Luke realized that his vigil had ended. There was nothing more he could do for the young man.

Luke sat by Billy's body for an hour, unwilling to accept the boy's death. Finally, he drew the blanket up over the young man's face. Then, he left the tent, idly throwing another piece of drift wood on the glowing embers of the campfire. The fire blazed up, and momentarily, drove the shadows back.

Luke slumped to the ground with his back to a boulder and stared into the burning coals. A deep weariness crept through his body, drawing the strength from his limbs, and sapping his energy. The dancing flames mesmerized him, and he closed his eyes for just a moment. His thoughts flew back to another time, eons ago it seemed, when he was home with his wife. He smiled when he remembered the rustle of her dress when she walked, and the smell of her perfume after she had passed. In his thoughts, Mary called to him. He opened his eyes, and saw her standing in the shadows. She walked toward him. He rose to greet her, speaking her name. They embraced, and Luke clung to her.

Finally, she stepped back and spoke. "My love," she said in a voice that only Luke could hear. "You have been sad too long."

He hung his head. "But I don't want to--I can't--live without you," he replied, tears welling up in his eyes.

Mary grasped his hand held it tightly. With a firm tenderness, she replied, "You must look for happiness. Life is for the living, and it is time for you to live again."

Luke whispered, "Mary, I'm sorry. I should have been there."

Mary gazed at Luke for a long time, and then she kissed him lightly on the cheek. "It's forgiven, my love. It's always been forgiven. You must know that." Then, she stepped back, and her face took on a sad expression. "Promise me that you'll look for happiness in this life." Luke gazed into her radiant face, but in a moment, she was gone. Feelings that had long been suppressed burst from Luke's heart in a flood of tears. Overcome, he lay down on the hard ground and wept.

#

At sunrise the next morning, Luke climbed the high bluffs above the river and found a level site overlooking the valley. Using the shovel Howard had given him, he set to work digging a grave. The day was warm, the earth soft, and his work went quickly. When he was satisfied that the grave was deep enough, he walked back down to the tent.

"It's time, Billy," he said softly, and he rolled the young man's body up in his bedroll. Taking a piece of leather strapping, he secured the shroud and hoisted the boy's body to his shoulders, surprised at how light he was. Luke carried his burden up the bluff where the warm earth waited, and placed it gently into the grave. Then, from his coat pocket he retrieved the Bible Howard had given him, opened it up, and began to read aloud.

An hour later, he closed the book. Turning his eyes skyward, he took off his hat and spoke. "Lord, Billy never asked for much. All he wanted was for his mother to have peace. I've never said many prayers, but if you can hear this one, grant her the peace he asked for. Let her know that Billy was a good boy, no, a good man, and a good cowhand, Lord, and I commend his soul to heaven." Luke looked down. "God rest your soul, Billy," he said.

Luke tucked the Bible into his pocket and jammed his hat back on his head. Then, he shoveled the warm dirt back into the grave, mounding it up over the young man's body. Gathering a pile of large flat stones, he placed them over the fresh soil, rolling one big rock to the top of the grave to serve as a headstone. When he was finished, he stood for a few minutes surveying his work. Satisfied, he threw the shovel over his shoulder and strode purposefully back down the hill to where they had spent the night. Striking camp, he headed north.

The herd had made only about fifteen miles since they had left yesterday morning, but Luke was in no hurry to rejoin the drive. He ambled along, thinking about the night before, about Billy's death, and about Mary. At noon, he urged his horse into a trot, and three hours later, he caught the tail end of the herd. Walker rode out to greet him.

"I don't see Billy. I guess it's over," was all he said.

Luke nodded.

"Take the pack horse over and throw the bags and tent in the hoodlum wagon," Walker said. "You can ride point today."

CHAPTER 15. JESSE'S TREK

A half-continent away from the prairies of Wyoming, Jesse slipped across an alley to the side door of Carson's livery stable. Pausing for a moment, she cast a glance over her shoulder, pushed the door open, and stepped inside.

Henry Carson, the proprietor, stood in a horse stall at the far end of the stable, forking straw into a wheelbarrow. Hearing the door open, he leaned his pitchfork against a sidewall. A customer, he thought, and walked toward the front of the livery. The early morning light filtered dimly through open slats on the walls, and he strained his eyes trying to see who had entered the livery, "Hallo," he called out. "Can I help you?"

The visitor, standing in the shadows, responded. "Henry, how would you like to buy a good team and wagon?"

The liveryman scowled. The voice was definitely feminine, and sounded vaguely familiar, but he couldn't quite place where he had heard it before. Wiping his grimy hands on his pant legs, the stableman replied, "Whose team and wagon?"

"Mine," replied the voice, and the figure stepped closer. Henry let out a low chuckle and slapped his thigh. "Jesse McGill," he said. "Doesn't this beat all. One of the Branscom boys was in here last week. Said that your cabin caught fire up there in the Holler. You, your pa, and the boy, Travis, were kilt. Burnt up,"

I'd suspect that would be Bakky," Jesse replied, her voice low.

Henry nodded.

"They were only partly right," said Jesse. "They burned the cabin and shot Pa, but I'm still here. I don't know where Travis is."

Henry looked over his shoulder. "What do you want?" he asked. "I don't want any trouble with those polecats, or with that devil they work for, that Ben Santelli."

"Will you take the wagon and team?" asked Jesse.

"Well, let's see," Henry said as he removed his hat to scratch his head revealing a pate as devoid of hair as the ice on a frozen lake. "You've got two fine looking mules, not too well matched, though. One's black, and the other's a gray. The gray is bigger than the black, too. I watched that team when your Pa come into town 'bout a month ago. The little one is letting the big one do all the pullin'," I said to myself then. Nope, not a well-matched pair there, Miss Jesse. I couldn't give you top dollar for 'em. As for the wagon, it squeals a little, probably been run without greasin' the wheels. Most likely, the axle is worn, but seein's you're needing to sell, I'll tell you what." He looked slyly at Jesse. "I'll give you a hundred dollars for the team and wagon."

"Henry," Jesse countered, "I said I'd sell it, not give it away. How about a hundred and fifty dollars for the team horses and the wagon."

Henry scratched his head again, and stuck out his jaw. "Just because I like you, Jesse McGill, and I know you're needin' to get out of town, I'll give you a hundred and twenty-five."

"It's yours," Jesse replied, her voice laced with disgust, "but you're stealing it."

Henry grinned, unfolded his arms, and strode into the enclosure he used as his office, shutting the door behind him. A few minutes later, he returned carrying a leather bag. Reaching deep inside, he withdrew a handful of shiny gold coins, laying them one by one in Jesse's hand until he had counted out one hundred ten dollars in gold coin.

"There it is," he said.

"Henry," said Jesse, "You're fifteen dollars short."

Henry's face took on the look of a stubborn mule. "That's all I'm giving. Do you want it or don't ya?"

Jesse's eyes flashed, but she put the coins in her coat pocket. "If Pa were here, he'd thrash you good for taking advantage of a woman in need," she said.

Henry smirked. "But, he ain't, Jesse McGill, and I suggest you keep a civil tongue in yer head."

Jesse glared at the stable man. "Have it your way then," she said. "Now, I need two horses. Good ones. One to ride, and one to pack. Let's see what you have."

A wide grin lit up Henry's face, exposing a set of crooked yellow teeth. "Sure," he said, spinning and walking toward the far end of the stable. "I've got just the horse flesh for ya. Follow me out back."

Henry led Jesse to the corrals at the back of the livery. "Take a look at these horses here," he said, climbing up on one rail and waving his arm at the animals milling around inside.

Jesse peered at the horses through the corral rails. A big roan looked good, but he walked with a barely noticeable limp. A small buckskin had good legs, but didn't look strong enough for a long journey. Jesse mentally picked out two of the better-looking animals, a sorrel gelding and a pinto mare. The gelding was sleek and muscular and appeared to be about six years old. He would be a good one to ride, Jesse thought. The mare was small and rangy and looked like she had spent some time on the trail. Both horses looked at Jesse with curiosity.

Jesse asked about several of the other horses first, paying only scant attention to Henry's responses. Finally, she pointed toward the mare, "How about that pinto?" she asked. "Has she ever packed anything?"

"Tyler, there? Of course!" replied Henry. "Why, she just came off the trail. Look here. I'll bet she weighs a thousand pounds anyway. Look at those legs. She could pack off my barn today and be back for more tomorry."

Jesse rolled her eyes, but bit her lip. "The sorrel looks like he could travel," she said. "What do you know about him?"

"Buck? Why, he's premium stock, might be the best I've got." Henry responded, warming up to the sale. "He's a good saddle horse. Gentle as a lamb. Why, a babe could ride him to church on Sunday."

Jesse glanced at Henry from beneath her broad brimmed hat, and gave an incredulous smile. "Sure," she quipped in a voice laden with skepticism. After watching both animals in the corral for a few minutes, she asked, "what's the price for both the pinto and the sorrel?"

"A hundred and forty dollars," Henry replied.

Jesse shook her head. "That's a lot. I need to look at them closer," she said.

Henry retrieved a rope from the barn and lassoed the sorrel. Leading him out of the corral, he tied the gelding to the fence. Then, he did the same with the pinto mare. Jesse circled the horses, inspecting them closely and peppering Henry with questions about their health.

Satisfied, she turned to Henry. "Grab my pack out of the wagon, would you? Let's see if the mare is as good as you said." Henry waddled over to the wagon, returning with Jesse's pack. A minute later, Jesse had the pack tied onto the mare's back.

"Do you have a bridle and saddle?" She asked.

Henry nodded and hurried back into the barn. He returned in a few minutes with a worn saddle and a bridle.

Jesse took the bridle and approached Buck slowly. She stroked his neck, and then circled his body, touching him lightly on the legs and along the flanks. The gelding flinched, but stood quietly as Jesse placed a bridle on its head. She retrieved the saddle, and threw it up and onto Buck's back. The gelding danced sideways, but her soft voice soothed the animal, and soon she had the saddle cinched up tight.

Henry watched. "A good one, ain't he?" he beamed, spitting a stream of tobacco juice into the corral.

"Maybe," Jesse replied. Stepping a foot in the stirrup, she mounted the gelding and guided him over to the where the pinto stood. Reaching down, she untied the pinto's halter rope from the corral fence.

"Wa'al, I'll be," said Henry in admiration. "You have a right good way with animals there, Jesse McGill. Ole Buck has taken a likin' to ya. Usually, he don't take too kindly to strangers."

Jesse smiled. "Henry, I don't have time to haggle. I'll give you a hundred and twenty-five dollars for the two horses and the saddle," she called out as she headed down the dirt street.

"Done," Henry replied, but his expression faded from a lopsided grin to a scowl as Jesse spurred the horse into a canter. Breaking into a run, he caught up with her retreating figure and trotted alongside the sorrel, gasping for air. "Hey, what about my money? You haven't paid me yet," he panted.

Jesse reined Buck to a stop in the middle of the street and looked down at the stableman. Fishing inside her pocket, she pulled out the coins Henry had given her for the team and wagon and tossed them to the ground. "There's your payment," she said.

"But...but," Henry spluttered, "we agreed on a hundred twenty-five dollars. This is only a hundred and ten."

"I suppose," Jesse replied. "But you lied to me about the pinto. She's never packed anything in her whole life. I'll have to break her in on the trail. And, this sorrel is meaner than an old black bear in the spring. I'll be lucky if he doesn't kill me on the trail. Take the money, Henry. It's all you're getting." Henry went to his knees and began retrieving the coins from the dust. "Just you wait, Jesse McGill," he complained angrily. "Sheriff Branscom will hear about this soon as I see 'im. Yes ma'am, jist as soon as I see 'im."

Leaving Henry grubbing in the dust, Jesse spurred Buck, and the big horse broke into a canter. Casting a glance over her shoulder, she saw Henry stalking back down the street to his livery. The weasel will make good on his threat, she thought, and kicking Buck with her heels, urged the gelding into a faster pace.

A mile out of town, Jesse struck off toward the base of the mountain that loomed ahead. Though the travel would be more rugged, the forested hills would hide her from unwelcome eyes.

Pushing hard, she rode until dusk, checking her back trail often. Before darkness enveloped them, Jesse found an overhanging cliff that would provide shelter for the night. Nearby, a small meadow and an open spring provided grass and water for the horses. After taking care of the animals, she built a small fire, warmed her meal, and heated some coffee. Rolling out her bedroll, she picked a soft place in the sand at the bottom of the cliff and curled up to spend the night. Though confident that she was alone, she kept her pistol close at hand.

#

When Jesse woke the next morning, the dusky hills were shrouded in mist, and a cold rain soaked everything it touched. Protected by the rock overhand, she worked to kindle a flame in a small fireplace, and soon had the fire blazing high enough to warm her hands and heat up two hard biscuits fished from her pack.

Buck and Tyler stood with their backs to the wind, clearly unwilling to travel in the cold rain. As she threw the saddle on his back, Buck turned skittish. He's gonna be a challenge today, she thought, but she realized she had no choice. This rain could last for two or three days, and she couldn't stay in one place that long. Buckling her coat tight around her body, Jesse mounted the gelding and set out on the trail again, trekking along the base of the mountain until she encountered an old road that wound upward to the ridges high above. Deeply worn, it had been trod for millennia by the moccasin-shod feet of the native tribes, but there were no signs that it had been traveled lately, except by wild animals that found the worn track easier than the thickets and deadfalls of the forest.

Jesse pointed Buck up the trail and two hours later, they were a thousand feet above the valley below. At the higher elevation, the wind blew harder, cutting Jesse to the bone and driving the rain through every thread of her slicker. Head down, Buck plodded on until the bedraggled travelers came to a junction where another road rose up from the valley below. At the confluence of the two roads, imprinted on the sodden ground, was the fresh sign of two riders. They were heading west at a fast clip.

Jesse reined in the gelding and dismounted to take a closer look at the tracks. *Hours old, she thought. Surely, Henry could not have told the sheriff about my being in town yet, so these riders couldn't be Santelli or his minions, could they? And whoever made the tracks should be long gone by now, shouldn't they?* Placing her foot in the stirrup, she crawled back into the saddle and urged her charges west, and though she tried to convince herself that all was well, nagging questions dogged her thoughts.

Late in the afternoon, Jesse stopped on the leeward side of a large pine tree to rest. "Buck," she said, rain dripping from the brim of her hat, "whether anybody is following us or not, we've got to get off this mountain before we freeze to death. By my calculations, we're about five miles from the river ferry." Giving Buck a nudge with the heel of her boots, she guided

113

him back onto the trail. "We can start down here. Once we hit the ferry and make the other side of the river, we're out of Sheriff Branscom's territory. That'll make us both happy."

The further they dropped below the high-country ridges, the thinner the cloud bank became. The rain turned to a light mist, and a thousand vertical feet lower, they rode out onto the road that paralleled the Ohio River. Jesse figured that she was not more than three miles from the ferry landing that would take her across to the other side of the Ohio. The sky above the valley was clearing, and the late afternoon sun beamed down strong. She basked in its warmth, and before long, she had shed her coat, letting the sunlight dry her rain-soaked clothes.

An hour before sunset, Jesse arrived at the ferry's dock. The craft was preparing to make its last run of the day. "Are ye goin' across?" yelled the ferry boat operator.

Jesse scanned the boat's deck. It was crowded with passengers, and freight was stacked precariously in scattered places on the deck, but there was still some room at the back of the craft for her and her horses. She nodded.

"Git on board, then," the boatman yelled. "The ride's a dollar. The sun's a settin'. We need to shove off now so we can git across the river before dark. Ain't good to be on the river after sundown."

Nudging Buck forward, Jesse guided the sorrel onto the ferry's wood deck. Tyler plodded along behind. As soon as both horses were aboard, the boatman threw off the mooring lines, and pushed the ferry out into the river current.

The ferry was heavy-laden, and a wave crested over the boat's edge, rolling onto the wooden deck and splashing against Buck's hooves. The gelding moved uneasily, but Jesse stroked his long face and fed him the remnants of an apple she had left over from breakfast. Slipping a scarf from beneath her coat, she tied it like a blindfold around his eyes. Buck quieted, and Jesse took a few moments to check Tyler. The pinto mare stood with her head low, too tired to cause trouble. Holding Buck's reins with one hand, Jesse tugged at Tyler's pack with the other. Satisfied that it was good and tight, she relaxed for a moment and stood at the ferry's wooden rail, gazing back at the shore line and the life she was leaving behind.

The ferry churned across the river slowly as the dusk deepened. Near the river's mid-point, the boat master shouted out, "We're half-way there!" The sudden shout frightened Buck, and he skittered across the deck, scattering several passengers in his wake. Jesse pulled hard on the gelding's bridle, bringing him to a standstill against the boat rail. Still blindfolded, he stood, nervously blowing hard.

Jesse patted Buck's neck. "Quiet. We'll be back on dry land soon," she said softly, squinting into the gloom toward the dock, barely visible on the distant shore, but as her eyes left the far side of the river, they fell on two men standing against the rail at the ferry's bow. Buck's unruliness had drawn their attention, and now they were staring at her and her horses. Suddenly, a shiver ran from the nape of her neck to the tips of her toes. Even through the twilight, she recognized the evil visages of Ben Santelli and Sheriff Branscom.

Santelli said something to the sheriff, and the two men started working their way toward the back of the ferry. Jesse ducked, and looked for a way to escape, but with the dock still minutes away, she was trapped. She slipped up and onto Buck's back, pulling her hat low over her eyes and turning to gaze out over the river.

Moments later, Santelli stood in front of Buck, staring at his markings. He peered closely at Jesse but her hat covered her long, dark hair, and twilight shadows hid the fine lines of her face.

"Where did you get these horses?" Santelli asked.

"They're my Pa's," replied Jesse, feigning a deeper voice and hoping that her hat concealed her face.

"A stable man upriver told me two horses like these were stolen from him," Santelli said as he came around to the side of the sorrel.

"These aren't them, mister," Jesse replied, biting her tongue to keep her voice from quivering. "Like I said, they belong to my Pa."

Santelli frowned. He rubbed his chin, suspicious but unwilling to draw more attention to their conversation. Just when he was about to turn away, a gust of wind grabbed Jesse's hat and sent it whirling into the river. A pile of jet-black hair cascaded from the top of her head to the middle of her back.

Santelli's evil eyes narrowed, and he edged closer to the woman. "Why, Jesse McGill," he said, "I've been looking all over for you. You've something that belongs to me, and we got some unfinished business to attend to, you and I."

"You stay away from me!" she shouted, kicking out at the big man. From a sheath beneath her coat, she drew the horn handled knife and brandished it menacingly.

Santelli's eyes fixed on the knife. Like a chameleon, he changed tones. "Now Jesse," he said, his words flowing like syrup, "there's no sense in getting excited. Come along peaceably, and you'll come to no harm."

"No harm!" she shouted. "After killing my Pa, and Travis, and shooting me, you say you mean me no harm."

Santelli glanced around. The other passengers on the ferry were starting to take notice of the ruckus. He pressed closer. "Travis wasn't killed," he hissed. "He headed west somewhere, last I knew. Why don't you just give me back my knife, and come along with the Sheriff and me. Henry just wants his horses back."

Before Jesse could answer, Santelli's hand snapped out and grasped Buck's bridle. Startled, the gelding skittered sideways, and Tyler jerked her head up and backed away, pulling Buck off balance. Sliding on the wet deck, the gelding slammed into the edge of the boat, splintering the railing and knocking pieces into the river. Several men rushed forward, intending to help, but the added weight on that side of the ferry caused it to dip precariously. Water washed up over the deck and swirled around Buck's hooves.

Santelli lunged forward and grabbed at Jesse's arm. She screamed and fought his steel grip like a wildcat as the ferry's deck erupted into chaos and shouting men rushed to see what was happening. In the commotion, Buck whinnied and thrashed around while Santelli crowded close, trying to pull Jesse from the saddle. The extra weight on Jesse's side of the ferry cause the barge to dip steeply and suddenly, a heavy, wooden barrel broke loose from its moorings. It rolled across the floor of the ferry, scattering passengers left and right and knocking Santelli to the deck.

Now thoroughly frightened, Buck reared, pawing the air with his hooves. Jesse jammed the knife back in its sheath and fought to stay with the gelding, holding on to the saddle-horn with all her strength, but the wild-eyed animal slipped on the wet deck and lost his balance. With Jesse still clinging to his back, the horse crashed through the broken railing and toppled into the black water of the river.

Crushed by Buck's weight, Jesse went under. She struggled to kick out of the stirrups as icy water sucked the breath from her body. Just before she thought her lungs would burst, she floated free of the saddle and swam upward, finally breaking the surface of the river and gasping for air. A moment later, Buck surfaced beside her, his hooves still flailing as he began to swim. Jesse tried to push away, but one of Buck's hooves grazed her skull. She fought against the blackness that spread across her mind, and with one last effort, she to grasped the horn of Buck's saddle and held on, even as the rushing water carried her away from the ferry. Instinctively, Buck swam towards the far back of the river, his strong muscles pushing them closer to the shore with every stroke of his hooves. Exhausted, Jesse clung to the saddle until her feet touched bottom. Wading to the riverbank, she gave the horse a hug, and spoke a silent prayer.

CHAPTER 16. THE NEW JOB

As Luke rolled out of his damp bedroll, he cast his eyes skyward. Heavy clouds scudded across the sky. Thirty long days after leaving Cheyenne, he mused, and the last morning of the drive is fit only for a duck.

The sound of Howard muttering refocused Luke's attention. The cantankerous old cook was complaining to nobody in particular as he stirred a pot. Luke smiled and strode to the campfire, crowding as close as he could to soak up the heat.

Several of the cowboys were already up, standing with their backsides to the fire. Vapor rose from their clothes as the moisture was driven out by the heat.

Howard served breakfast a bit later than usual, and by the time everyone was fed, the sun had already pulled itself a respectable distance above the eastern horizon. Luke polished off the last biscuit and ambled out to the remuda. After roping a rangy buckskin, he threw a saddle on its back and cinched it up tight. Mounting, he rode out to where John Walker was waiting. The other cowboys arrived singly and in pairs, laughing and joking with one another, and soon all sat waiting for the final day's orders.

When the trail boss cleared his throat, every hand stopped to listen. "Kelly," he said, "you ride drag today."

"At least there won't be no dust," the Irishman snarled as he wheeled his mount and spurred hard toward the back end of the herd.

"Banister and McGill," Walker continued, shifting his gaze, "you two ride point." Grinning, Travis tipped his hat to the rest of the crew, and the two bent into the cutting wind and trotted out to their assigned spots. When everyone was in place, Walker gave a signal, and the herd began to move.

The early morning rain had left a thin veneer of mud on the ground, and for a while, even the sure-footed steers slipped and slid as they trekked northward. Hours passed. Occasionally, a long-eared jack rabbit would erupt from beneath a clump of sage and loped across the green prairie, its lean, gray body soon lost from sight in the underbrush.

As the sun rose higher in the sky, however, the air warmed, and the trail began to dry. Luke unbuttoned his coat and scanned the vast countryside that stretched before him. To the east, hidden in a haze, lay the Black Hills of the Dakotas. To the west, the Big Horn Mountains rose from the prairie, crystalline white snows crowning its peaks. Ahead of him stretched miles of greening prairie. Only weeks before, icy winter gales stormed across the lands, but now the warm breath of spring had driven the cold winds back to the Arctic north, and tuffs of tender green grass grew up through the hardened yellow skeletons of last year's stems.

The longer Luke rode, the more a feeling of coming home grew within him. But this was a different home than he had known before. It carried a different sense of beauty. Gardens enclosed by white picket fences were replaced by miles of open rangeland. Instead of the greens of hardwood forests, prairie golds and the smoky, blue tinges of distant mountains held sway.

By mid-afternoon, the herd had arrived at the crossing of Crazy Woman Creek. The stream was shallow, making it easy to ford, and they pushed across its clear waters easily. Walker's ranch lay only two miles to the north and an hour later, the last steer was turned loose on the grass of the Bar X.

The cowboys gathered together to watch the cattle drift away. Most were glad the drive was over, but some wondered what they would do next. Their questions were answered when Walker rode up and stopped in their midst. "Follow me up to the house, gentlemen, and I'll settle up with ya'll there," he said, and he turned his horse north. The drovers fell in line, following Walker as he rode toward the buildings in the distance.

The trail boss rode up to the porch of a trim log cabin and dismounted. Tying his horse to a rail, he stepped into the house, returning moments later with a heavy canvas bag. Pulling a small table from the kitchen, he sat down with an accounting book and began calling the men by name. As each man stepped forward, Walker counted out his due in paper bills and coins, meticulously noting the name and amount in his book.

When he called Travis' name, the boy eagerly bounded up the steps of the porch to where John Walker sat. "Travis," Walker said as he handed him his wages, "I'd like you to come work for me on the ranch. Are you interested?"

Travis' eyes widened, and he nodded his head vigorously.

"Then, welcome aboard, son. Throw your gear in the bunkhouse over there. Grab a bed, and we'll get you started in the morning."

With a whoop, Travis bounded down the stairs to pick up his gear.

Next, Walker called out Luke's name. Luke stepped forward, and Walker handed him his month's wages. "Luke," he said earnestly, "I could use your expertise in certain areas, not always areas concerned with cattle ranching. If you're interested, I'd like to talk."

Luke nodded thoughtfully as he pocketed his money. "Depends on the job, I guess, but I could use some work," he replied.

"Stay here tonight, and we'll talk in the morning," Walker replied, and he stood to shake Luke's hand.

Next, Walker called out Frank Kelly's name. When the Irishman stepped forward, Walker handed him his wages, politely thanking him for his service on the drive, but saying nothing else. For a moment, Kelly stood without speaking. Then his face flushed. "Ain't I good enough to work for ya?" he growled.

Walker looked up. "Kelly," he replied without smiling, "you're a good cow hand, but nothing but trouble when you drink. I don't have a place for a man who looks for trouble."

Kelly glowered at Walker. "You'll be sorry," he snarled at the cattleman. Jamming the roll of bills deep in his pocket, he stomped off the porch and mounted his horse. Raking his spurs viciously along the animal's ribs, he sped away.

#

The next morning, Luke and Travis turned out of the bunkhouse in time for breakfast. Walker introduced both men to his ranch foreman, Jim Barker. "Travis," Walker drawled, "you go with Jim today. He'll show you the ropes. Luke, you come with me."

Luke followed Walker to the main house. Though not large, the house was comfortable and well-appointed. "Take a seat, Luke," Walker said, motioning toward a straight-backed chair standing next to a polished oak table.

Luke pulled out the chair and sat down. Walker retrieved a black metal coffee pot from the wood stove, poured Luke a fresh cup, and set the pot down on the table. Then, he took a chair. "There's some things about this country that you should know," he said, sipping his hot, black brew.

"And what's that?" asked Luke, curious.

"There's a range war brewing along Powder River."

"Range War?"

Walker gazed out the window, and a faraway look crept across his eyes. "When I first came to this country in the late '70's, I was a young man," he said. "Hell, we were all young men then, fresh out of Texas and ready for anything. We trailed herds of longhorns up the Bozeman into Wyoming and on to Montana, and we loved every day of the adventure, hard work and all. Most of the boys I knew drew their wages and drifted on, but some of us stayed and made our lives in this wilderness. I'm about the last of the original ranchers, Luke. There are only a couple of us left. All the others have been bought out by investors from the east coast, and English and Scottish land barons. These folks don't have the same outlook on life as we did. They don't live on this land. They're businessmen, Luke. They're here to make fast money."

"I've heard that before," Luke said ruefully, remembering the gambler on the Golden Girl.

"The problem is, they're not making any money. Over the past several years, drought's been bad and we've suffered some terrible rough winters. Despite it all, these folks just turn more cattle loose on the range. This country just won't support the number of cows these folks want to run. It's over-grazed. And, then, there's the problem with rustlers."

"Rustlers?" Luke asked.

"Well, most of 'em ain't breaking any law," Walker shrugged. "They're just cowboys who realized it was more profitable to rope and brand a maverick for themselves than for another outfit. A lot of them took up homesteads figuring they had as much right to the land as the barons. Most have built their own herds, legally or illegally, through branding mavericks, buying cows, or simply appropriating unbranded cattle running loose on the range. Can't say as I blame 'em much," chuckled Walker. "That's how I got my start."

When John paused, Luke swirled his coffee in his cup. "Why are you telling me all this?" he asked.

"Two reasons, really," answered John. "First, the west is disappearing, Luke. I've seen it in my lifetime. Why, in nine years, we'll be in the twentieth century. You're new to this land, but you're smart, and you're gonna stay. I can feel it in my bones. We need men like you to settle here. Would you consider staying on at the Bar X?"

"The second reason?" asked Luke.

"Well, the barons blame their cattle losses on the rustlers and small ranchers. I know men who have been tolerant of one another for years that now finger their pistols when they pass on the trail. And, visitors to outlying ranches are met with warning shots instead of a hot meal. The small ranchers, of course, have a different opinion, but the two sides are going to war soon enough. You'll be asked to choose sides, Luke."

Luke thought for a moment. "What side are you on John?"

"My own, Luke, my own," the big red-head said, taking a sip of coffee. "Luke, I feel like I can trust you. If anything happens to me, I want you to know that beneath that old desk over there, in a hole beneath the floorboards, are my valuables. There's no gold, or silver—nothing worth stealing. What I keep are some documents—letters mostly, but they are invaluable to some very particular folks."

Luke looked across at the piece of furniture, but before he could ask any more questions, Walker stood up. "Well, I've given you fair warning about the job," he said. "Do you want to stay, or go?"

"Got no place else to go," Luke responded with a grin.
"Good, then," Walker said. "Let's get started. He threw back the last swallow of coffee, donned his hat, and strode out the door. Luke followed close behind.

CHAPTER 17. THE RED WALL COUNTRY

For Luke and Travis, June blew by faster than a rain cloud in the vast Wyoming sky. Spring became summer, and almost overnight, the prairie turned brown and dry.

One morning in mid-July, John Walker and Luke set out before daylight to check on cattle. They rode west, straight toward the eroded canyons that fell like ribbons from the upturned limestone cliffs in the distance. As the sun rose higher in the cloudless sky, the sun boiled the moisture from the ground and the hooves of their horse kicked up a fine clay dust that hung in the still air of the ravines like a thick, choking fog.

For the better part of the morning, Luke and John searched the sagebrush patches and dusty arroyos for stray cows. Finally, just before midday, they scared up a small herd. Bawling and snorting, the animals scattered, but Walker chased after one yearling and dropped a rope over its neck. He pulled up and brought the calf to a sudden halt. With his horse pulling the rope taut, Walker vaulted to the ground and ran where the calf stood. With a grunt, he threw the yearling to the sod.

Walker called Luke over and pointed to the calf's hide. It bore the fresh scar of a running iron on its left flank. "Rustlers," he said, removing the lariat's noose and turning the calf loose.

Luke watched the calf run off into the brush. "I saw a fresh trail heading south, towards the Red Wall Country. Looks like they took about twenty head with them, John."

Walker mounted his horse. "In my younger days, I would have tracked down the men that did this myself," he said, "but I can't leave the ranch that long anymore. I need somebody to bring these cows back."
Luke gazed at the hazy foothills that stretched southward as far as he could see. "When do you want me to ride?"

"Today," Walker replied grimly. Mounting their horses, the two men rode back to the Bar X headquarters.

Luke roused Howard, and the old cook packed a knapsack with enough grub for three days. Luke saddled a fresh horse, and as he mounted up, Walker brought out two extra boxes of rifle cartridges. "Good luck," he offered, stuffing the cartridges into Luke's saddle bag.

"Thanks, gentlemen," Luke responded, giving Howard and Walker a quick salute. "I'll see you in a few days." Wheeling his horse, he headed back toward where they had last seen the rustler's tracks.

For three days Luke tracked the stolen cattle, following the herd beneath a blistering July sun. The morning of the fourth day found Luke deep in the Red Wall Country, a part of the county long known as an outlaw haven. The ground was baked hard, but the tracks he followed were fresh, only hours old. On cresting a red sandstone ridge, he stopped and scanned the trail before him. Ahead lay endless canyons and ravines, havens for rustlers and bandits, and they were also an excellent place from which to ambush an unwary pursuer.

The bawling of a heifer brought his eyes to a brushy draw a half-mile away. Luke dismounted and tied his horse to a stand of sage. Retrieving his rifle and a pair of binoculars, he snaked through the brush until he came to a knoll from which he could see the whole of the countryside. Lifting the binoculars, he focused on the draw. It didn't take long to spot a herd of cattle penned in a makeshift corral. Two men lazed against the trunk of an old cottonwood tree. Luke chuckled. One of the men was Frank Kelly.

Luke laid the binoculars aside and picked up his rifle, resting its barrel atop a small rock. Planting his sights just above the heads of the two rustlers, he levered off three blasts in quick succession. The slugs slammed into the tree's trunk just inches above the rustler's heads, raining bark and splinters down on their hats. Shouting in surprise, the two men scrambled to their feet and ran for their horses. In a wild panic, they threw themselves into the saddle and raced away into the sage, triggering off a dozen wild shots as they ran.

Luke had no intentions of killing anyone, but with methodical fire, he kept the two men moving until they finally hightailed it up and over the next ridge. Once sure the men were gone, he retrieved his horse and rounded up the cattle, starting the long drive back to the Bar X.

The Red Wall Incident, as it came to be known, became legend at the Bar X, and then, at surrounding ranches. Luke became the ranch's full-time range rider, and with each success, his notoriety grew. But a growing reputation also brought danger. As a result, he grew cautious, taking routes across the range that allowed him to travel unseen, and often turning up unexpectedly in rustler territory. On one occasion, he rode up on a lone rider who whispered to him about a planned ambush up ahead. But, regardless of who it was, he never turned his back on men he met on these lonely trails.

#

Jesse knocked on the door of May Bell Lee's house in Kansas City. When May Bell came to the door, Jesse introduced herself. "My lands, girl" exclaimed May Bell Lee. "Why, I've seen more relation in the past few months than I've seen in the last ten years. Your brother was through here not more than two months ago."

"Travis?" questioned Jesse, her eyes opening wide. "My brother, Travis?"

"Yes, child. Headed west, he was, towards Wyomin' he said. Traveling with some nice gentlemen from back east. I think he said his name was Luke Banister, I believe. Travis said he'd write as soon as he was able." "But Travis can't write," replied Jesse incredulously. "Are you sure it was him?"

#

When September arrived, the cool tang of autumn laced the prairie air. Early mornings grew crisper; the succeeding nights cooler, and with each sunrise, the day lost a few more moments of life. The Big Horn Mountains wore a sheer veil of azure haze while prairie grass carpeted the hills in yellow gold. Cattle moved restlessly from the high country to the lowlands in ever growing numbers, and occasionally, a flock of geese a half mile long could be heard honking in the blue skies overhead, heading south to their winter's retreat.

September found Luke a physically changed man. Months of riding mountain valleys and outlaw canyons under the high- country sun had turned his skin a dark brown. Shaggy, black hair nearly concealed his piercing gray eyes. All vestiges of the bullet wound he received in West Virginia were gone, and now he walked with the sleek assurance of a large mountain cat.

Travis discovered he had a knack for breaking horses. On his way to being the best rider on the ranch, he could grip a bronc so tight between his two knees that it seemed to groan each time it jumped. Even the other cowboys took great delight in watching him fork a horse while it pitched and bucked around a corral, and with his skills, he had become a valuable hand around the Bar X.

Travis had also developed into an eager and able student. At night, by lantern light, he voraciously devoured every book he could beg or borrow from friends and neighbors. As promised to May Belle Lee, he proudly penned a letter to her as soon as he was able to write.

John Walker was appointed foreman of the annual fall roundup by the Association ranchers, and preparations for that event had been consuming his time for weeks. This year, the roundup came on the 5th day of September, a bit later than usual. The Association had elected to set up roundup camp in a large flat meadow along the banks of Crazy Woman Creek just a short ride from The Bar X. By Association rules, each large spread was allowed five men to ride the roundup. Walker chose Luke, Travis and three other hands to ride for his brand.

On the first day of the roundup, the Bar X hands rose at dawn and made the short ride to camp. They were the first to arrive, but chuckwagons, buckboards and roundup crews from the rest of the brands soon rolled in to join them. By midmorning, all the cowboys were gathered in the meadow to await instructions. In high spirits, the men sat astride fine-looking horses and, with good natured banter, greeted seldom seen friends. Once in a while, one of the high-strung mounts would blow up and take to bucking in the tall grass, giving the other cowboys a good, hearty laugh.

Luke took in all the activities with detached interest until his eyes fell on an approaching entourage made up of buggies, wagons, and single riders. As the entourage drew closer, Luke could see that it was led by a man riding an English saddle and wearing knee breeches. The dandy was followed closely by another man Luke had seen several times, the foreman of the Cross K.

As the menagerie rolled into roundup camp, Luke burst out laughing, and he was still chuckling when John Walker walked by. "What is that?" Luke asked the big red-head, pointing toward the entourage.

"That, Mr. Banister, is Lord James Atherton," sighed Walker, shading his eyes as he gazed at the oncoming band. "He owns the Cross K. I'll tell you about him later. Right now, I've got work to do."

Walker strode over to a nearby wagon and climbed into its box. "Good morning, gentlemen," he said, his voice echoing over the assembled crews. "Welcome to the Association's fall roundup. Now, gather round so I can make assignments."

The cowboys crowded closer and grew quiet.

"Pedro," Walker boomed out, pointing at a dark-skinned caballero, "you take the 76 brand and go west. Cover the foothills and up the arroyos. K brand, take half your men and ride north toward Buffalo. Go as far as Clear Creek. The other half of the Cross K, ride with the Bar C and head south. The rest of the brands represented here today, head east. If you need to split up, do so as the opportunity presents itself. Howard serves supper at 6:00 sharp, so be back by then if you expect any hot grub. Any questions?"

No one said a word.

"And, one more thing," Walker said with a frown, looking straight at the hands gathered around. "On this roundup, there'll be no gambling around the wagons, no horse racing on company horses, and no whiskey. Is that clear to everyone?"

An audible groan rose from the cow hands. "Aw, John," yelled someone from the back of the crowd. "You take all the fun out of it."

Walker began to climb out of the wagon when the general foreman of the Cross K Ranch stepped forward and tugged on his coat sleeve. Walker bent down, and the man whispered excitedly in his ear, gesturing at Lord Atherton, and then toward the cowboys standing impatiently nearby. Luke watched as Walker and the Cross K foreman argued back and forth. Finally, John Walker shook his head and angrily pushed past the man, stepping off the platform and striding away toward the Bar X wagons.

Red-faced, the Cross K Foreman clambered up into the bed of the wagon and reaching into his breast pocket, withdrew a paper. Looking out over the assembled cowboys, he began to read. "By order of the fall roundup committee, if any man here has homesteaded government land, or if any man has bought a homesteader's ranch or land of his own, or if any man has bought cattle of his own, then that man is banned from working this round-up for any of the outfits."

For several moments, everyone was quiet as the edict sunk in. Then, an angry murmur spread through the ranks. The cowhands knew that the big cow outfits carried ill will toward the settlers who had taken up land along the creeks and meadows, but many of the cowboys were homestead-ers themselves, or had friends and neighbors who ran their own cattle. "We have a right to be in this roundup!" shouted one cowboy angrily from the back of the crowd.

"These rules were put together by the Association and this is an Association roundup. If you've done any one of these things, then you'll have to get on your horse and ride out of here," replied Atherton's foreman. "You're black-balled. No rancher here will let you ride for them, and if we catch any man cutting out cattle for himself during this roundup, the justice will be swift and sure."

Shouts and curses were hurled at the Cross K foreman, but about ten of the hands spurred their horses and sped away. The men who remained glowered at the Cross K foreman and whispered among themselves. When it was time to go, they sullenly fell in behind their own foremen, trotting off in the direction given. Luke followed Walker's foreman, Jim Barker, and they rode east.

By sundown three days later, less than a thousand head of cattle had been gathered by the roundup crew, the worst roundup on record. After supper, Luke sat with several old-timers around the campfire, and they began talking about days long past. One of the gray-haired cowboys spoke about roundups that had taken place only four or five years ago where there were at least twenty-five or thirty wagons and 10,000 cattle herded to the rail heads. Some men speculated privately that the low herd numbers this year were because many of the remaining cow hands sympathized with those who had been black-balled. Some even boasted openly that not all the cattle they had seen were gathered and herded back to Crazy Woman.

Finally, one cowhand by the name of John Smith spoke up. "The old range is gone," he lamented, puffing on his pipe. "After this roundup, some of the boys are gonna take off for Montana. Some are headed west to Idaho. We won't see them back this way again for sure."

"Well, I can't say as I blame 'em," pitched in Albert Brewster as he kicked at the dirt with the toe of his boot. "The big outfits are making it tough on smaller ranchers. My brother proved up on 160 acres on the Little North Fork, but this country is getting dangerous. He'd sell out, homestead and everything, for $500.00."

"I'm neighboring up creek from him," chimed in an older cowboy named Joseph Hansen. "I don't like the looks of things right now, and I didn't come here to get all shot up. I'd sell out as well. Go on to Oregon, or California, maybe."

Luke sat and listened. He liked the looks of the Little North Fork; the meadows were wide and the grass was deep. He said nothing, but resolved to talk with Albert Brewster and Joseph Hansen the first chance he had.

CHAPTER 18. CHIEF WALKING BEAR

After breakfast on the fourth day of the roundup, John Walker finished his instructions to the other crews. Then he turned to Luke and grinned. "You come with me today," he said. "I'll show you something today that you might find interesting."

"Lead the way, cowboy," Luke laughed.

Walker cantered toward the herd of cattle the roundup crew had gathered. Riding up to the cowboy in charge of the herd, he said, "I'm cutting out twenty head. Mark them up to the Bar X account."

"Suit yourself," replied the cowboy.

"Help me out here, Luke," said Walker, and between the two of them, they cut out twenty of the better-looking steers. "See that mountain, there," Walker said, pointing westward. "That's Sisters Hill. We're gonna trail these cows into the canyon on the south side." Luke nodded, and they headed the steers westward along the top of the mesa, toward Sister's Hill that lay about four miles distant.

Over the eons, the mesa had eroded away at the base of the front range, leaving a series of hills and gulleys. Walker pushed the steers over the mesa's edge, and they made their way through the ravines to the creek bottom below.

As the steers moved up the creek, the men rode along with little conversation. Then, Walker began to speak. "Next year may be the last big roundup this country will ever see," he said, a hint of sadness in his voice.

"Why do you say that?" asked Luke.

"We used to have several hundred cowboys," Walker replied. "Some of our boys would ride as far east as Niobrara—150 miles—and as far south as the Platte. It would take us a month to round up the cattle and send them off to market. But, no more. Fences, homesteaders, rustlers all are closing in this frontier. It's good to have progress, I guess, but it sure do make a man feel old when he sees his way of life fading away."

Walker reined in his mount and pointed toward a red rock hill about a quarter mile away. Luke squinted into the sun and spotted a lone figure sitting like a stone statute astride a pinto pony.

"That's Chief Walking Bear of the Crow tribe," said Walker.

Suddenly, a dozen young Indians on ponies raced over a nearby hill, galloping hard toward the two men. Luke reined in his horse, but in the blink of an eye, the young braves surrounded the two men. Walker sat in his saddle, suppressing a grin, and soon, both he and the young braves were laughing loudly. Luke smiled, sure that the fun was at his expense.

When his laughter had subsided, Walker spoke. "Chief Walking Bear and his band have set up their hunting lodges here on the Little Crazy in late summer for years, but since Wounded Knee, they have been confined to the reservation. They have to get special permission to come here. He helped me out plenty when I first came here twenty-five years ago, and every year since, I've brought twenty head of cattle to him and his people." Walker waved at the steers with his hand and, immediately, the young men took over the herding chores, driving the steers toward a grassy meadow at the base of the cliffs.

Chief Walking Bear rode up to Walker. "My friend," said the Chief, raising his hand in a solemn greeting. "It is good to see you again."

"And, you as well," replied Walker. "The year has been good to you?"

"It has been. It is good to come here."

As the two men talked, Luke studied the old chief. Walking Bear's face was dark and weathered, and long, gray braids hung from beneath a battered cowboy hat and fell to his back, though he was clad in white man's clothes. He appeared to be ancient, though Luke guessed him to be at least seventy years of age.

"Come," the chief said, and the struck out toward the base of the mountain, motioning for the two cowboys to follow. Shortly, they came upon the Indian village situated at the mouth of the canyon where the stream furnished clear mountain water for drinking. As they rode into the camp, women stepped out of the lodges and stared. Youngsters peaked from behind their mother's skirts to watch as the strangers passed.

At the center of the encampment, the Chief reined his horse to a stop and dismounted. Walker came to a halt a few yards back and sat silently. Chief Walking Bear said. "This is a good place for a man to pitch his teepee, my friend. My bones are old. They punish me when I lie on the hard ground, but here the grass is thick. It is easy to sleep, and my bones are happy. But enough. Leave your horses. You will stay with us tonight."

Luke leaned toward Walker. "What's he asking us to do?" he asked.

"The Chief has invited us to stay tonight," Walker replied without turning to look at Luke.

"I don't know about this," replied Luke looking around at the Indians.

"If we don't, we'll embarrass him in front of his people," answered

Walker. "Don't worry. I've stayed with his people for twenty-five years, and I still have my hair." Then, speaking to the Chief, Walker said, "We would be honored."

The Chief smiled. "It is good," he said. Then, he said something in a strange tongue to a small boy. The boy stepped forward and held out his hand. Walker dismounted and handed the youngster the reins of his horse. With some misgivings, Luke did likewise.

"Come," the Chief said as he turned. "We have prepared a lodge for you."

The two men followed the Chief as he made his way toward a teepee covered with tanned hides.

"Come on, Luke," Walker said, pulling aside the entrance flap. "This is where we sleep tonight."

Luke followed Walker into the teepee. Inside, it was warm. Red ocher hand prints adorned the leather walls, along with paintings of horses, deer and buffalo. The smells of many campfires permeated the air. It was strange to Luke, but also comforting in an odd way, and he began to relax.

That afternoon, the young men butchered one of the steers. By evening, the Indian women were busily cooking the meat, and when it grew dark, the band feasted around the camp fire. When they had finished dining, one older man produced a leather- covered drum and started thumping the taut skin with carved stick. He beat the drum slowly at first, but then, the rhythm picked up speed, and several of the young Indians began dancing around the fire. One stopped and waved for Luke to join in. He shook his head, but then Walker nudged him. Luke kicked off his boots and joined the men in the circle. With his tanned face and dark hair, he was barely distinguishable from his hosts.

The feast lasted until the moon began to fall toward the western sky. By then, the fire had died down low, and many of the band had already slipped away to their own lodges. Finally, the drum stopped, and the Chief stood up. "It is time for rest," he said simply.

Luke thanked his hosts and returned to his lodge. Exhausted, he dropped onto a skin bed. His eyes grew heavy, and he fell asleep.

Luke awoke the next morning to the sound of a dog barking. He threw aside his blankets, and pushed through the flap covering the teepee entrance, stepping out into the encampment. It was early morning, and from the position of the sun, he gauged the time to be about 7:00 o'clock. Except for a stray dog or two, he appeared to be the only one awake.

Stretching, Luke walked down to the creek and knelt on its bank. Stripping off his shirt, he dipped his hands into the stream and threw cold water onto his face and chest. The clear water washed away the dust and sweat and the lingering smoke smell from the pine fire.

Refreshed, he ambled back to the encampment where he found John Walker talking with Walking Bear near the Chief's lodge. Walker broke off the conversation, and asked, "Are you ready to go back to work?"

Luke nodded, and an hour later, they were on their way back to the roundup camp.

CHAPTER 19. THE HANGING

As soon as Luke and Walker left the canyon, they began working the brush in the ravines along the Little Crazy, and by the sun reached its midday zenith, they had built a small herd of strays. The sun blazed furnace-hot from a cloudless sky, turning the still air of the arroyos into a miserable torment of heat and sweat.

Luke met up with Walker at the confluence of two ravines. "This is like working in Hades," Luke complained, wiping the sweat from his forehead.

Walker squinted at the sun. "It's noon. Let's take a break," he suggested. Luke nodded in assent. Leaving the still air behind, they turned up a hill, hoping to find a cool breeze higher on the mesa.

As they crested over the edge of the ravine, the steady drum of hoofbeats heralded the arrival of a lone, hard-riding cowboy. When the man spotted Walker and Luke, he angled his route to intercept theirs, and coming in fast, pulled his horse to a stop in a cloud of dust. Luke recognized Bill Smith, or Smithy as he was known, one of the cowboys from the Bar C. Smithy's horse was lathered and hot, but the cowboy seemed not to notice. "They told me you'd be out this way," he panted.

"What's the matter, Smithy?" Walker asked.

"I had nothin' to do with it. I swear on my mother's grave, John. I tried to stop it but I couldn't."

"You're not making any sense," Walker replied. "Now slow down and tell me again what happened."

Smithy pointed back toward a small grove of cottonwood trees that stood tall and lonely on the hillside about a mile distant. "They hanged him, John," he said, the words spilling frantically from his mouth. Without waiting for a response, he wheeled his horse and headed off in the direction of the roundup camp.

Scowling, Walker watched the rider dash away. "Go see what Smithy's talking about," he said to Luke. "I'll catch him before he stirs up the entire crew." Walker laid his quirt on the rump of his mount and chased after the fleeing rider.

Luke spurred his horse and galloped toward the distant cottonwoods. Five minutes later, he rode over a small rise less than fifty yards from the grove. Strangely, a half-dozen mounted cowboys sat motionless in front of him, hardly noticing his arrival. Luke rode forward, scanning the area for signs of trouble.

About half-way to the band of cowboys, Luke noticed that the cottonwood cast an inviting shadow, and while sweat ran in rivulets down the backs of the cowboys, not one man moved into the shade to escape the sun's heat. Rather, they sat motionless, as if images in a tin-type photograph.

Luke pushed his mount past the huddled mass of men and horseflesh. They gave way, but when he reached the line where the light of day turned to shade, his horse stopped as if pulled up short by an invisible barrier. Puzzled, Luke looked back at the cowboys, but all averted their eyes, staring instead at something hidden by the low hanging branches and leaves. Luke followed their gaze until he beheld a sight that made him gasp. There, hanging from a gnarled limb and a long rope, was the body of a man bound hand and foot. He swayed gently in the prairie breeze, the toes of his boots nearly touching the ground.

At that moment, one of the cowboys broke ranks and rode up alongside Luke. It was Travis. "Atherton and his foreman, along with men from the Cross K. They're the ones that did this," the young man said.

Luke felt a cold anger rising in his gut. "Ride and get Sheriff Angus," he said grimly. Obediently, Travis wheeled his mount and disappeared over the top of the hill.

Luke lightly spurred his horse. The big animal pushed forward, but skittered sideways when he reached the shadows cast by the tree. Maybe it's the smell of death, Luke thought. Dismounting, he handed his reins to another rider and walked toward the swaying body.

A quick inspection showed the man had been tied, his mouth covered with a neckerchief, and then hoisted into the air with a lariat. He had struggled before he died, and the thin rope cut deeply into the flesh of his neck leaving it black and swollen. From the tracks on the ground, it looked like there were four, maybe five riders involved. They had come in from the east, and it appeared they had returned the same direction. A bay horse stood off at a distance, his reins caught up in a clump of sage, and Luke surmised it belonged to the man at the end of the rope.

The breeze brought a strong, cloying stench to Luke's nostrils. He pulled his neckerchief up around his mouth and nose and turned to another cowboy, "Walt, cut this man down," he said. "The rest of you boys stay back." Luke steadied the body while Walt urged his horse in close. Grabbing the rope just above the corpse's head, Walt pulled out a Bowie knife and sawed at the lariat until the hemp parted. Heavy in death, the man slipped through Luke's grasp and fell face down to the ground.

Luke stood over the body for a moment, choking back an urge to vomit. Hating what he had to do next, he sucked in a deep breath and knelt beside the body. Grasping the corpse's arm, he turned the dead man over. Quickly, he straightened up and backed away.

"What's the matter?" queried Walt.

Luke stood for a moment, breathing hard. "It's a man I know," he said.

"Who?" asked Walt.

"Sam Miles. A man I rode with for a month or more," Luke replied. Turning to another cowboy, he barked out an order, "Jim, go round up that horse over yonder. Most likely, Sheriff Angus won't arrive for a day, maybe two. We'll have to take him into town."

One of the cowboys retrieved an old, worn camp blanket from his saddlebags and tossed it to Luke. They used it like a shroud to wrap Sam's corpse. Luke pulled down the hanging-rope and wrapped it tightly around the body to keep the blanket on. The shroud seemed to lessen the smell.

By the time they had finished their work, Jim had returned with the bay. Luke wiped his brow. "Help me out here," he asked Walt. "We'll throw him up and over the saddle and tie him on. I'll take him into town."

The two men hoisted Sam's body over the saddle and tied the corpse so that it would not slip off. Luke retrieved his mount. "Gentlemen," he said, swinging into the saddle. "I'm heading back to camp with Sam's body. Somebody is going to answer for this."

#

A half-hour later, Luke led the bay carrying Sam's corpse into round-up camp. He didn't have to look for Lord Atherton. The man was standing at the campfire and talking animatedly to John Walker. Luke strode purposefully toward him, reaching the Englishman with one long bound. Grabbing Atherton's shoulder, he spun the man around and unloaded a solid punch that caught the English lord square on the jaw.

Atherton fell backwards over the fire, knocking over a cooking pot. Covered with ash and dripping blood from his mouth, he rolled away from the flames, and scrambled to his feet. With hatred blazing in his eyes, he reached inside his jacket, his fingers closed over the small pistol he carried in a vest pocket. Before he pulled it free, his eyes fell on Luke's right hand. It hovered over the butt of the black pistol, ready to draw and fire at the slightest move.

Atherton had fought pistol duels before, but not at close range, and even he had heard of Luke's prowess with a gun. Not eager to engage in a shoot-out, the Lord slowly withdrew his hand from his vest pocket.

"That's for Sam," Luke said, glaring at the Englishman.

"If you're talking about that rustler we hung," Atherton retorted angrily, "we caught him red-handed. He was branding a maverick out on the open range. He's a known thief. He's on the list."

"What list?" asked Luke as he took a step toward Atherton, but before Atherton could respond, John Walker stepped in between the two men. "Enough!" he commanded.

"What list?" Luke demanded again, his curiosity rising even in the face of his anger. Atherton's face burned red, but he closed his mouth and turned to walk away. After a few steps, he spun on his heel and turned back to Luke. With cold intensity, he said, just loud enough for Luke to hear, "I thought you might be one of us, but you're nothing but a peasant, Banister. You've not heard the end of this." Then, he turned and continued on to his wagon, rubbing his jaw and brushing cinders from his jacket.

Walker watched the Englishman disappear behind one of the assembled wagons. A strange look stole over the red-head's face, but there was no mistaking his order. "Mr. Banister, grab your bedroll and a horse and light out of here. You're no longer in the employ of the Bar X!"

Luke looked at Walker, stunned at his reaction, almost at a loss for words. "John, we lived with Sam Miles for a month coming up from Cheyenne," he finally stuttered, his voicing rising angrily. "He was a good man, a friend, but Atherton and his gang of cutthroats hung him..., no, murdered him, like some kind of animal. Is a maverick the same value as a human life, John? Sam was at least entitled to a fair trial! That's the law of this State, not this vigilante justice!"

Walker lowered his gaze. Then he looked up defiantly. "I gave an order, Mister Banister. Now, grab your gear and clear out."

Luke looked Walker in the eyes. The trail boss was a man of his word, and there was no changing his mind. Luke strode over and retrieved his bedroll. By the time he had returned to his horse, Albert Brewster was standing there holding the reins of Luke's mount and that of Sam Miles. He handed the leads to Luke. Luke nodded and threw his leg over the saddle. "Listen," said Luke, bending close to Brewster, "about that brother of yours. If he's still thinking of selling after the roundup, tell him to come and see me. Hansen, too. I might be interested."

"I guess you're not working for John Walker anymore," he said.

"I can't agree on hanging a man without a trial," Luke responded. "And, there's no law that says a man can't run his own cattle, is there?"

Brewster shook his head. "Guess not, but you know if you go to buying land and cattle, you'll be black-balled. You heard it from Atherton's foreman."

"Maybe," Luke replied, "but it's time this country changed. It's a free land. The laws apply equally to everybody."

"I suppose," Brewster replied, "but I'm sure sorry to see you go."

Luke spurred his horse and left the roundup camp behind, riding north until he came to a shallow creek meandering through a green meadow. Dismounting, he led his horse to a clear pool of water and let him drink his fill. When his mount had finished, Luke knelt and splashed cold mountain water on his face, but he stood ramrod straight when he heard the steady clip clopping of horses' hooves pounding toward him on the hard-baked ground. Placing his hand on the butt of his pistol, he waited until the rider topped the creek bank and headed down into the meadow. He relaxed when he recognized Albert Brewster.

Brewster reined in his horse. "Next Saturday my brother will be in town," he said looking behind him. "You bring the five hundred dollars to the Burlington Hotel at noon; he'll bring the deed. Hansen said he'd do the same."

Luke nodded. "I'll see them there," he replied as he mounted his horse. Brewster turned and headed back the way he had come at a gallop. Luke mounted up, and continued on into town, leading Sam Miles horse behind him.

#

Luke was within a mile of the town of Buffalo when he encountered Travis and Sheriff Angus riding hard toward the roundup camp. They reined their mounts to a stop on the road beside him. It took only a few minutes for Luke to fill the Sheriff in on the details of Sam's hanging.

Usually, Angus' face was clad in a grin. Today, the grin was gone. "Damn people," he cursed, shaking his head. "I should hang 'em all. Guess we'd better get out there before the sun sets. Are you coming Mr. Banister?"

Luke shook his head. "No, I can't, Sheriff. I'm going to take Sam into the undertaker. Besides, I had a run in with Lord Atherton and John Walker fired me. I'm persona non grata at the roundup right now."

"Ya mean ya ain't welcome no more?" replied the Sheriff with a wry smile. "Well, if that's the case, I hope you knocked Atherton on his ass, but good."

"I did that, Sheriff. I did that," Luke replied with satisfaction.

"Watch him. He won't do anything himself, but he might pay someone else to dry gulch you," Angus said. Then, he turned in his saddle. "How about you, son?" he asked. "Are you coming along?"

Travis looked undecided. "You go ahead. I'll catch up," he said.

Angus gave a slight nod. A man of few words, he spurred his horse and sped off toward the roundup camp.

As soon as Angus left, Travis reached into his shirt pocket and withdrew an envelope, brandishing the folded document excitedly. "Luke," Travis said, "I got a letter from Jesse. She's alive and in Kansas City with Aunt May Bell Lee."

"Jesse's alive?" Luke echoed, surprise coloring his voice. "Are you sure?"

"Yep!" replied Travis. "Letter says so right here." Then his voice quieted. "Luke, she wants me to come and get her. She wants to come out to Wyoming."

"Here?" Luke asked, his eyebrows arching just a little. "Wyoming's a long way from West Virginia."

By this time, Travis had calmed down. "Maybe, but I'm the only close kin she's got," he replied. "Where else could she go?" Then, looking a bit confused, he asked, "Did you say that Walker fired you?"

"Lost my temper when I saw Atherton, I guess," Luke said.

"Well, I guess that makes my mind up for me," Travis said with finality. "If you're fired, then I ain't gonna work for that man neither. I'll draw my pay and take the train back to Kansas City to get Jesse."

"Travis," Luke said. "Go help the Sheriff. I'll see you in town in a few days. We'll talk some more then."

Travis nodded and sped off after the Sheriff.

CHAPTER 20. THE CHURCH SOCIAL

A day after the roundup ended, Travis drew his pay and took the train back to Kansas City. A month passed without a word from Travis. Now October, Luke concluded that he might not hear from him, or Jesse, ever again.

In the weeks following the roundup, Luke met with Brewster's brother and Joseph Hansen. Their ranches lay ten miles south of Buffalo on the Little North Fork of the Crazy Woman Creek. He bought both, including the cattle.

"The Little Crazy", as some folks referred to the location, lay in prime cattle country—tall grass prairies, mountain meadows, and snow-fed streams. To the east lay miles of open range; to the west, wide creek bottoms narrowed into deep ravines and canyons. While many ranchers claimed more land, few spreads were located better. In the spring, cattle would begin grazing up one creek until they reached the foot of the mountains. Then, they would cross a dividing mesa and work their way back down stream.

Luke's predecessor, Joseph Hansen, had built a small, but comfortable cabin on a hill overlooking the confluence of two creeks. Over the years, he had added a sturdy barn and several log outbuildings built with rough sawn yellow pine.

From the moment he arrived on the Little Crazy ranch, Luke rode from sunup to sundown, his days taken up by fixing fence or herding cattle. It was a solitary life, though, occasionally, a rider would stop in for a cup of coffee, bringing gossip and news about the outside world.

One sunny day, towards the end of October, Luke looked up from his work to see Silva Cook ride into the ranch yard. Silva was about sixty, Luke guessed, and the man straddled his mount like he had been born there. A good judge of horseflesh, he always rode the finest looking horses in the territory.

Silva came abreast of where Luke was working and reined in his high-stepping paint. "Luke," he said, "Are you a going to the Congregational Church social tomorrow? Gonna be some good food and some purdy girls." Silva also possessed a rascally charm that women seemed to love.

Luke struck one more blow at the nail he was driving into the corral rail and set his hammer down. He pushed back his hair and smiled at his visitor. "Now Silva," he said teasingly, "every time I go to some kind of social, you've got all the pretty women gathered around you. It makes all us young boys jealous."

"Ah," Silva retorted, "the women like to hang around me just because they know I'm harmless."

"Anyway," Luke scoffed, "there's only one woman for every five men in this country, so when one comes of age, they're roped and branded about as fast as a slow maverick out on the range. I doubt there's any available ladies left around these parts."

"Maybe," Silva drawled, "but I hear tell there's a new woman in town, a fine-looking Norwegian gal waiting tables down at the Burlington. She's supposed to be strong, and a looker. You might ought to go take a gander. Winter's comin' on. It'll be mighty cold out here, and lonely too. A good woman would keep a man warm all winter long."

"First off, you old coot," Luke replied with a grin, "I've got fences to mend and stock to take care of. I haven't got time to run after every woman that shows a pretty ankle."

Silva guffawed loudly. "Suit yourself, cowboy, but when the old winter wind's a howlin' through them logs, you'll be remembering what old Silva told you about keeping warm."

After a few more words of conversation, Silva excused himself and rode on.

#

October mornings can be especially pleasant in Wyoming, and Saturday was no exception, dawning warm and sunny with the smell of fall permeating the air. Luke rose early, checked the stock and completed his chores. By mid-morning, he was basking in the sunshine on his porch, trying to chew a particularly tough piece of dried beef without much success. Disgusted, he spit the stringy gristle out and tossed his plate into the yard. "I'm darned tired of my own cooking," he muttered to himself.

Luke tipped his chair back against the wall of his cabin and retrieved a shriveled apple from his coat pocket. Holding it up, he eyed a suspicious wormhole with disdain. His thoughts turned to Silva's comments about the church social. I guess there's no reason I shouldn't check out the new Norwegian woman, he thought to himself, if there really is one, and the church social. Maybe somebody will bring an apple pie that I can actually eat.

Luke rocked forward and the front legs of his chair thumped onto the wooden deck. Stepping off the porch, he strode purposefully to the barn. Tossing the shriveled apple into a feed bunk, he threw open the barn door and entered its dim interior.

The Hansens had left an old buggy parked against the barn wall. Luke dragged it out into the sunlight and dusted off the dust and stray. The buggy was black, a single seater, with thin wooden spokes supporting wheels bound by a slender iron ring. It's a little raggedy, he thought, but serviceable.

Luke lassoed his best bay mare, hitched her to the buggy, and drove to the cabin door. He bounded out of the seat and disappeared inside. The bay mare stood waiting, stamping her hooves and swishing her tail impatiently.

When Luke reappeared, he was freshly groomed. Dressed in a white shirt and black pants, he wore a long black coat and carried a brown leather bag in his hand. Throwing the bag in the seat beside him, he clambered into the buggy, slapped the reins and guided the mare toward Buffalo.

The mare trotted along smartly, and in less than an hour they were at the outskirts of town. Luke wasn't sure how long the social would last, but he didn't want to travel back late at night, so he checked his rig at the livery and ambled down the street to the Burlington Hotel. Entering the lobby, he rented a room, left his bag, and sauntered back up the street to the church.

The Congregational Church was a whitewashed, frame structure that lay on the south side of the main street, up a slight hill. As Luke approached, he was mildly surprised at the number of people who had already gathered. On entering the church yard, he mingled with the crowd, nodding to several cowboys he knew or had met over the past several months. Most of the town women were there, and many of the young, single girls were standing shyly by the food table where they knew each of the young cowboys would be drawn sooner or later.

Luke grabbed a plate and stacked it high with meats, potatoes, and salad greens. Balancing a glass of water, he turned to look for a place to sit, finally picking a sunny spot against the south-facing wall of the building. He ambled over and made himself comfortable. The first bite of steak made him realize how bad his own cooking really was. At the second bite, he was beginning to think that maybe old Silva was right.

Luke ate slowly, savoring each morsel, but eventually he swallowed the last bite, and set the plate on the ground. Content, he leaned back against the wall of the building and enjoyed the warmth and sunshine of the October afternoon. A young girl about eight or nine flitted by like a nervous sparrow and retrieved his plate, flashing him a grin, minus a front tooth, as she carried it off.

A few acquaintances wandered by and struck up polite conversations, but then moved on. As Luke sat quietly watching the people, he spotted John Walker talking with another rancher. Scowling, Walker broke off the conversation and turned in Luke's direction.

Preoccupied with his thoughts, the big red-head approached to within ten feet of where Luke sat when he looked up and caught Luke's gaze. Startled, he stopped in mid stride. For a moment, Luke thought he was going to walk on by without saying a word. Instead, Walker stepped over to where Luke sat.

"How have you been, Luke?" Walker asked, apprehension in his voice.

"I've been good, John, and yourself?"

"Good, I guess," Walker replied with a look back at the rancher he had been conversing with. Then, Walker looked directly at Luke. "I've been meaning to look you up to talk about what happened during the roundup," he said, his eyes showing he was not sure of what kind of response Luke would give him. "But, I haven't been able to catch up with you."

Luke stood up. "Nothing needs to be said," he responded. "I respect your position. No hard feelings. Though, I've got something that needs to be said anyway."

Walker arched an eyebrow.

"You probably know I bought out Albert Brewster's brother down on the Little Crazy," Luke continued, "and, Joseph Hansen as well. We're neighbors now, you and I."

Walker stood for a moment, and then a look of sadness crept over his face. "I had heard that."

"John," Luke continued. "I appreciate everything you have done for me over the past months. I count you as a friend, and regardless of what happened at the roundup, I would still help you out anytime you ask. But, it's time to strike out on my own. You know how the law reads. Anybody who runs cows on this range is entitled to their fair share of the roundup cattle. I intend to buy my own cows from reputable sources and run them on the range just like everyone else."

"I guess it doesn't take a man with any smarts long to figure that out, and I take no offense with that," Walker said solemnly. "Any man is as good as another in this state." He paused. "I guess I knew it would come to this, Luke, but you're too good a friend to let you go without explanation. So, listen, you need to know that I signed a contract with the Association. If one of my hands takes up buying mavericks, then I'm obligated to fire him from the outfit. He'll be black-balled. And, if I give that man any help, Luke, then I'll be black-balled as well. That said, I want us to be good neighbors."

Walker gazed off toward the distant horizon a few moments before he spoke again. "I knew you were right back there during the roundup. Atherton should not have hung Sam Miles. He should have brought him in, or held him for the sheriff. So, Atherton deserved what you gave him." He lowered his voice. "But, let me tell you one thing. You've made a powerful enemy in James Atherton, Luke. He's not one to easily forget the kind of humiliation you gave him during the roundup."

Luke frowned. "At the roundup, Atherton referred to 'the list?'" he asked. "What did he mean."

Walker glanced over his shoulder, and when he spoke, Luke detected a tinge of fear in his voice. "I can't say. I would be signing my own death warrant." With that, Walker turned and began to walk away, but then he stopped and turned back toward Luke. "All I can tell you is to watch your back. And, if anything happens to me, remember what I told you about the papers in my house." Without another word, he strode back in the direction he had come, leaving Luke pondering a host of unanswered questions.

#

Twilight had settled over the town when Luke bid goodbye to friends and made his way back down the hill to the Burlington. He walked slowly through the dusk thinking of Walker's statements. His words make no sense, he reasoned as he pushed open the door to the hotel and stepped into its dimly lit interior. Luke put Walker's words out of his mind and strode through the saloon, intent on turning in for the night. He had not yet reached the hotel stairs when a man stepped in his way, stopping him cold.

"Well if it ain't the dude," sneered Frank Kelly. The Irishman stood legs spread apart, a nasty grin on his flushed face.

Luke measured Kelly from top to bottom. He didn't relish a confrontation with the brawling Irishman, but he stood his ground. The bartender attempted to intervene. "Never mind him," he said, scowling at Kelly. "He's had too much to drink. Can I get something for you?"

Luke narrowed his gray eyes and stared straight into Kelly's face. "No," he replied. "I just want to go to my room, but this fellow seems to be standing in my way."

The bartender stepped from behind the bar. "You two aren't bustin' up the place on my shift," he said as he disappeared into the back room. "I'm getting the Sheriff."

Kelly stepped closer. "I'm a better cowhand than ten of you," he snarled with whiskey-tainted breath. "Walker was an idiot to offer you a job and not me."

Luke didn't blink. "It happened because you can't hold your liquor." he said.

Kelly squinted through bloodshot eyes. "Keep talking Banister," he said. "It ain't good for your health."

"I should be afraid of you?" Luke asked the Irishman derisively. "You're nothing but a coward and a cow thief."

"I ain't stole no cattle," spat out Kelly.

"You lie, Kelly. I trailed you down into the red wall country after you'd rustled Walker's cattle," Luke retorted. "You high-tailed like a scared jack rabbit when I put a couple of slugs over your head."

Kelly seethed with red-eyed hatred. "I could kill you with my bare hands right now," he said, edging closer.

Luke spoke softly. "If I die, Kelly, it won't be by your hand. You're not killing anyone today."

"And why not?" Kelly snarled through tobacco-stained teeth. "John Walker ain't here to save you this time."

Luke pulled back his coat to reveal the pearl handled revolver slung low on his hip. Fixing his eyes on the Irishman, he said evenly, "Because if you take one more step, I'm going to put a slug through your heart."

The color drained from Kelly's pock-marked face. His whiskey-fueled courage failed and he retreated toward the bar, making room for Luke to pass.

Considering the confrontation over, Luke stepped toward the stairs, but from the corner of his eye he caught a blur of motion. He whirled around just as Frank Kelly jerked a small Derringer from his coat pocket. The drunk leveled it at Luke and sauntered forward, stopping ten feet from where Luke stood. "I should've killed you that night on the trail, Banister, and would've if it hadn't been for Walker. No matter. I'll do it now," he hissed through clenched teeth.

Before Kelly could pull the trigger, the bartender stepped back into the saloon. Spotting Kelly's Derringer, he shouted, distracting the Irishman's attention for just a split second.

Before Kelly could refocus, Luke's pistol cleared its holster and boomed twice in rapid succession. The first slug tore the Derringer from Frank Kelly's right hand. The second smashed into his shoulder and spun him around. Kelly fell to his knees, howling as blood trickled from the angry, red hole in his arm.

Luke stared at the wounded man for a moment, his eyes growing dark and merciless. Without taking his gaze off the wounded Irishman, he thumbed back the hammer on his pistol again and walked forward, his finger tightening on the trigger.

Suddenly, Sheriff Angus burst through the hotel door brandishing a short-barreled shotgun. "Hold it," Angus shouted loudly, and he leveled the shotgun at Luke's belly.

CHAPTER 21. THE FINAL PLAN

It was early November, and a winter squall raged down the muddy track Cheyenne called a street, pummeling everything in its path. A lone cowboy, blown along the boardwalk by the storm, halted at the door of the Cheyenne Social Club. Bracing himself, he shouldered the door open, but a gust of wind ripped it from his grasp and slammed it hard against the interior wall of the room. Accompanied by a flurry of snow, the cowboy stepped inside and pushed the door shut.

The man removed his snow-covered hat and wiped the ice crystals from his moustache with the sleeve of his coat. When his eyes refocused, he was startled by the sight of a half-dozen pistols drawn and aimed at his chest by the room's hard-eyed occupants. Slowly, the cowboy raised his gloved hands, palms out, to show he had no weapon.

"Holster your iron, gentlemen," a voice called out. "It's John Walker from up Johnson County way." The pistols disappeared and the men returned to their earlier pursuits.

"Thanks, gents," Walker said, taking a deep breath. Stomping his boots hard on the wooden floor, he walked toward a pot-bellied stove standing in the middle of the room, leaving a trail of water and ice behind him. The comforts of the social club were a welcome respite from the howling blizzard outside, and Walker watched the patrons closely as he crowded close to the stove. When his body warmed, he unbuttoned his long coat, revealing a six-gun hanging from his right hip. The pistol was not worn low on his leg, like a gunslinger, but more like a working tool for shooting a rattle snake, perhaps, or a coyote.

After warming for a few minutes, John raised his eyes to the second floor of the club, and set out for the long flight of stairs that lead to the upper level, tipping his hat to the sloe-eyed ladies he passed.

Walker was not the only person out that bitter night. Another cowboy, warm woolen coat hanging loose to mid-calf and wearing a battered gray Stetson hat, arrived next. A well-dressed businessman in a three-piece suit, vest pocket adorned by a gold watch chain, followed him in the door. Over the next half hour, twenty men came. Some were alone. Others were in groups and pairs. All were plastered with snow and battered by the storm.

The men represented a wide cross section of Wyoming society. Each acknowledged the presence of the others with a nod or a brief "hello", and then made his way through the fleshly distractions of the social club to climb the long narrow staircase. When each reached the landing at the top of the stairs, a guard armed with a six-gun stepped forward and inquired as to their name and purpose. After a satisfactory answer, the guard opened a set of double doors into a large open meeting room and ushered the visitors inside.

The meeting chamber itself was ornately decorated and boasted high tinned ceilings. Hung around the room were a series of tintype photographs of men—judges, politicians, and other leaders of frontier society. A red carpet covered the floor. At the front of the room stood a large oak table, and facing the table were five rows of chairs separated by an aisle.

New arrivals were greeted by a corpulent red-faced man sporting bushy muttonchops. The fat man would call each guest by name and vigorously pump his hand. Occasionally, he would slap one of the guests on the back and guffaw at some private joke.

Each of the visitors chose a hard backed chair and sat down, greeting those around him as if they were old acquaintances. Soon, there were groups of three or four carrying on quiet conversations throughout the room.

At the stroke of seven, the fat man waddled through the double doors and spoke to the guard. Then, he came back into the room, lumbering down the aisle to the huge table at the front. After adjusting a large leather chair, he plopped down with a great exhalation of breath, his round face flushed pink with exertion.

Pulling a large kerchief from his pocket, the obese man wiped his forehead and pulled a watch from his vest pocket, glancing at the dial. Looking up, he caught the eye of a man standing at the back of the room and gave a nod. The guard strode over to the doors and stepped out into the hallway to look for late arrivals. When he was satisfied no one else was coming, he stepped back into the room and closed the doors securely.

The fat man faced the crowd and banged a large gavel on the table. The crowd quieted, and the man spoke in a surprisingly authoritative voice.

"Gentlemen, you all know me, but let me introduce myself again. I'm Raymont Jaynes. This meeting of the Cattlemen's Association is now in session. As you know, we're here to discuss the problem with rustlers up in Johnson County, so let's not waste any time. These bandits have plagued us all. If we don't band together to protect ourselves, they will put us out of business one by one."

Jaynes paused for a moment, and looked around. "We voted last summer to go after these thieves like Montana did in '72--to hang 'em or run 'em out of the country. Now, gentlemen, it's time to act. Bill Falmouth, here, is going to lay out our plan."

A thin, balding man stood. "It's like Mr. Jaynes says," Bill Falmouth began. "We have to do something about the lawless element in the north, especially Johnson County. They've taken mavericks off the range, costing us about 3000 head of cattle, we figure, at the last roundup. Many of these men have taken up homesteads along the creeks, fencing off the best grass and water. We've black-balled them from the roundups, but several rode right into the roundup demanding a share of the calves. We've hired range detectives. We've done everything to prevent them from bankrupting us. Nothing has worked. So now, we'll have to take another kind of action. You are all familiar with how Montana took care of their rustlers and outlaws in '72. We are going to do the same."

The men stirred and looked at their neighbors. One man spoke out and said, "Bill, just how do you propose to take care of the element in Johnson County? You know the locals support the rustlers. And the Sheriff up there seems to be on the side of the bandits, as well."

"Joe," Falmouth replied, "we have a list of men who are reputed to be the main rustlers in the county. Sheriff Angus is on our list, too. We'll deal with him just like we do the others."

Another man spoke up "Bill, who's going to do this? We all have our own ranches to take care of. We can't go to gallavantin' off to northern Wyoming this time of year."

"Gentlemen," Bill replied. "That's the essence of this plan. We're putting together an expedition—a vigilante group of about 50 men. Texans mostly. We have been recruiting down that way for months. We'll leave Cheyenne secretly and travel by Union Pacific to Casper. There, we'll disembark with horses and supplies enough to reach Johnson County. We'll surprise the town and capture the men on our list. It'll be a quick strike, and a clean one.

"How many rustlers do you think we'll get?" asked another man from the audience.

"We have about thirty on the first list." answered Falmouth, "but there are again as many that could be hung or run out of the country."

"How long will this take?" asked another cowboy.

"The first raid will start in April, and will take about a month," Falmouth replied. "Then, the fifty men will divide up into groups of five squads. They'll ride over the country to clean out all the rustler nests we missed. We'll deal with them our way, gentlemen. All in all, we think that the action can be complete in four or five months."

An older man dressed in riding clothes spoke up "How much do you think this will cost Mr. Falmouth? We've all lost money in recent years and we can't afford a tremendous expense."

"Ah, Charlie, always thinking of the bottom line, aren't you?" Falmouth said. "We have agreed to pay five dollars a day for each man hired for the raid plus fifty dollars for each rustler hung or shot while on the raid."

A cowboy at the back of the room rose and spoke. "I don't know Bill. With only fifty men against several hundred armed locals...," and his voice trailed off.

Falmouth replied, "When we get to Johnson County, we'll be supported by our friends. They'll supply food and horses, and once we eliminate the outlaw element, we'll control the town. No one will dare come against us. If they do, we'll deal with them just like we do the rustlers."

John Walker had been listening quietly. Finally, the lanky cowboy stood, holding his hat in his hands. "Mr. Jaynes, you know me, and for the folks here that don't, my name's John Walker. I'm from Johnson County. Rode two days to get on the train in Casper so I could be here for this meeting. Men, I think this is a bad plan. We don't have any evidence against these fellas. Many are just small ranchers eking out a living on hardscrabble ground. Some are my friends. We'll be breaking the law riding into Johnson County, and to kill men who are just trying to provide for their families is just plain murder. If an innocent man gets hung or shot, what then? We're no better than they are."

"Gentlemen," boomed a voice from the back of the room. The cattlemen went quiet. A distinguished gent of about fifty strode to the front of the room. A shock of white hair graced his head, falling to his shoulders like a powdered wig. "For those of you who don't know me, I'm James Atherton," he said in a cultured English accent. My cousin, Robert Oglethorpe is standing at the back of the room. We have interests in the Cross K up in Johnson County. Rest assured that we have many friends in both the federal and state governments. Our force will be comprised of Deputy U.S. Marshals as well as other law enforcement officers. We intend to abide by the law, of course."

Atherton paused for a moment, looking around the room at the assembled men. "Let me remind you, gentlemen, that we have had several bad years. Our financial backers in New York and in England are pressuring us. They know we have had problems; they've been patient, but they won't act with restraint forever."

Atherton paused again. The room was deathly quiet when he began to speak once more. "We didn't say this would be easy, but this land belongs to us. Mr. Walker, you have been here since the first drives. We all have invested money to establish the ranches, buy stock and to create the cattle districts. We've brought order to this wild country, and we can't slink away with our tails between our legs like a whipped dog." Atherton's voice rose. "We are at war here, gentlemen, and in all wars some innocent lives are lost in pursuit of victory. It's regrettable, but it's a small price to pay to maintain the rule of law in this land, and to maintain our livelihoods. Now, it's time to cast your lot. Are you with us, or are you against us?"

The room exploded as men shouted to be heard. Raymont Jaynes banged his gavel on the table, and it took several minutes to restore order. When the room had quieted, Jaynes called for a voice vote. The room was polled. Only John Walker dissented.

Raymont Jaynes lumbered to a standing position and spoke. "Gentlemen," he concluded. "It appears that the plan has passed. No sense to worry yourselves about the details from here on. We'll take care of those. Now each man in this room must swear to secrecy. Is there any here that cannot do that?"

No one moved as Walker rose to his feet. Gathering his coat and hat, he strode to the dark oak doors standing closed at the back of the room. He placed his hand on the shiny brass handle, paused for a moment, and turned back to the assembled men. "Gentlemen," Walker said grimly. "I will not be a part of this plan. You're talking of killing my friends and neighbors. I won't stand by and let that happen. I, here and now, resign my membership in this association." With that, he shoved the door open and left the chambers.

The men in the room were stunned. Finally, Falmouth cleared his throat and spoke quietly to Atherton. "Obviously, there are men in Johnson County who know about our plan. They'll spread the word about this expedition just as soon as we start the march north from Casper."

Atherton replied. "We've always had concerns about two or three men, but we've taken steps to ensure our friends there speak with these men as soon as possible. I'm sure we can convince them to remain silent, or to leave the country for a time. If not..." and Atherton's voice trailed off.

The room went quiet. Each of the remaining men looked at his neighbor. Finally, Raymont Jaynes rapped his gavel on the table. "Gentlemen," he said in a business-like tone. "If there is no more discussion, this meeting is adjourned."

No one spoke, and one by one the men stood and left in the same manner in which they had arrived, slipping out and disappearing into the swirling snow.

When the dark oak doors shut on the last man, Lord Atherton turned to Falmouth and Jaynes. "Gentlemen," he said gravely, "we have a dissenter in our midst. If we don't deal with him quickly, our whole plan will go for naught." They nodded in assent. Atherton strode forward and pushed open the oak doors, stepping out into the hall. He approached a man who had been sitting unnoticed in the shadows of the hallway, hat pulled low over his eyes. Leaning close, he spoke quietly, and with surprising swiftness, the man rose to his feet. Motioning to one of the other men who had stood guard during the meeting, they threw on their coats and hurried down the stairs.

Stepping back inside the room, Atherton faced Jaynes and Falmouth. "The man I spoke with is a colleague newly arrived in Wyoming. He is quite discreet and possesses certain ... ah ... shall I say, skills that are useful in circumstances such as these. He and one of my men will ensure that Mr. Walker holds his tongue."

Falmouth and Jaynes stood without moving, their thoughts unspoken. Finally, Falmouth spoke to no one in particular, "Do you think it will work?"

Atherton replied with a confidence bordering on arrogance, "Yes. It will work. We have the government on our side, and money. In England, we have controlled the country for a thousand years with that sort of combination. The commoners can't get together enough to change anything, even if they could agree on what they wanted."

Jaynes listened. "Yes, but this is not England, my dear Atherton. The people here don't have the peasant mentality. They consider each man an equal regardless of what family he was born into. They believe they have just as much right to the land as anyone else."

Robert Oglethorpe, who up to now had been silent, intruded on the conversation. "I have experienced such thoughts here in this country. Revolutionary thinking, it is, but contrary to the natural order of things. In England, we have inherited our birthrights from our fathers, and our fathers from their fathers for centuries. We are the rightful owners of the earth. We have a God-given right to control this land. As romantic as some might make them out to be, these commoners, these rustlers, are simply highwaymen and thieves. They deserve to be hunted and dispatched like the wolves in the high country."

Falmouth picked up his hat and fingered the brim. "One thing you must remember about this country, he said thoughtfully. "We are quite familiar with wolves, and personally, sir, I don't want to be in a corner with a wolf." He looked directly at Oglethorpe. "It's quite possible that he could bite more out of us, then we of him."

Atherton smiled. "Enough of this talk, gentlemen. Let us go downstairs and have dinner. The ladies are awaiting our arrival."

At that, Falmouth threw his coat over his arm, and the men left, closing the doors behind them.

#

John Walker paused at the door of the Cheyenne Social Club and buttoned his coat tightly around his body. Turning, he took one last look at the Club's warmth and pleasures. He was a marked man now, that he knew, and for a moment, regret flitted through his mind. No. This is the right way, the way it should be, he thought to himself. Setting his jaw resolutely, he opened the door and stepped out into the howling wind.

CHAPTER 22. BACK FROM CHEYENNE

Walker pushed through the storm to the Union Pacific depot, hoping to catch the last train of the afternoon before it rolled north. As he blew into the doorway of the station, he breathed a sigh of relief. There, smoking like a giant black dragon, sat the engine being made ready for its overnight run. He hurried to the ticket window and shoved a handful of paper bills at the agent. "I'm going to Casper," John said, "and I need a ticket. Is the train going through?"

"Sure 'nuff, mister," the ticket agent replied. "Train goes through rain or shine."

"This ain't exactly rain," John replied, brushing away the ice plastered to his coat.

The agent pushed a paper ticket across the counter. "Nope," he said cheerfully as he closed the ticket window.

Walker hurried out of the depot and strode to the waiting passenger car. Scrambling aboard, he stood for a moment scanning its dim interior, but the coach was empty. Guess no one's crazy enough to get out in this blizzard, John thought. He made his way to the back of the car and sat down, turning to gaze out the frosty window at the gathering darkness.

A minute later, the muffled sound of a shrill whistle cut through the night air and slowly, the iron wheels began to turn. John relaxed, but from the corner of his eye he picked up the figures of two men who suddenly appeared out of the storm. The men sprinted along the platform, catching the slow-moving coach and swinging up onto its steps. Pushing open the door, they entered the car as the station faded into the night.

John shifted his position and eyed the two strangers curiously. One was short with stringy, white hair. He wore a snow-covered leather coat. Dull blue eyes peered from a hatchet-shaped face. The second man was larger. A nose like a chicken hawk's beak erupted from a week-old beard. Intense black eyes peered restlessly from beneath a battered hat. He was clad in a gray, woolen coat that hung to his knees.

The big man scanned the car, his gaze quickly coming to rest on John Walker. Expressionless, he locked eyes with the big red-head for a moment. John's muscles tensed. He placed his hand on his holstered Colt 45, while his thumb found the Colt's hammer. An audible click of steel-on-steel cut through the confines of the coach. The stranger's eyes narrowed, but he broke his stare and muttered something to dull blue eyes. The men turned and nonchalantly retreated to the far end of the car.

John breathed a low sigh of relief and eased the hammer of the pistol back into a resting position. Leaning against the wall of the train car, he pulled his hat low over his eyes, positioned so that he could see both men from beneath the brim. As the train picked up speed and began to roll through the snow-covered countryside, John settled in for a long night.

Hours passed and raucous snores drifted through the passenger car from where the men sat. John fought to keep his eyes open, but finally, exhaustion set in and he fell into a restless sleep.

#

Toward sunrise, a whistle blast startled John from his slumber. Opening one eye, he threw a darting glance in the direction of the men who had boarded in Cheyenne, cursing himself quietly when he saw they were already awake. Without moving, he watched them talk together quietly for a few minutes, but they appeared to have no interest in him. Relaxing, he turned to gaze out the window as a second whistle announced the train's arrival in Casper.

Minutes later, the engine and cars clattered into the station. Before the train could squeal to a complete stop, the two men, who had so hurriedly swung aboard the night before, just as hurriedly left, jumping from the coach onto the platform. John watched as they disappeared into the telegraph office. He gathered his gear and exited the train as well.

The morning was clear and warming. Catching a ride on a freight wagon to a nearby hotel, John ate a quick breakfast. Afterward, he made his way to the livery stable where he had left a rangy, black stallion three days before. Roscoe, the liveryman, greeted him as he stepped in the door, and scurried to get his horse, a big black stallion.

"Thanks. What do I owe you?" Walker asked.

Roscoe wrinkled his brow. "A dollar," he replied.

Walker pulled a silver coin from his pocket and flipped it to the liveryman. He threw on his saddle, and cinched up.

"Say, did I tell you that a couple of men were in here, not more than an hour ago, asking after you?" asked Roscoe.

"Was one a big man--tall? The other, shorter with white hair?"

"Now that you mention it, one did have white hair. An odd lookin' gent."

"Friends of mine," Walker replied. "I'll be on the look-out for them." It was a little more than a hundred miles back to his ranch in Johnson County. Walker could make it in a day and a half if he pushed hard. Crossing the Platte River at Casper Creek, he headed north at an easy gait and soon the lanky rancher found himself alone under the wide Wyoming sky. He could see no one ahead of him and, though he checked his backtrail often, he spotted no one trailing him. Hours passed. The black ate up ground tirelessly and nightfall found them at the Powder River, nearly sixty miles to the north.

John rode along the banks of the wide but shallow stream until he found a patch of willows that provided some cover from prying eyes and a respite from the wind. A small meadow lay nearby, and an open spring provided water. He built a fire, large enough to brew a pot of coffee. A cup of steaming java and a mouthful of hardtack later, he settled in for the night.

John awoke shivering just before dawn. A cold front had dropped over the front range of the Big Horns, and ice crystals filled the air. He ate the last of his biscuits. After saddling the black stallion, he crossed the Powder River and headed north. He was more than half-way home, but he had another forty miles yet to travel before he reached the Bar X.

The stud set a fast pace, and for three hours the big stallion pushed into the teeth of the wind. John kept his pistol ready, skirting ravines and stands of pine—places a bushwhacker might lie in wait. He stopped often to scan the prairie, but saw no one else on the trail, and when he finally crossed Crazy Woman Creek onto Luke Banister's Little Crazy ranch, the tenseness left his face. Almost home, he thought, looking forward to a warm fire and a hot meal to fill his belly.

A quarter mile further on, however, John came upon a set of frozen tracks—riders on the same trail as his. Reining the black to a halt, he dismounted and squatted down on his haunches, studying the sign on the ground. He ran his fingers over the deep indentations. Two horsemen, he figured, and the tracks were fresh, probably not more than an hour old.

Scowling, Walker rose and climbed back into the saddle, scanning the trail ahead. Rustlers occasionally rode these parts, but they usually ran like scared rabbits if faced with a fight. Nevertheless, John checked his carbine, and spurred the stud. If someone is lying in some gulley waiting to dry gulch me out on the prairie, they're gonna get mighty cold before the day's over, he thought. I'll take the old Indian trail in. With that, he veered off the main road and headed straight west, toward the mountains that lay several miles away.

Walker skirted the south rim of the Little North Fork mesa, stopping often to scan the ravines and dry washes that were carved like long, sinewy fingers into its surface. To the west, limestone escarpments stood like jagged shark's teeth along the foothills of the mountains, making an impassable barrier for a mile or more, and scrub pine and huge boulders covered the mountain's flank.

Walker intersected the ancient Indian trail at the point where the prairie met the foothills. He turned north, following the ancient trace for perhaps a mile or more when it disappeared into a boulder field nearly concealed by a stand of jack pine.

A good place for an ambush, John thought, pulling his revolver. Warily, he urged his horse on until he came upon a natural corral surrounded by rocks and trees. Frozen scat showed that it had been used recently, but the place now seemed to be deserted. Walker paused, his intense eyes scanning the surrounding area. Seeing nothing, he un-cocked his pistol and let a nervous smile play across his face, but the smile froze when he spotted the metallic glint of a hidden rifle barrel only a heartbeat before the shootist dropped the hammer on his first round.

CHAPTER 23. MURDER

Howling like a banshee hunting a dead man's soul, the first slug slammed into a limestone boulder just beyond John Walker's left ear, sending a dozen shards of silvery metal screaming into the mountain sage. A second later, the second slug came in quiet and high and plowed a hot, red furrow across his cheek.

Pain hammered at Walker's skull, but the thunder of rifle fire forced his clouded eyes to focus on two horsemen racing toward him, fire flashing from the muzzles of their carbines. Instinctively, he spun the stud and raked his spurs across the animal's ribs. The rangy black stallion exploded onto the frozen prairie at a dead run.

Walker clung to the stallion's back and pushed the pain from his mind. He scanned the terrain ahead and, to his dismay, saw that the stallion was racing straight for the rim of Crazy Woman Canyon. From years of chasing cows on this range, he knew that in many places the canyon rim dropped off a sheer limestone wall hundreds of feet high. Trying to turn the stud, John sawed on the reins, but the frightened animal only gripped the bit harder and picked up his pace. "Looks like it's your play, you crazy cayuse," Walker shouted. "Just pick the right spot, or the coyotes will be gnawing our bones for sure."

If the stud heard John's plea, he showed no sign. In one stride, the rangy black covered the last few yards of turf and plunged over the mesa's edge at full speed. Walker leaned back and gripped the saddle with both knees, and with eyes bigger than a hoot owl's, braced himself for the ride of his life.

John could have sworn they were airborne for an eternity, but the stud finally hit the ground, front feet first like a stag bounding over a forest deadfall. An instant later, the stallion's back feet followed. Walker clung precariously to his back as the powerful animal skidded down a steep slope, deftly side-stepping boulders and leaping over fallen pines. In a cloud of dust, man and animal ran out onto the canyon floor, finally coming to a halt amid a grove of trees.

Thankful they had not ended up at the bottom of a hundred-foot cliff, Walker half fell from the saddle and leaned against the silvery bark of a quaking aspen. Emotions knotted his gut, and he gagged, emptying his stomach of swallowed blood. When the spasms subsided, he stood upright and wiped his mouth with his sleeve. Gingerly, he touched the wound on his face. It was still oozing blood. Just a scratch, he thought. Then, he turned his attention to the stud. The stallion was blowing hard, but the wildness had left his eyes. John managed a weak smile when he realized that the ride had consumed even the stud's fearsome strength.

Walker pulled himself back into the saddle and rode out of the aspen grove into open ground. Scanning the canyon's slope, he caught a flash of motion and picked out the two cowboys who had tried to run him down. They were pushing their horses down the steep trail as fast as they could. John recognized the leather jacket and the gray woolen long coat worn by the men who had entered the train car in Cheyenne. By his estimation, they were yet some minutes away from coming out on the creek bottom.

"I should give those good for nothin' bushwhackers a taste of lead they'll never forget," John muttered to himself as he reached one long arm over his saddle to withdraw the 44-40 rifle resting snuggly in its scabbard. He lay the long barrel over one arm and centered the gun's iron sights on the chest of the lead cowboy. His finger tightened on the trigger, and he was just about to fire when he frowned and looked up. A third rider had joined the other two. Are there more?

Not liking the odds, Walker lowered the rifle. The three bushwhackers had the high ground and plenty of cover in the rocks. They would pin him down until he ran out of cartridges, and then they would come and get him. He eyed the slope across the creek. It was steep and open. They would be able to pick him off before he made his way to the upper rim. This is not the place to make a stand, he concluded. Ramming his rifle back into the scabbard, he mounted and spurred the stud west.

Walker's route led directly into the maw of Crazy Woman Canyon. Over eons, Crazy Woman Creek had wound its way through the fault in the earth, eroding the limestone rock and carving out a narrow riverbed. Towering limestone cliffs guarded each side of the stream, forming an impenetrable barrier for miles and shrouding the canyon in perpetual shadow.

An ancient Indian trail wound its way through the canyon, climbing steadily through pine forests and aspen groves until it day-lighted on top of the Big Horns, about six miles from where it began. This time of year, however, snow could lay a foot deep in the lower reaches of the canyon and towards the top, it could be deeper than a horse's chest.

Walker did not much like riding into the dark recesses of the gorge, but he knew there was no other way. From certain points where the canyon walls converged to make narrow openings, he could hold off an entire army. If the bushwhackers dared follow him there, he planned on making them pay dearly.

John had traveled more than a mile into the canyon before he encountered ever deepening snow. The stud plowed through the drifts using his great strength, but soon even he was slowed to a walk. John paused for a moment to look back. His pursuers, taking advantage of the broken trail, were rapidly gaining ground.

"Stud," John said softly, "Let's find us a place to hole up here somewhere." The words had barely left John's lips when he heard a rifle blast. Almost simultaneously, he felt the stallion shudder and exhale explosively as if kicked in the ribs by an angry mule. Looking down, he gasped when he saw a steady stream of bright red blood spurting out of a small red hole between two of the stallion's ribs. A slug had torn through his stirrup hanger just in front of his right boot, and burrowed deep into the stallion's chest.

Ripping the kerchief from his neck, John bent low in the saddle and with his right hand tried to stuff the cloth into the gaping wound in the stallion's dark hide, but the hot blood seeped from around the edges of the bandana and dripped to the snow, staining it a dark red. The stud's head fell, and he slowed and stumbled.

Walker slid from the horse's back just before the valiant animal fell to his knees. The big man reached out and touched his dying companion, whispering words of encouragement as the stud swayed back and forth in the cold air, his strength ebbing away. But, moments later, the stud's rear legs buckled beneath him. Slowly, the stallion toppled over into the snow, his body crashing into a stand of tall, blue-stemmed sage.

In disbelief, Walker stared at the body of the stud. Mechanically, he swiped at the blood trickling down his face with a gloved hand, but the sound of pounding hooves and another rifle blast returned him to reality. Dropping into the snow, he reached across the stud's body and grasped the butt of his Winchester 44-40 rifle, drawing it from the scabbard in one swift motion.

With his thoughts turning to his own survival, Walker raised his head and scanned the surrounding terrain. Two cowboys were charging up the trail, close enough that John recognized them as the men who had shared the train with him from Cheyenne to Casper. Suddenly, the cowboys cut loose with a volley of bullets that boiled over the body of the little stud. A second volley skipped through the nearby brush, clipping stems of sage as they zipped by.

John raised his rifle and triggered off a shot. "That was for the stud," he shouted. Swiftly, he levered another cartridge into the chamber and fired again. This time, his aim was deadly, and the slug from the 44-40 hit the white-haired stranger like an iron first. The man screamed and fell backward off his horse, disappearing in the snow. The man's partner skidded to a halt, spun his horse, and spurred back up the trail in the direction he had come.

For long moments, the valley lay in silence. Hunkered down behind the stallion's body, Walker listened as the stud struggled for breath. He thought that each rasping exhalation would be the animal's last. He considered using one of his bullets to end the stallion's pain, but he had only the cartridges in his 44-40 and those in the cylinder of his pistol. When he ran out of ammunition, John knew the vultures would close in.

The sound of a stone rolling downhill refocused John's attention. He raised his head and caught a brief glimpse of the two remaining cowboys. One had worked his way up the south facing slope of the canyon to a large boulder. There, the man hunkered down and began sniping at John's position. The other used the rifle fire to scurry through stands of sage, coming closer with each passing moment.

"Damn," Walker cursed, hugging the frozen ground as bullets zipped past. He snapped off a shot in the direction of the sniper, sending the man ducking for cover behind the rock.

John took advantage of the brief lull to reconnoiter the canyon bottom and didn't like what he saw. The sagebrush was sparse and scraggly, providing little cover. The snow was deep and soft, making quick movement difficult. He was cold and running out of ammunition.

The grim realization of his predicament set in. He had thwarted death once today, but he was going to be hard pressed to escape it again, and for the first time, Walker felt fear in his gut. "Cowboy, this one is going to be tough," he reflected aloud.

His only chance of surviving was to find a defensible position, and he focused on a huge pile of house-sized boulders that had fallen to the foot of a cliff about fifty yards away. The boulders had formed a maze of openings, small caves, and crevasses that might provide cover. If I make it to those boulders, he concluded, I can hole up a long time.

Walker checked the chamber of his rifle to make sure that he had a fresh cartridge. Patting the still warm body of the stud, he said, "So long, partner." Taking a deep breath, he raised his rifle and triggered off two shots in the direction of the sniper. Then, he jumped to his feet and began sprinting through the knee-deep snow.

The first twenty strides were easy as his pursuers were taken by surprise. Then, the bullets started buzzing past, smacking into the snow and throwing up sprays of crystalline ice. On reaching a large patch of brush, he threw himself to the ground and lay still, breathing hard. With thirty more yards to cover, across a part of the canyon floor that was void of cover, he knew the next run would be more dangerous.

Allowing himself only seconds of rest, Walker crawled forward until he came to the open area. Gathering his courage, he leaped to his feet and sprinted toward the boulders. He was only ten yards from safety when he felt a slug tear into his right leg. Then, a second ripped deep into his back. Walker fell face first, but pushed himself to his hands and knees and crawled through the snow until he reached the rock fall. His heart beating wildly, he snaked into one of the crevasses formed by the jumbled boulders, making his way deep into its dark recesses. Slugs smashed into the limestone and whined away into the brush, but the mass of rock surrounded him like a protective cocoon.

Deep inside the rockfall, Walker stopped and rolled to his back, opening his coat to expose the wound. He gasped when he saw the blood-stain expanding from around a ragged hole in his flesh. Grimacing, he ripped a jagged square of cloth from his shirt and stuffed the fabric into the hole. Propping himself up with his back against the hard limestone, he lay his rifle between two rocks and pointed its deadly barrel at the entrance to his lair. This will do, he thought. Only one person at a time can get through the entrance, and I'll get him before he even sees me. He took out his pistol and laid it on his lap. With his breathe coming hard, he rested and waited.

Over the years, John had seen several men bleed to death for one reason or another. Taking stock of his condition, he figured that might be his destiny. As his body slowed, shock pushed to envelope his mind, clouding his thoughts like a heavy fog. He struggled to push it back, determined to live as long as he could and do whatever he had to send the bushwhackers to hell.

John didn't know how long he had been lying among the rocks when the sound of voices and hard leather heels scraping the rock outside his cave penetrated his brain. Though he was stiff and cold, his eyes flew open and his focus sharpened. He had left a blood trail when he crawled into the crevasse, so the ambushers knew where he was, but they did not know exactly how far back in the rock pile he lay. And, he was sure none of them wanted to crawl in on hands and knees to get him. It would be like crawling into the den of a wounded grizzly.

Minutes passed. The voices quieted, and the silence was deafening; yet no one braved his fortress. Finally, he heard a rough voice from the mouth of the cave shouting to him, "Hey, you in there. Come on out. If you come out, we won't hurt ya."

John said nothing, but tossed a pebble toward the entrance to the rock fall. As it rattled among the rocks, a volley of pistol shots blasted into the darkness shattering bits of limestone that peppered his legs. He lay still. After a few moments, John could hear more conversation from his attackers. This time the voices were louder and angrier. He suspected his pursuers were arguing about who would go into the cave after him. The argument was settled by gun, or by words, because it wasn't long before he could hear the rustling in the opening of the cave.

Whoever had drawn the unlucky straw would crawl a few feet into the cave, and then wait. After a few minutes, the person would move a few feet more. What the intruder didn't know was that John had set up so that he could see a good part of the tunnel, but unless the intruder had a sixth sense, he could not see John's position in the darkness until it was too late.

The man's head came into view, but John waited until the intruder's body was fully exposed; then he fired his rifle. The bullet smashed into the limestone and splintered into shrapnel. The intruder screamed and clutched at his face as bits of lead and rock peppered his eyes.

"Did you get 'im?" a rough voice shouted.

The intruder just moaned. Then, the voice shouted into John's burrow. "Listen, I'm going to pull my friend out, and then we are leaving. Do you hear? Don't shoot, and we'll move on." Again, John said nothing, but soon, someone came into the hole far enough to grab the man by the ankles. A moment later, the wounded man was gone.

After that exchange, there was silence. Walker lay still for what seemed to be an eternity, all the while feeling his life ebbing from him. Sticking his hand beneath his shirt to reposition the cloth stuck into his wound, he felt his tally book and pencil. Pulling the pamphlet out, he opened it, and positioning himself so that one small ray of light illuminated its pages. He leafed through the book until he came to the last one. Then he wrote: "Last Will of John Walker".

Minutes later, Walker heard a "hallo" from the entrance to his hole. Weak, but still coherent, he answered back. The voice shouted down the tunnel again. "John, John Walker, are you alright? Come on out. You've got friends out here."

Walker hesitated, but he knew he had little choice if he stayed in the hole. He would surely die. Sticking his tally book back into the pocket of his duster, he crawled slowly toward the tunnel's entrance. When he finally crawled from the rock fall into the light, he rolled to his back. The sunlight blinded him for a moment, but when he finally was able to focus his eyes, he found himself looking straight down the barrel of a forty-four held by a mysterious stranger with coal black eyes.

As the gunman pulled back the hammer on the weapon, John asked, "Who are you?"

The man curled his lip in an ugly sneer. "Doesn't matter. Ain't nothin' personal."

The single blast echoed among the rocks, reverberating over and over until it eventually grew faint and died away, leaving the canyon engulfed in silence. But the brown faces that had been watching the events from a place of concealment on the cliffs above the rock fall silently mounted their ponies and faded into the brush.

CHAPTER 24. FOUND

Artic air whipped along the slopes of the limestone cliffs, swirling snow into whirlwinds of crystalline ice that cut and seared exposed flesh. Luke pulled the long leather coat tighter around his body and adjusted the woolen scarf protecting his face.

Intending to check on cattle, Luke had left his cabin at sunrise, riding north into the pummeling winds. Now, it was mid-morning, and though he found himself at the northern boundary of his ranch, he had yet to see more than a few scattered steers.

The storm had moved away from the Big Horns and out onto the open prairie, but its trailing edge still stretched from north to south across the sky. Luke let the rangy buckskin pick his way through the frozen sage until he spotted a cut bluff some hundred yards distant. He made his way across a windblown ridge, reining the buckskin to a stop on the leeward side of the bank.

Protected from the worst of the wind, Luke surveyed the valley of Crazy Woman Creek several hundred feet below. A slight movement caught his eye. Squinting, he spotted a small herd of steers huddled together in willows along the creek bottom, plastered white with wind driven snow. He counted those he could see, and retrieving a small black tally book from the pocket of his duster, meticulously added his count to a column of numbers on one of the book's blue-lined pages. Frowning, he touched his horse lightly and moved fifty yards to the west. He recounted and checked his figures again. He was twenty head short of the count he had made last week.

Luke was about to make his way down the hillside to the valley below when the north wind brought the muffled drum of hoof beats to his ears. Startled, he turned and spotted three men, still a half mile away, but coming fast. A man has to have a special reason to be calling on a day like this, Luke thought, and it may not be just a neighborly call. He reached beneath his coat and drew his pistol, stuffing it in the pocket of his long coat where it would be handy.

The riders veered toward Luke, bringing their mounts to a stop about a dozen feet away and sending Luke's buckskin dancing sideways. The men had dressed for the cold. Layered wool clothing covered their bodies, while their faces were covered with woolen scarves to protect them from frostbite. Only their eyes were exposed.

Luke fingered the trigger on his revolver nervously until the riders pulled the scarves from their faces. With relief, he recognized the weathered features of Sheriff Angus, Jim Barker, the foreman of Walker's Bar X Ranch, and Billy Samuels, a range detective hired by the Association.

Luke turned his attention back to the sheriff. "Mr. Angus, it's a mighty cold day to be out wandering the countryside."

Before the sheriff could answer, Jim Barker spoke up brusquely. "We're looking for John Walker, Banister. He was supposed to have ridden through here yesterday on his way home from Cheyenne. You seen him?"

Luke didn't answer directly, but shifted slightly to look at the sheriff. "That true?" he asked.

"That's the story from Jim here," the sheriff said, tilting his head in the direction of Walker's foreman. "Says he should've been in yesterday afternoon, but he didn't show. We thought you might a' seen sign of him?"

"Fact is, Sheriff, I haven't seen anybody pass through here," Luke said, "though I did see some sign of a horse and rider over yonder about an eighth mile or so. Trail is not good, pretty well covered with snow."

Samuels, the range detective, held Luke's gaze for a moment. Then he shifted his focus to Angus. "Sheriff, maybe Banister here had something to do with Walker's disappearance. There was some bad blood between the two of them at the roundup this fall."

Luke narrowed his eyes and glared at the range detective. "I don't know what you're driving at, Mr. Samuels, but John Walker was a friend of mine," he said in a low voice. "If he came through here, he certainly would not have met any harm at my hands, and I don't take kindly to your insinuations."

Angus spurred his horse and cut in between the two men. "Hold on there, boys. No one is accusing anybody of anything. Luke, if you saw tracks, I'd suggest we take a look."

"I'll ride along if you don't mind," Luke declared, not liking the tone of the encounter. "You could always use another pair of eyes."

"Sure. Glad to have ya. You can start by showing us where the tracks were."

Luke turned his horse and headed west. The trio of riders trailed behind until they came upon the tracks Luke had described. Angus dismounted, studying the sign for a short time. Then he remounted and turned his horse west. The others fell into line behind him.

The tracks were faint and hard to follow. Often, they were filled with snow, and occasionally, a drift would obliterate all sign for hundreds of feet, but they kept on. Luke rode beside Jim Barker, and though sporadic conversation, Barker related the story of how Walker had gone to Cheyenne for an

Association meeting five days ago. He was scheduled to be back at the ranch by late afternoon yesterday. When he did not return, Barker sent a rider to summon the sheriff.

Angus had responded quickly to the summons, riding into the Bar X that very morning. The range detective had ridden into the ranch soon thereafter, and after being apprised of Walker's disappearance, volunteered to join the search.

The four men followed the hoof-prints until they turned west, directly toward the limestone crags that loomed in the distance. Eventually, the trail came to a stand of dense scrub pine at the base of the mountain. As they cleared the outside stand of timber, the party came upon the makeshift corral, nearly hidden from view among the rocks and trees. Sheriff Angus motioned for the men to proceed quietly, and in single file they wound their way through the scrub pine and boulders.

Abruptly, Angus held up his hand. The riders halted. "Looks like a rifle slug struck here," Angus said, pointing at an irregular black mark on one boulder that towered over the riders. "And look there, there's blood," he added, nodding toward drops of red, frozen in the snow.

Barker opened his mouth to speak, but Angus raised his hand and warded off any conversation. Like a wolf on scent, he followed the blood trail across the prairie to the edge of the mesa, and without hesitation, disappeared down the steep slope. The search party followed.

The snow made the slope treacherous, and it took some time before the last man slid out onto the canyon floor. By then, Angus had dismounted and was squatted beside a trail of torn up earth. "Gentlemen," he said, running his finger along the edge of a hoofprint. "There were four riders here. Three were on range ponies. The shoes on their horses are old and rounded on the edges. One rider rode a horse with new shoes. See, the edge of the depression is sharp."

"That means nothing," Samuels said impatiently, "only that some cowboy just had his horse shod. We're wastin' time. Let's move on."

"Not so fast," Barker said, dismissing the detective's statements with a wave of his hand. "John had his horse shod just before he left for Cheyenne. He didn't want to throw a shoe someplace between here and Casper and be afoot. Those could be his tracks."

Angus stared at the canyon's entrance. "Might be. I guess we'll find out soon enough. There are four sets of tracks going in, but the horse with the new shoes didn't come back out."

The sheriff walked his horse slowly along the trail, combing the ground with his eyes. The rest of the men followed at a distance. As the party approached the high cliffs guarding the canyon mouth, Sheriff Angus set his foot into the stirrup, and swung into the saddle. "We'll follow the trail," he said as he headed into the maw looming before him, "and see where it ends."

Angus entered the canyon, stopping now and then to examine the tracks, but he offered little comment on what he saw. The trail wound its way upward, crossing the creek and treacherous talus slope. Barker's mount struggled to maintain his footing on the rocks, while Samuels elected to stay lower and push through knee-deep snow alongside the creek. Luke maintained his spot directly behind the sheriff, scanning the canyon bottom as he rode.

They traveled about a mile until they came upon a jumble of house-sized rock slabs that lay piled atop one another like a child's building blocks. Its surface glazed by winter ice, the creek disappeared in darkness under the giant slabs, only to re-emerge into the light further downstream. Two hundred yards past the slabs, they found the body of the black stud.

Sheriff Angus scanned the area from the back of his horse. Then, he dismounted and tied his horse to a scrub pine. Reaching inside his coat, he pulled a small black book and pencil from his vest pocket. Motioning to the other three men to stay back, he approached the horse's carcass carefully, making notes as he moved closer in.

Luke's eyes swept the valley floor until he noticed a set of boot tracks in the snow. They led toward another huge rock fall that lay higher up the slope of the canyon wall. Angus caught Luke's eye and followed his gaze. Without hesitation, he moved off in the direction of the tracks. Luke dismounted and followed at a distance.

"Don't walk in the same tracks, stay off to the side several yards," Angus cautioned.

Luke complied, pushing uphill through undisturbed snow. They had gone only twenty yards when they spotted the place John Walker had dove into the snow the first time to rest. Ten yards further on, the white snow became spotted with red spots. As the two men neared the rock fall, the spots grew larger and came more often.

By now, Angus was puffing hard and icy crystals streamed from his mouth and nostrils. Luke took the lead and forged on, cresting a slight ridge just ahead of the Sheriff. There, he stopped, and his eyes locked on to what looked like a rag doll tossed carelessly among the limestone rocks.

Angus plowed through the snow to stand by Luke. He leaned over with his hands on his knees, panting hard. "Looks like we found him," he said. After catching his wind, he stepped forward and squatted down beside the body, taking care not to disturb any more of the area than necessary.

Walker's eyes stared vacantly into the azure sky. "Looks like he's been shot at close range," the sheriff stated, noting the neat bullet hole between his eyes. Moving the body slightly, the Sheriff added, "He was also shot in the back; maybe in the leg as well."

Straightening up, the Sheriff scanned the area with a practiced eye. "Must have been the three that followed him into the canyon. Looks like he fought 'em pretty good."

At that moment, Samuels arrived, panting and wheezing from the climb up the hill. "Rustlers!" he exclaimed. "It was those damned rustlers that did this. We saw their corral up on the top of the mesa and all those cattle tracks. We've all been having trouble. I'll bet he surprised those coyotes up in the rocks on the mesa, and they ran him down and killed him."

Sheriff Angus responded. "That's certainly one theory, Mr. Samuels. Evidence might suggest such a thing, but it might have been someone else. Before we rush to a conclusion, let's make sure we have all the facts."

"I have all the facts I need," Samuels replied angrily.

"Maybe so, but for now," Angus continued, "you gentlemen step back and let me inspect the area." With that, the Sheriff took the small notebook and pencil from his vest pocket and began to draw diagrams and write notes upon its white pages.

Leaving the Sheriff to his work, Luke scoured the immediate vicinity, noting the boot tracks and the second blood trail. Looks like John put some lead in somebody before he got his, Luke thought with grim satisfaction. Luke returned to the area where Walker's body lay just about the time Sheriff Angus was wrapping up his investigation. "What now?" he asked.

"Mr. Samuels, you get Barker and the two of you make up a travois. Bring the horse up here and we'll load up ole John and take him to town. Doc needs to take a look at 'im. He might find something we missed." Samuels frowned, but headed down the hill to get Walker's foreman.

Luke noticed Walker's battered old black hat. He stepped over to pick it up, but when he lifted it from the ground, a black book fell from its brim, burying itself in the snow. Luke bent down and retrieved the object, and brushing off the white flakes. Flipping through the pages, he saw that the first page bore John's name. Subsequent pages were filled with notes, mostly on cattle counts and weather. The last page, however, bore the following writing:

"Last Will of John Walker. I hereby give all I have to my niece Grace West. I want Luke Banister to take care of everything for me." - John Walker

Luke studied the writings for a moment, and then he handed the book to the Sheriff. "You might want to take a look at this," he said.

"Now ain't that interesting," mused the sheriff as he leafed through the pages. "It looks like John scratched out a last will and testament right here in his tally book. Let's keep this quiet for just a bit and see what turns up here."

Luke nodded, looking at John's battered old hat with its eagle feather in the hatband. "Sheriff," he said, "John always told me this feather reminded him of the wild birds and how they could soar in the air. Somehow, he knew he would soar up there himself someday."

With that, they sat down to wait for Samuel's return.

CHAPTER 25. FILING

The Rock Creek Stage rumbled into Buffalo, wallowing through a sucking mire that clutched at its iron-rimmed wheels. Perched atop the stage in the driver's seat was a wizened old man, his flowing white hair partially hidden by a battered Stetson hat. Next to him sat a tow-headed boy of about twelve, hanging onto the seat for dear life.

Shouting a series of "gees" and "hahs," the driver guided the team into town, edging ever closer to a boardwalk that ran the length of the narrow street. With each revolution, the wheels threw up a drenching spray of mud and water, scattering passersby, and drawing curses from unlucky victims. Ignoring any and all recriminations, the driver skillfully jockeyed the stage to within inches of the walkway, and brought his charges to a halt in front of a two-story frame building. The words Burlington Hotel were freshly painted in big block letters on the upper story.

After tying his lines to the seat, the driver clambered to the ground. He was followed by the tow-headed boy who leaped from the seat onto the boardwalk.

"Tanner," said the driver to the boy, "fetch the board." The boy trotted into the hotel to tend to his errand.

By this time, the bystanders who habitually loitered around the hotel entrance had returned to their stations. "Damn, Roy," growled one whiskered old gent as he retook his chair in the warm sunshine at the front of the hotel, "you should slow that team down coming into town. You're gonna kill somebody someday."

"Oh hell!" said the driver as he pulled a dirty cloth from his trouser's pocket and wiped his weathered face. "Cain't slow down. I've a schedule to keep."

Stuffing the grubby cloth back into his hip-pocket, the driver hitched his pants up over his bony hips and bent to test the traces, oblivious to the jibes of the other old men who had returned to their haunts at the hotel entrance.

In a few moments, the young boy returned lugging a long, rough-sawn plank. He set one end on the boardwalk and dropped the other in the muck under the stage door. The driver stepped on it with a muddy boot, grunting his approval as it held firm.

"Now, Tanner," he ordered, "unload the bags while I attend to the passengers." Dutifully, the lad turned to his task.

By this time, the first passenger had stuck his head out the open coach door. Clad in black pin-stripe pants, a vest and matching long black coat, it was plain that the man was not a regular visitor to this outpost on the fringes of civilization. Grasping his hat with one hand, the man gauged the distance from the stage to the ground and then stepped onto the rough plank, cursing as muddy water ran over the board and lapped against his shiny black boots.

The man turned back to the stage and held up a hand. An attractive, well-dressed woman appeared at the door and took the man's hand. Lifting her skirt high enough to reveal a set of well-turned ankles, she lightly stepped down onto the board and nimbly traversed the plank to the boardwalk.

"Your luggage, ma'am," said Tanner, as he dragged a trunk down the boardwalk toward the hotel door.

The woman nodded to the boy, turning her attention to the small crowd of onlookers gathered on the boardwalk.

"Robert," she said as she looked over the crowd, "I don't see my uncle. His telegram said that he would meet us here."

"Grace, dear, from the size of this town, I don't think he could be too far," said the man. Then he turned to the driver. "Take our bags into the hotel," he ordered. "We'll wait there."

The stage driver looked up from checking his team and spit into the mud. Drawing himself up to his full height, he replied. "Mister, you're gonna have to carry your own bags. I'm a driver, not a mule."

One of the old whiskered men sitting at the door of the hotel placed his hands on his belly and guffawed. "Well, that's debatable," he interjected, grinning widely. "Perhaps "jackass" would be a better term," quipped another. A chorus of laughter sounded from the other bench sitters.

The driver glared at the laughing men and launched a stream of tobacco spit onto the boardwalk near their perch. He climbed back up into the driver's seat of the stage. "Come on, Tanner," he hollered. "We're behind schedule already." He cracked his whip and set the team in motion. The boy ran and grabbed hold of the back of the luggage platform as the stage moved out. He swung himself aboard as the stage angled out into the street and picked up speed.

Taken back by the driver's impertinence, Robert Oglethorpe stood with his mouth agape watching the stage depart. Finally, in a cultured English accent, he commented acidly, "Grace, dear, it looks like these peasants could be taught a lesson in manners."

"It seems that way, doesn't it?" replied Grace, shivering as she spoke.

"Let's go inside," Oglethorpe said irritably. "At least we'll be able to warm up a bit, and maybe get some valet to take the bags to our rooms." Leaving the bags on the boardwalk, he entered the hotel. Walking purposefully to the front desk with Grace West in tow, he banged hard on counter bell. A man's voice responded from the back room. "Hold your horses," it said. "I'll be there in a jiffy." Moments later, a short, bespectacled man appeared and hurried to the counter.

"I'm Robert Oglethorpe, and this lady is Grace West. We were supposed to meet Grace's uncle here, a Mr. John Walker. He owns the Bar X ranch. He knew we were arriving today, and he sent a telegram several weeks ago stating that he would be here. I assume it's appropriate to wait here until Mr. Walker arrives?"

The clerk's eyes widened behind his wire rimmed glasses. "Sure, sure," he stuttered. "Any kin of John's is welcome in my place." Pointing to a large divan standing along one wall, he continued, "If you and Miss West wish, you can wait over there."

Oglethorpe glanced at the scruffy horsehair couch and frowned, but when he turned back to the desk, the clerk had already vanished. From the backroom, he heard a muffled conversation followed by the slamming of a door. Annoyed, Oglethorpe stepped over to the divan and sat down beside Grace.

Five minutes later, the door to the Burlington Hotel opened and into the lobby stepped a stocky, dark-complexioned man. A bushy moustache grew wild beneath his nose. He was dressed in coarse brown trousers, a heavy coat and worn boots, but a shiny, metal star adorned the lapel of his coat. A blond woman followed him in the door.

The man ambled over to where the couple sat on the divan. Removing his hat, he spoke. "Miss West, I presume. My name is Angus. I'm the Sheriff of Johnson County." Motioning toward the blond woman, he continued. "Miss Higgins told me you just arrived on the stage."

Oglethorpe rose to his feet. "To what do we owe the honor of your visit, Sheriff?" he asked.

"Well," replied the Sheriff, "I would like to speak to Miss West, if you don't mind?"

"What about?"

"It's private."

"Sir, I'm Miss West's fiancée and also her attorney," Oglethorpe retorted arrogantly. "So, her business is also my business."

"Then, Mr. Oglethorpe," stated the Sheriff stepping forward, "advise her as you wish, but I'm going to ask her a few questions."

Oglethorpe balled his fists, but the Sheriff laid his calloused hand lightly on the butt of the forty-four pistol hanging from his belt. Seconds ticked by. Finally, Grace stood and laid her hand on the arm of her fiancée. Oglethorpe gave one last glaring challenge to the Sheriff, but he unclenched his fists and stepped back. "Sheriff, what is this all about?" Grace asked.

"Miss West," the sheriff stated calmly, "your visit is somewhat surprising. What brings you to Wyoming this time of year?"

"I received a letter from my uncle about three months ago, inviting me out to his ranch."

"Do you have the letter with you?"

"No, I don't," Grace replied, tossing her ash-blond hair.

"Did he mention anybody he might be having trouble with?"

"Not that I recall."

The Sheriff lowered his eyes and played with his hat for a moment. "Miss West, I guess with your traveling and all, you haven't heard. I'm afraid I have some unpleasant news about your uncle, John Walker." The Sheriff raised his eyes and looked directly at Grace. "Miss West, your uncle was murdered two days ago down on the Little Crazy Woman Creek."

Grace gasped, and with a soft moan, swooned against her fiancée. Oglethorpe caught her and carried her to the divan. She slumped into the seat, a dazed look in her eyes.

Oglethorpe turned to the Sheriff. "How did this happen?" he asked angrily.

Sheriff Angus shook his head. "There's still a lot we don't know, Mr. Oglethorpe, but I suggest you and Miss West stay in town for a few days. We will need to talk more."

The hotel clerk, who had been busying himself at the counter, suddenly spoke up. "I happen to have two rooms available. No better place in town than the Burlington, I want you to know." Withdrawing a pen from an inkwell, he pushed it and the registration book toward Oglethorpe. "Just sign here," he directed, pointing to the next open line on the page with a bony finger.

The Englishman put his arm around Grace's shoulders. "Dear, we have been traveling for three days. Staying in town for a day or two would give us an opportunity to attend to this business, don't you agree?"

Grace nodded her head. The hotel clerk smiled broadly, and tapped the hotel register again with his finger. Oglethorpe strode over and signed his name, and followed with hers. Looking up at the clerk, he asked, "The keys?"

The clerk turned, eyed the board behind him, and chose two metal keys. Handing them to his guests, he pointed at the stairs leading to the second floor. "Just go to the top of the stairs. Your room is on the left ma'am. Mr. Oglethorpe, your room at the end of the hall, first room to the right. I'll have your bags brought right up. Rooms are made up with fresh linens every third day. We serve breakfast at 6:00 a.m., dinner at 5:00 p.m. You can ring for hot water or whatever else you might need before 8:00 pm. After 8:00 you can ring, but nobody will answer."

The clerk stepped from behind the counter and disappeared down a lower hall into a backroom, returning moments later with a lad of about twelve. "Young Nick here'll take your bags up for you mister," the clerk said.

Oglethorpe looked contemptuously at the boy and then turned to the clerk. "I don't think this truant can carry these heavy bags."

"Sure I can, mister," the young boy retorted. "It cain't be much heavier than a calf and I carry those all the time. Just watch." With that, he reached for the handle of Oglethorpe's black leather valise, but like a striking snake, Oglethorpe's hand snapped out and caught the boy by the wrist.

"Ow, ow," yelped the boy as he danced around, tethered to the Englishman by the man's long-armed grasp.

"Don't ever touch my bags without asking," Oglethorpe hissed through clenched teeth as he pulled the boy close.

The boy's howls of pain brought Grace out of her daze. "Robert!" she said, rising from the divan. "What's wrong with you?"

Oglethorpe let go of the boy's wrist and grabbed his black valise from the floor. "I couldn't be sure that this miscreant wasn't a thief," he said, a mask of calm sliding over his face.

"I wasn't gonna steal your bags, mister," the boy said, "but you can darn sure carry 'em yourself." Before anyone could say a word, the youngster drew back his foot and kicked Oglethorpe squarely on the shin. The Englishman howled in pain as the boy raced down the hall and disappeared around the corner. In his wake, he left Robert Oglethorpe angrily hopping around on one foot, Grace West staring open mouthed, and Sheriff Angus hiding a big grin behind his moustache.

CHAPTER 26. PETITIONING

The rooster crowed twice before Luke raised his head and cast a tired-eyed glance out the square paned cabin window. He was greeted by a reddish orange ball of sun. Reluctantly, he swung his legs over the edge of his bunk, shivering when a cold draft wafted over his bare skin. "Damn," he chided himself, "I should chink those logs or stock the fire higher at night."

Luke high stepped across the icy wooden floor to retrieve a pair of trousers and a shirt from the back of a slatted chair, hurriedly throwing them on. A touch on the top of his old black iron stove revealed its coals were long cold, so he jammed two sticks of wood into the stove's firebox, along with a handful of wood shavings, and held a match to the kindling. The wood slivers flared to life, and soon the pine was popping merrily.

Pulling a tin of ground coffee from an open cupboard, Luke measured out several scoops of the dark bean. After pouring them into the top of a smoke-stained pot, he set the pot on the stove and sat down with his legs propped up on the kitchen table, pondering the events of the last several days.

Why was John killed? he mused, hoping some thought would trigger a rationale for his death. *He was a rough old guy, but he didn't have many sworn enemies, at least any that I know of. Were his killers rustlers? Or was it somebody else? And, more curious, why did he name me executor of his will?*

The coffee began to perk, interrupting his thoughts. He stood and poured himself a cup. It was only a little colored, but hot. He leaned against the stove, soaking up its warmth, and his thoughts wandered back to the words John spoke at the church social. *He was worried then. Maybe it had something to do with the list, or the papers he told me about the first day at the ranch.*

With no ready answers, Luke threw down the last swig of coffee and strode over to an ancient steamer trunk that sat at the end of his bed. More than two months ago, he had wired his former law partner back in Pennsylvania and asked him to send the trunk out west. It had arrived three weeks later. Luke knelt and opened its domed lid. At the very top of its neatly arranged contents sat a photograph of a beautiful dark-haired woman with a winsome smile.

Luke lifted the picture from its resting place, and gazed at the image for several moments. He stroked the glass, and then carefully laid the picture aside. Next, he focused on a set of books, running his finger along the spine of each until he came to the title he wanted. He pulled the volume from its resting place and set it aside. Then he rummaged through the trunk's contents once again until he came to a package tied up with string. He pulled it out and unwrapped the paper, revealing a nicely tailored black suit, white shirt, and tie.

Luke stepped to the window and held the suit up to the light, brushing dust from the suit's shoulders and lapels. Hanging the garments from a hook above the cook stove, he positioned the tea kettle so that the steam from its spout permeated the suit and shirt, hoping some of the wrinkles would be smoothed.

The book Luke had selected was a leather-bound legal volume, one of the few remaining memories of Luke's past life—a probate book that detailed the procedures for passing a man's property after his death. He laid the volume on the table and fished a pad of legal sized paper from a lower drawer of the wall cabinet, along with a pen and a bottle of black ink. After consulting the legal text, he dipped his pen into the black liquid and began writing on the clean white paper.

Luke worked slowly at first, concentrating on every word, but soon his thoughts began flowing like water. The tea kettle quit steaming and the only sound that disturbed the quiet was the scratching of the pen as it raced across the paper.

#

Sunlight streamed through the glass window, waking Grace West from an uneasy sleep. The room was cold, and for long moments she lay buried beneath the heavy blankets on her bed, enjoying their warmth. As the events of the night before filtered into her consciousness, a flurry of questions filled her head. *Her uncle murdered. How did that happen? Who would have wanted to kill him?* Grace pondered the questions for a moment, but each question begged another, and only a gray cloud of uncertainty that gave neither clarity nor answer.

Frustrated, Grace threw aside the blankets and rose from her bed. Throwing a robe around her shoulders, she tiptoed across the icy floor to a water bowl and splashed cold water on her face. Pulling a rough cloth from a drawer, she toweled away the moisture that clung to her skin while staring at her reflection in the tin-rimmed oval mirror that hung from the wall. She grimaced when she noticed the slight crow's feet lines at the corners of her eyes, and the ever increasing hairs of gray hair hidden amongst the blond.

Her mind focused on Robert Oglethorpe, but even those thoughts couldn't dampen the sense of loneliness that spread across her being. *Is it time for me to settle down? she wondered. Is he the right one. I've known men before him, better men, perhaps, and maybe too many. Why had no man stayed around? Was it me? Or, was it them?* Shrugging her shoulders, she retrieved a hair brush from her trunk, pulled the it through her thick, blond hair, and tossed it carelessly on the vanity top when she was finished.

Stepping over to her trunk, she knelt and rummaged around until she found a pair of riding pants, boots, and a blouse. She dropped her robe to the floor, revealing a trim, shapely figure, and methodically pulled on the clothes and boots. Catching one more quick glance into the mirror, she opened her hotel room door and walked down the long flight of stairs to the hotel lobby.

As Grace stepped off the staircase, she paused for a moment to survey the dining room. The walls were papered an off-yellow, and dark oak woodwork trimmed doors and windows that rose to a high, ornate ceiling. Though the room was not overly spacious, eight tables were neatly arranged in the dining area. She was mildly surprised to spot Oglethorpe seated with a stranger towards the rear of the room. They were engaged in a quiet, but earnest, conversation.

Grace crossed the hotel dining room toward the seated men, the heels of her boots clicking rhythmically against the wooden floor. Oglethorpe caught her eye as she drew closer.

"Good morning, Grace," he said, standing with a slight bow. "We've been waiting for you." He reached for her hand, and gripping it lightly, pulled her toward him. "Grace, I'd like you to meet an acquaintance, Phineas Standbury," he said, gesturing toward the stranger. "Mr. Standbury is an attorney who also represents my cousin, Lord Atherton. I happened to run into him this morning during an early walk."

The short, potbellied lawyer stood, offering his hand. Grace shook it politely. Oglethorpe pulled out a straight-backed wooden chair and Grace sat down, noting the empty breakfast plates covered with crumbs on the table, and an open leather briefcase on the floor. *Apparently, the two men have been here for some time,* she thought.

Grace's thoughts were interrupted when the same blond woman who had brought the sheriff the night before, appeared. "Good morning', I'm Mary," the waitress said spritely. "Looks like the men-folk started without you, but what can I get for you this morning?"

There was something about the waitress' impertinence that Grace liked. She smiled. "I'll have a cup of coffee, black, please."

"Comin' right up," Mary said. She turned on her heel and disappeared through a pair of swinging doors into the kitchen.

As soon as the waitress left, Oglethorpe took Grace's hand. "My dear," he said, "Mr. Standbury has some news about your uncle's ranch."

"What would that be?" asked Grace, arching her brows and turning her green eyes toward the rotund lawyer.

"Miss West," began Standbury, clearing his throat impressively, "first, I must extend my condolences to you concerning your uncle. He was a good man."

"Thank you," Grace replied demurely.

"Miss West," the lawyer repeated, "I know this might be sudden, and I apologize if it sounds...ah...tawdry in view of the recentness of your uncle's death, but news, especially bad news, travels fast around here. To say it forthrightly, Miss West, I represent certain business interests who heard you were in town and didn't want to miss the opportunity to make you a business proposition—a fair offer for your uncle's place."

"Dear," Oglethorpe interjected, "it would be so beneficial if we, that is if you, could sell the ranch as soon as possible. We could have this messy business all wrapped up and be back to Boston in less than a month."

"Robert," Grace responded, gazing out the window of the hotel, "we only arrived in town yesterday. I haven't even been out to the ranch. I don't know what it looks like. I'll consider all offers, but I can't agree to sell anything—not right now, not today."

Robert Oglethorpe said nothing for a moment, but then he spoke, his words controlled. "Yes, of course, you are most certainly right. Considering the circumstances, we should discuss it more before we entertain any offers. My enthusiasm for selling was only in hopes that we could be back in Boston in plenty of time to get married before Christmas."

"Why, Robert, are you setting a date?" Grace asked, her voice tinged with sarcasm.

Robert Oglethorpe reddened. "Well, Grace," he stammered, "I guess I am..." and his voice trailed off.

At that moment, the waitress reappeared with a mug of hot coffee and a heavy plate bearing Grace's breakfast. She set them on the table and returned to the kitchen.

"Oh my," exclaimed Standbury glancing at a gold watch he had pulled from his vest pocket. "Look at the time. Miss West, Mr. Oglethorpe," he said as he stood. "I certainly understand your reluctance to discuss business so early after your uncle's passing, Miss West. But, if you need anything, please come and see me. The sooner you attend to this business, as unpleasant as it might be, the better off you are." With that, he threw on his coat, grabbed his briefcase. "Now, if you'll excuse me, I must be on my way." Tipping his hat, he hurried out the front door of the hotel.

Through the hotel window, Robert Oglethorpe watched Standbury zig-zag across the muddy street until the lawyer disappeared in the door of a frame building directly across from the Burlington. Almost as an after-thought, Oglethorpe commented to Grace, "In the case of our legal business here in Wyoming, Mr. Standbury comes highly recommended."

"Does he?" she queried, quietly.

"We should consider his kind offer to help in matters related to your uncle's ranch and estate," Oglethorpe continued, "and we should get started right away."

Grace was silent for a moment. Then she turned to look directly at Oglethorpe with fire in her eyes. "Robert," she said, "we are not married, yet, and this is my uncle's ranch. I am rather disappointed that you are dis-cussing a sale when I am not here. Before I agree to anything, I need--no, I want--to know more about it. I want to see it."

Robert Oglethorpe said nothing for a moment, but then he spoke, his words controlled. "Yes, of course, you are most certainly right. We should ride out there today and look it over. But, first, let's engage Mr. Standbury and at least get the process started."

"I can agree to that, but only on the condition that I be appointed executor of the estate." Grace responded.

Oglethorpe protested, but Grace held firm. "Fine," he said, finally. "But, you must let me advise you through this process."

"Good. I'll be ready in an hour," she said. Excusing herself, she went back upstairs to her room, leaving her breakfast untouched.

#

True to her word, Grace met Oglethorpe at the bottom of the stairs an hour later. The couple exited the front door of the hotel, stepping out onto the main street.

"Grace," Robert admonished as they started across the muddy track. "While Mr. Standbury is trustworthy, be wary. These country lawyers have to work with the townsfolk long after we're gone, so be careful of what you might say."

"That's positively amusing coming from a fellow barrister. Isn't there any honor among thieves? Besides, a big city lawyer like you should be able to outsmart any old country lawyer, shouldn't he?" Grace responded, batting her long lashes in mock astonishment.

Oglethorpe simply grunted. Soon, they arrived in front of the law office. "Phineas Standbury" was painted in bold black letters on the window. They entered, and the thick-bodied lawyer came from a back room to greet them.

"Mr. Standbury," began Oglethorpe. "Miss West has considered your offer of legal services and has decided that she wants you to represent her here. As the sole heir to Mr. Walker's estate, she would like to appoint me as the personal representative. Also, we would like to have the petition filed today."

Standbury pulled a gold watch from his vest pocket and flicked open the cover. Glancing at the open face, he frowned. "Well, its nine o'clock now," he said. "The judge leaves for the day at five." Snapping the watch cover shut, he continued, "We have much work to do before then."

Standbury led Oglethorpe and Grace West into his inner office. It was sparsely decorated--a desk darkened with age, a table cluttered with papers, several chairs, and a small legal library. He motioned for them to sit. Withdrawing a pad of paper from the desk, he sat down opposite them at the table, and began asking questions, writing down the answers as Grace responded.

After a half hour, Standbury finished his note taking. Standing, he said to Robert Oglethorpe, "Why don't you take Miss West back to the hotel. These documents will take me several hours to prepare. I'll come there when I'm finished."

Oglethorpe nodded and escorted Grace out the door.

#

It was midday before Luke lay the pen down and leaned back in his chair. He had vowed to quit practicing law when he left Philadelphia, but this was a special occasion, and though it had been a long time, this simple legal document should accomplish what he wanted it to do.

If I'm going to go to court, I might as well look the part, he concluded and drug out a washtub, one luxury he afforded himself via a purchase in town. He poured hot water into its bowl, and after adding enough cold water to make it tolerable, soaked in its cramped interior until the water started to cool. After drying off, he scraped away days of rough, black stubble with a razor.

Satisfied, Luke put on the white shirt and the black suit. Buckling on his gun belt, he pulled the pistol from its holster and spun the cylinder to ensure it was loaded. He didn't expect any trouble, but he counted on the sight of the weapon dissuading anybody who might think otherwise. Retrieving a leather satchel from beneath his bunk, he placed the documents within its folds and stepped through the cabin door.

With purposeful strides, Luke headed to the barn. Wasting little time, he saddled up his favorite buckskin and turned the gelding in the direction of Buffalo. The circuit court judge was holding court this week, and Luke needed to file his documents before he left for the next county.

CHAPTER 27. THE JUDGE

Promptly at 3:30 in the afternoon, Phineas Standbury left his office and crossed the street to the Burlington. He found Grace West and Robert Oglethorpe waiting in the lobby.

"I've come early," Standbury said, motioning to a nearby table. "We need to go over the petition before we see the judge."

The three sat down, and Standbury withdrew a stack of legal documents from his valise. Setting them on the table, he picked one and explained its purpose. After the last document was discussed, he stuffed all the papers back into his leather case. "We need to move quickly," he said, looking at his pocket watch. The courthouse closes at 5:00 pm. The Judge is a circuit judge and is leaving at the end of the week. He'll be gone for a month. If we file our petition by 4:00, there's a chance that he will see us before he leaves, and we can get the probate of Mr. Walker's estate started."

Oglethorpe suppressed a smile. "Then, let's not waste any more time."

The three exited the Burlington and climbed the sandstone steps to the courthouse. On entering the red brick building, they walked down the long hall to a narrow flight of wooden stairs, climbing to the second floor. There, puffing and panting, Standbury stopped at the Clerk of Court's office. "Is the judge in?" asked Standbury, addressing the short, matronly-looking gray haired woman tending the counter as he struggled to catch his breath. "We need to talk with him about the John Walker estate."

"He just finished a hearing," the Clerk responded, "I'll ask if he has time to see you." The Clerk stepped to the judge's chamber and knocked on the door. From within, a voice responded "Who is it?"

The Clerk pushed the door open and stuck her head inside. "Mr. Standbury would like to speak with you about the John Walker matter," she said. "He has some clients with him."

"Send them in."

The Clerk opened the judge's door and waved the trio through. Judge Saufley sat at his desk clad in a long black robe that did little to hide his robust body. He leaned back in his chair and surveyed Standbury from deep set eyes shaded by bushy eyebrows. "What can I do for you, Mr. Standbury?" the judge growled.

"Your honor," said Standbury, "let me introduce Mr. Robert Oglethorpe and Miss Grace West. Mr. Oglethorpe is a lawyer with business interests here in Wyoming. Miss West is the niece of John Walker. They were traveling here to visit with John when he met his untimely death only two days ago."

"I was sorry to hear about your uncle," the judge said, turning his gaze on Grace. "He was a good man."

"Thank you," Grace responded.

Standbury set his leather valise on the judge's desk and withdrew the legal documents, laying them in front of the black-robed jurist. "Judge, Miss West is Mr. Walker's sole heir and beneficiary. At her request, I prepared a petition appointing her as executor of the Walker estate. If you could sign it here today, your honor, we could take control of the property and start managing the estate immediately."

A curious look crossed the judge's face, and he leaned back in his chair, rubbing his chin thoughtfully. "Well, Mr. Standbury," he drawled. "Miss West may be John Walker's sole heir, but someone else has also filed a petition to be executor, along with a will."

"What!" exclaimed Standbury. "That can't be."

The judge retrieved a file from the corner of his desk and withdrew a hand written document. "Mr. Standbury, I have here a petition that was filed just a few hours ago by a gentleman named Luke Banister. According to this petition, John Walker made a will before his death and appointed Mr. Banister as executor of his estate." The judge turned the folder around and let Standbury read the petition.

"This...this doesn't meet the statutory requirements!" sputtered Standbury, a look of incredulousness crossing his face. "There is no will here."

The judge pulled a brown, dog-eared tally book from the file. "I believe there is. Look for yourself, Mr. Standbury. The will is written on the back page. If I read it right, it says:

"Last Will of John Walker. I hereby give all I have to my niece Grace West. I want Luke Banister to take care of everything for me." -
John Walker

"This is no will," retorted Standbury. "It's just some scratchings on an old book. Surely, judge, you won't accept this as a valid will."

"Mr. Standbury," replied Judge Saufley, "you're as familiar with the law as I. If the writing is John Walker's, and it's his signature, then it may meet all the elements required of a holographic will."

"A holographic will?" asked Grace West, frowning.

Oglethorpe broke in. "Grace, a holographic will is a type of will, signed by the deceased and written entirely in his hand."

"Why, this is preposterous," sputtered Standbury. "Who knows whether this writing, or this signature, is really Walker's or not."

"Mr. Standbury," said the Judge, "at this point, neither of us know for sure. But there is a procedure to prove the signature in court, as you well know counselor. You used the process last year with old Ben Johnson."

Robert Oglethorpe cut in. "Now look, judge, I don't know what kind of cow town justice this is, but Miss West is the only living relative of the deceased. According to the will, she is his only beneficiary as well. Miss West has filed a petition with this court to be named the executor, and most civilized courts would hold that she should have that right. I demand that you issue a decision in her favor on this today."

The judge glared. Then in slow measured tones, he stated, "I don't know how it is in England or more civilized states, Mr. Oglethorpe, but in Wyoming, the person designated by the testator has first preference, absent some disqualifying circumstance. Do you know of any circumstance that would disqualify Luke Banister, Mr. Oglethorpe?"

"I don't even know the man," responded Oglethorpe angrily. "How can I comment on his qualifications?"

The judge looked at Grace West. "How long did it take you to get here from Boston, Miss West?"

"About five days."

"And, how long do you think it will take you to settle your uncle's estate?"

"I think that we can settle the cattle, and the land, and close out all the business in about one month, maybe two at the most."

"Then it may take you two months or so to conduct this business?"

"Yes."

The judge wrinkled his forehead for a moment, and then said, "I'm leaving the county at the end of the week. I do find that there is a need for a quick decision in this matter, so I am setting this case for a hearing three days from today at 1:00 P.M. Bailiff, send word to Mr. Banister."

"We will challenge this petition, your honor, if we lose," Standbury declared.

The judge smiled at the two men standing before him. "Well, Mr. Standbury," he said in his best country drawl, "you haven't lost yet, but if you do, you're entitled to an appeal, according to the rules, of course. I think that it probably will take nine months at least to get a decision from the Wyoming Supreme Court, depending on when I get the file sent down. Until then, I suggest you prepare for the hearing. Good day, gentlemen, Miss West." With that, the judge closed the file, rose from his desk, and walked to the door, holding it open. Standbury, Oglethorpe and Grace West exited, and the door slammed behind them.

#

"Who is this Luke Banister, anyway?" fumed Robert Oglethorpe as he stormed past the Clerk of Court's office.

Standbury held up his hand. "Wait here a moment," he said. He ducked into the Clerk of Court's office, returning a few minutes later with a perplexed look on his face. "The Clerk doesn't know much about him. Story is that he drifted in here last spring with John when he drove that herd up from Cheyenne. For some reason, John took a liking to him and hired him on at the Bar X. The man claims to be an attorney, but he's never practiced around here, that I know."

"Why would this, this...imposter, want to put his nose in our business?" Grace West asked, her green eyes flashing.

Standbury shrugged his round shoulders. "He told the Clerk that he was filing the petition because your uncle asked him to."

Oglethorpe patted Grace on the arm. "He's just an annoyance, Grace dear. We'll find some way to persuade him to step aside, whether he wants to or not."

Phineas Standbury pulled a big white handkerchief from his vest pocket and wiped the sweat from his forehead. Glancing over his shoulder, he lowered his voice. "Getting rid of the man might not be that easy. Clerk says he made something of a name for himself this summer tracking rustlers down in the Red Wall country. Rumor is that he's tough and can use a gun pretty well."

"We have tough men ourselves," replied Oglethorpe impatiently. "But, no matter. If we can't run him off, we'll buy him out. By the end of the week, he'll be just another nameless drifter."

"One more thing, Mr. Oglethorpe," Standbury said as he pushed back his sparse hair. "Luke Banister worked for your uncle until the round-up last fall. They had a falling out, and your uncle fired him, right there on the spot—something about hanging a man without a trial. Though it's only speculation, an argument could be made that Banister might have had something to do with John's death. There was bad blood between the two, so he had motive. And, he was in the area when Sheriff Angus went out looking for John, so he had opportunity. Rumor is that he even helped the

184

sheriff find John's body."

"That could be a disqualifying consideration," Oglethorpe said thoughtfully. "We'll work on that."

Grace spoke up. "Certainly, we don't want this Luke Banister to watch over my uncle's cattle. That would be like putting a fox to guard the hen house, wouldn't you agree?"

Robert Oglethorpe smile and patted Grace's arm. "Not to worry, my pet, we can deal with Luke Banister, and I know a man who can help us do just that."

#

The dark-coated stranger loitered at the bottom of the back stairway to the Burlington Hotel, leaning nonchalantly against the weathered hand-rail. It was twilight and the evening shadows revealed only a dark silhouette to passersby. The stranger rolled a cigarette, jamming the finished product between his teeth. Striking a match, he lit the paper and drew the first puff, holding the tobacco smoke in his lungs for long seconds before he blew twin streams from his nostrils. He took only a few drags before flicking the cigarette to the ground. Grinding out the embers with the heel of his boot, he turned with catlike stealth and bounded up the staircase, letting himself in the back door of the hotel.

#

Robert Oglethorpe paced back and forth in his hotel room, his thin fingers clutching a crumpled telegram. "Creditors!" he snarled under his breath. "Always demanding money." A noise on the street below brought him nervously to the window. It was only the evening stage arriving, and he returned to his pacing. He needed more time for his plan to work, but with Luke Banister handling Walker's estate, it could take months to sell the Bar X. That was more time than he could spare. Cursing, Oglethorpe ripped the telegram in bits and threw it into the pot-bellied stove. Banister was no longer just an inconvenience. He needed to be dealt with, and quickly.

The Englishman's pacing was interrupted by a rapping at his door. He stomped to the door and threw it open, preparing a tongue-lashing for whomever might be stupid enough to disturb him at this hour, but he swallowed hard when he recognized Lord Atherton.

"Well, my dear cousin, are you going to ask me in?" Atherton inquired politely.

"James!" stuttered a red-faced Oglethorpe. "Certainly. Come in, by all means."

Atherton entered the room and strode to the window overlooking the street below. He drew the curtains, and then turned back to Robert Oglethorpe. "I've heard things did not go as well as you might have hoped at the hearing today."

"Bad news certainly travels fast," Oglethorpe said, wondering how his cousin had received the news of the court action so quickly. "But I think I can remedy the situation."

"Maybe, but it will be harder now and it will take longer," Atherton said. The Englishman walked across the room to a bottle of brandy that stood on the dresser. "Do you mind if I pour myself a drink?" he inquired as he poured two fingers of the amber liquid in a glass. "It's most effective in cutting the dust from a man's throat." He touched the glass to his lips and tossed the contents down. Atherton poured another brandy, replaced the cork in the neck of the bottle and settled in a nearby chair.

"Frankly, my dear cousin, it is imperative that you come up with financing quickly," Atherton said, turning the brandy glass around and around in his slender hands. "I can hold off our creditors only another month, maybe two, before...,"

"A man named Luke Banister is holding me up," interrupted Oglethorpe, seething with anger and frustration. "He's blocking everything I need to do, but Standbury thinks we'll get him removed as executor at the hearing on Friday."

"Luke Banister?" said Atherton, raising an eyebrow. "I have a score to settle with that man myself." He sipped the brandy. "More importantly though, cousin, the Association's plans to eliminate the rustler element here in Wyoming are at a critical stage. Your fiancée's uncle, Mr. Walker, had resigned the Association and certain members are still concerned that some rather embarrassing letters written to Mr. Walker might surface. We need to prevent that from happening."

"How?" asked Oglethorpe.

Atherton rose from his chair and walked to the hotel room door, swinging it open. There, leaning against the wall, stood Ben Santelli.

"Come in, Ben," Atherton said.

Santelli grunted and stepped into the room, closing the door behind him.

"I trust you two know one another," asked Atherton.

Oglethorpe gave Santelli a nod. "We do," he said.

Atherton turned to the big man. "Frankly, Mr. Santelli, things are not going well for us here. A man by the name of Luke Banister is causing us problems."

"Luke Banister?" interjected Santelli, his forehead wrinkling in thought. "I've heard that name before."

"I trust he's not a friend," said Atherton.

"I don't keep friends," replied Santelli. "But if it's the man I'm thinking of,

I know a Sheriff in West Virginia who would issue a warrant for his arrest—on murder charges. We chased the man all the way down the Ohio River before he disappeared."

"The Ohio River?" Oglethorpe said slowly. "Now I remember where I heard that name. A Luke Banister was a card dealer on The Golden Girl, the riverboat where you, Mr. Santelli, and I met. It couldn't be the same man, could it? He jumped off the boat. Everyone was sure he drowned."

Atherton waved his hand. "It's possible this is the same man. But whether he is or isn't, we want him to go away."

"It would be my pleasure to see it done," Santelli replied as he turned toward Oglethorpe. "Before I start another job though, I want to be paid for my last one. Do you have the rest of my money?"

Oglethorpe frowned. Stepping to his traveling chest, he opened it, withdrew an envelope, and tossed it to Santelli. "That's all I have," he said. "You could have told me you were coming."

Santelli caught the package in midflight, but he kept his eyes riveted on the thin Englishman. "I never announce my arrival to men who owe me money," he growled. "It gives them too much time to think." The big man opened the envelope and riffled through the bills. Then he shoved the envelope deep into his coat pocket. "Banister will cost you the same."

"Good," Atherton broke in, politely walking to the door and opening it wide. "I'll see that you get paid. Now, you may go, Mr. Santelli, before somebody sees you."

Santelli's eyes gleamed. He started to say something else, but thought the better of it, so he spun on his heel and left.

Atherton kept his eyes on the big man until he was gone. "I've used that man a long time, but I don't trust him anymore," he said, coldly. "He knows too much, and he can be bought." Atherton tossed down the remainder of his brandy and rose to his feet. "After he disposes of Banister, you need take care of him, one way or another."

Oglethorpe blanched. Stammering, he replied, "I'll figure out some way to...", but he couldn't finish the sentence.

"Good," Atherton said with satisfaction. "And, one more thing, Cousin," he continued, "I will be back on Friday evening to take the stage to Gillette, and then the train back to Boston. I have business there, and so do you. I trust you will be successful on Friday. A bit of success is just what you need to reassure your creditors. But, whatever happens, be prepared to go with me when the stage leaves, Robert. You have pressing business in Boston that can no longer wait."

CHAPTER 28. THE FIRE

After filing his documents with the court, Luke left Buffalo just before the early spring sun vanished behind the distant peaks of the Big Horns. A full moon rose to take its place, hanging in the sky like a golden apple and covering the prairie with a soft, white radiance. Only the occasional howl of a lonely coyote broke the night quiet.

The buckskin set a rhythmic pace. In less than an hour, his long legs had carried Luke to the outskirts of Walker's Bar X Ranch. The ranch buildings lay still and quiet. Like a corpse, Luke thought. Vivid memories of Walker lying cold and stiff in the mountain snow crept unbidden into his mind causing an involuntary shiver that prickled the hair at the back of his neck. He urged his mount to a faster pace.

Luke had nearly passed Walker's house when the faintest glimmer of light caught his eye. He reined the buckskin to a stop and peered intently through the darkness, scanning the ranch buildings. There was nothing. Just a reflection of the moon against a window pane, he told himself. Spurring the buckskin back onto the trail, he cast one last look back, but this time he fixed his eyes on a light that flared, held steady for a moment, and then died out. The light came from a window in Walker's house.

"That's not moonlight," Luke whispered to the buckskin. He nudged his mount toward the Bar X. "Let's go take a look. John wanted me to take care of his place, I might as well start now."

Luke rode quietly past the ranch outbuildings, guiding the buckskin to the rear of the log barn where both would be hidden from the sight of anyone who might be in the house. Sliding to the ground, he tied the horse to a corral rail and pulled his revolver from its holster. Holding it up to the night sky, he spun the cylinder, noting the dull glint of moonlight off each chambered cartridge as it whirled past. With the pistol at ready, he slipped through the shadows toward the silent house.

When Luke reached the cabin's porch, he stepped onto the wooden deck, but each footfall seemed to reverberate through the night like the beat of a giant drum. He stopped. You're waking the dead, he chided himself, but the only sound he heard was the beating of his own heart. Steadying his nerves, he traversed the last few steps to Walker's front door. It stood slightly ajar. Luke gave it a push, and it swung open. He ducked inside.

Though the cabin's interior was nearly black, Luke hugged the cabin's wall. Moonlight poured through the open door frame, and while it provided little illumination, he didn't want to be silhouetted by the dim light. For what seemed to be an eternity, he held motionless, but there was no sound and no light.

Luke cursed. *I can't stay here forever, he thought.* Fishing in his pocket, he produced a wooden match and scratched it against the log wall. It flared, lighting the room dimly. No other person was visible, but the match light revealed a kerosene lantern hanging from a hook an arm's reach away. Luke lifted the lantern from its hanger and lit the wick. When the lantern burned steadily, he held it high and surveyed the room. He was stunned. Overturned chairs littered the floor. Drawers were pulled out and their contents scattered. An overstuffed leather sofa had been sliced with a knife and the stuffing hung out like the guts of a wounded animal.

Luke moved to the next room. It, too, had been ransacked. Whoever did this was looking for something—maybe something so valuable they would kill for it—but what? The question brought back memories of his first morning at the Bar X, and John's conversation about valuables hidden under the floor of his cabin. Luke holstered his pistol and set the lantern on the floor. Stepping quickly to the dresser, he shoved it aside, and then knelt to push on one end of the newly exposed floor planking. It swung open to reveal a gray, metal box sitting snugly in a cavity beneath the floor.

Luke pulled the box from the hole and carried it back to the lantern, deftly opening the lid. Inside the box were three documents. He fished them out, scanning each in the dim light. The first was a deed to the ranch. The second, a paid mortgage on property. But the third was a letter from the Wyoming Stockgrowers Association.

Luke unfolded the letter and held it close to the lantern's light. Seconds later, he let out a low whistle, scarcely able to believe what he had just read. Did the letters tie in with John's conversation at the church social. Is that what Walker kept hidden? Folding the document again, he stuffed it into his coat pocket. Then, as he reached for the other documents, from the upper floor, he heard the unmistakable creak of weight shifting on a wooden floor.

Luke froze, his heart pounding. Slowly pulling his pistol from its holster, he thumbed back its hammer and stepped to the stairway. Placing one foot above the other, he inched up the stairs. With each step, his heart raced faster.

At the upper reaches of the stairwell, the lantern's light faded, leaving the second story lit only by moon light that poured through a small gable window. Luke paused. Nothing moved. Gathering himself, he dove forward and rolled across the floor, coming to his feet with his pistol ready to fire at the slightest movement.

Too late, he sensed movement behind him and swung his pistol, firing just before a right cross sent him reeling. He went face down on the floor as lights exploded in his brain and then dimmed out. The last thing he saw before he lost consciousness was a shiny silver boot buckle arcing toward his ribs.

#

Silhouetted in the moonlight, Ben Santelli circled Luke's prostrate form, waiting for any movement, any sign of life. But Luke lay still. After a moment, the big man grasped Luke's arms and dragged him to a spot where moonlight pooled on the wooden floor. He knelt and jerked the unconscious man to his back. When the moonlight fell on Luke's face, Santelli began to laugh, and his laughter grew loud and maniacal and echoed through the night until, abruptly, it subsided.

"I think you have something I want," Santelli whispered, his face now grim. The big man bent over Luke and methodically rifled through his pockets, finding the letter Luke had retrieved from the metal box.

With an evil grin, Santelli stood up and shoved the letter beneath his shirt. "This is working out far better than I expected, Mr. Banister," he said with a sneering chuckle. Santelli nudged Luke's body with the toe of his boot, but Luke failed to move. Satisfied that his prey was helpless, Santelli turned and hurried down the stairs of Walker's cabin.

Retrieving a can of kerosene from near the stove, Santelli splashed it onto the debris strewn about the floor of Walker's house. He stepped through the doorway to the porch outside and struck a match. The phosphorus flared brightly. With a flick of the wrist, Santelli sent the burning matchstick sailing into the cabin toward the kerosene soaked pile. The fuel exploded, and like wildfire, spread along the floor.

Santelli walked to the barn. Gathering his horse, he mounted and sat in the shadows, watching the voracious blaze lick at the cabin walls. Satisfied that the fire would consume everything in the house, including Luke Banister, the big man spurred his mount and headed north. Just before he reached the road, he stopped and cast a fleeting glance back at Walker's burning ranch. Flames tinged the night sky a deep orange, and turbulent black smoke blotted out the stars. "Nothing personal, Banister," he chuckled. Spinning his horse, he laid a quirt to its ribs, intending to be far away before daylight revealed the destruction he had set in motion.

Slowly, consciousness returned to Luke's brain. When he finally opened his eyes, he found himself lying face down on a hard wooden floor. He pushed himself to a sitting position, cursing when the floor beneath him burned his flesh. He took a deep breath. Hot air seared his throat and a choking heaviness settled in his chest. Coughing, he squinted through the roiling smoke, and with horror, realized that the cabin was on fire.

Gasping for air, Luke spotted a faint beam of moonlight that marked the location of the tiny gable window. On hands and knees, he crawled toward the light as flames began to lick at the top of the stairwell. He had crawled only a few yards when his hand touched something hard. Instinctively, he grasped the object and pulled it toward him, touching it with both hands before he realized it was the barrel of his own pistol. He held on to it and continued to crawl until he found himself at the window. Lifting the pistol over his head, he hammered it into the window pane, shattering the glass. He hammered at the window again; this time the entire sash fell out of the wall to the ground below.

Luke looked back at the smoke billowing up the stairwell. The flames would follow at any moment, exploding into an inescapable inferno. Kicking out the remaining shards of glass, he tossed the pistol out, and then wriggled through the window himself, dropping to the ground below. He rolled to his hands and knees and crawled into the darkness. When he could no longer feel the heat of the fire, he sprawled out on the ground and lost consciousness.

CHAPTER 29. THE NOTICE

A razor's edge of red light slit the eastern horizon from end to end when a pair of calloused hands shook Luke awake. Numb from the November cold, Luke forced his eyes open and gazed into the rough, moustached face of Sheriff Angus.

"Seems we meet at interesting times, Mr. Banister," the lawman drawled with a tinge of irony in his voice.

Luke opened his mouth to answer, but his teeth chattered so hard he couldn't speak.

"You ain't froze solid yet, but a chunk of ice off the Powder couldn't be much colder," Angus offered as he pulled Luke to a sitting position. "Let's get you over to the cabin, or what's left of it anyway." He anchored his arm around Luke's shoulders, helping him to his feet and half carrying him toward the charred ruins of Walker's house. A dozen feet from the cabin, Angus lowered Luke onto a log.

"You alright?" the lawman asked.

"Ankle is sprained some, my hands hurt, and my ribs feel like I was kicked by a mule, but I think I'll survive otherwise."

A slight breeze stirred the glowing embers lightly, carrying their warmth toward Luke. "Those coals are still hot enough to cook a buffalo steak," Angus said, holding his gnarled hands out toward the fire. "They should get some warmth back into your bones soon enough."

The Sheriff removed a pouch of tobacco from his pocket, along with a booklet of thin, white paper. With deft fingers, he rolled a cigarette, stuck it in his mouth, and lit it with an ember from the cabin. He took a deep draw while his restless eyes scanned the area. "If you're up to it, maybe you could tell me what happened here?" he said, blowing a cloud of smoke into the sky.

Luke surveyed the smoking remnants of John Walker's cabin. Anger flooded his mind when he thought that some animal had left him in the house to die when the house burned to the ground. "Sheriff," he began slowly, stumbling over words as memories of the previous night's events roiled around in his brain, "I saw a light over here in Walker's cabin last night on the way home. I rode over to investigate. Someone had broken in and ransacked the house. The same person, I assume, jumped me in the dark-- sucker punched me good. Next thing I know, I wake up and the house is on fire. I crawled out the upstairs window just before the place exploded."

Angus listened closely. "Did you see the fella who punched you?"

"Never saw the man's face," replied Luke, rubbing his jaw, "but he hit me harder than if I'd been kicked by a mule."

"Anything else?"

"One more thing, Sheriff," Luke said as he felt in his pocket for the letter he had taken from Walker's gray metal box. Finding nothing, he cursed. "Damn!

"Problems?" Angus inquired politely.

"When I first hired on at the Bar X, Walker told me a letter he had stashed away in his house, under the floor beneath an old desk. Told me that if anything ever happened to him, then I should get it and keep it in a safe place. It was the most valuable thing he had. Last night, I found the letter, but whoever cold-cocked me must have taken it."

"Most likely, whatever the letter said, it's nothing but ashes now," the Sheriff responded.

"Maybe," Luke replied, "but I did read it."

"Remember what it said?" Angus asked, curiosity lacing his voice.

"It said something about an army, and it mentioned 'the destroying angel.' It contained a list of names."

"Do you remember any of the names on the list?"

"Only a few. Nate Champion was there. You were too."

Angus shook his head. "Don't know what that would be about," he said, rising to his feet, "but I'll ask around."

By now, Luke had begun to feel more human. He stood up and stretched his muscles, wincing as they protested. Changing the subject, he said, "Don't mean to sound ungrateful, Sheriff, but what brings you out this way so early in the morning?"

"I'm headed down toward the crossing on Powder River," the Sheriff replied, the cigarette dangling precariously from his lips. "Got some business there. And, that reminds me," he continued, unbuttoning his coat. "The Judge asked me to deliver this." Reaching into his shirt pocket, he withdrew an envelope and handed it to Luke. "He wants a hearing on the Walker probate in three days."

"Three days!" Luke exclaimed. "I can't possibly be ready in three days."

"You'll have to tell that to the judge," replied the lawman. "A niece of John Walker's showed up yesterday. Goes by the name of Grace West. Has a friend by the name of Oglethorpe, Robert Oglethorpe, I believe."

Luke scowled. "This friend doesn't happen to be English, does he?"

Angus tossed a curious glance at Luke, but continued with his story. "Yep," he said, "a tall, skinny fella. They didn't waste a minute. Hired Phineas Standbury to represent them on Walker's estate. Filed a petition with the court, same as you. Now they're all fired up about getting this estate done quickly, and the woman wants to be named executor. Why, I'll bet that woman don't know nothin' about cows."

Luke listened, but said nothing.

Angus stood up and turned his backside to the smoking cabin. "I ain't the suspicious sort, but it seems just a little bit strange and all, them showing up like that, don't you think?" he opined, watching Luke's reaction closely.

"Maybe it's just coincidence, Sheriff. On the other hand, maybe there is a reason John wanted me to handle his estate if something happened to him. He may not have trusted his niece, or her companion for that matter." Angus grunted and took another drag on the cigarette. "Maybe," he replied, flicking the butt to the dirt and grinding it out with his heel. "Listen, I'd like to stay and chew the fat, but sun's up, and I've got a day's ride ahead of me if I'm gonna get to Powder River. Is your horse still around?"

Luke nodded toward the barn. "Horse should be tied down at the corrals," he said.

"Well, if you're healthy enough to walk down and get him, I'll take a look around the place," the Sheriff said.

"Sure," Luke said, rising to his feet. With every part of his body hurting, he limped toward the barn. There, still tied to a corral post, stood the buckskin. The horse raised his head and perked up his ears when Luke appeared. Luke climbed into the saddle and rode back to the burned out remains of Walker's house.

Angus rounded the corner of the charred building just as Luke returned. "I did find one thing," the Sheriff said, holding up a black revolver. "Look familiar?"

"It's mine, Sheriff," Luke said with relief. "I must have lost it last night when I crawled out the window."

Angus handed the pistol to Luke. "Thought so. I remember seeing it when you had that run-in with Frank Kelly."

Angus glanced sideways at Luke. "Didn't see anything else," he said, "ceptin' some foot prints. Looked like a big man from the size of the boot."

"With a silver buckle," Luke said thoughtfully.

"A what?" asked Angus.

"On his boot. The last thing I saw was a strap across the man's boot and a silver buckle on one side," said Luke. "It looked custom made. I know I've seen a boot like that somewhere before."

Angus stepped into the stirrup, and threw a leg over his saddle.

"Well, if you remember where, let me know. Now if you're ready, I'll ride with you as far as your place. Ain't nothing I can do here now."

"Glad for the company," Luke said, turning the buckskin toward home.

The Sheriff set a fast pace, and it wasn't long before the two men crested the ridge overlooking Luke's spread. Angus reined in his mount, and turned to look at Luke. "You look mighty rough in the daylight, Mr. Banister." he said, raising an eyebrow. "Your hands might be burnt. You should ride into town and see the Doc."

Luke nodded. "I'll survive, replied Luke. "There's nothing that old horse doctor could do for me that I can't do for myself."

Angus grinned. "Guess you're right there," he chuckled. The Sheriff wheeled his horse and headed south. "If you think of anything else, you can let me know on Friday at the hearing. I'll see you then, if you're still alive, that is."

"Thanks for thinking of me," Luke said sarcastically. "I don't mind dying, but I'm not going to die like that.

The Sheriff spurred his mount into a canter and headed south. Luke watched until the lawman disappeared over a slight rise. Then, he turned the buckskin toward his homestead, letting the rangy horse pick his way through the sage down to the barn.

He turned the buckskin loose and trudged to his cabin. Withdrawing the summons the Sheriff had given him, he tossed it onto the small wooden table, and then walked across the kitchen to the cast iron stove. After jamming several chunks of split pine into the fire box, he struck a match and kindled a flame. Soon the pine was blazing and throwing off welcome warmth.

Luke stifled a yawn. The night had left him exhausted, and almost as if someone had pulled a plug, the strength drained from his body. He shuffled over to his bunk and lay down, falling asleep before his head hit the pillow.

CHAPTER 30. THE FRAME

Carrying a leather case filled with legal documents, Luke shouldered the courtroom doors open and stepped inside. It was hearing day, and at the far side of the room, his adversaries were gathered around a counsel's table—Phineas Standbury, a rotund lawyer Luke had seen around town but never met, Grace West, and Robert Oglethorpe. When Luke entered the courtroom, they looked up and grew quiet.

Luke pushed through the bar separating the court from the gallery and tossed his hat and leather bag on a counsel's table. Striding toward the trio, he held out his hand. "Mr. Standbury," he said. "I'm Luke Banister."

Standbury stood. "I know who you are," he replied, leaving his hands dangling at his side. "We were not sure you would make it today. Sheriff Angus told us you almost met with a terrible accident down at Mr. Walker's cabin."

"Almost," Luke replied. He turned to Grace West. "And, you must be John Walker's niece, Grace West."

Grace tossed her blond curls. "I am," she answered, her pouting blue eyes appraising Luke from head to toe.

Luke smiled, but when his eyes locked onto the tall, thin frame of Robert Oglethorpe, the smile faded. "So, we meet again, Mr. Oglethorpe."

Oglethorpe's cheeks flushed, but he never moved from behind the table. Luke's voice hardened. "You might recall a poker game on the Ohio River some six months ago aboard a paddle-wheel called The Golden Girl. Oglethorpe's eyes narrowed. "Of course, I remember. You cheated me in the card game, and tried to rob me afterward."

Anger boiled up in Luke's belly. He laid his hand lightly on the butt of his pistol. "I never like being called a cheater, mister," he said, "especially by a poor card player. And I've never liked a thief."

Oglethorpe reddened, but Grace West laid her hand on her fiancée's arm. Turning to Luke, she said, "I remember you. You were the card dealer that night Robert was cheated and robbed, aren't you? You tried to murder him. The whole river was looking for you, but we thought you drowned."
"With all due respect, Miss West, I'm sure his version of what happened that night is much different than mine."

Grace's smile faded and her voice took on a sharper edge. "I don't know who you think you are, Mr. Banister, though you certainly look different today that you did six months ago. No matter. My fiancée here is a highly respected attorney with a practice in Boston and London. I think after this hearing, you will rue the day that you tried to butt into our affairs."

"We shall see," Luke replied, but at that moment, the bailiff opened the door leading to the judge's chambers and somberly intoned, "Hear ye! Hear ye! The Court in and for Johnson County, Wyoming, is now in session. The Honorable Judge Saufley presiding. All rise."

Bedecked in a black robe, the judge stepped into the courtroom and mounted the bench. Rapping the gavel, he called the court to order. "Gentlemen," he began, "Would you please be seated. This is a hearing in the estate of John Walker. Because no one has had much time to prepare, I'm not going to stand on much formality today. We are simply here so that I can put someone in charge of Mr. Walker's estate during the probate." The judge peered over the top of his glasses, gazing at the people assembled before him. "Mr. Banister, you've filed a petition to be appointed executor of the estate. Is that right?"

"Yes, your honor," replied Luke.

Mr. Standbury, you filed a petition on behalf of Miss West to appoint Robert Oglethorpe as executor, is that correct."

"Yes, your honor."

"Mr. Standbury, I'm going to let you go first."

Standbury rose to his feet. "Your honor," he began, "Grace West is the only living relative of the deceased, John Walker. We are arguing that the preferred executor of the estate should be Robert Oglethorpe, a man of Miss West's choosing rather than Luke Banister. Mr. Banister is only an acquaintance of Mr. Walker's, and one of very short duration, at that. Further, we are going to raise questions about his character, and his qualifications to serve."

"Is that all, Mr. Standbury?" inquired the Judge.

"No, your honor. Miss West would like to testify here today on her own behalf, as well."

Luke, who had been taking notes, dropped his pencil on the table and looked up. This was a turn of events that he had not expected.

Judge Saufley leaned back in his chair. "This is a hearing on the applicable law, Mr. Standbury. I did not anticipate witnesses today."

"I realize that, your Honor," said Standbury, his voice turning syrupy. "But Miss West wants an opportunity to talk to the court about her uncle, Mr. Walker, and what he meant to her."

The Judge looked at Luke. "Do you have any objections, Mr. Banister?" he asked.

Luke thought for a moment. He anticipated that Grace would be an emotional witness, and it was always hard to handle an emotional woman on the stand. "Yes, I do, your Honor," he responded, finally. "Based on Mr.

Standbury's explanation of her testimony, I expect Ms. West's testimony to be irrelevant to this matter."

"Overruled, Mr. Banister," replied the judge. "You may proceed, Mr. Standbury."

"If it pleases the court, I would like to call my first witness, Miss Grace West," replied Standbury with a theatrical flourish.

Grace West rose from the table and walked to the witness chair. After being sworn in, she took her chair and immediately, took out a handkerchief, dabbing at her eyes. Standbury took a moment for the effect to set in. Then he began his line of questioning.

Grace recounted how she had come to Wyoming to visit her favorite uncle, but had arrived too late. At the end of her testimony, she broke down and sobbed. Standbury stood close and patted her on the arm.

When Grace composed herself again, Standbury asked if there was anything else she wanted to say. Grace pointed toward Luke, and spat out angrily, "I know that man. He is a vile person, that Luke Banister."

Surprised by the sudden attack, Luke rose from his chair. "Objection, your honor."

"Overruled," replied the judge. "Please continue, Miss West."

Grace turned toward the judge, wiping her eyes with a kerchief. "Judge Saufley," she said, "I've met this man before. He's a thief and a card cheat. Please don't let this villain take over my dear uncle's ranch."

It was a good performance, all that Luke expected and more. Luke conducted little cross examination, simply asking if she had ever lived or ranched in Wyoming. Grace professed little experience or knowledge of either. Then, she was dismissed.

Standbury stood and faced the judge. "I have one more witness," he stated.

"Counselor," said the Judge a little irritably, "you said you were only going to have one witness testify."

"Judge," answered the rotund lawyer, turning to face the bench, "it is imperative that we call this second witness. We have reason to believe that Mr. Banister may be linked to heinous crimes in West Virginia and that he is a wanted outlaw. It goes towards his qualification as the executor in this matter."

The judge raised an eyebrow. "Quite unusual, Mr. Standbury. I'll be interested in hearing what your witness has to say."

Without hesitating, Standbury turned toward the back of the courtroom, looking at a man who had slipped in quietly. "Your honor, I would like to call my second witness, Mr. Ben Santelli, deputized by the State of West Virginia."

At the mention of Ben Santelli's name, Luke's mouth dropped open. He spun around, catching sight of Santelli's leering grin as the man arose at the back of the courtroom. Santelli sauntered toward the witness stand, staring malevolently at Luke as he passed. He stopped in front of the bailiff and held up his hand.

"Baliff, swear in the witness," Judge Saufley commanded.

Luke finally overcame his surprise and rose to his feet. "I object to this witness, your honor!" he blurted out.

"Mr. Banister," said the judge with curiosity. "This is an informal hearing. May I ask on what grounds you are objecting?"

"It was my understanding that this hearing was called to argue the legal basis of appointing an executor to John Walker's estate. Over objection, Ms. West's testimony was allowed though it was hearsay and irrelevant. Mr. Santelli's testimony is the same. With due respect, your honor, I request a continuation."

The Judge turned toward Phineas Standbury. "Mr. Standbury," he inquired, "what is the relevancy of this witness, and the basis of his testimony?"

Standbury cleared his throat before he spoke, looking sideways at Robert Oglethorpe. "My witness will testify, your honor, of personal knowledge that he has about two murders Mr. Banister is charged with committing in the State of West Virginia."

The judge raised one eyebrow. "Those are serious charges. I do hope you have proof of this Mr. Standbury."

"I do."

Judge Saufley glowered at Standbury. "I'm warning you, Mr. Standbury, if this is some kind of shenanigan, then I'm going to hold you in contempt."

"No trick, your honor," Standbury replied.

The Judge turned his gaze back to Luke. "This is only a hearing," he replied. "As you might know, hearsay evidence is allowed in a hearing. And other testimony as well. Objection overruled. Judge Saufley turned to the bailiff. "Swear in the witness," he ordered, his voice slow and deliberate.

"Do you swear to tell the truth, the whole truth and nothing but the truth so help you God?" the bailiff asked.

"Yes," Santelli replied. Turning, he stepped to the witness stand, a smirk flickering across his face. Stunned, Luke dropped into his chair

Standbury covered all the preliminary foundational questions with his new witness; then, he began his direct exam in earnest.

"Have you ever been to the State of West Virginia?" inquired Standbury.

"Yes," Santelli answered.

Standbury turned and looked directly at Luke. "Do you know a Sheriff Branscom in Hancock County, West Virginia," Standbury asked Santelli.

"Yes," replied Santelli.

"How did you come to know him?" asked Standbury.

"I worked for Sheriff Branscom running down moonshiners and bootleggers in his county."

"What brings you out to Wyoming," asked Standbury.

"I was offered a job with the Wyoming Stockgrowers Association."

"Let's focus on your job in West Virginia, Mr. Santelli," stated Standbury. "What, if anything, did your job there have to do with Mr. Luke Banister?"

Santelli cleared his throat. "Luke Banister murdered two people in Hancock County last year," answered Santelli, "a Samuel McGill and a Jesse McGill. Sheriff Branscom had reason to believe that Mr. Banister had fled to Wyoming."

"I object," shouted Luke.

"Overruled," replied the judge. "Go on Mr. Standbury."

"Have you been in touch with Sheriff Branscom recently?" asked Standbury.

"I sent him a telegram telling him that I had found the man he was looking for," Santelli replied, his eyes gleaming.

"Did you get a reply?" asked Standbury.

"I did. It's right here," Santelli answered, holding up a yellow telegram.

"Would you read the telegram to the court," Standbury asked triumphantly.

"Of course," Santelli replied, relishing the moment. "It says:

"West Virginia warrant issued for the arrest of Luke Banister. Wanted for the murder of Jeremiah McGill and Jesse McGill."

"Is Mr. Luke Banister in the courtroom today?" asked Standbury.

"Yes. He's sitting there," Santelli replied pointing an accusing finger at Luke.

Luke leaped to his feet again. "I object," he shouted. "This is all a lie!"

The judge banged his gavel on the desk. "Sit down, Mr. Banister, before I find you in contempt."

Luke dropped into his chair--his mind numbed by the turn of events.

When the court had quieted, Standbury turned to the judge. "No more questions, your honor," he said and sat down at the counsel's table, a self-satisfied look on his face.

It was Luke's turn to cross-examine Santelli. He stood for a moment, unable to form any words. The judge looked at him expectantly, until finally Luke stammered, "Judge Saufley, may I have a one-hour recess?"

Judge Saufley gazed at Luke over the tops of his glasses. "We'll take a one-hour noon break, Mr. Banister. I suggest you use the time to review your case, and by the way, don't even consider leaving town." With that, the judge rapped the bench with his gavel. "Court recessed until 1:00 o'clock," he ordered, and then he stepped down from the desk and disappeared in his chambers.

#

Luke slumped at the counsels' table; his shoulders hunched over in despair. He was a fool for taking this hearing so lightly, he thought to himself. After the others had left, Luke descended the stairs, and trudged out the door of the courthouse, finally sitting down on a bench on the courthouse lawn. Head in his hands, he hardly noticed the afternoon stage as it rumbled by. He was about to go back to the courthouse when Mary Higgins, the waitress from the Burlington, walked past.

"Good afternoon, Mr. Banister," she said.

"It's hardly good," Luke responded dejectedly.

"Anything I could help with?"

"A court case that I'm involved in," he said. "It's not going well."

"Is it the judge? Can't you just talk to him and tell him your side of the story?" asked Mary.

Luke thought for a moment, then spoke. "Mary, you're a genius. It would be highly unusual, but this is an unusual matter. Listen, I must go back to the courthouse. If you will excuse me, I have some work to do over the next hour."

Luke hurried back to the brick building, bounding up the stairs to the courtroom. He pulled a set of legal volumes from a bookshelf and began leafing through them, page after page. The hour passed quickly, and soon people began filtering into the courtroom for the afternoon session. Word had spread that Luke Banister had been accused of murder by an Association range detective, and every man and woman with an idle afternoon began to arrive, anxious to see the drama.

Standbury, Santelli, Oglethorpe and Grace West returned with the others. Sheriff Angus followed them, a grim and unhappy look on his rough face. Luke took his place at counsel's table just before the Judge reentered the courtroom. Santelli walked back to the witness stand for cross examination. Luke stood up and approached him as he sat smiling.

200

"Mr. Santelli, you testified that you were in West Virginia at the time of the McGill murders." Luke asked directly.

Santelli shifted in his chair, but the smile never left his face. "Yes," he replied confidently, "and so were you!"

"Please, just answer the question," cautioned Luke. "Mr. Standbury will have an opportunity to ask additional questions after I'm finished. Now, did you know the McGill family, the family that you said was murdered?" Luke continued, probing further.

"I knew them," Santelli answered, looking at Standbury.

Luke paused for a moment. "What were their names?" he asked.

Santelli turned questioningly toward the judge.

"Answer the question, Mr. Santelli," the judge ordered.

Santelli frowned. "As I recall, they were Samuel McGill, Jesse McGill, and Travis McGill."

"Would you recognize them if you saw them again?" asked Luke.

"I doubt it, they're dead. You killed them," replied Santelli with a smirk.

A few onlookers sniggered in the back of the courtroom.

"Get to your point, Mr. Banister," ordered the judge.

Luke nodded, continuing. "This morning, you testified that you were in the employ of one Sheriff Branscom while you were in West Virginia. Is that correct?"

"I was deputized by Sheriff Branscom," stated Santelli with great authority.

"Well, Mr. Santelli, isn't it true that Sheriff Branscom is a corrupt politician who committed cold-blooded murder while trying to take over the illegal moonshine trade in his county?"

"I object!" shouted Standbury.

Luke ignored the legal challenge, raising his voice to be heard over the courtroom commotion. "Isn't it true, Mr. Santelli, that while you were in Hancock County of West Virginia, you and Sheriff Branscom attempted to take over the moonshine business of Jeremiah McGill!"

"I object, your honor!" shouted Standbury rising from the counsel's table.

Santelli half rose in the witness box, and reached into his shirt pocket. "No, Mr. Banister, it's not true," he bristled, waving a piece of paper at Luke. "The truth is that I received in the morning post a warrant for your arrest, sent by Sheriff Branscom himself."

Luke's blood chilled, but he ignored Santelli's statement and moved forward, his voice continuing to rise. "Mr. Santelli, while trying to take over the moonshining business in Hancock County, you attacked and murdered Jeremiah McGill, and you attacked and tried to kill Jesse McGill. Isn't that true, Mr. Santelli?"

Standbury rose to voice another objection, but he was drowned out when the crowd erupted with shouts and yells. Judge Saufley pounded his gavel on the bench until order was restored. Then, looking over his horn-rimmed glasses at Luke, the Judge said angrily, "Objection sustained! Mr. Banister," he continued, his eyes hardening. Mr. Santelli testified that you murdered a man in West Virginia, and a duly constituted authority there is seeking your arrest for that murder. My patience with you is about gone. If you don't have anything else, then I'm going to..."

Suddenly, the courtroom door flew open and slammed hard against the courtroom wall. "What the Sam Hill…," growled a startled Judge Saufley as a slender, dark-haired woman walked through the door. She crossed the bar and stood at the counsel's table next to Luke, her head held high. The woman was followed by a young, blond-haired man. Luke stared at the newcomers as if they were ghosts.

"Who is this woman, and what is the meaning of this intrusion into my courtroom?" asked Judge Saufley.

In a voice that rang out loud and clear, the woman replied. "I'm Jessie McGill. The woman that man tried to kill." Then, with fiery green eyes blazing, she pointed an accusing finger at the man in the witness box. "It was you who murdered my father," she shouted at Ben Santelli, "and it was you who tried to kill my brother and me. Luke Banister had nothing to do with it!"

Color drained from Santelli's face. He rose from the witness chair, a look of madness distorting his features. Then, with cat-like quickness, he rushed toward Jesse McGill, his eyes blazing with hatred. Sheriff Angus stepped in front of Santelli, knocking him sideways, but the enraged man stayed on his feet. Spinning, Santelli let loose with a roundhouse punch that caught the Sheriff on the side of the head. Angus went down to the floor as men from the courtroom gallery sprang to their feet and pushed forward. Santelli fought like a cornered animal, striking with fists of iron at any man who came close, but he retreated until he found his back against a long, courtroom window. Suddenly, he grasped hold of a stout wooden chair, and raising it high above his head, swung it like a club, smashing the clear pane of the courtroom window to smithereens.

Growling like a rabid dog, he clubbed at the mob with the remnants of the chair while he clambered onto the windowsill. For a moment, he stood to face the throng. Then, he jumped from the window to the ground below. Howling in pain, he rose to his feet and limped away.

CHAPTER 31. JESSE'S STORY

Sheriff Angus, who had recovered from Santelli's blow, ran to the shattered window. Pulling his pistol, he leaned over the casing and triggered off two rounds at the fleeing killer just as he rounded the corner of the court-house. The slugs missed their mark, but left two long streaks of black on the red brick.

In the meantime, Judge Saufley pounded the bench with his gavel. "Order," he shouted. "There will be order in this court!" Quickly, the court room calmed. "Sheriff," the Judge said solemnly, "looks like you ought to get together a posse and go after Mr. Santelli."

"Headed there now," Angus replied, hurrying out of the courtroom.

The judge narrowed his eyes. "Any more witnesses, Mr. Standbury?" he asked in a voice dripping with sarcasm.

Standbury stood open mouthed. "I...I don't know that man!" he stammered. Fear flooded across his face, and he turned toward Robert Oglethorpe. "You were the one who wanted me to use him as a witness," he screeched. Oglethorpe's face flushed, but he said nothing.

The Judge turned to Luke. "Do you have anything else to say, Mr. Banister?" he asked.

Luke seized his chance. "Your honor," he began, "my legal memorandum is on your desk. As you know, there is no preference in Wyoming for a relative to be executor of a person's estate. Indeed, there are many instances when a deceased did not want any of his or her relatives to be handling his property after death. In this case, the reason Mr. Walker wanted me to run the ranch is because he knew that I know the land and the livestock. I daresay that neither Miss West nor Mr. Oglethorpe knows anything about cattle. Ranching is a business, and to put someone in charge of a business who is not familiar with the market, the land or the stock would seem to be unwarranted."

"Miss West," intoned the judge, "do you know anything about cattle prices, or cattle marketing?"

"Well, not exactly, your honor," replied Grace West. "But I do have a ranch foreman who does. Mr. Barker here has run cattle both in Texas and Wyoming as well as a few states in between."

The Judge scribbled some notes on his tablet, and then asked, "Miss West, have you ever lived in Wyoming or on a ranch before?"

"No, your honor," Grace West answered, "but..."

The judge cut her off and turned to look at Luke.

"Mister Banister, do you see any reason why you can't discharge this executorship in a timely and efficient manner?"

"No, your honor, no reason whatsoever."

"Fair enough, then. I see no reason to deviate from the terms of Mr. Walker's last wishes. I hereby appoint you, Mr. Banister, as executor of the John Walker estate."

Turning to Standbury, the judge authoritatively stated. "It is the judgment of this court, that the petition filed on behalf of Grace West be denied. Mr. Banister's petition is approved. Mr. Banister, if you'll prepare the order I'll sign it. You do know how to draw up an order, don't you?"

"Yes, your honor, I do," Luke replied.

"Bring it to me when you have it ready," the Judge said with finality, and with that, he arose, stepped down from the bench, and disappeared into his chambers leaving Oglethorpe, Standbury and Grace West standing in stunned disbelief.

Luke grinned broadly and turned toward Travis and Jesse McGill. "Am I ever glad to see you two," he said, clasping Travis on the shoulder and giving Jesse a hug.

By this time, Phineas Standbury had regained his composure. He stepped toward Luke and pointed a pudgy finger at Jesse McGill. "Is this woman your client?" he asked brusquely.

Luke hesitated for a moment, and then turned to face Standbury, "I guess she is," he replied matter-of-factly.

Drawing himself up to his full height, Standbury puffed out his chest. "Well, I must inform you that if she in anyway attempts to link that... that Ben Santelli with Mr. Oglethorpe or Miss West, we will consider such an attempt slanderous, and we will sue."

"Of course, my clients will only tell the truth", replied Luke courteously. "If Mr. Oglethorpe, or Miss West, find the truth uncomfortable, that is their problem."

"Humph," Standbury sniffed, and he pushed his way through the door. Oglethorpe followed him, Grace trailed. As she passed, she stopped to look Jesse up and down. Then, tossing her blond hair, she grasped Robert Oglethorpe's arm. Together they swept out of the courtroom.

As the trio disappeared down the stairway, Luke turned back to Jesse. "When Travis and I left West Virginia, we thought you were ... you know."

"Dead?" Jesse asked pointedly.

"Yes, I guess that's it," Luke stammered.

"Well, I'm not as you can see," Jesse said, her green eyes sparkling with amusement.

Luke smiled. "How did you get here?"

"We came in on the stage about an hour ago. I must admit, Mr. Banister, this is long way from McGill Holler. It took us the better part of a week to get here after we left Kansas City."

"How did you know to come here, to the courtroom?" asked Luke.

"When we arrived at the hotel," Travis broke in, "we went into the restaurant to get something to eat. Jesse overheard the waitress tell someone about talking with you outside the courthouse. She said you were in a terrible fix, so we came up to see if we could help. It looks like we got here just in time."

"That you did," Luke responded. "I'm grateful that you came." He pulled out his pocket-watch and looked at the time. "I know you're tired. Why don't you go down to the hotel and freshen up. I'll finish up here and buy you dinner at the Burlington, say in an hour."

Before Jesse could respond, Travis interjected, "Can't we eat sooner? I'm starved."

"In an hour," Luke grinned, and he turned to gather his papers from the table.

#

The evening stage appeared out of the twilight, rolling to a stop in front of the Burlington Hotel. The driver crawled down from his perch, and slapping the dust from his coat, stepped to the coach door, opening it wide. One lone passenger disembarked. The man strode to the front door of the Burlington, but before entering, he turned back to the driver. "What time does the stage leave?" he inquired in a clipped English accent.

The driver pulled out a pocket watch and studied the dial for a moment. "At 8:00 P.M. sharp, Mr. Atherton," he replied. "An hour. Jist as soon as we hitch up a new team and git the stage checked out."

Atherton strode into the hotel, heading directly up the stairs to Robert Oglethorpe's room, tapping lightly on the door. Oglethorpe answered. "We leave at 8:00 p.m. sharp," Atherton said, looking at his pocket watch. "I trust you have your things together. I'll meet you downstairs." Spinning on his heel, he left Oglethorpe standing in the doorway of his room.

Oglethorpe cursed. Time had run out. There was no refusing Lord Atherton. He could not avoid going, and only after he had soothed things over in Boston would he be able to return. Inwardly, the Englishman raged. It'll be my great pleasure to see that Luke Banister dead, he told himself, but it will have to wait until I finish my business back east.

Oglethorpe left his hotel room and hurried down the hall to Grace West's room. He knocked. No one answered. "Where is she?" he muttered, anger rising in his throat. He turned and ran down the stairs to the restaurant, finding her at a table talking with Mary Higgins.

Oglethorpe hurried to where the two women sat. Casting a glance at the waitress, he said coldly, "Grace and I need to speak for a moment, alone."

"Well, Mr. Oglethorpe," Mary exclaimed. "I can see when I'm not welcome." She rose and disappeared into the back room.

"Robert!" exclaimed Grace. "You were rude. You've hurt Mary's feelings."

Oglethorpe brushed aside Grace's comment as he sat down. "I have urgent business in Boston, Grace, and must leave tonight. I want you to come with me."

Grace stared at her fiancée. "Robert," she said, "I thought that everything was in order before you left. You have clerks in your firm that can take care of most everything. What business could be so urgent?"

"It concerns things I can't discuss. Things that I must personally attend to."

Oglethorpe's answer triggered Grace's intuition, and for some reason, she knew he was not being truthful. When she replied, she spoke deliberately. "Robert, if you need to go back, then please do so. It's insane to ask me to go back with you on such short notice. And, even if I could go, I do not want to leave uncle John's cattle at the mercy of Luke Banister. I must stay here."

Oglethorpe cursed, and his hand snaked across the table, grabbing Grace's wrist. "You're going back to Boston with me," he snarled. "I want you there."

"Ow, you're hurting me," Grace cried out as she twisted away from Oglethorpe's grasp.

Oglethorpe's face reddened, but at that moment Lord Atherton appeared at the table and put his hand on his relative's shoulder. Tipping his hat to Grace West, he said quietly, "Good evening, Grace. I see that Robert has told you that he and I must leave tonight on urgent business. I hope that this change of plans does not inconvenience you."

Atherton's presence changed Oglethorpe's demeanor in an instant. He softened his voice. "I'm sorry Grace," he said, "Will you please forgive me? This client's business is very important to me, and I had so planned on having you for a companion when we went back to Boston that I simply lost my head. When you said you were going to stay, I just became distraught."

With ice in her voice, Grace replied, "Robert, I'm staying here. There is nothing you can do or say to make me go. Is that clear?"

Just at that moment, the stage driver poked his head in the door of the hotel. "Five minutes!" he shouted loudly.

Oglethorpe seethed, but he had no time to argue. Pushing back his chair, the Englishman stood. Mustering a modicum of his usual charm, he tipped his hat. "Grace, my dear," he said, "then I shall see you when I get back. I advise you to let Mr. Standbury look after your legal interests. He's a knowledgeable man, in his own way." Then, without so much as a backward glance, he hurried across the floor of the restaurant and bounded up the staircase to get his bags.

Lord Atherton watched Oglethorpe disappear. "You must forgive Robert tonight, Miss West," he said. "He has several pressing business matters that seem to have affected him. After he attends to his business, I'm sure he will be himself again."

"What business would so disturb Robert that he would act like an animal?" she asked.

Before Atherton could answer, Mary Higgins arrived with a freshly brewed pot of coffee. "Coffee?" she inquired.

"No, thank you. I must be going," Atherton replied. He bowed slightly and exited the hotel.

Grace smiled. "Mary, I would like one more cup, please," she said, and watched as the waitress poured a stream of steaming, black coffee into the mug. Raising the cup to her lips, Grace took a sip and contemplated the events that had just occurred. When she had first met Robert Oglethorpe, he was the perfect gentlemen, courteous and polite. But it troubled her that this encounter revealed a more menacing side to the man she had pledged to marry.

#

Oglethorpe exited the hotel and stood unhappily beside Atherton as the travel bags were loaded. Following his cousin into the coach, he slumped into the corner and pulled his hat low over his eyes. Things had not gone as planned, but there were new days ahead. He would attend to his business in Boston, and then be back. The next time, he would do things differently.

#

The delicious aroma of cooked beef assailed Luke's nose as he stepped into the Burlington Hotel behind Jesse and Travis. They chose a table by the window, and ordered their meal.

"Travis has been telling me all about your travels since you left McGill Holler," Jesse said. "I dare say, Mr. Banister, you have led my baby brother on a series of adventures over the past few months."

"Please call me Luke," Luke replied. "And, I think Travis is no longer a 'baby brother'. He has grown into a man, and a good man at that. But you have heard all about our travels and adventures by now. You must tell me about yours, Miss McGill."

"Nothing would please me more," Jesse said happily, and she plunged into the events that had transpired with her since the Branscom raid on McGill Holler. Luke listened with great interest to her account of meeting Santelli on the ferry, of falling overboard, and especially to the account of her rescue by a passing raft.

Before long, the restaurant began to darken with evening shadows. "Truly, Miss McGill, it has been a pleasure" Luke said politely, but it's a long ride home yet. Now that you've found Travis, what are your plans? Are you going back to West Virginia or McGill Holler?"

Jesse's head came up, and her eyes locked onto Luke's. "No, Mr. Banister," she said, her eyes fiery and proud. "San Francisco, but we have unfinished business yet. Ben Santelli is out there somewhere, and he won't stop hounding us until he's sure we're dead. Travis and I talked it over. We will not run anymore, so we've proposition that might work out for both of us."

"So," Luke inquired, "what would that be."

"We need a place to stay," Jesse continued, "and you need a man to help run your ranch, especially if you take on the Walker property. I'm proposing that we stay at your ranch for a while. I can cook and Travis can help out on the place."

Travis cut in. "Luke, we can look out for one another this way."

"And one more thing," Jesse continued with a mischievous smile playing on her lips, "I've heard your coffee is like molasses. Certainly, I can do better than that."

Luke reflected on the McGills' proposal. It made sense—some sense anyway—fences had to be built, buildings maintained, and livestock attended to. And Santelli was still at large. The three of them together would be a harder target than just one or two alone. "All right," he said, thinking of his own close encounters with the madman. "Gather your bags. We'll go out to the ranch tonight. Travis and I can sleep in the bunkhouse. Jesse, you can have the cabin, at least until you decide what you want to do from here. We'll see how it works out."

Jesse looked at Luke with relief. Travis jumped up grinning and did a jig around the hotel floor. "This is great," he said. "I knew we'd be partners someday."

"The 'day' starts at sunup tomorrow," replied Luke with a smile. "We'll see how you like it then."

\#

Sheriff Angus and his posse pursued Santelli through the ravines and hills south of Buffalo, but as night fell, his tracks were lost. Vowing to regroup the next morning, the posse turned back toward Buffalo.

Hidden in a thick stand of willows alongside Clear Creek, Santelli peered through the glass window of the Burlington Hotel at Luke, Jesse and Travis. He hated them all. They were laughing at him, he knew that, but, he would make these people pay. Not now, but when the time was right.

As the night grew blacker, the air grew colder. Shivering, Santelli turned up the creek, following a pathway through the willows made by small boys fishing the pools and riffles of stream. The big man emerged from the willow curtain onto a darkened back street and furtively scanned the road. Seeing no one, he made his way to an alley where a saddled horse stood tied to a post. Mounting, he rode west and vanished into the night.

CHAPTER 32. THE KNIFE'S STORY

Luke woke Travis at dawn the next morning, and they trudged to the barn to tend to the animals. Before long, Jesse opened the cabin door and stepped out onto the porch. "Luke, Travis," she called out, "I've made breakfast. Come in and wash up."

"Best offer I've had all day," Luke answered, and he ambled up to the cabin door and stepped inside. Travis followed closely behind. The smell of bacon sizzling in a big black frying pan on the cookstove made his mouth water. He picked up a fork and headed toward the pan.

"Oh, no you don't," Jesse chided, steering him toward a straight-backed kitchen chair. "You sit down over here."

She returned to the stove and busied herself with the eggs popping in another skillet. Walking over to her travel bags, she rummaged around until she found the horn-handled knife she had taken from Ben Santelli months ago. Returning to the table, she sliced off two generous slabs of bread, laying the knife on the edge of the pan. Placing the bread on two plates, she mounded up a pile of eggs, bacon, and cooked potatoes and set the plates in front of the hungry men.

Luke prepared to dig in, but before he could take the first bite, there came a light rap on the cabin door. Putting down his fork, he rose from his chair, stepped to the door and opened it wide. With great surprise, he found Chief Walking Bear and a young Indian boy standing awkwardly on the porch. A solemn look covered the old Chief's leathery face.

"Chief, won't you come in," Luke asked, motioning the two inside.

Walking Bear stepped into the cabin's interior. His bearing proud, his shoulders square, he stood for a moment before he began to speak. "Luke Banister, my people were saddened when words arrived of John Walker's death. He was a friend. A good man, and a brave warrior. We spoke of him around our campfires, and when my grandson, White Eagle, heard, he came to me and told me a story about what he had seen on the mountain ten days ago. I have asked him to tell you what he told me."

"What is that?" asked Luke, turning his attention to the young Indian boy.

White Eagle hung his head shyly. His black hair fell forward to hide his face. "He is afraid," Chief Walking Bear said. "Indians do not trust the white man's justice. We have our own ways. He is afraid that he will be blamed for the killing of our friend."

"Tell him I will see that no harm comes to him," replied Luke.

Chief Walking Bear said something to the boy in his native tongue, and after a little more coaxing, the boy looked up and began to speak in English. "My friend, Gray Wolf, and I were hunting on the mountain, about ten days ago now," he said, "when we heard shooting below us in the canyon of the Crazy Woman. We crawled to look over the canyon's edge, and we saw a white man with a gun standing over John Walker." White Eagle paused to look up at the Chief.

"Go on," urged Walking Bear.

"We watched for only a few seconds, and before we could do anything, the man shot Mr. Walker," the young boy blurted out.

Luke's interest was now piqued. "What did this man look like?" he asked.

"He was a big man. He rode a gray horse," White Eagle answered.

"Is that all you saw?" Luke asked.

"Well, there was one other thing. As he rode away, I could see the sun reflecting off something on the side of his boots."

"Could it have been a buckle, a silver buckle on the side of his boot?"

"It might have been. We were so far away that we could not see clearly."

"Santelli!" Luke exclaimed, half to himself. "I should have guessed that he would be in on this."

"Santelli," echoed Travis.

"It's a long story," Luke said, but the pieces are beginning to fit together. Luke turned to the Chief. "Excuse me for my lack of manners, Chief. These are my friends, Jesse and Travis McGill. We were just sitting down for breakfast. We would be honored if you and your grandson would join us."

Jesse rose and took two extra plates from the cupboard, placing them on the table. Motioning for the Chief and the boy to sit, she stepped around to pick up the bone-handled knife from the edge of the pan and prepared to cut more bread.

Chief Walking Bear eyes were drawn to Jesse's knife, and as he stared, his face took on a strange look. Suddenly, his gnarled old hand reached out and grasped Jesse's arm. Startled, she dropped the knife on the table.

"Chief, what is it?" asked Luke, astonished at the Indian's action.

"Luke Banister, I would very much like to see the knife your woman has," Walking Bear said, his eyes never leaving the blade lying on the table in front of him.

"The knife Jesse has?" asked Luke, confused by the request.

"Yes," replied the Chief. "Where did you get that knife?"

Luke looked at Jesse's stricken eyes, but nodded his assent. The old warrior let go of Jesse and slowly reached for the blade. Picking it up, he held it in the palm of one hand while running the fingers of his other over the eagle carved into one side of the handle. A faraway look came over his face, and he said nothing for long moments. Then, he spoke. "This brings back memories of a place I have long forgotten," he said quietly. "A place I have not visited, even in my mind, in many winters."

"What do you mean?" asked Luke, perplexed.

"Many years ago," began Walking Bear, "only a short while after I had become Chief, I lead my youngest brother, Wolf's Claw, and the young men from my tribe into the mountains to look for the great bear—the grizzly bear as the white men call him. After two days, we found sign and tracked the bear deep into our sacred hunting grounds, to a valley hidden high above the waters of the Crazy Woman. The bear eluded us, but our search led us to a band of white men who had built a cabin in the valley. These men were digging for gold with shovels and metal tools. Wolf's Claw became angry because they were defiling sacred ground and he wanted to kill them then, but I convinced my brother to steal their horses only, thinking that would force the white men to leave. But the men stayed. My braves grew angrier, and demanded we go back and fight them. As Chief, I led them back. We killed all but two of the white men that day, but we lost seven young men of our own, including my brother, Wolf's Claw."

Walking Bear stopped, and looked closely at the carving on the knife. Then, he looked up at Luke. "I made this knife for my brother," he said quietly, "just before we went hunting for the great bear. I carved the eagle on this side to represent his becoming a man. He carried it into battle on that day, but when we found his body, the knife was gone. I believed that one of the white men took it with him, but I had a dream that it would find its way home someday."

Jesse leaned close to hear every word that Walking Bear's spoke. When he finished, her green eyes took on a strange gleam. "Chief, the other side of the handle has a carving as well. What does it represent?" she asked. The aged man turned the knife handle over, and studied it closely. "I did not carve this in the handle," he said. "It has been cut there by someone else. Walking Bear stared at the carving intently, and then he continued. "If you stood on top of the canyon wall overlooking the hidden valley, and looked back to the north, this carving looks like the two peaks that lie on either side of that valley."

"And, what about this," asked Jesse, pointing toward a square carved into the handle with an "X" in one corner of the square.

"I do not know what that means," Walking Bear responded, shaking his head.

"Where are you taking this?" asked Luke, shifting his gaze toward Jesse.

Jesse ignored Luke, and continued to focus on the Chief. "Where is this canyon?" she asked. "I must know!"

Walking Bear looked curiously at Jesse. "I guess it should no longer be a secret where the bones of the white men lie," he said, frowning slightly. "All of our land has been taken. None is sacred anymore." The Chief sat back in his chair, and continued. "If you go almost to the head of the Crazy Woman Creek, you will find a large stone, a stone larger than ten lodges together. Behind the stone is a gap in the rock wall that will let you climb to the hidden valley. The white man's cabin is there, but you must be careful. Nearby, a small stream falls from high on the wall of the canyon to the valley below, and the mist from the stream causes moss to grow on the rocks in the gap. They are very slick and hard to climb."

Everyone was silent for a moment, and then Chief Walking Bear spoke again. "I wish to have this knife so I can take it back to my brother," he said.

Jesse nodded. "It is your brother's," she said quietly. "I will give it to you as a gift on one condition."

"And that is?" responded the Chief.

"The condition is you let me go to the hidden valley with you—tomorrow."

Luke jumped to his feet. "What!" he exclaimed. "You can't go up there this time of year. The snow is probably already a foot deep or more. And what about Santelli?"

Chief Walking Bear spoke calmly. "I have been to the canyon recently. The snow does not yet block the trail. I will show you the way if you meet me in the morning at the place where the river leaves the mountain."

Luke turned to look at the aged Indian. "Why would you want to go the mountains this late in the year?" he inquired, frowning.

Walking Bear sat upright, and squared his stooped shoulders. "Already, it has been too many years since my last visit. By the time another winter has come and gone, I may not be able to return."

Jesse sat back down, but after toying with her food for a moment, she put down her fork, and looked Luke in the eye. "Luke, I'm going with Chief Walking Bear."

"Jesse," Luke pleaded, "It's a hard ride. The headwaters of the Little Crazy Woman are ten miles from here. It'll take a day to get there, climb into the valley, and get back. It's no place for a woman."

Thrusting out her chin, she said stubbornly, "You don't have to go with me, but I'm going."

Luke could see he was not going to talk the woman out of her plan right then. "We can discuss this later," he replied

Jesse rose and served Walking Bear and his grandson breakfast. As they ate, they discussed the next day's excursion, and at the end of the meal, Chief Walking Bear, his grandson, and Luke stepped outside. For several minutes, Luke and the chief engaged in conversation. Then, the Chief and boy left.

Luke watched the grandfather and grandson leave. Then, he came back inside. "Why are you so intent on doing this?" he asked Jesse.

"I have my reasons."

"If you can't tell us what they are, then we can't help."

Jesse pondered for a moment, and then spoke reluctantly. "When Santelli cornered me on the ferry the day I crossed the Ohio, he said this knife was the key to a fortune in gold, a treasure that lay buried in Wyoming. He said it was enough gold to make seven men rich. Luke, I know in my heart that this is the place that Santelli was talking about. The treasure is there somewhere in that valley."

Luke scratched his head, a skeptical look on his face. "Jesse," he said, "I've heard stories of a lost mine in these mountains ever since I came here. There are similar stories all over the west, Arizona, Colorado, dozens in any one of those places. Mostly, they're told by half-mad prospectors who've been out in the wilderness by themselves way too long."
Jesse's face fell. "I believe this one is true," she said.

"Luke opened his mouth for a sharp retort, but one look into Jesse's determined eyes changed his mind. "I can see I'm not going to win this argument," he muttered. "Get your things together. We'll meet the Chief tomorrow morning, early."

For the remainder of the day, they made preparations for the trek. Travis inspected the wagon; Luke checked and repaired the team harness, and Jesse prepared enough food to last the day.

CHAPTER 33. ICY DEATH

At daylight the next morning, Luke threw a saddle on the buckskin and helped Travis hitch a team to the wagon. By the time they had finished their tasks, Jesse had stepped out of the cabin into the early morning sunshine. Clad in long pants and one of Luke's heavy coats, she cradled a basket heaped with food in her arms.

Luke studied her as walked toward him. Her long black hair was brushed back and fell to the middle of her back. The sunlight seemed to make her green eyes sparkle, and even so early in the morning, she looked fresh and vibrant.

"Good morning," she said as she handed Luke the basket.

"And the same to you, Miss McGill," he replied, setting the food in the back of the wagon.

She gave him her hand, and he helped her up onto the hard wooden seat. "Thanks," she said as she settled in, "but I could have got in by myself."

Luke studied her for a moment. "I know," he responded. "I was just being a gentleman." She flashed him a smile, but further conversation was interrupted when Travis appeared and clambered aboard the wagon.

"You all ready?" Travis asked.

"Looks like we have everything," Luke answered.

Travis clucked at the team. The horses leaned into their traces and with a groan, the wagon rolled forward. Luke watched it rattle away for a moment before he walked to the buckskin and mounted. They had covered about a mile when Jesse turned and spoke. "What were you talking with Walking Bear about yesterday?" she asked.

"Oh, he was wanting to know if you were for sale," Luke replied.

"For sale," Jesse asked incredulously. "He asked if I was for sale?"

"Well," Luke replied, "he thought you looked strong and healthy, and would be able to have many children, so he wanted to buy you for his wife." Jesse sputtered. "Well, I am not for sale like a cow. That is barbaric. What did you tell him?"

"Well, it is part of their culture, and old Chief Walking Bear is pretty persuasive. Offered me two horses and a dog," Luke said without cracking a smile. "I thought I had a deal, but he backed out when I told him that you were stubborn as an old mule." With that, Luke grinned and spurred his horse, galloping ahead and leaving a laughing Travis and a speechless Jesse in his wake.

#

Half-mad, Ben Santelli grasped Phineas Standbury by the throat. "Where are they?" he roared, a deep guttural sound coming from his throat. The pudgy little man's face turned purple, and he worked his jaw, but no sound came out except a strange gargling noise.

Santelli lifted Standbury clear of the office floor. "I sold my soul for that gold, and that she-devil will not cheat me out of it!" he screeched. "Where did they go?"

Standbury's eyes bulged in his head, and he raised an arm to point south. Santelli dropped the gagging barrister's feet back to the floor. "They... they went to Luke Banister's ranch," Standbury choked out, trying to catch his breath.

A dark sneer crossed Santelli's face. "Banister," he muttered to himself, "and the McGills. All in one place. I'll take care of them once and for all." Striking like a rattler, the big man back-handed Standbury, knocking him to the ground. "Don't think about telling the Sheriff I was here," Santelli said, "or I'll be back. Is that clear?"

Standbury nodded his head as he lay gasping for breath. Santelli stomped out of the law office onto the main street and strode down the boardwalk to a saddled horse. Leaping onto its back, he spurred his mount, and raced headlong through town, headed south.

Santelli pushed his mount hard until he reached Luke Banister's ranch. With a madness that made him oblivious to danger, he rode straight to the cabin and dismounted. Pulling his pistol, he strode to the cabin door and kicked it open. The door fell from its hinges, but no one was inside. Retreating to the yard, he stood, and like a wild beast, bellowed out Luke Banister's name, but no one answered.

He scouted the area, chortling when he spotted the wagon tracks heading west toward the mountains. Mounting his sweating horse, he laid a quirt along its flanks and galloped toward the towering, snow covered peaks.

#

The trio traveled west toward Crazy Woman Canyon. Luke lead the wagon across the top of the mesa until they came to its western most edge. There, a steep, narrow wagon trail wound its way down slope to the river bottom below.

Luke reached the edge of the mesa first, and sat waiting for the wag-

216

on to catch up, his keen eyes scanning their back trail.

"Are we being followed?" asked Jesse.

"No, but it pays to be careful. There are a few folks around here who aren't happy with us right now, Ben Santelli being one of them."
It was another mile to the mouth of the canyon which they covered with good speed. When they arrived, Chief Walking Bear was waiting. Together, the four travelers headed into the canyon's maw.

A rocky trail wound its way through the canyon, and they pushed the team and wagon into the canyon's confines until its path was finally blocked by huge, impassable boulders. There, they left the wagon, trekking through the fallen rocks and across steep slopes on foot. Sometimes, the walking was easy, but at other items, they found themselves blazing a trail through knee-deep snow.

In the distance, Luke picked up the sound of falling water, and before long they came to the cabin-sized boulder that Chief Walking Bear had described. Above, a small stream rushed through a notch in the ancient limestone cliff and fell thirty feet or more into a deep pool at its base.

Chief Walking Bear pointed at a gap in the ragged limestone escarpment. "There," he said, "is the way to the hidden valley. Now, we must climb."

Together, the travelers traversed the rocky slope, always ensuring that they had a secure handhold before reaching for the next. After an hour of climbing, Luke was the first to reach the top of the overhanging cliff. He turned, and grasping Travis by the hand, pulled him up and over the limestone ledge. They secured a rope to an aged pine, and threw it down, pulling Chief Walking Bear and Jesse up and over the ledge in turn.

#

Ben Santelli rode silently into the canyon, scanning the trail ahead for any sign of movement. He saw none, but smiled inwardly. His quarry was further ahead, but they were there somewhere, and would be trapped by the rocks and snow. He slowed his pace, following the track until he reached the wagon and horses. With growing excitement, he tied his own mount to the wagon wheel, took out his carbine, and began tracking the foursome on foot.

#

For a half-hour, Luke and his companions walked upstream through snow and carpets of brown, pine needles. Suddenly, Walking Bear stopped and held up his hand. The carcass of a freshly killed deer lay across their path.

Sniffing the air, the old warrior turned to his companions. "Grizzly bear," he whispered. "Fresh kill. Bear close by."

Luke jacked a cartridge into the chamber of his rifle and continued on, making sure he was far enough away from the brush that a grizzly would not be able to take them by ambush. Ten minutes later, they arrived at what remained of the mining camp.

The Sioux had failed to burn the cabin that fateful day, and all four walls and half the roof were still intact. Luke strode forward and stepped past a slab door that lay rotting on the ground. Inside, the cabin's dirt floor was now littered with weeds and debris. A rusted shovel stood against one wall.

Chief Walking Bear stood for long minutes, gazing over the valley. With his eyes misting, he spoke to Jesse. "I brought you to this place as I promised," the old warrior said. "Now I go to return White Eagle's knife." With that, Walking Bear turned and disappeared into the aspens.

Jesse looked around the meadow. "Everything is here," she said excitedly. "The cabin. The sluices. This is the place Chief Walking Bear remembers. This is the place Ben Santelli was talking about."

Travis spoke up. "Well, even if the story of gold is true, it could be anywhere in this valley. How would we find it?

Jesse knelt down and spoke while she drew a picture in the dirt. "One of the miners who escaped took the knife. On the handle, there were two picture carvings," she said. "One was a picture of the two mountains that flanked this valley. I think that was so the man could find his way back. The second was just a square with an "X" in the corner, like this. If we can figure out what that means, then we could find the gold."

Travis studied the square for a moment, and then scanned the surrounding area. "The only thing square around here is the cabin," he remarked.

"Travis, you're a genius," Luke exclaimed. "That's it! The "X" shows where the gold is buried. It's in the cabin."

"Let's find out," Travis said, and he grabbed the rusted shovel and began to dig.

It wasn't long before the shovel's rusty blade clanked against something hard. Jesse fell to her knees and brushed away the loose soil with her hands. The top of a glass jar appeared. With a stick, she pried it out of the hole, drawing in a deep breath when she saw that it was filled to the brim with gold dust.

Travis stood open-mouthed, but Luke took the shovel from Jesse and continued to dig. Soon, seven more jars sat on the ground in front of them, each gleaming with a lustrous yellow color. Jesse sat on a log and stared at the precious metal, a broad smile covering her face.

Luke's elation at finding the gold cache was tempered by his realization that the sun was fast falling toward the horizon. Exuberance gave way to practicality, and he scanned the woods. It had been more than an hour since Chief Walking Bear had left. If he did not get back soon, Luke mused, they would be traveling home in the dark.

Luke's thoughts were interrupted when Jesse stood. "I'll gather firewood if you'll start a fire," she said.

"Fair enough," Luke agreed.

Jesse tugged on Travis' sleeve, and the pair headed out the weather ravaged door of the miner's cabin. Travis walked up the hillside toward a stand of downed pine, while Jesse wandered back down the trail in the direction they had come.

Luke scavenged a few dry limbs that littered the ground and piled them up on the ground inside the cabin. He was trying to coax the kindling into a flame when he heard Jesse scream.

Luke sprang to his feet and grabbed his rifle. As he ran out the doorway, he spotted Jesse standing in the snow some sixty yards distant, but his eyes passed over Jesse's form and came to rest on a grizzly bear not more than thirty steps beyond. Rearing up on its hind legs, the bear roared and sliced the air with six-inch claws. Panic-stricken, Jesse turned and ran.

Luke slammed the rifle to his shoulder and levered a cartridge into the chamber as the bear dropped to all fours and focused its beady eyes on Jesse's fleeing figure. He squeezed off a shot just as the grizzly charged.

The first slug hit the bear in the ribs, stopping the enraged animal's momentum, but only for a moment. Bawling and slobbering, it gathered itself and surged forward again. Luke levered another cartridge into the rifle chamber, and squeezed the trigger a second time. This time, the slug struck the bear in the shoulder. Crippled and bleeding, the animal slowed. Once more, Luke jacked a bullet into the rifle chamber, but this time, he aimed carefully. The third slug slammed into the bear's heart and stopped the animal in its tracks. Like a towering tree, the bear wavered for a moment while the life blood ebbed from its body, and then it slumped hard to the ground.

#

Ben Santelli's head jerked up as he heard the rifle blast—once, twice, three times. A sneer appeared on his face, and he increased his pace.

#

Chief Walking Bear heard the rifle shots and rose from the burial mounds of his brother and his fellow warriors. Lifting his eyes skyward, he said, "I must go now, but I will be back, my brother. I will be back." He turned and hurried back the way he had come.

#

Jesse stood frozen, the crumpled bear at her feet. Luke ran to her, and she threw her arms around his neck, trembling like a leaf. He held her until she had calmed, and then he walked her back to the cabin, sitting her by the smoldering fire.

By this time, Travis had sprinted back to the cabin to help, but the attack by the bear had lasted only a few seconds. After ensuring that Jesse was unhurt, Travis picked up the rifle and walked back to where the grizzly lay. The bear was still, but Travis eyed the carcass warily. Standing with his back toward the woods, he shouted to Luke. "Looks like this bear won't bother...," but before Travis could finish his sentence, a rifle roared from the darkness of the woods, and the young man pitched forward into the snow.

The blast echoed from valley wall to valley wall like rolling thunder, and at first, Luke thought that Travis had fired again, maybe finishing off the bear. He leaped to his feet, hurrying to the cabin door. He stopped and scanned the meadow, but the young man was nowhere to be seen. The bear lay where it had dropped.

"Stay here," Luke commanded Jesse.

Pulling his pistol, Luke stepped from the cabin and moved cautiously toward the bear's carcass. He spotted Travis lying in the snow. Blood was pooling beside his chest, but the young man was still alive. Luke raced forward and knelt beside his young friend. Travis opened his eyes and tried to mouth a warning, but it was too late. A blow from behind knocked the pistol from Luke's hand, and sent him sprawling as Ben Santelli attacked.

Luke clambered to his feet, deflecting Santelli's blows. The big man waded in, but Luke fought back ferociously, landing a punch to Santelli's forehead and one to his midsection.

Momentarily taken back by Luke's counter-attack, Santelli circled, looking for an opening. "I'm going to kill you with my bare hands, Banister," the madman snarled. "And then, I'm going to kill that she-devil you have with you."

Luke jabbed, but Santelli absorbed the hit and counter-punched, hitting Luke solidly in the chest. Luke danced away, parrying punch after punch as the big man tried to bull in, and landing blows of his own. Frustrated, Santelli swung wildly, grazing Luke on the side of the head. Luke tripped and went down, and Santelli pounced, pinning his adversary to the ground and pummeling him with his fists.

Frozen, Jesse watched the fight from the doorway of the cabin, but when Luke tripped, she abandoned all caution and ran toward forward. Throwing herself on Santelli's back, she clawed at his eyes and face, but he swatted her away like a fly. She attacked again, but this time he balled up his fist and punched her on the jaw. Moaning, she went down into the snow beside Travis.

With Santelli distracted, Luke brought his knee up in the man's groin with all the strength he could muster. Santelli groaned and rolled aside, grabbing his crotch, but he came at Luke again. Bloodied, Luke gave ground until Santelli suddenly stopped. His eyes locked on Luke, Santelli reached into the snow and pulled out the rifle Travis had dropped. He pointed the barrel at Luke's chest.

"Looks like you've toughened up a little since we last met," Santelli snarled, grinning sadistically. "I'm disappointed, Banister, it won't be as much fun to shoot you as it would have been to kill you with my bare hands. No matter. I'll git over it. The Englishman's only paying me when I kill you, not for how. So, say your prayers. You'll be joining old man Walker soon." Santelli's finger tightened on the rifle's trigger.

Luke steeled himself, but instead of lead slicing into his body, a slashing piece of bone and steel cut through the air, landing with a "thunk" in Santelli's chest. Stunned, Santelli reached up and closed his hand over the knife that ripped at his heart. His tried to speak but no words came from his mouth. He took one step forward and fell face first into the snow.

Luke looked up to see a grim-faced Chief Walking Bear standing at the edge of the aspen grove, a warrior in battle one last time.

CHAPTER 34. ONE MONTH LATER

The December sun hung low in the winter sky turning Travis' breath into tiny crystals of ice. Grasping the last of Jesse's bags, he lugged them over to where she stood talking with Luke in the front of the Burlington Hotel. "Are you sure you want to go on," he overheard Luke ask. "You're welcome to stay at the ranch for as long as you like."

"I know," Jesse replied, her cheeks reddening from more than the cold, but before she could say anything else the stage driver popped out of the hotel door and called, "All aboard."

"Oh, it's time to go," she said. Her clear, green eyes staring at Luke. "I've always wanted to see San Francisco, and now that I have money to do that...," and her voice trailed off.

"You should go, then," Luke responded, "but you should think about coming back some time. Wyoming's a fine place."

The driver, who had been waiting, coughed loudly and said "I'm sorry ma'am. But the stage is leaving on time today. It's time to board, if you're going."

Jesse looked one more time at Luke. Stepping forward, she kissed him on the cheek. Then, she gave Travis a hug. "You two boys tame Wyoming, if you can," she said perkily, and hurried to the stage door. Luke helped her step up and she disappeared into the stage's interior.

Suddenly, a commotion arose at the hotel door and Grace West bustled out with her bags. The stage driver frowned. "I'm not sure we can git all those on board," he said, scratching his head.

"Then get what you can, and have the rest shipped," Grace snapped back. "I'm leaving on this stage today!"

"Yes ma'am," answered the driver, smirking at Grace's words, and with the help of several men, he hoisted the trunk and bags to the top of the stage.

"Well, Miss West," said Luke politely, tipping his hat. "It's so good to see you."

The lady stiffened. "I don't believe a word of what you told the sheriff about my fiancé," replied Grace haughtily, "and I'm going to have Mr. Standbury look into suing you for slander."

"I would be pleased if you did," responded Luke. "More often than not, an investigation brings many facts to light. People want to know the truth about this matter, though I think you're going to have to find another lawyer to do the suing. I'm not sure Mr. Standbury relishes another client like Robert Oglethorpe."

"Hmmph," Grace responded tersely. Tossing her blond curls, she clambered into the coach and slammed the door behind her.

"Do you think they'll kill one another?" asked a voice, and Luke turned to see Sheriff Angus standing at his elbow.

"Who do you mean?" asked Luke.

"Grace West and Jesse McGill," said Angus. "They're going to have to ride together all the way to the rail station."

"Sheriff, I'm sure there'll be a thousand cuts between here and there," Luke answered with a grin, "though it's unlikely any blood will be spilled."

Angus roared with laughter.

At that moment, the driver cracked his whip, and the team leaned into their harnesses. Creaking and groaning, the stage eased away from the hotel. "So," said Angus, watching the stage move away, "mind if I ask you just a few more questions about John Walker's killing?"

"Not a problem," replied Luke.

"You're sure Ben Santelli killed John?"

"I am," answered Luke. "Ben Santelli admitted so much just before his...uh, untimely death."

"What part did Robert Oglethorpe play?"

"I don't have any direct evidence, Sheriff," replied Luke, "but my contacts back east tell me that Oglethorpe desperately needs money. Desperate men do desperate things, and my theory is that he knew Grace West had an uncle in Wyoming with a big ranch and lots of cattle. Grace was John's sole heir. Knowing that, Oglethorpe developed a plan whereby he would have John Walker killed. With John out of the way, he would marry Grace and have access to a fortune to pay off his debt."

"Well, what about Atherton?" asked Travis. "What part did he play in this whole thing, if any."

Luke watched the stage gather speed as it rolled down the street. "I'm not sure," he replied slowly. "I have a hunch that Atherton was somehow involved in John's murder, at least indirectly, but there is something bigger going on here that I can't put my finger on. John Walker alluded to it several times. Where are the two Englishmen anyway?"

"I telegraphed Boston's constable," Angus responded, "but neither Oglethorpe nor Atherton went back there. The last time they were seen was in New Orleans booking passage on a ship to Barbados in the Caribbean, an English colony. They are well connected in England, and in this country, so unless there's iron clad proof of their involvement in something illegal, it would be next to impossible to extradite them for any crime once they set foot on English soil."

"It does seem strange that they both left the country so quickly," opined Luke.

"What about the list of people?" asked Angus. "Do you have that figured out yet?"

Luke shook his head. "No," he replied. "But there must be some kind of connection."

Angus stood quietly for a few seconds. "One last question; then I'm going to get some of Mary Higgins' apple pie. You can join me if you want."

"I'm game," replied Luke.

"Me too," echoed Travis.

"The knife that killed Santelli," stated the Sheriff as he began walking to the hotel entrance. "Jesse said she took it from him in West Virginia when he killed her Pa. Santelli tried to kill her several times to get it back. Is it true that it was the map to a fortune in gold?"

This time Luke and Travis both laughed. "No, not a fortune for sure," they replied together.

Luke threw open the door to the Burlington. "Let's get that pie, Sheriff. It's on me," he said, grinning widely. And, with that, the three men walked through the door of the Burlington, their thoughts turning to a piece of Mary's fresh baked apple pie.

About the Author

Steven R. Laird was born and raised in Wyoming, and while he has traveled extensively throughout the state, he loves the storied history of Johnson County, the home of the famed Johnson County Range War. His work in the state has ranged from political analysis to mining projects and legal activities. And, while the times and events in this book might seem familiar, anything in this book notwithstanding, the events, people and names in this book related to this account are purely fictional.